OXFORD WORLD'S CLASSICS

RUDYARD KIPLING

The Jungle Books

Edited with an Introduction and Notes by
W. W. ROBSON

OXFORD
UNIVERSITY PRESS

OXFORD
UNIVERSITY PRESS

Great Clarendon Street, Oxford OX2 6DP

Oxford University Press is a department of the University of Oxford.
It furthers the University's objective of excellence in research, scholarship,
and education by publishing worldwide in

Oxford New York

Athens Auckland Bangkok Bogotá Buenos Aires Calcutta
Cape Town Chennai Dar es Salaam Delhi Florence Hong Kong Istanbul
Karachi Kuala Lumpur Madrid Melbourne Mexico City Mumbai
Nairobi Paris São Paulo Shanghai Singapore Taipei Tokyo Toronto Warsaw

with associated companies in Berlin Ibadan

Oxford is a registered trade mark of Oxford University Press
in the UK and in certain other countries

Published in the United States
by Oxford University Press Inc., New York

Introduction, Explanatory Notes © Wallace Robson 1987
General Editor's Preface, Select Bibliography, Chronology
© Andrew Rutherford 1987
Updated Bibliography © Andrew Rutherford 1996
Appendix © Aubrey Manning 1987

The moral rights of the author have been asserted
Database right Oxford University Press (maker)

First published as a World's Classics paperback 1992
Reissued as an Oxford World's Classics paperback 1998
Reissued 2008

British Library Cataloguing in Publication Data

Data available

Library of Congress Cataloging in Publication Data
Kipling, Rudyard, 1865–1936.
The jungle books/Rudyard Kipling; edited with an introduction by W. W. Robson.
p. cm.—(Oxford world's classics)
Includes bibliographical references (p.).
Summary: Presents the adventures of Mowgli, a boy reared by a pack of wolves
and the wild animals of the jungle. Also includes other short stories set in India.
1. Mowgli (Fictitious character)—Fiction. 2. Animals—Fiction.
3. India—Fiction. [1. Jungles—Fiction. 2. Animals—Fiction.
3. India—Fiction. 4. Short stories.] I. Robson, W. W. (William
Wallace), 1923– . II. Title. III. Series.
PR4854.J6 1992 823'.8–dc20 91–8905

ISBN 978–0–19–953645–0

7

Printed in Great Britain by
Clays Ltd, St Ives plc

CONTENTS

GENERAL PREFACE

RUDYARD KIPLING (1865–1936) was for the last decade of the nineteenth century and at least the first two decades of the twentieth the most popular writer in English, in both verse and prose, throughout the English-speaking world. Widely regarded as the greatest living English poet and story-teller, winner of the Nobel Prize for Literature, recipient of honorary degrees from the Universities of Oxford, Cambridge, Edinburgh, Durham, McGill, Strasbourg, and the Sorbonne, he also enjoyed popular acclaim that extended far beyond academic and literary circles.

He stood, it can be argued, in a special relation to the age in which he lived. He was primarily an artist, with his individual vision and techniques, but his was also a profoundly representative consciousness. He seems to give expression to a whole phase of national experience, symbolizing in appropriate forms (as Lascelles Abercrombie said the epic poet must do) the 'sense of the significance of life he [felt] acting as the unconscious metaphysic of the time'.[1] He is in important ways a spokesman for his age, with its sense of imperial destiny, its fascinated contemplation of the unfamiliar world of soldiering, its confidence in engineering and technology, its respect for craftsmanship, and its dedication to Carlyle's gospel of work. That age is one about which many Britons—and to a lesser extent Americans and West Europeans—now feel an exaggerated sense of guilt; and insofar as Kipling was its spokesman, he has become our scapegoat. Hence, in part at least, the tendency in recent decades to dismiss him so contemptuously, so unthinkingly, and so mistakenly. Whereas if we approach him more historically, less hysterically, we shall find in this very relation to his age a cultural phenomenon of absorbing interest.

[1] Cited in E. M. W. Tillyard, *The Epic Strain in the English Novel*, London, 1958, p. 15.

Here, after all, we have the last English author to appeal to readers of all social classes and all cultural groups, from lowbrow to highbrow; and the last poet to command a mass audience. He was an author who could speak directly to the man in the street, or for that matter in the barrack-room or factory, more effectively than any left-wing writer of the thirties or the present day, but who spoke just as directly and effectively to literary men like Edmund Gosse and Andrew Lang; to academics like David Masson, George Saintsbury, and Charles Eliot Norton; to the professional and service classes (officers and other ranks alike) who took him to their hearts; and to creative writers of the stature of Henry James, who had some important reservations to record, but who declared in 1892 that 'Kipling strikes me personally as the most complete man of genius (as distinct from fine intelligence) that I have ever known', and who wrote an enthusiastic introduction to *Mine Own People* in which he stressed Kipling's remarkable appeal to the sophisticated critic as well as to the common reader.[2]

An innovator and a virtuoso in the art of the short story, Kipling does more than any of his predecessors to establish it as a major genre. But within it he moves confidently between the poles of sophisticated simplicity (in his earliest tales) and the complex, closely organized, elliptical and symbolic mode of his later works which reveal him as an unexpected contributor to modernism.

He is a writer who extends the range of English literature in both subject-matter and technique. He plunges readers into new realms of imaginative experience which then become part of our shared inheritance. His anthropological but warmly human interest in mankind in all its varieties produces, for example, sensitive, sympathetic vignettes of Indian life and character which culminate in *Kim*. His sociolinguistic experiments with proletarian

[2] See *Kipling: The Critical Heritage*, ed. Roger Lancelyn Green, London, 1971, pp. 159–60. *Mine Own People*, published in New York in 1891, was a collection of stories nearly all of which were to be subsumed in *Life's Handicap* later that year.

speech as an artistic medium in *Barrack-Room Ballads*
and his rendering of the life of private soldiers in all their
unregenerate humanity gave a new dimension to war
literature. His portrayal of Anglo-Indian life ranges from
cynical triviality in some of the *Plain Tales from the Hills*
to the stoical nobility of the best things in *Life's Handicap*
and *The Day's Work*. Indeed Mrs Hauksbee's Simla,
Mulvaney's barrack-rooms, Dravot and Carnehan's
search for a kingdom in Kafiristan, Holden's illicit, star-
crossed love, Stalky's apprenticeship, Kim's Grand Trunk
Road, 'William''s famine relief expedition, and the Maltese
Cat's game at Umballa, establish the vanished world of
Empire for us (as they established the unknown world of
Empire for an earlier generation), in all its pettiness and
grandeur, its variety and energy, its miseries, its hard-
ships, and its heroism.

In a completely different vein Kipling's genius for the
animal fable as a means of inculcating human truths opens
up a whole new world of joyous imagining in the two
Jungle Books. In another vein again are the stories in which
he records his delighted discovery of the English country-
side, its people and traditions, after he had settled at
Bateman's in Sussex: 'England,' he told Rider Haggard in
1902, 'is the most wonderful foreign land I have ever been
in';[3] and he made it peculiarly his own. Its past gripped his
imagination as strongly as its present, and the two books of
Puck stories show what Eliot describes as 'the develop-
ment of the imperial . . . into the historical imagination'.[4]

In another vein again he figures as the bard of engineering and technology. From the standpoint of world history,
two of Britain's most important areas of activity in the
nineteenth century were those of industrialism and imperialism, both of which had been neglected by literature
prior to Kipling's advent. There is a substantial body of
work on the Condition of England Question and the socio-
economic effects of the Industrial Revolution; but there is

[3] *Rudyard Kipling to Rider Haggard*, ed. Morton Cohen, London,
1965, p. 51.
[4] T. S. Eliot, *On Poetry and Poets*, London, 1957, p. 247.

comparatively little imaginative response in literature (as opposed to painting) to the extraordinary inventive energy, the dynamic creative power, which manifests itself in (say) the work of engineers like Telford, Rennie, Brunel, and the brothers Stephenson—men who revolutionized communications within Britain by their road, rail and harbour systems, producing in the process masterpieces of industrial art, and who went on to revolutionize ocean travel as well. Such achievements are acknowledged on a sub-literary level by Samuel Smiles in his best-selling *Lives of the Engineers* (1861–2). They are acknowledged also by Carlyle, who celebrates the positive as well as denouncing the malign aspects of the transition from the feudal to the industrial world, insisting as he does that the true modern epic must be technological, not military: 'For we are to bethink us that the Epic verily is not *Arms and the Man*, but *Tools and the Man*,—an infinitely wider kind of Epic.'[5] That epic has never been written in its entirety, but Kipling came nearest to achieving its aims in verses like 'McAndrew's Hymn' (*The Seven Seas*) and stories like 'The Ship that Found Herself' and 'Bread upon the Waters' (*The Day's Work*) in which he shows imaginative sympathy with the machines themselves as well as sympathy with the men who serve them. He comes nearer, indeed, than any other author to fulfilling Wordsworth's prophecy that

If the labours of men of Science should ever create any material revolution, direct or indirect, in our condition, and in the impressions which we habitually receive, the Poet will sleep then no more than at present, but he will be ready to follow the steps of the Man of Science, not only in those general indirect effects, but he will be at his side, carrying sensation into the midst of the objects of the Science itself.[6]

This is one aspect of Kipling's commitment to the world of work, which, as C. S. Lewis observes, 'imaginative

[5] *Past and Present* (1843), Book iv, ch. 1. cf. ibid., Book iii, ch. 5.
[6] *Lyrical Ballads*, ed. R. L. Brett and A. R. Jones, London, 1963, pp. 253–4.

literature in the eighteenth and nineteenth centuries had [with a few exceptions] quietly omitted, or at least thrust into the background', though it occupies most of the waking hours of most men:

And this did not merely mean that certain technical aspects of life were unrepresented. A whole range of strong sentiments and emotions—for many men, the strongest of all—went with them ... It was Kipling who first reclaimed for literature this enormous territory.[7]

He repudiates the unspoken assumption of most novelists that the really interesting part of life takes place outside working hours: men at work or talking about their work are among his favourite subjects. The qualities men show in their work, and the achievements that result from it (bridges built, ships salvaged, pictures painted, famines relieved) are the very stuff of much of Kipling's fiction. Yet there also runs through his *œuvre*, like a figure in the carpet, a darker, more pessimistic vision of the impermanence, the transience—but not the worthlessness—of all achievement. This underlies his delighted engagement with contemporary reality and gives a deeper resonance to his finest work, in which human endeavour is celebrated none the less because it must ultimately yield to death and mutability.

ANDREW RUTHERFORD

[7] 'Kipling's World', *Literature and Life: Addresses to the English Association*, London, 1948, pp. 59–60.

INTRODUCTION

The Jungle Books, the most popular of Kipling's prose works, were written in the eighteen-nineties, the second phase of his literary career. Rudyard Kipling (1865–1936) was a young English journalist who had enjoyed a spectacular success as fiction-writer and poet, first in India and then in London, in the previous decade. Now began what literary historians have called his American period. It was a happy time in his life, when, fresh from his Indian and British triumphs, he seemed to be on the verge of making a settled home in the United States with his American wife. Ahead still lay the much publicized vendetta with his eccentric brother-in-law Beatty Balestier, the flight from the United States in dismay and anger, the near-fatal illness, the death of his young daughter Josephine (the much loved 'Taffimai'), the embitterment over the South African War which embroiled Kipling in a mutually hostile relationship with the English liberal intelligentsia that to this day has never quite been resolved. All this was to make the last years of the century the worst period of his literary life. But none of it is foreshadowed in *The Jungle Books,* which still retain traces of that idyllic atmosphere of the early nineties that was never to return to Kipling's work.

The Jungle Books (1894–5), like two other great English books, Lewis Carroll's *Alice in Wonderland* (1865) and Kenneth Grahame's *The Wind in the Willows* (1908), can be regarded as stories told by an adult to children. Kipling's younger daughter Elsie (Mrs George Bambridge) described to Dr A. W. Yeats in 1955 how Kipling recited the tales to the children with the lights out in a semi-dark room, and 'the cold narratives of *The Jungle Books* and *Just So Stories* in book form left so much to be desired that she could not bear to read them or hear them read'. (See an article by D. H. Stewart in *The Journal of Narrative Technique,* vol. 15, no. 1, Winter 1985). But a father's rigmarole for children is only part of the composition of *The Jungle Books*. They constitute a complex work of literary art in which the whole of Kipling's philosophy of life is expressed in miniature. Many influences, some reasonably certain, others at most probable, have been at work on the narrative, and it would require a substantial book to take the road to Xanadu. Kipling discusses the book in his autobiography, *Something of Myself* (1937), but, as usual in that work, makes no attempt to analyse or explain. It must be remembered that he believed his writing to proceed from a source which was not under conscious control, which he called his Daemon (i.e. his genius or inspiration), and so he was as suspicious of talk about his or any other writer's intentions as any disciple of Wimsatt and Beardsley. However, he did leave on record two interesting pieces of inside information. The first reveals what C. S. Lewis has called Kipling's preoccupation with the Inner Ring. '. . . somehow or other I came across a tale about a lion-hunter in South Africa who fell among lions who were all Freemasons, and with them entered into a confederacy against some wicked baboons. I think that . . . lay dormant until *The Jungle Books* began to be born.'[1] The second takes us to Kipling's first home in Vermont where many of the stories were written. 'My workroom in the Bliss Cottage was seven feet by eight, and from December to April the snow lay level with its window-sill. It chanced that I had written a tale about Indian Forestry which included a boy who had been brought up by wolves. In the stillness, and suspense, of the winter of '92, some memory of the Masonic Lions of my childhood's magazine, and a phrase in Haggard's *Nada the Lily*, combined with the echo of this tale. After blocking out the main idea in my head, the pen took charge, and I watched it begin to write stories about Mowgli and animals, which later grew into *The Jungle Books* . . . Two tales, I remember, I threw away and was better pleased with the remainder.'[2]

[1] *Something of Myself* (London, 1937), p. 8.
[2] Ibid., pp. 113-14.

It is possible to gloss and expand Kipling's own account a little, but only a little. One point to bear in mind is that, like most people, he thinks of *The Jungle Books* as stories about Mowgli. But in fact, like many of his other books, they are collections of miscellaneous short stories. The Mowgli stories form a coherent sequence, telling the story of Mowgli's childhood and youth, from his adoption by the wolves in 'Mowgli's Brothers' to his departure from the Jungle in 'The Spring Running'. But in the first *Jungle Book* only the first three stories are about Mowgli; the other four deal with different characters and settings, and they do not form a sequence, while in the second the first four stories about Mowgli are alternated with non-Mowgli stories, the volume closing with the last Mowgli story, 'The Spring Running'. Nor is it the case that only the Mowgli stories are good, the rest being inferior. One or two of the Mowgli stories would be agreed by most readers not to be as good as the best of the other stories. Nevertheless, *The Jungle Books* are rightly remembered for the Mowgli motif, which is the most original thing in them.

The next matter requiring comment is the question of which was the first Mowgli story (i.e. the first to be written, not the first in the fictional life of the wolf boy). As we have seen, Kipling says that he had written a tale about 'Indian Forestry', including Mowgli, before 'the pen took charge' and wrote *The Jungle Books*. Kipling is here referring to the story called 'In the Rukh', which appeared in *Many Inventions* (1893)—in this edition it is reprinted at the end of the second *Jungle Book*. All this seems clear enough, though many readers, without necessarily being able to articulate their reasons, must find it difficult to believe that 'In the Rukh' and 'Mowgli's Brothers' and its successors really belong to the same imaginative or daemonic impulse. The Mowgli of 'In the Rukh' is not only fully grown-up and (rather unromantically) a forest ranger in government service, he seems somehow different in conception from the character in *The Jungle Books*. C. E. Carrington put it well when he called 'In the Rukh' 'realistic and pseudo-rational . . . not quite successful, not vintage Kipling. You don't really believe it, in spite of its verisimilitude, while "Mowgli's Brothers" is a masterpiece. It shows genius and forces a complete suspension of disbelief, so that mere verisimilitude is irrelevant.' Carrington was allowed access to Kipling's diaries of the period, and they convinced him that the first motion towards 'Mowgli's Brothers' was a landmark, something new in his career. 'I suspect that "In the Rukh" and "Mowgli's Brothers" were two alternative experiments in a new mode, very likely taken up and dropped, in turn, "Mowgli's Brothers" proved to be by far the better to follow, but "In the Rukh" was too good for the waste-paper basket . . . Publication dates mean very little. Either or both of the stories might have lain by him in typescript for years.'[3]

Study of the sources of the Mowgli stories must always be accompanied by the recognition that they are works of imagination, fancy, fantasy, fiction, not credible anecdotes of jungle life. It is symbolically of some significance that Kipling transferred the setting of the stories from forests of Northern India which he knew well, and which are depicted in 'In the Rukh', to the Seoni district of Central India where he may never have set foot. The stories were written in the study, not in the jungle. Their chief literary sources are undoubtedly the anecdotes of Rudyard's father, Lockwood Kipling, in his *Beast and Man in India* (1891), full of Indian village- and jungle-lore (and these surely will have been coloured and enriched by Lockwood's table-talk), together with *Mammalia of India* (1884) and other books by Robert Armitage Sterndale. Here, for instance, we learn of the 'red dog of the Deccan' with hair between its toes. Sterndale also alludes to wolf-child stories, e.g. that of Romulus, and thinks them not impossible. (On this matter Carrington's opinion, based on expert advice, seems plausible; there could in real life be an individual, X, who was suckled as a baby by a

[3] C. E. Carrington, in *The Readers' Guide to Rudyard Kipling's Works*, ed. R. E. Harbord, vol. 7 (Bournemouth, 1972), pp. 3025–6.

wolf, and there could be an individual, Y, who was a wild man of the woods, but X and Y could not be the same person.) Another source that may be mentioned, perhaps as much of value to Kipling as their conversation, was probably the photographs of the Seoni district (now in the Carpenter Collection in Washington, DC) which his friends Professor and Mrs Hill took during their vacations there in the late eighteen-eighties.

A few other possible minor sources or allusions in the Mowgli stories will be touched on in the Explanatory Notes. But one requires special mention here, since it is the only stimulus Kipling himself acknowledged. This is *Nada the Lily* (1892), a novel by his friend Sir Henry Rider Haggard (1856–1925). Kipling wrote to Haggard that it was a 'chance sentence' in that book—well worth reading for its own sake, a powerful study of Chaka, a sort of Zulu Napoleon—that 'started me off on a track that ended in my writing a lot of wolf stories. You remember in your tale [i.e. on p. 103] where the wolves leaped up at the feet of a dead man sitting on a rock. Somewhere on that page I got the notion.'[4] For fuller discussion of this, and many other elements in the concoction of *The Jungle Books*, the reader is referred to chapter 6 of that excellent book *Kipling and the Children* (1965), by Roger Lancelyn Green.

But no study of sources, known or hypothetical, can be of more than peripheral importance when we are dealing with so distinguished an artist as Kipling at his best, and discussion of *The Jungle Books* should be made to centre not on their origins, of which we can know little, but on their meaning. This is something, of course, that readers will find out for themselves. It will be one thing if and when the reader is a child discovering the stories for the first time; another thing if the reader is an adult in that situation; yet another thing if the adult re-reads them, remembering his childhood reading. And of course one child, or one adult, or one adult remembering childhood,

---

[4] H. Rider Haggard, *The Days of My Life* (London, 1926), vol. 2, p. 17.

is very different from another. All the same, those readers who have reported on their readings—the critics—do seem very often to converge in their interpretations and judgments, and (whether this was their purpose or not) concur in one observation at least: *The Jungle Books* are very *odd* works, not really quite like anything else by Kipling, or any other writer. A little conjecture why this is so may perhaps be permitted.

Even when they are read only as fairytales, it is clear that the Mowgli stories are the expression of a powerful myth. They tell the story of how the baby abandoned in the jungle by his parents when the tiger attacks them is brought up by animals: (he is adopted by the wolves, a mighty people, and secures strong protectors, the head wolf Akela, the bear Baloo and the black panther Bagheera), and through a combination of what they have to teach him about the Jungle with his own innate capacities as a human being he becomes Master of the Jungle. The boy reader identifies with Mowgli and enjoys the transformation into joyful fantasy of the impulse to dominate. But at the same time the stories are carrying a message to him, which is only partly explicit. The explicit message is educational. Elliot L. Gilbert in *The Good Kipling* (1972) points out that the Mowgli stories are what he calls a *Bildungsroman*. In realistic fiction this genre is concerned with the struggle of a young man or woman to discover his or her 'identity', to discover as far as may be possible the truth about themselves. Gilbert shows how this kind of story is told in *The Jungle Books* in a fairytale, fabulous form. Mowgli spends his whole life among animals. But as he approaches manhood he begins to find that he is not like the animals. A central symbol for this is Mowgli's eyes. They are the source of his power over the beasts, who cannot meet his gaze. From the beginning they have been the sign that he is not one of the beasts: '. . . the look in [Mowgli's] eyes was always gentle. Even when he fought, his eyes never blazed as Bagheera's did. They only grew more and more interested and excited.' Mowgli has passed through a preliminary training which in many ways is like that suitable to animals. But a time comes when he must move beyond his animal 'brothers', and realize the truth about himself, and accept the responsibility of being a man, and the recognition that it sets him apart.

This theme of growing up, of becoming a new self, runs through much of *The Jungle Books*. Rikki-tikki-tavi, the mongoose, washed away from his parents by a summer flood, the White Seal discovering how to release his people from the threat of death, and finding himself at the end occupying on the new beach the position his father had held on the old, Purun Bhagat leaving the life of a Westernized statesman to take up the totally different existence of an ascetic hermit—all these stories, so different in setting and circumstances, are all exploring the theme of self-discovery and the realization that a new life has begun.

Much of Kipling's fiction for children and young people can be described as educational. The didacticism of *Just So Stories* (1902), meant for little ones, is only playful, a parody of Victorian 'instructional' pabulum, but the pedagogic element in *Captains Courageous* (1896–7) and the *Puck* books (*Puck of Pook's Hill*, 1906, and *Rewards and Fairies*, 1910) is meant seriously and is part of the meaning of those books. Obviously Baloo, Bagheera etc. are schoolmasters in animal costume, and a good deal of the subject is the acculturation of a late-Victorian child, put into symbolic form. But in other ways the Mowgli stories are not really like the educational books, but belong with another area of Kipling's fiction that came from deeper down in him, something more personal, and with more potent 'unconscious' or latent content; belong, in short, with 'Baa Baa, Black Sheep' (in *Wee Willie Winkie*, 1888), known to be based on the terrible experiences of Rudyard's own childhood, and, above all, with *Kim* (1900–1), the novel-poem which was the supreme imaginative correlate of all that India had meant to him. In other words, Mowgli belongs with Punch of 'Baa Baa, Black Sheep' and with Kim, as a study of the Waif. He belongs with Kim, and not with Punch, in so far as he is a waif who finds helpers and an environment which is co-operative with him and which he can eventually control. In this respect—the achievement of domination—Mowgli differs from another famous waif of late nineteenth-century literature, Mark Twain's Huck Finn. Both boys feel the lure of the uncivilized, the freedom from the restraints of the man-made world, but while Huck 'lights out for the Territory' Mowgli ends in the government service, like Kim.

It cannot be denied, then, that the message of the Mowgli stories is political. In much of his fiction of the eighties Kipling had studied various casualties of the imperial system in India. He had projected an unfavourable view of the activities at the top of the Indian government, in the summer capital of Simla. He had written stories showing the weakness of the imported 'sahibs', some of whom became too remote, in their clubs and other British dominated institutions, from the life of the people they were trying to govern. He had also seen the opposite weakness, the ruler who identifies too much with the subject people and 'goes native', like McIntosh Jellaludin in *Plain Tales from the Hills*. In the nineties Kipling was putting forward a positive project for the salvation of the Indian Empire through the improvement of its administration. The key figures would be people with a similar background to Kipling's own, the English born in India, who knew both worlds, and could pass from one to another, and back again, without being compromised.

We can see something of these ideas at the back of the Mowgli stories. As John A. McClure points out (in *Kipling and Conrad*, 1981), they can be read as an allegory of imperialism. Mowgli is learning the art of a colonial ruler, and the animals represent the natives, the subject people. He enforces his domination by what in the political jargon of the time was called Orientalism. He moves freely among the people, they are his 'brothers', yet at the same time he is not of them. Similarly Kim is the

'Little Friend of all the World', but in the last resort he uses the inside knowledge he has gained from living with the Indians to serve the imperial government. The problem for the reader about this consciously dual role played by the hero, slipping back and forwards across the border, is partly one of political (and moral) judgment. 'Fraternalism' (as it may be called) can be, and is, made very attractive by Kipling's literary art in the mutual happiness of Mowgli and the animals, Kim and the Indians. But it clearly begs the question of why the country-born figure has to dominate at all, or why, if he has to, he should not be in truth fully one of his own people, 'Jungle-dwellers' or 'Indians', according to which symbolism is being used. And we may wonder whether 'fraternity' in the end can really mean very much apart from the 'liberty' and 'equality' with which the slogan of French republicanism associates it. There is also the imaginative difficulty that in practice fraternalism seems to amount to the hero's behaving like a spy (which is what Kim, in the Great Game, actually becomes). McClure, writing as an American very consciously in the post-Vietnam-war perspective, is very severe on this aspect of the Mowgli stories, and it is not necessary to take such a harsh view of Kipling's politics to feel rather uncomfortable in those scenes between Mowgli and Bagheera in which the human hero asserts his superiority over the panther who is the 'natural' king of the Jungle. The appeal to fraternalism ('We be of one blood, ye and I') which is the key to Mowgli's success, looks a bit strained when it is juxtaposed with the naked assertion of power, as in this passage from 'Letting in the Jungle':

... Once more Mowgli stared, as he had stared at the rebellious cubs, full into the beryl-green eyes [of Bagheera] till the red glare behind their green went out like the lighthouse shut off twenty miles across the sea; till the eyes dropped, and the big head with them—dropped lower and lower, and the red rasp of a tongue grated on Mowgli's instep.

'Brother—Brother—Brother!' the boy whispered, stroking steadily and lightly from the neck along the heaving back ...

This tableau of the mighty panther licking the feet of the boy who calls him 'Brother' is psychologically convincing, but the ethical and political implications—if we take it as of symbolic significance—are problematic. That at least must be conceded to McClure's view.

Those who would prefer a more inclusive, less tendentious reading of the stories, one that does more justice to the magical atmosphere, the moralized fantasy, characteristic of *The Jungle Books*, should concentrate less on their function as sweetening the pill for the indoctrination of a Victorian imperialist, and more on the manifest theme of the stories, one central to Kipling's philosophy. This word does not seem entirely inappropriate, though it must be kept in mind that his philosophy was largely intuitive and not worked out on a systematic logical basis. We have come here, of course, to 'The Law', and what it meant to Kipling. McClure sees it merely as a formulation of Social Darwinism. But a more sympathetic, profounder and perhaps truer view of this concept is taken by Shamsul Islam in his book *Kipling's 'Law'* (1975). He shows the reiterated emphasis, and the religious seriousness and solemnity, with which Kipling invests it.

'Listen, Man-cub,' said the Bear, and his voice rumbled like thunder on a hot night. 'I have taught thee all the Law of the Jungle for all the peoples of the Jungle—except the Monkey-Folk who live in the trees. They have no Law. They are outcasts.'

In the words of Kipling's most notorious line of verse (from 'Recessional', 1897) they are 'lesser breeds without the Law'. But what does this *mean*? Whatever it means exactly, it permeates *The Jungle Books*, and not only the Mowgli stories. Purun Bhagat, going about with his begging bowl, passes through a busy Simla street and is stopped by a Muslim policeman for obstructing the traffic, and 'Purun Bhagat salaamed reverently to the Law, because he knew the value of it, and was seeking for a Law of his own'. We think of *Kim* (for which the story of Purun Bhagat is in some ways a 'trailer'), in which the Lama says

'I follow the Law—the Most Excellent Law.' In the animal stories we constantly 'hear the call—Good hunting all/That keep the Jungle Law!' ('Night-song in the Jungle'.) It is said to be 'the oldest law in the world ... arranged for almost every kind of accident that may befall the Jungle People, till now its code is as perfect as time and custom can make it'. Baloo told Mowgli that the Law was like the Giant Creeper, because it dropped across everyone's back and no one could escape. On the day of the Water Truce, Hathi the elephant tells the story of 'How Fear Came', a Jungle parallel to the story of the Fall of Man in the Garden in *Genesis*. 'The first of your masters has brought Death into the Jungle, and the second Shame. Now it is time there was a Law, and a Law that ye must not break.'

All this makes it sound as if the Law were a matter of the arbitrary commands of a god. But it is not. Nor is it simply a collection of prudential or 'utility' principles. It has something in it of both the prescriptive and the descriptive, but it is not fully reducible to either. In an extended discussion Dr Islam identifies the essential elements of the Law. The most important of these is that it is rational, the antithesis of *dewanee* (Urdu for 'madness', 'irrationality'). All the Jungle People fear this, 'the most disgraceful thing that can overtake a wild creature'. The rational basis of the Law is shown, for instance in the reason why the Law of the Jungle forbids the killing of Man:

The Law of the Jungle, which never orders anything without a reason, forbids every beast to eat Man ... The real reason for this is that man-killing means, sooner or later, the arrival of white men on elephants with guns, and hundreds of brown men with gongs and rockets and torches. Then everybody in the Jungle suffers.

The Law of the Jungle is geared to the attainment of the common good. 'The strength of the Pack is the Wolf, and the strength of the Wolf is the Pack.' ('But every wolf has full right under the Law to fight', as cross Mowgli once forgot when he tried to stop two young ones fighting.) In case of danger to the community the Law prescribes immediate offensive action to protect society from disintegration. In 'Kaa's Hunting' the lawless monkeys intrude into the Jungle, and the followers of the Law take immediate action against them. In 'Red Dog' the Pack decides, on the advice of Mowgli and Akela, to fight rather than surrender to the enemy. Similarly Rikki undertakes grave dangers in fighting against the cobras, symbols of lawlessness, to restore the peace and harmony of the whole community of the bungalow and its garden. The Law enjoins ethical values: moderation; respect for elders; kindness to both young and old; fortitude; the value of keeping one's word; the danger of pride and the need for humility. 'Hold thy peace above the kill', Bagheera advises Mowgli. Finally, devotion to duty and work are advocated.

In personal relationships, Mowgli and his friends go beyond the explicit code of the Seeonee Wolf Pack. Much is made of the love between Mowgli and the animals; the risks Baloo and Bagheera and Kaa take to rescue him from the Bandar-log; the willingness of the wolf brothers to sacrifice their lives for his sake; Mowgli's decision to stay with the pack when the red dogs attack. Love is shown in the emotion of grief at loss, as when the animals lament at Mowgli's departure from the Jungle. The scene is charged with emotion. 'It is hard to cast the skin,' says Kaa, as Mowgli sobbed and sobbed, with his head on the blind bear's side and his arms round his neck, while Baloo tried feebly to lick his feet.

Mowgli also goes beyond the code in his idea of justice. He hears the word from Messua's husband and he says, 'I do not know what justice is, but—come thou back next rains and see what is left.' Mowgli's concept of justice is close to revenge in 'Letting in the Jungle'. McClure comments on the savagery of this story, and suggests that it arises from Kipling's own hysterical vindictiveness, deriving from his days of impotent suffering in the House of Desolation. But we must also remember that this is a primitive society.

The thoughtful reader of the stories is reminded from time to time that not all the Law is natural law, the eternal law ordained by God. Some of it is positive law, and therefore requires law making, authority and promulgation. This aspect of the Law is shown by the proviso that the leader of the Pack can make new rules for a situation not already dealt with. 'The word of the Head Wolf is Law.' Finally, there is a good deal in the stories about the importance of custom and tradition. As Noel Annan has said, Kipling in much of his work is preoccupied with what holds society together.[5] In *The Jungle Books* it is clear that religion and custom, convention and morality, and laws, are forces of social control. The individual breaks these rules at his peril.

All this is communicated to the youthful reader in language which he can understand, and in terms of a morality which is second nature to him, a morality of 'just deserts' and 'just reward'. Yet it is conveyed by way of a masterpiece of story-telling, which can be enjoyed without a thought of the didactic content. Imaginative, aesthetic, and sensuous, the Jungle is 'there' as a complex evocative symbol, of which the full significance cannot be paraphrased.

The Jungle Books were once very popular, but are perhaps not much read now. This may be due to reasons for some of which Kipling was responsible, and for some of which he was not. One of the latter was the appropriation of the Mowgli theme by the American writer Edgar Rice Burroughs (1875–1950), with his series of stories, beginning with *Tarzan of the Apes* (1914), about the son of an English aristocrat abandoned in the jungle as a baby and reared by apes. (Kipling read *Tarzan* and remarks that the author had 'jazzed' the motif of *The Jungle Books* 'and, I imagine, had thoroughly enjoyed himself'.)[6] A later misfortune, also not Kipling's fault, was the Disney cartoon of *The Jungle Book*, harmless entertainment and

---

[5] See 'Kipling's Place in the History of Ideas', *Kipling's Mind and Art*, ed. Andrew Rutherford (Edinburgh and London, 1964), pp. 101–2.
[6] *Something of Myself*, p. 219

nothing to do with Kipling, but marred even as that by Disney's awful cuteness. More responsibility on Kipling's part may be assigned to the use made of Mowgli and his friends by Baden-Powell in the Boy Scout movement. Kipling was a friend of Baden-Powell and he had no objection to this, but the activities of those dear little boys called Wolf Cubs make it more difficult to see *The Jungle Books* as the profound works of literature which they really are. But above all it is Kipling's 'views' (which W. H. Auden said time would pardon)[7] that probably do most to turn readers away in the late twentieth century. Nor is it easy to separate the views from the art, nor what is distasteful from what is permanently valid in the views themselves. All that need be said of this here is that it would surely be a pity if any consideration of 'views' should prevent any reader, old or young, from flying through the air with Mowgli and the Bandar-log, or joining Mowgli in the 'armchair' of the aged python's coils, or savouring the tremendous scene in 'Red Dog' when the Bee People swarm among the ancient rocks.

Of the Mowgli stories in the first *Jungle Book*, 'Mowgli's Brothers' is in a class by itself. It creates the whole world of the Jungle, and by implication suggests essentially everything that is to follow in the other stories about him. From the moment when Father Wolf carries the 'naked brown baby' in his mouth to Mother Wolf in the cave we know that we are in the company of a great story-teller, like Aesop. The stories seem always to have existed. We do not think of anyone as making them up. Yet the Kipling ideology is slyly present. The baby already reveals his membership of the Master Race as he looks up into Father Wolf's face and laughs when the wolf was checked in

---

[7] See the stanza subsequently cut from 'In Memory of W. B. Yeats':

> Time that with this strange excuse
> Pardoned Kipling and his views,
> And will pardon Paul Claudel,
> Pardons him for writing well.

midspring, and when he is 'pushing his way between the cubs' to get to Mother Wolf's teats. Later,

Father Wolf taught him his business, and the meaning of things in the Jungle, till every rustle in the grass, every breath of the warm night air, every note of the owls above his head, every scratch of a bat's claws as it roosted for a while in a tree, and every splash of every little fish jumping in a pool, meant just as much to him as the work of his office does to a business man.

He is a citizen of two worlds by now, called 'Mowgli the Frog' (it has been suggested) because the frog is an amphibian. The simplicity of the writing, appropriate to the child reader, can take on a Swift-like mordancy when for a moment an adult reader is envisaged:

The Lame Wolf had led them for a year now. He had fallen twice into a wolf-trap in his youth, and once had been beaten and left for dead; so he knew the manners and customs of men.

'Mowgli's Brothers' has many fine things. But it has the inevitable defects of a pioneer work; the construction is a little jerky, compared with such masterpieces of flowing narration as 'Kaa's Hunting' or 'Red Dog'.

'Kaa's Hunting' is the rival of 'Red Dog' for the title of the best Mowgli story. The humour of Mowgli and his bear and panther schoolmasters, the humour of their relations with Kaa, will not be lost on the child reader, while the adult can relish how cleverly it is done. The imaginative symbols of the story are two, the Bandar-log and Kaa. It is fairly plain what the monkeys represent, though this is not a simple allegory: the Bandar-log may be a glance at the bad side of American democracy (we remember that the Seeonee Pack are pointedly called 'the Free People'); they may also remind us of London (or any other) literary circles. But essentially they are a standing metaphor, available for application according to the relevant experience of the reader. The symbolism of Kaa goes deeper. What do Kaa and his coils represent? Snakiness, coldness, the physical and moral strength of a power emancipated from passion; age, memory. ... Soon it becomes clear that the symbol is polyvalent, cannot be exhausted in a formula. The young reader, gripped by the story and the humour, is insensibly learning about new possibilities in *human* life (not really about pythons). With the Cold Lairs we have an imaginative extension that goes beyond the simple moral tale of the naughty boy who played with the monkeys. And in the powerful scene when Kaa hypnotises the Bandar-log, while Baloo and Bagheera too fall under the spell, and uncomprehending little Mowgli looks on untouched, the theme of *The Jungle Book*, in so far as it turns on Mowgli, is neatly dramatized.

'Tiger! Tiger!' is a disappointment. The showdown between Mowgli and Shere Khan has been long awaited; it is crucial to the saga. But the adult reader may be almost as puzzled as the child reader as to just how Shere Khan was killed. And it is a minor mystery why Kipling, having conceived Shere Khan as the second-rate, nasty character he is, should have reminded us in the title of Blake's Tyger, 'burning bright'. Perhaps there is an intentionally ironic effect here. Perhaps, also, the fact that (as in 'Red Dog') Mowgli gets others to do his killing for him, has something to do with the hidden unromantic theme: that getting things done in the real world is less a matter of personal heroics than of ingenuity and the capacity for collective organization. But none of this, even if it is meant to be there, makes the story very good. It is chiefly interesting for Mowgli's relations with the Man Pack. These (apart from the mysterious English at Khanhiwara) are portrayed unfavourably. The life of the village is one of mud walls, narrowness, superstition, prejudice. The exception is Messua. Here warm human feeling comes in, indicated with great tact and delicacy. Messua is clearly in love with 'Nathoo': is he with her? 'Nathoo', as Messua sees him, is someone who might well have grown up to be the Mowgli we meet in 'In the Rukh'. But this Mowgli is a more complex figure, with his ambiguous position between the Jungle and the human worlds, that is to be beautifully worked out in 'The Spring Running'.

'The White Seal' has probably been much less read than

the Mowgli stories. In a book by Edith Nesbit, a disciple of Kipling, it is remarked as an oddity that one of the characters knows it. 'The White Seal' has been underrated: it is superior to its counterpart, 'Quiquern', in the second *Jungle Book*, for although in both stories Kipling has mugged up a lot of information, it is worn more lightly in the earlier story. Kotick, the White Seal, is an anomaly, like Mowgli, and like Mowgli he saves his people. There is some delightful descriptive writing, and the humour of Sea Cow as an old gentleman is lively, though gentle; there is a flavour of Lewis Carroll's Mock Turtle about him. There is also a flavour in the whole story of Charles Kingsley's *The Water Babies* (1863), a work which Kipling knew well: a blend of sensuous realism with fantasy similar to Kingsley's water world. 'The White Seal' may also be called, on its smaller scale, a *Bildungsroman*. It is a charming story (the accompanying poetry has more charm than the verse in *The Jungle Books* usually has) and the work of a master writer, but we do not feel the Daemon as conspicuously present.

In contrast, 'Rikki-tikki-tavi' seems to be a story that was born, not made. The adults and children who enjoy it together are enjoying the same things. Also the story may be more obviously attractive than the Mowgli stories, though they are deeper and more powerful. Rikki has the moral virtues Kipling wants us to admire, but he is less part of the official machinery than Mowgli. There are no bears, etc. lecturing on civics; and the Law is only present by implication. The mongoose has his own law, he is an empiricist. The story beautifully creates the world of the Indian bungalow and the garden. The sinister Nag and his wife Nagaina render the Kipling aphorism: 'the female of the species is more deadly than the male.' There is humour in Darzee and his wife. The balance of sympathies is well held, the fallacies of Darzee, the realism of his wife, the timidity of Chuchundra versus the bravery of Rikki, the evil Nag, and Nagaina even more savage but more sympathetic, trying to save her children.

'Toomai of the Elephants' may have been the first *Jungle Book* story to be written. It is more in the tradition of the Ernest Thompson Seton animals stories: none of the elephants speak, and even Little Toomai cannot converse with Kala Nag. Toomai himself is pleasantly sketched, but he is a slight character. The story was made into a British film, *Elephant Boy* (London Films, 1937). Apart from the co-director, Zoltan Korda, and the Indian actor Sabu, there were intelligent people connected with it, the director Robert Flaherty and the actor Walter Huston, but it deserved Graham Greene's scathing review (reprinted in *The Pleasure Dome*, 1972). Greene says that 'Kala Nag's attack on the camp should have been the first great climax of the picture'. But the 'scene is thrown away'. The elephants do not dance as Kipling described them. Greene notes something crude and cruel in Kipling's mind. 'We are expected to feel satisfaction at the thought of the wild dancers driven into the stockade to be tamed.' Yet it is only when Kipling speaks, in his own dialogue, when Machua Appa apostrophizes Toomai, that 'the ear is caught and the attention held'.

'Her Majesty's Servants' is even more minor. It is enjoyable, but slight. The world of the pack-animals, with the human narrator hearing everything, lacks the secrecy and magic of the Jungle. The story is memorable only for the finale, which in its context amounts to a mighty peroration on Kipling's great theme of obedience—without which you cannot run an empire, conduct an orchestra, control the traffic, perform a surgical operation, etc., etc. Politics apart, this is the verbal music to which the reader, coming to it as the epilogue of the first *Jungle Book*, cannot but thrill.

'... Mule, horse, elephant, or bullock, he obeys his driver, and the driver his sergeant, and the sergeant his lieutenant, and the lieutenant his captain, and the captain his major, and the major his colonel, and the colonel his brigadier commanding three regiments, and the brigadier his general, who obeys the Viceroy, who is the servant of the Empress. Thus it is done.'

'Would it were so in Afghanistan!' said the chief; 'for there we obey only our own wills.'

'And for that reason,' said the native officer, twirling his moustache, 'your Amir whom you do not obey must come here and take orders from our Viceroy.'

The Second Jungle Book is superior to the first. Three at least of the Mowgli stories are first-rate, and there is at least one other story ('The Miracle of Purun Bhagat') which is unsurpassed in Kipling's work generally. 'How Fear Came' is chiefly valuable for deepening the myth of the Jungle, giving it the suggestion of a scripture and a theology. The horrors of drought are hinted at, without disturbing the atmosphere of a bedtime story—suitable for a bath night: '. . . Mowgli, lying on his elbows in the warm water, laughed aloud, and beat up the scum with his feet.' But Mowgli himself plays only a subordinate part in the story. And the suggestion that the Jungle is 'fallen' is not altogether in harmony with other stories, in which it is innocent and Eden-like in contrast with the greater corruptions—and greater opportunities—of human civilization.

In 'Letting in the Jungle' Mowgli plays the main part, but it is not one of the best of the stories. The dialogue between Mowgli and Hathi is impressive. But the process of arranging Mowgli's revenge seems to take a long time, and perhaps it drags a little. Again, as in 'Tiger! Tiger!', the human world comes off poorly; apart from the hostility of the villagers, the grown-ups lack magic, as in one of Edith Nesbit's stories; the fairytale fades into the light of common day. Once again Mowgli is not permitted to shed human blood: he gets others to wreak his revenge for him. There is no doubt that his conduct is savage and cruel, and this is an aspect of Kipling that admirers have to face. He wrote a number of revenge stories. But they come to an end with 'Dayspring Mishandled' (1928), one of Kipling's best stories, in which the avenger gives up his revenge. For the young Kipling, however, revenge was still sweet.

'The King's Ankus' needs no apologia, and no explanation. At least one critic has called it the best of the Mowgli stories. Two considerations could be urged against that view. First, it is less rich in atmosphere than 'Kaa's Hunting', or 'Red Dog'. The easy way in which the Jungle 'properties' are handled in the early pages suggests that if Kipling had decided to turn these stories into a series 'The King's Ankus' might have been the prototype. Secondly, Mowgli's role is somewhat marginal. He learns something—something very terrible—about human greed and wickedness, but we learn nothing new about him. The story, which is very well told, is a traditional one, and the analogy with 'The Pardoner's Tale' of Chaucer, about the men who went in search of Death, is apt. But, although Kipling greatly admired Chaucer, the two stories seem quite independent. The moral is equally forceful in both of them.

'Red Dog' is surely the masterpiece of the Mowgli stories in this book. Kaa is again impressive. He is *seen* wonderfully here:

For a long time Mowgli lay back among the coils, while Kaa, his head motionless on the ground, thought of all that he had seen and known since the day he came from the egg. The light seemed to go out of his eyes and leave them like stale opals, and now and again he made little stiff passes with his head, right and left, as though he were hunting in his sleep.

Kipling's poetic genius is kindled, as in 'The Mother Hive' (1908), by the opportunity to evoke the world of bees.

For centuries the Little People had hived and swarmed from cleft to cleft, and swarmed again, staining the white marble with stale honey, and made their combs tall and deep in the dark of the inner caves, where neither man nor beast nor fire nor water had ever touched them. The length of the gorge on both sides was hung as it were with black shimmery velvet curtains, and Mowgli sank as he looked, for those were the clotted millions of the sleeping bees.... As he listened he heard more than once the rustle and slide of a honey-loaded comb turning over or falling away somewhere in the dark galleries; then a booming of angry wings, and the sullen drip, drip, drip, of the wasted honey, guttering along till it lipped over some ledge in the open air and sluggishly trickled down on the twigs.

The story is the most 'epic' in quality in the Mowgli series. J. M. S. Tompkins compares it to scenes in Tolkien's *Lord of the Rings*. A precedent may be found in Macaulay's 'Horatius': the *Lays of Ancient Rome* are an earlier example of the use of legendary, mythic material in the education of the young Victorian imperialist. But the use of the beast-fable perhaps limits the power and scope of the story, whereas Macaulay's use of Livy and 'the brave days of old' enhances them. Roger Sale has complained that the destruction of the *dhole* by the wild bees is anti-climactic,[8] and perhaps Mowgli's craft and cunning a little eclipse his warriorhood. Otherwise the story is replete with the traditional motifs of heroic fable: the Lone Wolf, the death of Akela. Finally, it represents the climax of the Mowgli *Bildungsroman*: his victory over the red dogs makes him Master of the Jungle.

'The Spring Running' makes a better epilogue than the too 'arty' 'In the Rukh'. It may have too little 'story', perhaps, to attract the young reader. Yet it may be that he will sense dimly what it is about and respond to it without knowing why. The cold word 'puberty' is here replaced by this marvellous and delicate evocation of the upsurge of a new kind of life. As often in Kipling, it is through the use of *sound* that much of the effect is created.

There is one day when all things are tired, and the very smells, as they drift on the heavy air, are old and used. One cannot explain this, but it feels so. Then there is another day—to the eye nothing whatever has changed—when all the smells are new and delightful, and the whiskers of the Jungle People quiver to their roots, and the winter hair comes away from their sides in long, draggled locks. Then, perhaps, a little rain falls, and all the trees and the bushes and the bamboos and the mosses and the juicy-leaved plants wake with a noise of growing that you can almost hear, and under this noise runs, day and night, a deep hum. *That* is the noise of the spring—a vibrating boom which is neither

[8] *Fairy Tales and After* (Cambridge, Mass., 1878), p. 207.

bees, nor falling water, nor the wind in tree-tops, but the purring of the warm, happy world.

Of the non-Mowgli stories in this book the best is 'The Miracle of Purun Bhagat'. Possibly it is not really in place in *The Jungle Books*. It has the Indian setting of the Mowgli stories, and the animals, but they are part of the furniture, not protagonists. This may have led to the tendency of critics to forget about it when they are considering Kipling's claim to be the greatest short-story writer in English. At any rate, it is a very fine story. The theme resembles the Lama motif in *Kim*. The life-history of the Bhagat is the three 'Lives' of *Piers Plowman* in miniature: Do-Well, Do-Better, Do-Best. The Bhagat turns from the Active life of an Indian statesman to the Contemplative life of a hermit, and at the crisis of the story illustrates the Unitive life, when he emerges from his mystic solitude to save his people. Kipling's distinction comes out in his ability to grasp why men have turned to contemplation, though he himself is committed to the life of action. Yet, fine story though it is, 'The Miracle' does not rank with the greatest things in short fiction, such as Tolstoy's 'The Death of Ivan Illich', or Melville's 'Billy Budd'. Though it is not a fairytale, there is something of the distanced, frozen quality of a fairytale about it. The art with which nature is depicted suggests the art of Kipling's uncle-in-law, Burne-Jones. It is lovely, but somehow lacking the quality of major creation. Perhaps Kipling could only resolve the East/West opposition by giving it this distanced, 'framed' kind of setting? But the essential point of the story is its insight into the heart of Purun Dass:

Even when he was being lionised in London he had held before him his dream of peace and quiet—the long, white, dusty Indian road, printed all over with bare feet, the incessant, slow-moving traffic, and the sharp-smelling wood-smoke curling up under the fig-trees in the twilight, where the wayfarers sit at their evening meal.

'The Undertakers' has perhaps been too much ignored. The critics who have mentioned it, such as Roger Lancelyn Green, do not much like it, and it is not oriented towards the young reader. It is a rather slight story, told in an unusual way, largely through flashbacks, in the conversation of the three predators, the Mugger, the Jackal, and the Adjutant. They are all unpleasant characters, but there are some telling ironies, and the whole story can be relished for its sardonic, Ben Jonson-like comedy. There is also a possible complexity of feeling about 'progress', when the Mugger says: 'Since the railway bridge was built my people at my village have ceased to love me; and that is breaking my heart.' But in its context this has no pathos, because we cannot sympathize with the evil crocodile.

'Quiquern' is no one's favourite. The amassing of detail is both laborious and obvious, and the story must be a candidate for the weakest story in both *Jungle Books* (it is inferior to its charming opposite number in the first book, 'The White Seal'). That said, the anecdote on which the story turns is unusual and attractive. But it may be too slight for so much treatment. Indeed 'Quiquern' is almost all 'treatment'. One way to enjoy it is to see it as a story about story-telling. There were no limits to the sophistication and artifice with which Kipling could practise, and reflect on, the ancient art which he had mastered. At the end of 'Quiquern' he plays with the whole notion of 'fiction', and gently and humorously touches on the strangeness, and the chanciness, of it all.

... Kotuko ... scratched pictures of all these adventures on a long, flat piece of ivory with a hole at one end. When he and the girl went north ... he left the picture-story with Kadlu, who lost it in the shingle when his dog-sleigh broke down one summer on the beach of Lake Netilling at Nikosiring ... a Lake Inuit found it next spring and sold it to a man at Imigen ... he sold it to Hans Olsen, who was afterward a quartermaster on a big steamer ... [which stopped] at Ceylon, and there Olsen sold the ivory to a Cingalese jeweller ... I found it under some rubbish in a house at Colombo, and have translated it from one end to the other.

SELECT BIBLIOGRAPHY

THE standard bibliography is J. McG. Stewart's *Rudyard Kipling: A Bibliographical Catalogue*, ed. A. W. Yeats (1959). Reference may also be made to two earlier works: Flora V. Livingston's *Bibliography of the Works of Rudyard Kipling* (1927) with its *Supplement* (1938), and Lloyd H. Chandler's *Summary of the Work of Rudyard Kipling, Including Items ascribed to Him* (1930). We still await a bibliography which will take account of the findings of modern scholarship over the last quarter-century.

The official biography, authorized by Kipling's daughter Elsie, is Charles Carrington's *Rudyard Kipling: His Life and Work* (1955; 3rd edn., revised 1978). Other full-scale biographies are Lord Birkenhead's *Rudyard Kipling* (1978) and Angus Wilson's *The Strange Ride of Rudyard Kipling* (1977). Briefer, copiously illustrated surveys are provided by Martin Fido's *Rudyard Kipling* (1974) and Kingsley Amis's *Rudyard Kipling and his World* (1975), which combine biography and criticism, as do the contributions to *Rudyard Kipling: the man, his work and his world* (also illustrated), ed. John Gross (1972). Information on particular periods of his life is also to be found in such works as A. W. Baldwin, *The Macdonald Sisters* (1960); Alice Macdonald Fleming (*née* Kipling), 'Some Childhood Memories of Rudyard Kipling' and 'More Childhood Memories of Rudyard Kipling', *Chambers Journal*, 8th series, vol. 8 (1939); L. C. Dunsterville, *Stalky's Reminiscences* (1928); G. C. Beresford, *Schooldays with Kipling* (1936); E. Kay Robinson, 'Kipling in India', *McClure's Magazine*, vol. 7 (1896); Edmonia Hill, 'The Young Kipling', *Atlantic Monthly*, vol. 157 (1936); *Kipling's Japan*, ed. Hugh Cartazzi and George Webb (1988); H. C. Rice, *Rudyard Kipling in New England* (1936); Frederic Van de Water, *Rudyard Kipling's Vermont Feud* (1937); Julian Ralph, *War's Brighter Side* (1901); Angela Thirkell, *Three Houses* (1931); *Rudyard Kipling to Rider Haggard: The Record of a Friendship*, ed. Morton Cohen (1965); and '*O Beloved Kids': Rudyard Kipling's Letters to his Children*, ed. Elliot L. Gilbert (1983). Useful background on the India he knew is provided by 'Philip Woodruff' (Philip Mason) in *The Men Who Ruled India*

Simla: A Hill Station in British India (1978). Kipling's own autobiography, *Something of Myself* (1937), is idiosyncratic but indispensable.

The early reception of Kipling's work is usefully documented in *Kipling: The Critical Heritage*, ed. Roger Lancelyn Green (1971). Richard Le Gallienne's *Rudyard Kipling: A Criticism* (1900), Cyril Falls's *Rudyard Kipling: A Critical Study* (1915), André Chevrillon's *Three Studies in English Literature* (1923) and *Rudyard Kipling* (1936), Edward Shanks's *Rudyard Kipling: A Study in Literature and Political Ideas* (1940), and Hilton Brown's *Rudyard Kipling: A New Appreciation* (1945) were all serious attempts at reassessment; while Ann M. Weygandt's study of *Kipling's Reading and Its Influence on His Poetry* (1939), and (in more old-fashioned vein) Ralph Durand's *Handbook to the Poetry of Rudyard Kipling* (1914) remain useful pieces of scholarship.

T. S. Eliot's introduction to *A Choice of Kipling's Verse* (1941; see *On Poetry and Poets*, 1957) began a period of more sophisticated reappraisal. There are influential essays by Edmund Wilson (1941; see *The Wound and the Bow*), George Orwell (1942; see his *Critical Essays*, 1946), Lionel Trilling (1943; see *The Liberal Imagination*, 1951), W. H. Auden (1943; see *New Republic*, vol. 109), and C. S. Lewis (1948; see *They Asked for a Paper*, 1962). These were followed by a series of important book-length studies which include J. M. S. Tompkins, *The Art of Rudyard Kipling* (1959); C. A. Bodelsen, *Aspects of Kipling's Art* (1964); Roger Lancelyn Green, *Kipling and the Children* (1965); Louis L. Cornell, *Kipling in India* (1966); and Bonamy Dobrée, *Rudyard Kipling: Realist and Fabulist* (1967), which follows on from his earlier studies in *The Lamp and the Lute* (1929) and *Rudyard Kipling* (1951). There were also two major collections of critical essays: *Kipling's Mind and Art*, ed. Andrew Rutherford (1964), with essays by W. L. Renwick, Edmund Wilson, George Orwell, Lionel Trilling, Noel Annan, George Shepperson, Alan Sandison, the editor himself, Mark Kinkead-Weekes, J. H. Fenwick, and W. W. Robson; and *Kipling and the Critics*, ed. Elliot L. Gilbert (1965), with essays, parodies, etc. by Andrew Lang, Oscar Wilde, Henry James, Robert Buchanan, Max Beerbohm, Bonamy Dobrée, Boris Ford, George Orwell, Lionel Trilling, C. S. Lewis, T. S. Eliot, J. M. S. Tompkins, Randall Jarrell, Steven Marcus, and the editor himself. Nirad C.

Jeffrey Meyers, *Fiction and the Colonial Experience* (1972); Shamsul Islam, *Kipling's 'Law'* (1975); J. S. Bratton, *The Victorian Popular Ballad* (1975); Philip Mason, *Kipling: The Glass, The Shadow and The Fire* (1975); John Bayley, *The Uses of Division* (1976); M. Van Wyk Smith, *Drummer Hodge: The Poetry of the Anglo-Boer War 1899–1902* (1978); Stephen Prickett, *Victorian Fantasy* (1979); Martin Green, *Dreams of Adventure, Deeds of Empire* (1980); J. A. McClure, *Kipling and Conrad* (1981); R. F. Moss, *Rudyard Kipling and the Fiction of Adolescence* (1982); S. S. Azfar Husain, *The Indianness of Rudyard Kipling: A Study in Stylistics* (1983); Norman Page, *A Kipling Companion* (1984); B. J. Moore-Gilbert, *Kipling and 'Orientalism'* (1986); Sandra Kemp, *Kipling's Hidden Narratives* (1988); Norah Crook, *Kipling's Myths of Love and Death* (1989); and Ann Parry, *The Poetry of Rudyard Kipling* (1992); while further collections of essays include *Rudyard Kipling*, ed. Harold Bloom (1987); *Kipling Considered*, ed. Phillip Mallet (1989); and *Critical Essays on Rudyard Kipling*, ed. Harold Orel (1989). Among the most important recent studies are Edward Said, *Culture and Imperialism* (1991); Sara Suleri, *The Rhetoric of English India* (1992); Zohrah T. Sullivan, *Narratives of Empire: The Fictions of Rudyard Kipling* (1993); and Peter Keating, *Kipling the Poet* (1994).

Two important additions to the available corpus of Kipling's writings are *Kipling's India: Uncollected Sketches*, ed. Thomas Pinney (1986); and *Early Verse by Rudyard Kipling 1879–89: Unpublished, Uncollected and Rarely Collected Poems*, ed. Andrew Rutherford (1986). Indispensable is Pinney's edition of *The Letters of Rudyard Kipling*, of which Vols. I and II appeared in 1990, Vol. III in 1995, and Vol. IV in 1998.

A CHRONOLOGY OF KIPLING'S
LIFE AND WORKS

THE dates given here for Kipling's works are those of first authorized publication in volume form, whether this was in India, America, or England. (The dates of subsequent editions are not listed.) It should be noted that individual poems and stories collected in these volumes had in many cases appeared in newspapers or magazines of earlier dates. For full details see James McG. Stewart, *Rudyard Kipling: A Bibliographical Catalogue*, ed. A. W. Yeats, Toronto, 1959; but see also the editors' notes in this World's Classics series.

1865   Rudyard Kipling born at Bombay on 30 December, son of John Lockwood Kipling and Alice Kipling (*née* Macdonald).

1871   In December Rudyard and his sister Alice Macdonald Kipling ('Trix'), who was born in 1868, are left in the charge of Captain and Mrs Holloway at Lorne Lodge, Southsea ('The House of Desolation'), while their parents return to India.

1877   Alice Kipling returns from India in March/April and removes the children from Lorne Lodge, though Trix returns there subsequently.

1878   Kipling is admitted in January to the United Services College at Westward Ho! in Devon. First visit to France with his father that summer. (Many visits later in his life.)

1880   Meets and falls in love with Florence Garrard, a fellow-boarder of Trix's at Southsea and prototype of Maisie in *The Light that Failed*.

1881   Appointed editor of the *United Services College Chronicle*. *Schoolboy Lyrics* privately printed by his parents in Lahore, for limited circulation.

1882   Leaves school at end of summer term. Sails for India on 20 September; arrives Bombay on 18 October. Takes up post as assistant-editor of the *Civil and Military*

Gazette in Lahore in the Punjab, where his father is now Principal of the Mayo College of Art and Curator of the Lahore Museum. Annual leaves from 1883 to 1888 are spent at Simla, except in 1884 when the family goes to Dalhousie.

1884   *Echoes* (by Rudyard and Trix, who has now rejoined the family in Lahore).

1885   *Quartette* (a Christmas Annual by Rudyard, Trix, and their parents).

1886   *Departmental Ditties.*

1887   Transferred in the autumn to the staff of the *Pioneer*, the *Civil and Military Gazette*'s sister-paper, in Allahabad in the North-West Provinces. As special correspondent in Rajputana he writes the articles later collected as 'Letters of Marque' in *From Sea to Sea*. Becomes friendly with Professor and Mrs Hill, and shares their bungalow.

1888   *Plain Tales from the Hills.* Takes on the additional responsibility of writing for the *Week's News*, a new publication sponsored by the *Pioneer*.

1888–9   *Soldiers Three; The Story of the Gadsbys; In Black and White; Under the Deodars; The Phantom Rickshaw; Wee Willie Winkie.*

1889   Leaves India on 9 March; travels to San Francisco with Professor and Mrs Hill via Rangoon, Singapore, Hong Kong, and Japan. Crosses the United States on his own, writing the articles later collected in *From Sea to Sea*. Falls in love with Mrs Hill's sister Caroline Taylor. Reaches Liverpool in October, and makes his début in the London literary world.

1890   Enjoys literary success, but suffers breakdown. Visits Italy. *The Light that Failed.*

1891   Visits South Africa, Australia, New Zealand, and (for the last time) India. Returns to England on hearing of the death of his American friend Wolcott Balestier. *Life's Handicap.*

1892   Marries Wolcott's sister Caroline Starr Balestier ('Carrie') in January. (The bride is given away by

Henry James.) Their world tour is cut short by the loss of his savings in the collapse of the Oriental Banking Company. They establish their home at Brattleboro in Vermont, on the Balestier family estate. Daughter Josephine born in December. *The Naulahka* (written in collaboration with Wolcott Balestier). *Barrack-Room Ballads*.

1893　*Many Inventions*.

1894　*The Jungle Book*.

1895　*The Second Jungle Book*.

1896　Second daughter Elsie born in February. Quarrel with brother-in-law Beatty Balestier and subsequent court case end their stay in Brattleboro. Return to England (Torquay). *The Seven Seas*.

1897　Settles at Rottingdean in Sussex. Son John born in August. *Captains Courageous*.

1898　The first of many winters at Cape Town. Meets Sir Alfred Milner and Cecil Rhodes who becomes a close friend. Visits Rhodesia. *The Day's Work*.

1899　Disastrous visit to the United States. Nearly dies of pneumonia in New York. Death of Josephine. Never returns to USA. *Stalky and Co.*; *From Sea to Sea*.

1900　Helps for a time with army newspaper *The Friend* in South Africa during Boer War. Observes minor action at Karee Siding.

1901　*Kim*.

1902　Settles at 'Bateman's' at Burwash in Sussex. *Just So Stories*.

1903　*The Five Nations*.

1904　*Traffics and Discoveries*.

1906　*Puck of Pook's Hill*.

1907　Nobel Prize for Literature. Visit to Canada. *Collected Verse*.

1909　*Actions and Reactions*; *Abaft the Funnel*.

1910　*Rewards and Fairies*. Death of Kipling's mother.

1911   Death of Kipling's father.

1913   Visit to Egypt. *Songs from Books.*

1914–18 Visits to the Front and to the Fleet. *The New Army in Training, France at War, Sea Warfare,* and other war pamphlets.

1915   John Kipling reported missing on his first day in action with the Irish Guards in the Battle of Loos on 2 October. His body was never found.

1917   *A Diversity of Creatures.* Kipling becomes a member of the Imperial War Graves Commission.

1919   *The Years Between; Rudyard Kipling's Verse: Inclusive Edition.*

1920   *Letters of Travel.*

1923   *The Irish Guards in the Great War; Land and Sea Tales for Scouts and Guides.*

1924   Daughter Elsie marries Captain George Bambridge, M C.

1926   *Debits and Credits.*

1927   Voyage to Brazil.

1928   *A Book of Words.*

1930   *Thy Servant a Dog.* Visit to the West Indies.

1932   *Limits and Renewals.*

1933   *Souvenirs of France.*

1936   Kipling's death, 18 January.

1937   *Something of Myself For My Friends Known and Unknown.*

1937–9 *The Complete Works of Rudyard Kipling,* Sussex Edition. Prepared by Kipling in the last years of his life, this edition contains some previously uncollected items; but in spite of its title it does not include all his works.

1939   Death of Mrs Kipling.

1940   *The Definitive Edition of Rudyard Kipling's Verse.* This is the last of the series of 'Inclusive Editions' of his verse published in 1919, 1921, 1927, and 1933. In spite

The Jungle Book

PREFACE

THE demands made by a work of this nature upon the generosity of specialists are very numerous, and the Editor would be wanting in all title to the generous treatment he has received were he not willing to make the fullest possible acknowledgment of his indebtedness.

His thanks are due in the first place to the scholarly and accomplished Bahadur Shah,* baggage elephant 174 on the Indian Register, who, with his amiable sister Pudmini,* most courteously supplied the history of 'Toomai of the Elephants' and much of the information contained in 'Her Majesty's Servants.' The adventures of Mowgli were collected at various times and in various places from a multitude of informants, most of whom desire to preserve the strictest anonymity. Yet, at this distance, the Editor feels at liberty to thank a Hindu gentleman* of the old rock, an esteemed resident of the upper slopes of Jakko, for his convincing if somewhat caustic estimate of the national characterics of his caste—the Presbytes.* Sahi,* a savant of infinite research and industry, a member of the recently disbanded Seeonee Pack, and an artist well known at most of the local fairs of Southern India, where his muzzled dance with his master attracts the youth, beauty, and culture of many villages, have contributed most valuable data on people, manners, and customs. These have been freely drawn upon, in the stories of 'Tiger! Tiger!' 'Kaa's Hunting,' and 'Mowgli's Brothers.' For the outlines of 'Rikki-tikki-tavi' the Editor stands indebted to one of the leading herpetologists* of Upper India, a fearless and independent investigator who, resolving 'not to live but know,' lately sacrificed his life through over-application to the study of our Eastern Thanatophidia.* A happy accident of travel enabled the Editor, when a passenger on the *Empress of India*, to be of some slight assistance to a fellow-voyager. How richly his poor services were repaid, readers of the 'White Seal' may judge for themselves.

CONTENTS

Mowgli's Brothers

Now Rann the Kite brings home the night
    That Mang the Bat sets free—
The herds are shut in byre and hut
    For loosed till dawn are we.
This is the hour of pride and power,
    Talon and tush and claw.
Oh hear the call!—Good hunting all
    That keep the Jungle Law!
                    Night-Song in the Jungle

IT was seven o'clock of a very warm evening in the
Seeonee* hills when Father Wolf woke up from his day's
rest, scratched himself, yawned, and spread out his paws
one after the other to get rid of the sleepy feeling in their
tips. Mother Wolf lay with her big gray nose dropped
across her four tumbling, squealing cubs, and the moon
shone into the mouth of the cave where they all lived.
'Augrh!' said Father Wolf, 'it is time to hunt again'; and he
was going to spring down hill when a little shadow with a
bushy tail crossed the threshold and whined: 'Good luck
go with you, O Chief of the Wolves; and good luck and
strong white teeth go with the noble children, that they
may never forget the hungry in this world.'

It was the jackal—Tabaqui,* the Dish-licker—and the
wolves of India despise Tabaqui because he runs about
making mischief, and telling tales, and eating rags and
pieces of leather from the village rubbish-heaps. But they
are afraid of him too, because Tabaqui, more than any one
else in the jungle, is apt to go mad, and then he forgets that
he was ever afraid of any one, and runs through the forest
biting everything in his way. Even the tiger runs and hides
when little Tabaqui goes mad, for madness is the most
disgraceful thing that can overtake a wild creature. We call
it hydrophobia, but they call it *dewanee*—the madness—
and run.

'Enter, then, and look,' said Father Wolf, stiffly; 'but
there is no food here.'

'For a wolf, no,' said Tabaqui; 'but for so mean a person as myself a dry bone is a good feast. Who are we, the Gidur-log* [the jackal people], to pick and choose?' He scuttled to the back of the cave, where he found the bone of a buck with some meat on it, and sat cracking the end merrily.

'All thanks for this good meal,' he said, licking his lips. 'How beautiful are the noble children! How large are their eyes! And so young too! Indeed, indeed, I might have remembered that the children of kings are men from the beginning.'

Now, Tabaqui knew as well as any one else that there is nothing so unlucky as to compliment children to their faces; and it pleased him to see Mother and Father Wolf look uncomfortable.

Tabaqui sat still, rejoicing in the mischief that he had made, and then he said spitefully:

'Shere Khan,* the Big One, has shifted his hunting-grounds. He will hunt among these hills for the next moon, so he has told me.'

Shere Khan was the tiger who lived near the Waingunga River,* twenty miles away.

'He has no right!' Father Wolf began angrily—'By the Law of the Jungle he has no right to change his quarters without due warning. He will frighten every head of game within ten miles, and I—I have to kill for two, these days.'

'His mother did not call him Lungri* [the Lame One] for nothing,' said Mother Wolf, quietly. 'He has been lame in one foot from his birth. That is why he has only killed cattle. Now the villagers of the Waingunga are angry with him, and he has come here to make *our* villagers angry. They will scour the jungle for him when he is far away, and we and our children must run when the grass is set alight. Indeed, we are very grateful to Shere Khan!'

'Shall I tell him of your gratitude?' said Tabaqui.

'Out!' snapped Father Wolf. 'Out and hunt with thy master. Thou hast done harm enough for one night.'

'I go,' said Tabaqui, quietly. 'Ye can hear Shere Khan

below in the thickets. I might have saved myself the message.'

Father Wolf listened, and below in the valley that ran down to a little river, he heard the dry, angry, snarly, singsong whine of a tiger who has caught nothing and does not care if all the jungle knows it.

'The fool!' said Father Wolf. 'To begin a night's work with that noise! Does he think that our buck are like his fat Waingunga bullocks?'

'H'sh! It is neither bullock nor buck he hunts to-night,' said Mother Wolf. 'It is Man.' The whine had changed to a sort of humming purr that seemed to come from every quarter of the compass. It was the noise that bewilders wood-cutters and gipsies sleeping in the open, and makes them run sometimes into the very mouth of the tiger.

'Man!' said Father Wolf, showing all his white teeth. 'Faugh! Are there not enough beetles and frogs in the tanks that he must eat Man, and on our ground too!'

The Law of the Jungle, which never orders anything without a reason, forbids every beast to eat Man except when he is killing to show his children how to kill, and then he must hunt outside the hunting-grounds of his pack or tribe. The real reason for this is that man-killing means, sooner or later, the arrival of white men on elephants, with guns, and hundreds of brown men with gongs and rockets and torches. Then everybody in the jungle suffers. The reason the beasts give among themselves is that Man is the weakest and most defenceless of all living things, and it is unsportsmanlike to touch him. They say too—and it is true—that man-eaters become mangy, and lose their teeth.

The purr grew louder, and ended in the full-throated 'Aaarh!' of the tiger's charge.

Then there was a howl—an untigerish howl—from Shere Khan. 'He has missed,' said Mother Wolf. 'What is it?'

Father Wolf ran out a few paces and heard Shere Khan muttering and mumbling savagely, as he tumbled about in the scrub.

'The fool has had no more sense than to jump at a woodcutter's camp-fire, and has burned his feet,' said Father Wolf, with a grunt. 'Tabaqui is with him.'

'Something is coming up hill,' said Mother Wolf, twitching one ear. 'Get ready.'

The bushes rustled a little in the thicket, and Father Wolf dropped with his haunches under him, ready for his leap. Then, if you had been watching, you would have seen the most wonderful thing in the world—the wolf checked in mid-spring. He made his bound before he saw what it was he was jumping at, and then he tried to stop himself. The result was that he shot up straight into the air for four or five feet, landing almost where he left ground.

'Man!' he snapped. 'A man's cub. Look!'

Directly in front of him, holding on by a low branch, stood a naked brown baby who could just walk—as soft and as dimpled a little atom as ever came to a wolf's cave at night. He looked up into Father Wolf's face, and laughed.

'Is that a man's cub?' said Mother Wolf. 'I have never seen one. Bring it here.'

A wolf accustomed to moving his own cubs can, if necessary, mouth an egg without breaking it, and though Father Wolf's jaws closed right on the child's back not a tooth even scratched the skin, as he laid it down among the cubs.

'How little! How naked, and—how bold!' said Mother Wolf, softly. The baby was pushing his way between the cubs to get close to the warm hide. 'Ahai! He is taking his meal with the others. And so this is a man's cub. Now, was there ever a wolf that could boast of a man's cub among her children?'

'I have heard now and again of such a thing, but never in our Pack or in my time,' said Father Wolf. 'He is altogether without hair, and I could kill him with a touch of my foot. But see, he looks up and is not afraid.'

The moonlight was blocked out of the mouth of the cave, for Shere Khan's great square head and shoulders were thrust into the entrance. Tabaqui, behind him, was squeaking: 'My lord, my lord, it went in here!'

'Shere Khan does us great honour,' said Father Wolf, but his eyes were very angry. 'What does Shere Khan need?'

'My quarry. A man's cub went this way,' said Shere Khan. 'Its parents have run off. Give it to me.'

Shere Khan had jumped at a woodcutter's camp-fire, as Father Wolf had said, and was furious from the pain of his burned feet. But Father Wolf knew that the mouth of the cave was too narrow for a tiger to come in by. Even where he was, Shere Khan's shoulders and fore paws were cramped for want of room, as a man's would be if he tried to fight in a barrel.

'The Wolves are a free people,' said Father Wolf. 'They take orders from the Head of the Pack, and not from any striped cattle-killer. The man's cub is ours—to kill if we choose.'

'Ye choose and ye do not choose! What talk is this of choosing? By the bull that I killed, am I to stand nosing into your dog's den for my fair dues? It is I, Shere Khan, who speak!'

The tiger's roar filled the cave with thunder. Mother Wolf shook herself clear of the cubs and sprang forward, her eyes, like two green moons in the darkness, facing the blazing eyes of Shere Khan.

'And it is I, Raksha* [The Demon], who answer. The man's cub is mine, Lungri—mine to me! He shall not be killed. He shall live to run with the Pack and to hunt with the Pack; and in the end, look you, hunter of little naked cubs—frog-eater—fish-killer—he shall hunt *thee*! Now get hence, or by the Sambhur* that I killed (*I* eat no starved cattle), back thou goest to thy mother, burned beast of the jungle, lamer than ever thou camest into the world! Go!'

Father Wolf looked on amazed. He had almost forgotten the days when he won Mother Wolf in fair fight from five other wolves, when she ran in the Pack and was not called The Demon for compliment's sake. Shere Khan might have faced Father Wolf, but he could not stand up against Mother Wolf, for he knew that where he was she had all the advantage of the ground, and would fight to the death.

So he backed out of the cave-mouth growling, and when he was clear he shouted:

'Each dog barks in his own yard! We will see what the Pack will say to this fostering of man-cubs. The cub is mine, and to my teeth he will come in the end, O bush-tailed thieves!'

Mother Wolf threw herself down panting among the cubs, and Father Wolf said to her gravely:

'Shere Khan speaks this much truth. The cub must be shown to the Pack. Wilt thou still keep him, Mother?'

'Keep him!' she gasped. 'He came naked, by night, alone and very hungry; yet he was not afraid! Look, he has pushed one of my babes to one side already. And that lame butcher would have killed him and would have run off to the Waingunga while the villagers here hunted through all our lairs in revenge! Keep him? Assuredly I will keep him. Lie still, little frog. O thou Mowgli*—for Mowgli the Frog I will call thee—the time will come when thou wilt hunt Shere Khan as he has hunted thee.'

'But what will our Pack say?' said Father Wolf.

The Law of the Jungle lays down very clearly that any wolf may, when he marries, withdraw from the Pack he belongs to; but as soon as his cubs are old enough to stand on their feet he must bring them to the Pack Council, which is generally held once a month at full moon, in order that the other wolves may identify them. After that inspection the cubs are free to run where they please, and until they have killed their first buck no excuse is accepted if a grown wolf of the Pack kills one of them. The punishment is death where the murderer can be found; and if you think for a minute you will see that this must be so.

Father Wolf waited till his cubs could run a little, and then on the night of the Pack Meeting took them and Mowgli and Mother Wolf to the Council Rock—a hilltop covered with stones and boulders where a hundred wolves could hide. Akela,* the great gray Lone Wolf, who led all the Pack by strength and cunning, lay out at full length on his rock, and below him sat forty or more wolves of every size and colour, from badger-coloured veterans who could

handle a buck alone, to young black three-year-olds who
thought they could. The Lone Wolf had led them for a
year now. He had fallen twice into a wolf-trap in his youth,
and once he had been beaten and left for dead; so he knew
the manners and customs of men. There was very little
talking at the Rock. The cubs tumbled over each other in
the centre of the circle where their mothers and fathers sat,
and now and again a senior wolf would go quietly up to a
cub, look at him carefully, and return to his place on
noiseless feet. Sometimes a mother would push her cub far
out into the moonlight, to be sure that he had not been
overlooked. Akela from his rock would cry: 'Ye know the
Law—ye know the Law. Look well, O Wolves!' and the
anxious mothers would take up the call: 'Look—look well,
O Wolves!'

At last—and Mother Wolf's neck-bristles lifted as the
time came—Father Wolf pushed 'Mowgli the Frog,' as
they called him, into the centre, where he sat laughing and
playing with some pebbles that glistened in the moonlight.

Akela never raised his head from his paws, but went on
with the monotonous cry: 'Look well!' A muffled roar
came up from behind the rocks— the voice of Shere Khan
crying: 'The cub is mine. Give him to me. What have the
Free People to do with a man's cub?' Akela never even
twitched his ears: all he said was: 'Look well, O Wolves!
What have the Free People to do with the orders of any
save the Free People? Look well!'

There was a chorus of deep growls, and a young wolf in
his fourth year flung back Shere Khan's question to Akela:
'What have the Free People to do with a man's cub?' Now
the Law of the Jungle lays down that if there is any dispute
as to the right of a cub to be accepted by the Pack, he must
be spoken for by at least two members of the Pack who are
not his father and mother.

'Who speaks for this cub?' said Akela. 'Among the Free
People who speaks?' There was no answer, and Mother
Wolf got ready for what she knew would be her last fight,
if things came to fighting.

Then the only other creature who is allowed at the Pack

Council—Baloo,* the sleepy brown bear who teaches the wolf cubs the Law of the Jungle: old Baloo, who can come and go where he pleases because he eats only nuts and roots and honey—rose up on his hind quarters and grunted.

'The man's cub—the man's cub?' he said. '*I* speak for the man's cub. There is no harm in a man's cub. I have no gift of words, but I speak the truth. Let him run with the Pack, and be entered with the others. I myself will teach him.'

'We need yet another,' said Akela. 'Baloo has spoken, and he is our teacher for the young cubs. Who speaks besides Baloo?'

A black shadow dropped down into the circle. It was Bagheera* the Black Panther, inky black all over, but with the panther markings showing up in certain lights like the pattern of watered silk. Everybody knew Bagheera, and nobody cared to cross his path; for he was as cunning as Tabaqui, as bold as the wild buffalo, and as reckless as the wounded elephant. But he had a voice as soft as wild honey dripping from a tree, and a skin softer than down.

'O Akela, and ye the Free People,' he purred, 'I have no right in your assembly; but the Law of the Jungle says that if there is a doubt which is not a killing matter in regard to a new cub, the life of that cub may be bought at a price. And the Law does not say who may or may not pay that price. Am I right?'

'Good! good!' said the young wolves, who are always hungry. 'Listen to Bagheera. The cub can be bought for a price. It is the Law.'

'Knowing that I have no right to speak here, I ask your leave.'

'Speak then,' cried twenty voices.

'To kill a naked cub is shame. Besides, he may make better sport for you when he is grown. Baloo has spoken in his behalf. Now to Baloo's word I will add one bull, and a fat one, newly killed, not half a mile from here, if ye will accept the man's cub according to the Law. Is it difficult?'

There was a clamour of scores of voices, saying: 'What

matter? He will die in the winter rains. He will scorch in
the sun. What harm can a naked frog do us? Let him run
with the Pack. Where is the bull, Bagheera? Let him be
accepted.' And then came Akela's deep bay, crying: 'Look
well—look well, O Wolves!'

Mowgli was still deeply interested in the pebbles, and
he did not notice when the wolves came and looked at him
one by one. At last they all went down the hill for the dead
bull, and only Akela, Bagheera, Baloo, and Mowgli's own
wolves were left. Shere Khan roared still in the night, for
he was very angry that Mowgli had not been handed over
to him.

'Ay, roar well,' said Bagheera, under his whiskers; 'for
the time comes when this naked thing will make thee roar
to another tune or I know nothing of man.'

'It was well done,' said Akela. 'Men and their cubs are
very wise. He may be a help in time.'

'Truly, a help in time of need; for none can hope to lead
the Pack for ever,' said Bagheera.

Akela said nothing. He was thinking of the time that
comes to every leader of every pack when his strength goes
from him and he gets feebler and feebler, till at last he is
killed by the wolves and a new leader comes up—to be
killed in his turn.

'Take him away,' he said to Father Wolf, 'and train him
as befits one of the Free People.' And that is how Mowgli
was entered into the Seeonee wolf-pack for the price of a
bull and on Baloo's good word.

Now you must be content to skip ten or eleven whole
years, and only guess at all the wonderful life that Mowgli
led among the wolves, because if it were written out it
would fill ever so many books. He grew up with the cubs,
though they, of course, were grown wolves almost before
he was a child, and Father Wolf taught him his business,
and the meaning of things in the jungle, till every rustle in
the grass, every breath of the warm night air, every note of
the owls above his head, every scratch of a bat's claws as it
roosted for a while in a tree, and every splash of every little

fish jumping in a pool, meant just as much to him as the
work of his office means to a business man. When he was
not learning he sat out in the sun and slept, and ate and
went to sleep again; when he felt dirty or hot he swam in
the forest pools; and when he wanted honey (Baloo told
him that honey and nuts were just as pleasant to eat as raw
meat) he climbed up for it, and that Bagheera showed him
how to do. Bagheera would lie out on a branch and call,
'Come along, Little Brother,' and at first Mowgli would
cling like the sloth, but afterward he would fling himself
through the branches almost as boldly as the gray ape. He
took his place at the Council Rock, too, when the Pack
met, and there he discovered that if he stared hard at any
wolf, the wolf would be forced to drop his eyes, and so he
used to stare for fun. At other times he would pick the long
thorns out of the pads of his friends, for wolves suffer
terribly from thorns and burs in their coats. He would go
down the hillside into the cultivated lands by night, and
look very curiously at the villagers in their huts, but he had
a mistrust of men because Bagheera showed him a square
box with a drop-gate so cunningly hidden in the jungle
that he nearly walked into it, and told him that it was a
trap. He loved better than anything else to go with
Bagheera into the dark warm heart of the forest, to sleep all
through the drowsy day, and at night see how Bagheera
did his killing. Bagheera killed right and left as he felt
hungry, and so did Mowgli—with one exception. As soon
as he was old enough to understand things, Bagheera told
him that he must never touch cattle because he had been
bought into the Pack at the price of a bull's life. 'All the
jungle is thine,' said Bagheera, 'and thou canst kill everything that thou art strong enough to kill; but for the sake of
the bull that bought thee thou must never kill or eat any
cattle young or old. That is the Law of the Jungle.'
Mowgli obeyed faithfully.

And he grew and grew strong as a boy must grow who
does not know that he is learning any lessons, and who has
nothing in the world to think of except things to eat.

Mother Wolf told him once or twice that Shere Khan

was not a creature to be trusted, and that some day he must kill Shere Khan; but though a young wolf would have remembered that advice every hour, Mowgli forgot it because he was only a boy—though he would have called himself a wolf if he had been able to speak in any human tongue.

Shere Khan was always crossing his path in the jungle, for as Akela grew older and feebler the lame tiger had come to be great friends with the younger wolves of the Pack, who followed him for scraps, a thing Akela would never have allowed if he had dared to push his authority to the proper bounds. Then Shere Khan would flatter them and wonder that such fine young hunters were content to be led by a dying wolf and a man's cub. 'They tell me,' Shere Khan would say, 'that at Council ye dare not look him between the eyes';* and the young wolves would growl and bristle.

Bagheera, who had eyes and ears everywhere, knew something of this, and once or twice he told Mowgli in so many words that Shere Khan would kill him some day; and Mowgli would laugh and answer: 'I have the Pack and I have thee; and Baloo, though he is so lazy, might strike a blow or two for my sake. Why should I be afraid?'

It was one very warm day that a new notion came to Bagheera—born of something that he had heard. Perhaps Ikki* the Porcupine had told him; but he said to Mowgli when they were deep in the jungle, as the boy lay with his head on Bagheera's beautiful black skin: 'Little Brother, how often have I told thee that Shere Khan is thy enemy?'

'As many times as there are nuts on that palm,' said Mowgli, who, naturally, could not count. 'What of it? I am sleepy, Bagheera, and Shere Khan is all long tail and loud talk—like Mao, the Peacock.'

'But this is no time for sleeping. Baloo knows it; I know it; the Pack know it; and even the foolish, foolish deer know. Tabaqui has told thee, too.'

'Ho! ho!' said Mowgli. 'Tabaqui came to me not long ago with some rude talk that I was a naked man's cub and not fit to dig pig-nuts; but I caught Tabaqui by the tail and swung him twice against a palm-tree to teach him better manners.'

'That was foolishness; for though Tabaqui is a mischief-maker, he would have told thee of something that concerned thee closely. Open those eyes, Little Brother. Shere Khan dare not kill thee in the jungle; but remember, Akela is very old, and soon the day comes when he cannot kill his buck, and then he will be leader no more. Many of the wolves that looked thee over when thou wast brought to the Council first are old too, and the young wolves believe, as Shere Khan has taught them, that a man-cub has no place with the Pack. In a little time thou wilt be a man.'

'And what is a man that he should not run with his brothers?' said Mowgli. 'I was born in the jungle. I have obeyed the Law of the Jungle, and there is no wolf of ours from whose paws I have not pulled a thorn. Surely they are my brothers!'

Bagheera stretched himself at full length and half shut his eyes. 'Little Brother,' said he, 'feel under my jaw.'

Mowgli put up his strong brown hand, and just under Bagheera's silky chin, where the giant rolling muscles were all hid by the glossy hair, he came upon a little bald spot.

'There is no one in the jungle that knows that I, Bagheera, carry that mark—the mark of the collar; and yet, Little Brother, I was born among men, and it was among men that my mother died—in the cages of the King's Palace at Oodeypore. It was because of this that I paid the price for thee at the Council when thou wast a little naked cub. Yes, I too was born among men. I had never seen the jungle. They fed me behind bars from an iron pan till one night I felt that I was Bagheera—the Panther—and no man's plaything, and I broke the silly lock with one blow of my paw and came away; and because I had learned the ways of men, I became more terrible in the jungle than Shere Khan. Is it not so?'

'Yes,' said Mowgli; 'all the jungle fear Bagheera—all except Mowgli.'

'Oh, *thou* art a man's cub,' said the Black Panther, very tenderly; 'and even as I returned to my jungle, so thou must go back to men at last,—to the men who are thy brothers,—if thou art not killed in the Council.'

'But why—but why should any wish to kill me?' said Mowgli.

'Look at me,' said Bagheera; and Mowgli looked at him steadily between the eyes. The big panther turned his head away in half a minute.

'*That* is why,' he said, shifting his paw on the leaves. 'Not even I can look thee between the eyes, and I was born among men, and I love thee, Little Brother. The others they hate thee because their eyes cannot meet thine; because thou art wise; because thou hast pulled out thorns from their feet—because thou art a man.'

'I did not know these things,' said Mowgli, sullenly; and he frowned under his heavy black eyebrows.

'What is the Law of the Jungle? Strike first and then give tongue. By thy very carelessness they know that thou art a man. But be wise. It is in my heart that when Akela misses his next kill,—and at each hunt it costs him more to pin the buck,—the Pack will turn against him and against thee. They will hold a jungle Council at the Rock, and then—and then—I have it!' said Bagheera, leaping up. 'Go thou down quickly to the men's huts in the valley, and take some of the Red Flower which they grow there, so that when the time comes thou mayest have even a stronger friend than I or Baloo or those of the Pack that love thee. Get the Red Flower.'

By Red Flower Bagheera meant fire, only no creature in the jungle will call fire by its proper name. Every beast lives in deadly fear of it, and invents a hundred ways of describing it.

'The Red Flower?' said Mowgli. 'That grows outside their huts in the twilight. I will get some.'

'There speaks the man's cub,' said Bagheera, proudly. Remember that it grows in little pots. Get one swiftly, and keep it by thee for time of need.'

'Good!' said Mowgli. 'I go. But art thou sure, O my

Bagheera'—he slipped his arm round the splendid neck, and looked deep into the big eyes—'art thou sure that all this is Shere Khan's doing?'

'By the Broken Lock that freed me, I am sure, Little Brother.'

'Then, by the Bull that bought me, I will pay Shere Khan full tale for this, and it may be a little over,' said Mowgli; and he bounded away.

'That is a man. That is all a man,' said Bagheera to himself, lying down again. 'Oh, Shere Khan, never was a blacker hunting than that frog-hunt of thine ten years ago!'

Mowgli was far and far through the forest, running hard, and his heart was hot in him. He came to the cave as the evening mist rose, and drew breath, and looked down the valley. The cubs were out, but Mother Wolf, at the back of the cave, knew by his breathing that something was troubling her frog.

'What is it, Son?' she said.

'Some bat's chatter of Shere Khan,' he called back. 'I hunt among the ploughed fields tonight,' and he plunged downward through the bushes, to the stream at the bottom of the valley. There he checked, for he heard the yell of the Pack hunting, heard the bellow of a hunted Sambhur, and the snort as the buck turned at bay. Then there were wicked, bitter howls from the young wolves: 'Akela! Akela! Let the Lone Wolf show his strength. Room for the leader of the Pack! Spring, Akela!'

The Lone Wolf must have sprung and missed his hold, for Mowgli heard the snap of his teeth and then a yelp as the Sambhur knocked him over with his fore foot.

He did not wait for anything more, but dashed on; and the yells grew fainter behind him as he ran into the crop-lands where the villagers lived.

'Bagheera spoke truth,' he panted, as he nestled down in some cattle-fodder by the window of a hut. 'To-morrow is one day both for Akela and for me.'

Then he pressed his face close to the window and watched the fire on the hearth. He saw the husbandman's

wife get up and feed it in the night with black lumps; and
when the morning came and the mists were all white and
cold, he saw the man's child pick up a wicker pot plastered
inside with earth, fill it with lumps of red-hot charcoal, put
it under his blanket, and go out to tend the cows in the
byre.

'Is that all?' said Mowgli. 'If a cub can do it, there is
nothing to fear'; so he strode round the corner and met the
boy, took the pot from his hand, and disappeared into the
mist while the boy howled with fear.

'They are very like me,' said Mowgli, blowing into the
pot, as he had seen the woman do. 'This thing will die if I
do not give it things to eat'; and he dropped twigs and
dried bark on the red stuff. Half-way up the hill he met
Bagheera with the morning dew shining like moonstones
on his coat.

'Akela has missed,' said the Panther. 'They would have
killed him last night, but they needed thee also. They were
looking for thee on the hill.'

'I was among the ploughed lands. I am ready. See!'
Mowgli held up the fire-pot.

'Good! Now, I have seen men thrust a dry branch into
that stuff, and presently the Red Flower blossomed at the
end of it. Art thou not afraid?'

'No. Why should I fear? I remember now—if it is not a
dream—how, before I was a Wolf, I lay beside the Red
Flower, and it was warm and pleasant.'

All that day Mowgli sat in the cave tending his fire-pot
and dipping dry branches into it to see how they looked.
He found a branch that satisfied him, and in the evening
when Tabaqui came to the cave and told him rudely
enough that he was wanted at the Council Rock, he
laughed till Tabaqui ran away. Then Mowgli went to the
Council, still laughing.

Akela the Lone Wolf lay by the side of his rock as a sign
that the leadership of the Pack was open, and Shere Khan
with his following of scrap-fed wolves walked to and fro
openly, being flattered. Bagheera lay close to Mowgli, and
the fire-pot was between Mowgli's knees. When they were

all gathered together, Shere Khan began to speak—a thing he would never have dared to do when Akela was in his prime.

'He has no right,' whispered Bagheera. 'Say so. He is a dog's son. He will be frightened.'

Mowgli sprang to his feet. 'Free People,' he cried, 'does Shere Khan lead the Pack? What has a tiger to do with our leadership?'

'Seeing that the leadership is yet open, and being asked to speak—' Shere Khan began.

'By whom?' said Mowgli. 'Are we *all* jackals, to fawn on this cattle-butcher? The leadership of the Pack is with the Pack alone.'

There were yells of 'Silence, thou man's cub!' 'Let him speak. He has kept our Law'; and at last the seniors of the Pack thundered: 'Let the Dead Wolf speak.' When a leader of the Pack has missed his kill, he is called the Dead Wolf as long as he lives, which is not long, as a rule.

Akela raised his old head wearily:—

'Free People, and ye too, jackals of Shere Khan, for twelve seasons I have led ye to and from the kill, and in all that time not one has been trapped or maimed. Now I have missed my kill. Ye know how that plot was made. Ye know how ye brought me up to an untried buck to make my weakness known. It was cleverly done. Your right is to kill me here on the Council Rock now. Therefore, I ask, who comes to make an end of the Lone Wolf? For it is my right, by the Law of the Jungle, that ye come one by one.'

There was a long hush, for no single wolf cared to fight Akela to the death. Then Shere Khan roared: 'Bah! what have we to do with this toothless fool? He is doomed to die! It is the man-cub who has lived too long. Free People, he was my meat from the first. Give him to me. I am weary of this man-wolf folly. He has troubled the jungle for ten seasons. Give me the man-cub, or I will hunt here always, and not give you one bone. He is a man, a man's child, and from the marrow of my bones I hate him!'

Then more than half the Pack yelled: 'A man! a man!

What has a man to do with us? Let him go to his own place.'

'And turn all the people of the villages against us?' clamoured Shere Khan. 'No; give him to me. He is a man, and none of us can look him between the eyes.'

Akela lifted his head again, and said: 'He has eaten our food. He has slept with us. He has driven game for us. He has broken no word of the Law of the Jungle.'

'Also, I paid for him with a bull when he was accepted. The worth of a bull is little, but Bagheera's honour is something that he will perhaps fight for,' said Bagheera, in his gentlest voice.

'A bull paid ten years ago!' the Pack snarled. 'What do we care for bones ten years old?'

'Or for a pledge?' said Bagheera, his white teeth bared under his lip. 'Well are ye called the Free People!'

'No man's cub can run with the people of the jungle,' howled Shere Khan. 'Give him to me!'

'He is our brother in all but blood,' Akela went on; 'and ye would kill him here! In truth, I have lived too long. Some of ye are eaters of cattle, and of others I have heard that, under Shere Khan's teaching, ye go by dark night and snatch children from the villager's door-step. Therefore I know ye to be cowards, and it is to cowards I speak. It is certain that I must die, and my life is of no worth, or I would offer that in the man-cub's place. But for the sake of the Honour of the Pack,—a little matter that by being without a leader ye have forgotten,—I promise that if ye let the man-cub go to his own place, I will not, when my time comes to die, bare one tooth against ye. I will die without fighting. That will at least save the Pack three lives. More I cannot do; but if ye will, I can save ye the shame that comes of killing a brother against whom there is no fault,—a brother spoken for and bought into the Pack according to the Law of the Jungle.'

'He is a man—a man—a man!' snarled the Pack; and most of the wolves began to gather round Shere Khan, whose tail was beginning to switch.

'Now the business is in thy hands,' said Bagheera to Mowgli. '*We* can do no more except fight.'

Mowgli stood upright—the fire-pot in his hands. Then he stretched out his arms, and yawned in the face of the Council; but he was furious with rage and sorrow, for, wolf-like, the wolves had never told him how they hated him. 'Listen, you!' he cried. 'There is no need for this dog's jabber. Ye have told me so often to-night that I am a man (and indeed I would have been a wolf with you to my life's end), that I feel your words are true. So I do not call ye my brothers any more, but *sag* [dogs], as a man should. What ye will do, and what ye will not do, is not yours to say. That matter is with *me*; and that we may see the matter more plainly, I, the man, have brought here a little of the Red Flower which ye, dogs, fear.'

He flung the fire-pot on the ground, and some of the red coals lit a tuft of dried moss that flared up, as all the Council drew back in terror before the leaping flames.

Mowgli thrust his dead branch into the fire till the twigs lit and crackled, and whirled it above his head among the cowering wolves.

'Thou art the master,' said Bagheera, in an undertone. 'Save Akela from the death. He was ever thy friend.'

Akela, the grim old wolf who had never asked for mercy in his life, gave one piteous look at Mowgli as the boy stood all naked, his long black hair tossing over his shoulders in the light of the blazing branch that made the shadows jump and quiver.

'Good!' said Mowgli, staring round slowly. 'I see that ye are dogs. I go from you to my own people—if they be my own people. The Jungle is shut to me, and I must forget your talk and your companionship; but I will be more merciful than ye are. Because I was all but your brother in blood, I promise that when I am a man among men I will not betray ye to men as ye have betrayed me.' He kicked the fire with his foot, and the sparks flew up. 'There shall be no war between any of us and the Pack. But here is a debt to pay before I go.' He strode forward to where Shere Khan sat blinking stupidly at the flames, and caught him by the tuft on his chin. Bagheera followed in case of accidents. 'Up, dog!' Mowgli cried. 'Up, when a man speaks, or I will set that coat ablaze!'

Shere Khan's ears lay flat back on his head, and he shut his eyes, for the blazing branch was very near.

'This cattle-killer said he would kill me in the Council because he had not killed me when I was a cub. Thus and thus, then, do we beat dogs when we are men. Stir a whisker, Lungri, and I ram the Red Flower down thy gullet!' He beat Shere Khan over the head with the branch, and the tiger whimpered and whined in an agony of fear.

'Pah! Singed jungle-cat—go now! But remember when next I come to the Council Rock, as a man should come, it will be with Shere Khan's hide on my head. For the rest, Akela goes free to live as he pleases. Ye will *not* kill him, because that is not my will. Nor do I think that ye will sit here any longer, lolling out your tongues as though ye were somebodies, instead of dogs whom I drive out—thus! Go!' The fire was burning furiously at the end of the branch, and Mowgli struck right and left round the circle, and the wolves ran howling with the sparks burning their fur. At last there were only Akela, Bagheera, and perhaps ten wolves that had taken Mowgli's part. Then something began to hurt Mowgli inside him, as he had never been hurt in his life before, and he caught his breath and sobbed, and the tears ran down his face.

'What is it? What is it?' he said. 'I do not wish to leave the jungle, and I do not know what this is. Am I dying, Bagheera?'

'No, Little Brother. Those are only tears such as men use,' said Bagheera. 'Now I know thou art a man, and a man's cub no longer. The Jungle is shut indeed to thee henceforward. Let them fall, Mowgli. They are only tears.' So Mowgli sat and cried as though his heart would break; and he had never cried in all his life before.

'Now,' he said, 'I will go to men. But first I must say farewell to my mother'; and he went to the cave where she lived with Father Wolf, and he cried on her coat, while the four cubs howled miserably.

'Ye will not forget me?' said Mowgli.

'Never while we can follow a trail,' said the cubs. 'Come to the foot of the hill when thou art a man, and we will talk to thee; and we will come into the crop-lands to play with thee by night.'

'Come soon!' said Father Wolf. 'Oh, wise little frog, come again soon; for we be old, thy mother and I.'

'Come soon,' said Mother Wolf, 'little naked son of mine; for, listen, child of man, I loved thee more than ever I loved my cubs.'

'I will surely come,' said Mowgli; 'and when I come it will be to lay out Shere Khan's hide upon the Council Rock. Do not forget me! Tell them in the jungle never to forget me!'

The dawn was beginning to break when Mowgli went down the hillside alone, to meet those mysterious things that are called men.

Hunting-Song of the Seeonee Pack

As the dawn was breaking the Sambhur belled
    Once, twice and again!
And a doe leaped up, and a doe leaped up
From the pond in the wood where the wild deer sup
This I, scouting alone, beheld,
    Once, twice and again!

As the dawn was breaking the Sambhur belled
    Once, twice and again!
And a wolf stole back, and a wolf stole back
To carry the word to the waiting pack,
And we sought and we found and we bayed on his track
    Once, twice and again!

As the dawn was breaking the Wolf Pack yelled
    Once, twice and again!
Feet in the jungle that leave no mark!

Eyes that can see in the dark—the dark!
Tongue—give tongue to it! Hark! O hark!
    Once, twice and again!

Kaa's* Hunting

His spots are the joy of the Leopard: his horns are the
  Buffalo's pride.
Be clean, for the strength of the hunter is known by the
  gloss of his hide.
If ye find that the bullock can toss you, or the heavy-browed
  Sambhur can gore;
Ye need not stop work to inform us: we knew it ten seasons
  before.
Oppress not the cubs of the stranger, but hail them as Sister
  and Brother,
For though they are little and fubsy, it may be the Bear is
  their mother.
'There is none like to me!' says the Cub in the pride of his
  earliest kill;
But the jungle is large and the Cub he is small. Let him
  think and be still.

Maxims of Baloo

ALL that is told here happened some time before Mowgli
was turned out of the Seeonee wolf-pack, or revenged
himself on Shere Khan the tiger. It was in the days when
Baloo was teaching him the Law of the Jungle.* The big,
serious, old brown bear was delighted to have so quick a
pupil, for the young wolves will only learn as much of the
Law of the Jungle as applies to their own pack and tribe,
and run away as soon as they can repeat the Hunting
Verse:—'Feet that make no noise; eyes that can see in the
dark; ears that can hear the winds in their lairs, and sharp
white teeth, all these things are the marks of our brothers
except Tabaqui the Jackal and the Hyæna whom we hate.'
But Mowgli, as a man-cub, had to learn a great deal more
than this. Sometimes Bagheera, the Black Panther, would
come lounging through the jungle to see how his pet was
getting on, and would purr with his head against a tree
while Mowgli recited the day's lesson to Baloo. The boy
could climb almost as well as he could swim, and swim
almost as well as he could run; so Baloo, the Teacher of the
Law, taught him the Wood and Water Laws: how to tell a
rotten branch from a sound one; how to speak politely to
the wild bees when he came upon a hive of them fifty feet

above ground; what to say to Mang* the Bat when he
disturbed him in the branches at mid-day; and how to
warn the water-snakes in the pools before he splashed
down among them. None of the Jungle-People like being
disturbed, and all are very ready to fly at an intruder.
Then, too, Mowgli was taught the Strangers' Hunting
Call, which must be repeated aloud till it is answered,
whenever one of the Jungle-People hunts outside his own
grounds. It means, translated: 'Give me leave to hunt here
because I am hungry'; and the answer is: 'Hunt then for
food, but not for pleasure.'

All this will show you how much Mowgli had to learn by
heart, and he grew very tired of saying the same thing over
a hundred times; but, as Baloo said to Bagheera, one day
when Mowgli had been cuffed and run off in a temper: 'A
man's cub is a man's cub, and he must learn *all* the Law of
the Jungle.'

'But think how small he is,' said the Black Panther, who
would have spoiled Mowgli if he had had his own way.
'How can his little head carry all thy long talk?'

'Is there anything in the jungle too little to be killed?
No. That is why I teach him these things, and that is why I
hit him, very softly, when he forgets.'

'Softly! What dost thou know of softness, old Iron-feet?'
Bagheera grunted. 'His face is all bruised to-day by thy—
softness. Ugh.'

'Better he should be bruised from head to foot by me
who love him than that he should come to harm through
ignorance,' Baloo answered very earnestly. 'I am now
teaching him the Master Words of the Jungle that shall
protect him with the birds and the Snake-People, and all
that hunt on four feet, except his own pack. He can now
claim protection, if he will only remember the words, from
all in the jungle. Is not that worth a little beating?'

'Well, look to it then that thou dost not kill the man-
cub. He is no tree-trunk to sharpen thy blunt claws upon.
But what are those Master Words? I am more likely to give
help than to ask it'—Bagheera stretched out one paw and
admired the steel-blue, ripping-chisel talons at the end of
it—'still I should like to know.'

'I will call Mowgli and he shall say them—if he will. Come, Little Brother!'

'My head is ringing like a bee-tree,' said a sullen little voice over their heads, and Mowgli slid down a tree-trunk very angry and indignant, adding as he reached the ground: 'I come for Bagheera and not for *thee*, fat old Baloo!'

'That is all one to me,' said Baloo, though he was hurt and grieved. 'Tell Bagheera, then, the Master Words of the Jungle that I have taught thee this day.'

'Master Words for which people?' said Mowgli, delighted to show off. 'The jungle has many tongues. *I* know them all.'

'A little thou knowest, but not much. See, O Bagheera, they never thank their teacher. Not one small wolfling has ever come back to thank old Baloo for his teachings. Say the word for the Hunting-People, then—great scholar.'

'We be of one blood, ye and I,' said Mowgli, giving the words the Bear accent which all the hunting-people use.

'Good. Now for the birds.'

Mowgli repeated, with the Kite's whistle at the end of the sentence.

'Now for the Snake-People,' said Bagheera.

The answer was a perfectly indescribable hiss, and Mowgli kicked up his feet behind, clapped his hands together to applaud himself, and jumped on to Bagheera's back, where he sat sideways, drumming with his heels on the glossy skin and making the worst faces he could think of at Baloo.

'There—there! That was worth a little bruise,' said the brown bear tenderly. 'Some day thou wilt remember me.' Then he turned aside to tell Bagheera how he had begged the Master Words from Hathi* the Wild Elephant, who knows all about these things, and how Hathi had taken Mowgli down to a pool to get the Snake Word from a water-snake, because Baloo could not pronounce it, and how Mowgli was now reasonably safe against all accidents in the jungle, because neither snake, bird, nor beast would hurt him.

'No one then is to be feared,' Baloo wound up, patting his big furry stomach with pride.

'Except his own tribe,' said Bagheera, under his breath; and then aloud to Mowgli: 'Have a care for my ribs, Little Brother! What is all this dancing up and down?'

Mowgli had been trying to make himself heard by pulling at Bagheera's shoulder fur and kicking hard. When the two listened to him he was shouting at the top of his voice: 'And so I shall have a tribe of my own, and lead them through the branches all day long.'

'What is this new folly, little dreamer of dreams?' said Bagheera.

'Yes, and throw branches and dirt at old Baloo,' Mowgli went on. 'They have promised me this. Ah!'

'*Whoof!*' Baloo's big paw scooped Mowgli off Bagheera's back, and as the boy lay between the big fore-paws he could see the Bear was angry.

'Mowgli,' said Baloo, 'thou has been talking with the *Bandar-log**—the Monkey-People.'

Mowgli looked at Bagheera to see if the Panther was angry too, and Bagheera's eyes were as hard as jade-stones.

'Thou hast been with the Monkey-People—the gray apes—the people without a Law—the eaters of everything. That is great shame.'

'When Baloo hurt my head,' said Mowgli (he was still on his back), 'I went away, and the gray apes came down from the trees and had pity on me. No one else cared.' He snuffled a little.

'The pity of the Monkey-People!' Baloo snorted. 'The stillness of the mountain stream! The cool of the summer sun! And then, man-cub?'

'And then, and then, they gave me nuts and pleasant things to eat, and they—they carried me in their arms up to the top of the trees and said I was their blood-brother except that I had no tail, and should be their leader some day.'

'They have *no* leader,' said Bagheera. 'They lie. They have always lied.'

'They were very kind and bade me come again. Why

have I never been taken among the Monkey-People? They stand on their feet as I do. They do not hit me with hard paws. They play all day. Let me get up! Bad Baloo, let me up! I will play with them again.'

'Listen, man-cub,' said the Bear, and his voice rumbled like thunder on a hot night. 'I have taught thee all the Law of the Jungle for all the peoples of the jungle—except the Monkey-Folk who live in the trees. They have no law. They are outcasts. They have no speech of their own, but use the stolen words which they overhear when they listen, and peep, and wait up above in the branches. Their way is not our way. They are without leaders. They have no remembrance. They boast and chatter and pretend that they are a great people about to do great affairs in the jungle, but the falling of a nut turns their minds to laughter and all is forgotten. We of the jungle have no dealings with them. We do not drink where the monkeys drink; we do not go where the monkeys go; we do not hunt where they hunt; we do not die where they die. Hast thou ever heard me speak of the *Bandar-log* till to-day?'

'No,' said Mowgli in a whisper, for the forest was very still now Baloo had finished.

'The Jungle-People put them out of their mouths and out of their minds. They are very many, evil, dirty, shameless, and they desire, if they have any fixed desire, to be noticed by the Jungle-People. But we do *not* notice them even when they throw nuts and filth on our heads.'

He had hardly spoken when a shower of nuts and twigs spattered down through the branches; and they could hear coughings and howlings and angry jumpings high up in the air among the thin branches.

'The Monkey-People are forbidden,' said Baloo, 'forbidden to the Jungle-People. Remember.'

'Forbidden,' said Bagheera; 'but I still think Baloo should have warned thee against them.'

'I—I? How was I to guess he would play with such dirt? The Monkey-People! Faugh!'

A fresh shower came down on their heads and the two trotted away, taking Mowgli with them. What Baloo had said about the monkeys was perfectly true. They belonged to the tree-tops, and as beasts very seldom look up, there was no occasion for the monkeys and the Jungle-People to cross each other's path. But whenever they found a sick wolf, or a wounded tiger, or bear, the monkeys would torment him and would throw sticks and nuts at any beast for fun and in the hope of being noticed. Then they would howl and shriek senseless songs, and invite the Jungle-People to climb up their trees and fight them, or would start furious battles over nothing among themselves, and leave the dead monkeys where the Jungle-People could see them. They were always just going to have a leader, and laws and customs of their own, but they never did, because their memories would not hold over from day to day, and so they compromised things by making up a saying: 'What the *Bandar-log* think now* the jungle will think later,' and that comforted them a great deal. None of the beasts could reach them, but on the other hand none of the beasts would notice them, and that was why they were so pleased when Mowgli came to play with them, and they heard how angry Baloo was.

They never meant to do any more—the *Bandar-log* never mean anything at all; but one of them invented what seemed to him a brilliant idea, and he told all the others that Mowgli would be a useful person to keep in the tribe, because he could weave sticks together for protection from the wind; so, if they caught him, they could make him teach them. Of course Mowgli, as a woodcutter's child, inherited all sorts of instincts, and used to make little huts of fallen branches without thinking how he came to do it, and the Monkey-People, watching in the trees, considered his play most wonderful. This time, they said, they were really going to have a leader and become the wisest people in the jungle—so wise that every one else would notice and envy them. Therefore they followed Baloo and Bagheera and Mowgli through the jungle very quietly till it was time for the mid-day nap, and Mowgli, who was very much ashamed of himself, slept between the Panther and the

Bear, resolving to have no more to do with the Monkey-People.

The next thing he remembered was feeling hands on his legs and arms—hard, strong, little hands—and then a swash of branches in his face, and then he was staring down through the swaying boughs as Baloo woke the jungle with his deep cries and Bagheera bounded up the trunk with every tooth bared. The *Bandar-log* howled with triumph and scuffled away to the upper branches where Bagheera dared not follow, shouting: 'He has noticed us! Bagheera has noticed us. All the Jungle-People admire us for our skill and our cunning.' Then they began their flight; and the flight of the Monkey-People through tree-land is one of the things nobody can describe. They have their regular roads and cross-roads, up hills and down hills, all laid out from fifty to seventy or a hundred feet above ground, and by these they can travel even at night if necessary. Two of the strongest monkeys caught Mowgli under the arms and swung off with him through the tree-tops, twenty feet at a bound. Had they been alone they could have gone twice as fast, but the boy's weight held them back. Sick and giddy as Mowgli was he could not help enjoying the wild rush, though the glimpses of earth far down below frightened him, and the terrible check and jerk at the end of the swing over nothing but empty air brought his heart between his teeth. His escort would rush him up a tree till he felt the thinnest topmost branches crackle and bend under them, and then with a cough and a whoop would fling themselves into the air outward and downward, and bring up, hanging by their hands or their feet to the lower limbs of the next tree. Sometimes he could see for miles and miles across the still green jungle, as a man on the top of a mast can see for miles across the sea, and then the branches and leaves would lash him across the face, and he and his two guards would be almost down to earth again. So, bounding and crashing and whooping and yelling, the whole tribe of *Bandar-log* swept along the tree-roads with Mowgli their prisoner.

For a time he was afraid of being dropped: then he grew angry but knew better than to struggle, and then he began to think. The first thing was to send back word to Baloo and Bagheera, for, at the pace the monkeys were going, he knew his friends would be left far behind. It was useless to look down, for he could only see the top-sides of the branches, so he stared upward and saw, far away in the blue, Rann* the Kite balancing and wheeling as he kept watch over the jungle waiting for things to die. Rann saw that the monkeys were carrying something, and dropped a few hundred yards to find out whether their load was good to eat. He whistled with surprise when he saw Mowgli being dragged up to a tree-top and heard him give the Kite call for—'We be of one blood, thou and I.' The waves of the branches closed over the boy, but Rann balanced away to the next tree in time to see the little brown face come up again. 'Mark my trail,' Mowgli shouted. 'Tell Baloo of the Seeonee Pack and Bagheera of the Council Rock.'

'In whose name, Brother?' Rann had never seen Mowgli before, though of course he had heard of him.

'Mowgli, the Frog. Man-cub they call me! Mark my tra-il!'

The last words were shrieked as he was being swung through the air, but Rann nodded and rose up till he looked no bigger than a speck of dust, and there he hung, watching with his telescope eyes the swaying of the tree-tops as Mowgli's escort whirled along.

'They never go far,' he said with a chuckle. 'They never do what they set out to do. Always pecking at new things are the *Bandar-log*. This time, if I have any eyesight, they have pecked down trouble for themselves, for Baloo is no fledgling and Bagheera can, as I know, kill more than goats.'

So he rocked on his wings, his feet gathered up under him, and waited.

Meantime, Baloo and Bagheera were furious with rage and grief. Bagheera climbed as he had never climbed before, but the thin branches broke beneath his weight, and he slipped down, his claws full of bark.

'Why didst thou not warn the man-cub?' he roared to poor Baloo, who had set off at a clumsy trot in the hope of overtaking the monkeys. 'What was the use of half slaying him with blows if thou didst not warn him?'

'Haste! O haste! We—we may catch them yet!' Baloo panted.

'At that speed! It would not tire a wounded cow. Teacher of the Law—cub-beater—a mile of that rolling to and fro would burst thee open. Sit still and think! Make a plan. This is no time for chasing. They may drop him if we follow too close.'

'*Arrula! Whoo!* They may have dropped him already, being tired of carrying him. Who can trust the *Bandar-log?* Put dead bats on my head! Give me black bones to eat! Roll me into the hives of the wild bees that I may be stung to death, and bury me with the Hyæna, for I am the most miserable of bears! *Arulala! Wahooa!* O Mowgli, Mowgli! why did I not warn thee against the Monkey-Folk instead of breaking thy head? Now perhaps I may have knocked the day's lesson out of his mind, and he will be alone in the jungle without the Master Words.'

Baloo clasped his paws over his ears and rolled to and fro moaning.

'At least he gave me all the Words correctly a little time ago,' said Bagheera, impatiently. 'Baloo, thou hast neither memory nor respect. What would the jungle think if I, the Black Panther, curled myself up like Ikki the Porcupine*, and howled?'

'What do I care what the jungle thinks? He may be dead by now.'

'Unless and until they drop him from the branches in sport, or kill him out of idleness, I have no fear for the man-cub. He is wise and well-taught, and above all has the eyes that make the Jungle-People afraid. But (and it is a great evil) he is in the power of the *Bandar-log*, and they, because they live in trees, have no fear of any of our people.' Bagheera licked one fore-paw thoughtfully.

'Fool that I am! Oh fat, brown, root-digging fool that I am,' said Baloo, uncurling himself with a jerk, 'it is true what Hathi the wild Elephant says: "*To each his own fear*"; and they, the *Bandar-log*, fear Kaa the Rock Snake. He can climb as well as they can. He steals the young monkeys in the night. The whisper of his name makes their wicked tails cold. Let us go to Kaa.'

'What will he do for us? He is not of our tribe, being footless—and with most evil eyes,' said Bagheera.

'He is very old and very cunning. Above all, he is always hungry,' said Baloo hopefully. 'Promise him many goats.'

'He sleeps for a full month after he has once eaten. He may be asleep now, and even were he awake what if he would rather kill his own goats?' Bagheera, who did not know much about Kaa, was naturally suspicious.

'Then in that case, thou and I together, old hunter, might make him see reason.' Here Baloo rubbed his faded brown shoulder against the Panther, and they went off to look for Kaa the Rock-python.

They found him stretched out on a warm ledge in the afternoon sun, admiring his beautiful new coat, for he had been in retirement for the last ten days, changing his skin, and now he was very splendid—darting his big blunt-nosed head along the ground, and twisting the thirty feet of his body into fantastic knots and curves, and licking his lips as he thought of his dinner to come.

'He has not eaten,' said Baloo, with a grunt of relief, as soon as he saw the beautifully mottled brown and yellow jacket. 'Be careful, Bagheera! He is always a little blind after he has changed his skin, and very quick to strike.'

Kaa was not a poison-snake—in fact he rather despised the poison-snakes as cowards—but his strength lay in his hug, and when he had once lapped his huge coils round anybody there was no more to be said. 'Good hunting!' cried Baloo, sitting up on his haunches. Like all snakes of his breed, Kaa was rather deaf, and did not hear the call at first. Then he curled up ready for any accident, his head lowered.

'Good hunting for us all,' he answered. 'Oho, Baloo, what dost thou do here? Good hunting, Bagheera. One of us at least needs food. Is there any news of game afoot? A doe now, or even a young buck? I am as empty as a dried well. '

'We are hunting,' said Baloo carelessly. He knew that you must not hurry Kaa. He is too big.

'Give me permission to come with you,' said Kaa. 'A blow more or less is nothing to thee, Bagheera or Baloo, but I—I have to wait and wait for days in a wood-path and climb half a night on the mere chance of a young ape. Psshaw! The branches are not what they were when I was young. Rotten twigs and dry boughs are they all.'

'Maybe thy great weight has something to do with the matter,' said Baloo.

'I am a fair length—a fair length,' said Kaa, with a little pride. 'But for all that, it is the fault of this new-grown timber. I came very near to falling on my last hunt—very near indeed—and the noise of my slipping, for my tail was not tight wrapped round the tree, waked the *Bandar-log*, and they called me most evil names.'

'Footless, yellow earth-worm,' said Bagheera under his whiskers, as though he were trying to remember something.

'Sssss! Have they ever called me *that?*' said Kaa.

Something of that kind it was that they shouted to us last moon, but we never noticed them. They will say anything—even that thou hast lost all thy teeth, and wilt not face anything bigger than a kid, because (they are indeed shameless, these *Bandar-log*)—because thou art afraid of the he-goat's horns,' Bagheera went on sweetly.

Now a snake, especially a wary old python like Kaa, very seldom shows that he is angry, but Baloo and Bagheera could see the big swallowing-muscles on either side of Kaa's throat ripple and bulge.

'The *Bandar-log* have shifted their grounds,' he said quietly. 'When I came up into the sun today I heard them whooping among the tree-tops.'

'It—it is the *Bandar-log* that we follow now,' said Baloo; but the words stuck in his throat, for that was the first time in his memory that one of the Jungle-People had owned to being interested in the doings of the monkeys.

'Beyond doubt then it is no small thing that takes two such hunters—leaders in their own jungle I am certain— on the trail of the *Bandar-log*,' Kaa replied, courteously, as he swelled with curiosity.

'Indeed,' Baloo began, 'I am no more than the old and sometimes very foolish Teacher of the Law to the Seeonee wolf-cubs, and Bagheera here——'

'Is Bagheera,' said the Black Panther, and his jaws shut with a snap, for he did not believe in being humble. 'The trouble is this, Kaa. Those nut-stealers and pickers of palm leaves have stolen away our man-cub, of whom thou hast perhaps heard.'

'I heard some news from Ikki (his quills make him presumptuous) of a man-thing that was entered into a wolf-pack, but I did not believe. Ikki is full of stories half heard and very badly told.'

'But it is true. He is such a man-cub as never was,' said Baloo. 'The best and wisest and boldest of man-cubs—my own pupil, who shall make the name of Baloo famous through all the jungles; and besides, I—we—love him, Kaa.'

'Ts! Ts!' said Kaa, shaking his head to and fro. 'I also have known what love is. There are tales I could tell that——'

'That need a clear night when we are all well fed to praise properly,' said Bagheera, quickly. 'Our man-cub is in the hands of the *Bandar-log* now, and we know that of all the Jungle-People they fear Kaa alone.'

'They fear me alone. They have good reason,' said Kaa. 'Chattering, foolish, vain—vain, foolish, and chattering, are the monkeys. But a man-thing in their hands is in no good luck. They grow tired of the nuts they pick, and throw them down. They carry a branch half a day, meaning to do great things with it, and then they snap it in two. That man-thing is not to be envied. They called me also—"yellow fish," was it not?'

'Worm—worm—earth-worm,' said Bagheera, 'as well as other things which I cannot now say for shame.'

'We must remind them to speak well of their master.

Aaa-sssh! We must help their wandering memories. Now, whither went they with the cub?'

'The jungle alone knows. Toward the sunset, I believe,' said Baloo. 'We had thought that thou wouldst know, Kaa.'

'I! How? I take them when they come in my way, but I do not hunt the *Bandar-log*, or frogs—or green scum on a water-hole for that matter.'

'Up, Up! Up, Up! Hillo! Illo! Illo, look up, Baloo of the Seeonee Wolf Pack!'

Baloo looked up to see where the voice came from, and there was Rann the Kite, sweeping down with the sun shining on the upturned flanges of his wings. It was near Rann's bed-time, but he had ranged all over the jungle looking for the Bear and missed him in the thick foliage.

'What is it?' said Baloo.

'I have seen Mowgli among the *Bandar-log*. He bade me tell you. I watched. The *Bandar-log* have taken him beyond the river to the monkey city—to the Cold Lairs. They may stay there for a night, or ten nights, or an hour. I have told the bats to watch through the dark time. That is my message. Good hunting, all you below!'

'Full gorge and a deep sleep to you, Rann,' cried Bagheera. 'I will remember thee in my next kill, and put aside the head for thee alone, O best of kites!'

'It is nothing. It is nothing. The boy held the Master Word. I could have done no less,' and Rann circled up again to his roost.

'He has not forgotten to use his tongue,' said Baloo, with a chuckle of pride. 'To think of one so young remembering the Master Word for the birds too while he was being pulled across-trees!'

'It was most firmly driven into him,' said Bagheera. 'But I am proud of him, and now we must go to the Cold Lairs.'*

They all knew where that place was, but few of the Jungle-People ever went there, because what they called the Cold Lairs was an old deserted city, and lost and buried in the jungle, and beasts seldom use a place that men have once used. The wild boar will, but the hunting-tribes do not. Besides, the monkeys lived there as much as they could be said to live anywhere, and no self-respecting animal would come within eye-shot of it except in times of drouth, when the half-ruined tanks and reservoirs held a little water.

'It is half a night's journey—at full speed,' said Bagheera, and Baloo looked very serious. 'I will go as fast as I can,' he said, anxiously.

'We dare not wait for thee. Follow, Baloo We must go on the quick-foot—Kaa and I.'

'Feet or no feet, I can keep abreast of all thy four,' said Kaa, shortly. Baloo made one effort to hurry, but had to sit down panting, and so they left him to come on later, while Bagheera hurried forward, at the quick panther-canter. Kaa said nothing, but, strive as Bagheera might, the huge Rock-python held level with him. When they came to a hill-stream, Bagheera gained, because he bounded across while Kaa swam, his head and two feet of his neck clearing the water, but on level ground Kaa made up the distance.

'By the Broken Lock* that freed me,' said Bagheera, when twilight had fallen, 'thou art no slow goer!'

'I am hungry,' said Kaa. 'Besides, they called me speckled frog.'

'Worm—earth-worm, and yellow to boot.'

'All one. Let us go on,' and Kaa seemed to pour himself along the ground, finding the shortest road with his steady eyes, and keeping to it.

In the Cold Lairs the Monkey-People were not thinking of Mowgli's friends at all. They had brought the boy to the Lost City, and were very pleased with themselves for the time. Mowgli had never seen an Indian city before, and though this was almost a heap of ruins it seemed very wonderful and splendid. Some king had built it long ago on a little hill. You could still trace the stone causeways that led up to the ruined gates where the last splinters of wood hung to the worn, rusted hinges. Trees had grown into and out of the walls; the battlements were tumbled down and decayed, and wild creepers hung out of the windows of the towers on the walls in bushy hanging clumps.

A great roofless palace crowned the hill, and the marble of the courtyards and the fountains was split, and stained with red and green, and the very cobble-stones in the courtyard where the king's elephants used to live had been thrust up and apart by grasses and young trees. From the palace you could see the rows and rows of roofless houses that made up the city looking like empty honeycombs filled with blackness; the shapeless block of stone that had been an idol, in the square where four roads met; the pits and dimples at street-corners where the public wells once stood, and the shattered domes of temples with wild figs sprouting on their sides. The monkeys called the place their city, and pretended to despise the Jungle-People because they lived in the forest. And yet they never knew what the buildings were made for nor how to use them. They would sit in circles on the hall of the king's council chamber, and scratch for fleas and pretend to be men; or they woud run in and out of the roofless houses and collect pieces of plaster and old bricks in a corner, and forget where they had hidden them, and fight and cry in scuffling crowds, and then break off to play up and down the terraces of the king's garden, where they would shake the rose trees and the oranges in sport to see the fruit and flowers fall. They explored all the passages and dark tunnels in the palace and the hundreds of little dark rooms, but they never remembered what they had seen and what they had not; and so drifted about in ones and twos or crowds telling each other that they were doing as men did. They drank at the tanks and made the water all muddy, and then they fought over it, and then they would all rush together in mobs and shout: 'There is no one in the jungle so wise and good and clever and strong and gentle as the *Bandar-log*.' Then all would begin again till they grew tired of the city and went back to the tree-tops, hoping the Jungle-People would notice them.

Mowgli, who had been trained under the Law of the Jungle, did not like or understand this kind of life. The monkeys dragged him into the Cold Lairs late in the afternoon, and instead of going to sleep, as Mowgli would have done after a long journey, they joined hands and danced about and sang their foolish songs. One of the monkeys made a speech and told his companions that Mowgli's capture marked a new thing in the history of the *Bandar-log*, for Mowgli was going to show them how to weave sticks and canes together as a protection against rain and cold. Mowgli picked up some creepers and began to work them in and out, and the monkeys tried to imitate; but in a very few minutes they lost interest and began to pull their friends' tails or jump up and down on all fours, coughing.

'I wish to eat,' said Mowgli. 'I am a stranger in this part of the jungle. Bring me food, or give me leave to hunt here.'

Twenty or thirty monkeys bounded away to bring him nuts and wild pawpaws; but they fell to fighting on the road, and it was too much trouble to go back with what was left of the fruit. Mowgli was sore and angry as well as hungry, and he roamed through the empty city giving the Strangers' Hunting Call from time to time, but no one answered him, and Mowgli felt that he had reached a very bad place indeed. 'All that Baloo has said about the *Bandar-log* is true,' he thought to himself. 'They have no Law, no Hunting Call, and no leaders—nothing but foolish words and little picking thievish hands. So if I am starved or killed here, it will be all my own fault. But I must try to return to my own jungle. Baloo will surely beat me, but that is better than chasing silly rose leaves with the *Bandar-log*.'

No sooner had he walked to the city wall than the monkeys pulled him back, telling him that he did not know how happy he was, and pinching him to make him grateful. He set his teeth and said nothing, but went with the shouting monkeys to a terrace above the red sandstone reservoirs that were half-full of rain water. There was a ruined summer-house of white marble in the centre of the terrace, built for queens dead a hundred years ago. The

domed roof had half fallen in and blocked up the underground passage from the palace by which the queens used
to enter; but the walls were made of screens of marble
tracery—beautiful milk-white fret-work, set with agates
and cornelians and jasper and lapis lazuli, and as the moon
came up behind the hill it shone through the open work,
casting shadows on the ground like black velvet embroid-
ery. Sore, sleepy, and hungry as he was, Mowgli could not
help laughing when the *Bandar-log* began, twenty at a
time, to tell him how great and wise and strong and gentle
they were, and how foolish he was to wish to leave them.
'We are great. We are free. We are wonderful. We are the
most wonderful people in all the jungle! We all say so, and
so it must be true,' they shouted. 'Now as you are a new
listener and can carry our words back to the Jungle-People
so that they may notice us in future, we will tell you all
about our most excellent selves.' Mowgli made no objection, and the monkeys gathered by hundreds and
hundreds on the terrace to listen to their own speakers
singing the praises of the *Bandar-log*, and whenever a
speaker stopped for want of breath they would all shout
together: 'This is true; we all say so.' Mowgli nodded and
blinked, and said 'Yes' when they asked him a question,
and his head spun with the noise. 'Tabaqui the Jackal,
must have bitten all these people,' he said to himself, 'and
now they have the madness. Certainly this is *dewanee*, the
madness. Do they never go to sleep? Now there is a cloud
coming to cover that moon. If it were only a big enough
cloud I might try to run away in the darkness. But I am
tired.'

That same cloud was being watched by two good friends
in the ruined ditch below the city wall, for Bagheera and
Kaa, knowing well how dangerous the Monkey-People
were in large numbers, did not wish to run any risks. The
monkeys never fight unless they are a hundred to one, and
few in the jungle care for those odds.

'I will go to the west wall,' Kaa whispered, 'and come
down swiftly with the slope of the ground in my favour.

They will not throw themselves upon *my* back in their
hundreds, but——'

'I know it,' said Bagheera. 'Would that Baloo were here;
but we must do what we can. When that cloud covers the
moon I shall go to the terrace. They hold some sort of
council there over the boy.'

'Good hunting,' said Kaa, grimly, and glided away to
the west wall. That happened to be the least ruined of any,
and the big snake was delayed awhile before he could find
a way up the stones. The cloud hid the moon, and as
Mowgli wondered what would come next he heard Bagheera's light feet on the terrace. The Black Panther had
raced up the slope almost without a sound and was
striking—he knew better than to waste time in biting
—right and left among the monkeys, who were seated
round Mowgli in circles fifty and sixty deep. There was a
howl of fright and rage, and then as Bagheera tripped on
the rolling kicking bodies beneath him, a monkey shouted:
'There is only one here! Kill him! Kill.' A scuffling mass of
monkeys, biting, scratching, tearing, and pulling, closed
over Bagheera, while five or six laid hold of Mowgli,
dragged him up the wall of the summer-house and pushed
him through the hole of the broken dome. A man-trained
boy would have been badly bruised, for the fall was a good
fifteen feet, but Mowgli fell as Baloo had taught him to
fall, and landed on his feet.

'Stay there,' shouted the monkeys, 'till we have killed
thy friends, and later we will play with thee—if the
Poison-People leave thee alive.'

'We be of one blood, ye and I,' said Mowgli, quickly
giving the Snake's Call. He could hear rustling and hissing
in the rubbish all round him and gave the Call a second
time, to made sure.

'Even ssso! Down hoods all!' said half a dozen low
voices (every ruin in India becomes sooner or later a
dwelling-place of snakes, and the old summer-house was
alive with cobras). 'Stand still, Little Brother, for thy feet
may do us harm.'

Mowgli stood as quietly as he could, peering through

the open work and listening to the furious din of the fight round the Black Panther—the yells and chatterings and scufflings, and Bagheera's deep, hoarse cough as he backed and bucked and twisted and plunged under the heaps of his enemies. For the first time since he was born, Bagheera was fighting for his life.

'Baloo must be at hand; Bagheera would not have come alone,' Mowgli thought; and then he called aloud: 'To the tank, Bagheera. Roll to the water-tanks. Roll and plunge! Get to the water!'

Bagheera heard, and the cry that told him Mowgli was safe gave him new courage. He worked his way desperately, inch by inch, straight for the reservoirs, hitting in silence. Then from the ruined wall nearest the jungle rose up the rumbling war-shout of Baloo. The old Bear had done his best, but he could not come before. 'Bagheera,' he shouted, 'I am here. I climb! I haste! *Ahuwora!* The stones slip under my feet! Wait my coming, O most infamous *Bandar-log!*' He panted up the terrace only to disappear to the head in a wave of monkeys, but he threw himself squarely on his haunches, and, spreading out his fore-paws, hugged as many as he could hold, and then began to hit with a regular *bat-bat-bat*, like the flipping strokes of a paddle-wheel. A crash and a splash told Mowgli that Bagheera had fought his way to the tank where the monkeys could not follow. The Panther lay gasping for breath, his head just out of water, while the monkeys stood three deep on the red steps, dancing up and down with rage, ready to spring upon him from all sides if he came out to help Baloo. It was then that Bagheera lifted up his dripping chin, and in despair gave the Snake's Call for protection—'We be of one blood, ye and I'—for he believed that Kaa had turned tail at the last minute. Even Baloo, half smothered under the monkeys on the edge of the terrace, could not help chuckling as he heard the Black Panther asking for help.

Kaa had only just worked his way over the west wall, landing with a wrench that dislodged a coping-stone into the ditch. He had no intention of losing any advantage of the ground, and coiled and uncoiled himself once or twice, to be sure that every foot of his long body was in working order. All that while the fight with Baloo went on, and the monkeys yelled in the tank round Bagheera, and Mang, the Bat, flying to and fro, carried the news of the great battle over the jungle, till even Hathi the Wild Elephant trumpeted, and, far away, scattered bands of the Monkey-Folk woke and came leaping along the tree-roads to help their comrades in the Cold Lairs, and the noise of the fight roused all the day-birds for miles round. Then Kaa came straight, quickly, and anxious to kill. The fighting-strength of a python is in the driving blow of his head backed by all the strength and weight of his body. If you can imagine a lance, or a battering ram, or a hammer weighing nearly half a ton driven by a cool, quiet mind living in the handle of it, you can rougly imagine what Kaa was like when he fought. A python four or five feet long can knock a man down if he hits him fairly in the chest, and Kaa was thirty feet long, as you know. His first stroke was delivered into the heart of the crowd round Baloo— was sent home with shut mouth in silence, and there was no need of a second. The monkeys scattered with cries of—'Kaa! It is Kaa! Run! Run!'

Generations of monkeys had been scared into good behaviour by the stories their elders told them of Kaa, the night-thief, who could slip along the branches as quietly as moss grows, and steal away the strongest monkey that ever lived; of old Kaa, who could make himself look so like a dead branch or a rotten stump that the wisest were deceived, till the branch caught them. Kaa was everything that the monkeys feared in the jungle, for none of them knew the limits of his power, none of them could look him in the face, and none had ever come alive out of his hug. And so they ran, stammering with terror, to the walls and the roofs of the houses, and Baloo drew a deep breath of relief. His fur was much thicker than Bagheera's, but he had suffered sorely in the fight. Then Kaa opened his mouth for the first time and spoke one long hissing word, and the far-away monkeys, hurrying to the defence of the

Cold Lairs, stayed where they were, cowering, till the loaded branches bent and crackled under them. The monkeys on the walls and the empty houses stopped their cries, and in the stillness that fell upon the city Mowgli heard Bagheera shaking his wet sides as he came up from the tank. Then the clamour broke out again. The monkeys leaped higher up the walls; they clung round the necks of the big stone idols and shrieked as they skipped along the battlements, while Mowgli, dancing in the summer-house, put his eye to the screen work and hooted owl-fashion between is front teeth, to show his derision and contempt.

'Get the man-cub out of that trap; I can do no more,' Bagheera gasped. 'Let us take the man-cub and go. They may attack again.'

'They will not move till I order them. Stay you ssssso!' Kaa hissed, and the city was silent once more. 'I could not come before, Brother, but I *think* I heard thee call'—this was to Bagheera.

'I—I may have cried out in the battle,' Bagheera answered. 'Baloo, art thou hurt?'

'I am not sure that they have not pulled me into a hundred little bearlings,' said Baloo gravely, shaking one leg after the other. 'Wow! I am sore. Kaa, we owe thee, I think, our lives—Bagheera and I.'

'No matter. Where is the manling?'

'Here, in a trap. I cannot climb out,' cried Mowgli. The curve of the broken dome was above his head.

'Take him away. He dances like Mao the Peacock. He will crush our young,' said the cobras inside.

'Hah!' said Kaa, with a chuckle, 'he has friends everywhere, this manling. Stand back, Manling; and hide you, O Poison People. I break down the wall.'

Kaa looked carefully till he found a discoloured crack in the marble tracery showing a weak spot, made two or three light taps with his head to get the distance, and then lifting up six feet of his body clear of the ground, sent home half-a-dozen full-power, smashing blows, nose-first. The screen-work broke and fell away in a cloud of dust and rubbish, and Mowgli leaped through the opening and flung himself between Baloo and Bagheera—an arm round each big neck.

'Art thou hurt?' said Baloo, hugging him softly.

'I am sore, hungry, and not a little bruised; but, oh, they have handled ye grievously, my Brothers! Ye bleed.'

'Others also,' said Bagheera, licking his lips, and looking at the monkey-dead on the terrace and round the tank.

'It is nothing, it is nothing, if thou are safe, O my pride of all little frogs!' whimpered Baloo.

'Of that we shall judge later,' said Bagheera, in a dry voice that Mowgli did not at all like. 'But here is Kaa, to whom we owe the battle and thou owest thy life. Thank him according to our customs, Mowgli.'

Mowgli turned and saw the great python's head swaying a foot above his own.

'So this is the manling,' said Kaa. 'Very soft is his skin, and he is not so unlike the *Bandar-log*. Have a care, Manling, that I do not mistake thee for a monkey some twilight when I have newly changed my coat.'

'We be one blood, thou and I,' Mowgli answered. 'I take my life from thee, to-night. My kill shall be thy kill if ever thou art hungry, O Kaa.'

'All thanks, Little Brother,' said Kaa, though his eyes twinkled. 'And what may so bold a hunter kill? I ask that I may follow when next he goes abroad.'

'I kill nothing,—I am too little,—but I drive goats toward such as can use them. When thou are empty come to me and see if I speak the truth. I have some skill in these [he held out his hands], and if ever thou art in a trap, I may pay the debt which I owe to thee, to Bagheera, and to Baloo, here. Good hunting to ye all, my masters.'

'Well said,' growled Baloo, for Mowgli had returned thanks very prettily. The python dropped his head lightly for a minute on Mowgli's shoulder. 'A brave heart and a courteous tongue,' said he. 'They shall carry thee far through the jungle, Manling. But now go hence quickly with thy friends. Go and sleep, for the moon sets, and what follows it is not well that thou shouldst see.'

The moon was sinking behind the hills, and the lines of

trembling monkeys huddled together on the walls and
battlements looked like ragged, shaky fringes of things.
Baloo went down to the tank for a drink, and Bagheera
began to put his fur in order, as Kaa glided out into the
centre of the terrace and brought his jaws together with a
ringing snap that drew all the monkeys' eyes upon him.

'The moon sets,' he said. 'Is there yet light to see?'

From the walls came a moan like the wind in the tree-
tops: 'We see, O Kaa.'

'Good. Begins now the Dance—the Dance of the
Hunger of Kaa. Sit still and watch.'

He turned twice or thrice in a big circle, weaving his
head from right to left. Then he began making loops and
figures of eight with his body, and soft, oozy triangles that
melted into squares and five-sided figures, and coiled
mounds, never resting, never hurrying, and never stopping his low, humming song. It grew darker and darker,
till at last the dragging, shifting coils disappeared, but they
could hear the rustle of the scales.

Baloo and Bagheera stood still as stone, growling in
their throats, their neck-hair bristling, and Mowgli
watched and wondered.

'*Bandar-log*,' said the voice of Kaa at last, 'can ye stir
foot or hand without my order? Speak!'

'Without thy order we cannot stir foot or hand, O Kaa!'

'Good! Come all one pace nearer to me.'

The lines of the monkeys swayed forward helplessly,
and Baloo and Bagheera took one stiff step forward with
them.

'Nearer!' hissed Kaa, and they all moved again.

Mowgli laid his hands on Baloo and Bagheera to get
them away, and the two great beasts started as though they
had been waked from a dream.

'Keep thy hand on my shoulder,' Bagheera whispered.
'Keep it there, or I must go back—must go back to Kaa.
Aah!'

'It is only old Kaa making circles on the dust,' said
Mowgli; 'let us go'; and the three slipped off through a gap
in the walls to the jungle.

'*Whoof!*' said Baloo, when he stood under the still trees again. 'Never more will I make an ally of Kaa,' and he shook himself all over.

'He knows more than we,' said Bagheera, trembling. 'In a little time, had I stayed, I should have walked down his throat.'

'Many will walk by that road before the moon rises again,' said Baloo. 'He will have good hunting—after his own fashion.'

'But what was the meaning of it all?' said Mowgli, who did not know anything of a python's powers of fascination.* 'I saw no more than a big snake making foolish circles till the dark came. And his nose was all sore. Ho! Ho!'

'Mowgli,' said Bagheera angrily, 'his nose was sore on *thy* account; as my ears and sides and paws and Baloo's neck and shoulders are bitten on *thy* account. Neither Baloo nor Bagheera will be able to hunt with pleasure for many days.'

'It is nothing,' said Baloo; 'we have the man-cub again.'

'True; but he has cost us heavily in time which might have been spent in good hunting, in wounds, in hair—I am half plucked along my back,—and last of all, in honour. For, remember, Mowgli, I, who am the Black Panther, was forced to call upon Kaa for protection, and Baloo and I were both made stupid as little birds by the Hunger-Dance. All this, Man-cub, came of thy playing with the *Bandar-log*.'

'True; it is true,' said Mowgli, sorrowfully. 'I am an evil man-cub, and my stomach is sad in me.'

'*Mf!* What says the Law of the Jungle, Baloo?'

Baloo did not wish to bring Mowgli into any more trouble, but he could not tamper with the Law, so he mumbled: 'Sorrow never stays punishment. But remember, Bagheera, he is very little.'

'I will remember; but he has done mischief, and blows must be dealt now. Mowgli, hast thou anything to say?'

'Nothing. I did wrong. Baloo and thou are wounded. It is just.'

Bagheera gave him half a dozen love-taps; from a panther's point of view they would hardly have waked one of his own cubs, but for a seven-year-old boy they amounted to as severe a beating as you could wish to avoid. When it was all over Mowgli sneezed, and picked himself up without a word.

'Now,' said Bagheera, 'jump on my back, Little Brother, and we will go home.'

One of the beauties of Jungle Law is that punishment settles all scores. There is no nagging afterward.

Mowgli laid his head down on Bagheera's back and slept so deeply that he never waked when he was put down by Mother Wolf's side in the home-cave.

Road-Song of the Bandar-log

HERE we go in a flung festoon,
Half-way up to the jealous moon!
Don't you envy our pranceful bands?
Don't you wish you had extra hands?
Wouldn't you like if your tails were—*so*—
Curved in the shape of a Cupid's bow?
      Now you're angry, but—never mind,
      Brother, thy tail hangs down behind!

Here we sit in a branchy row,
Thinking of beautiful things we know;
Dreaming of deeds that we mean to do,
All complete, in a minute or two—
Something noble and grand and good,
Won by merely wishing we could.
      Now we're going to—never mind,
      Brother, thy tail hangs down behind!

All the talk we ever have heard
Uttered by bat or beast or bird—
Hide or fin or scale or feather—
Jabber it quickly and all together!
Excellent! Wonderful! Once again!

Now we are talking just like men.
      Let's pretend we are ... never mind,
      Brother, thy tail hangs down behind!
      This is the way of the Monkey-kind.

Then join our leaping lines that scumfish through the pines,
That rocket by where, light and high, the wild-grape swings.
By the rubbish in our wake, and the noble noise we make,
Be sure, be sure, we're going to do some splendid things!

'Tiger! Tiger!'*

What of the hunting, hunter bold?
  Brother, the watch was long and cold.
What of the quarry ye went to kill?
  Brother, he crops in the jungle still.
Where is the power that made your pride?
  Brother, it ebbs from my flank and side.
Where is the haste that ye hurry by?
  Brother, I go to my lair—to die.

NOW we must go back to the first tale. When Mowgli left the wolf's cave after the fight with the Pack at the Council Rock, he went down to the ploughed lands where the villagers lived, but he would not stop there because it was too near to the jungle, and he knew that he had made at least one bad enemy at the Council. So he hurried on, keeping to the rough road that ran down the valley, and followed it at a steady jog-trot for nearly twenty miles, till he came to a country that he did not know. The valley opened out into a great plain dotted over with rocks and cut up by ravines. At one end stood a little village, and at the other the thick jungle came down in a sweep to the grazing-grounds, and stopped there as though it had been cut off with a hoe. All over the plain, cattle and buffaloes were grazing, and when the little boys in charge of the herds saw Mowgli they shouted and ran away, and the yellow pariah dogs* that hang about every Indian village barked. Mowgli walked on, for he was feeling hungry, and when he came to the village gate he saw the big thorn-bush that was drawn up before the gate at twilight, pushed to one side.

'Umph!' he said, for he had come across more than one such barricade in his night rambles after things to eat. 'So men are afraid of the People of the Jungle here also.' He sat down by the gate, and when a man came out he stood up, opened his mouth, and pointed down it to show that he wanted food. The man stared, and ran back up the one street of the village shouting for the priest, who was a big, fat man dressed in white, with a red and yellow mark on his forehead. The priest came to the gate, and with him at least a hundred people, who stared and talked and shouted and pointed at Mowgli.

'They have no manners, these Men Folk,' said Mowgli to himself. 'Only the gray ape would behave as they do.' So he threw back his long hair and frowned at the crowd.

'What is there to be afraid of?' said the priest. 'Look at the marks on his arms and legs. They are the bites of wolves. He is but a wolf-child run away from the jungle.'

Of course, in playing together, the cubs had often nipped Mowgli harder than they intended, and there were white scars all over his arms and legs. But he would have been the last person in the world to call these bites; for he knew what real biting meant.

'*Arré! Arré!*' said two or three women together. 'To be bitten by wolves, poor child! He is a handsome boy. He has eyes like red fire. By my honour, Messua,* he is not unlike thy boy that was taken by the tiger.'

'Let me look,' said a woman with heavy copper rings on her wrists and ankles, and she peered at Mowgli under the palm of her hand. 'Indeed he is not. He is thinner, but he has the very look of my boy.'

The priest was a clever man, and he knew that Messua was wife to the richest villager in the place. So he looked up at the sky for a minute, and said solemnly: 'What the jungle has taken the jungle has restored. Take the boy into thy house, my sister, and forget not to honour the priest who sees so far in to the lives of men.'

'By the Bull that bought me,' said Mowgli to himself, 'but all this talking is like another looking-over by the Pack! Well, if I am a man, a man I must become.'

The crowd parted as the woman beckoned Mowgli to her hut, where there was a red lacquered bedstead, a great earthen grain-chest with curious raised patterns on it, half a dozen copper cooking-pots, an image of a Hindu god in a little alcove, and on the wall a real looking-glass, such as they sell at the country fairs.

She gave him a long drink of milk and some bread, and

then she laid her hand on his head and looked into his eyes; for she thought perhaps that he might be her real son come back from the jungle where the tiger had taken him. So she said: 'Nathoo, O Nathoo!' Mowgli did not show that he knew the name. 'Dost thou not remember the day when I gave thee thy new shoes?' She touched his foot, and it was almost as hard as horn. 'No,' she said, sorrowfully; 'those feet have never worn shoes, but thou art very like my Nathoo, and thou shalt be my son.'

Mowgli was uneasy, because he had never been under a roof before; but as he looked at the thatch, he saw that he could tear it out any time if he wanted to get away, and that the window had no fastenings. 'What is the good of a man,' he said to himself at last, 'if he does not understand man's talk? Now I am as silly and dumb as a man would be with us in the jungle. I must learn their talk.'

It was not for fun that he had learned while he was with the wolves to imitate the challenge of bucks in the jungle and the grunt of the little wild pig. So as soon as Messua pronounced a word Mowgli would imitate it almost perfectly, and before dark he had learned the names of many things in the hut.

There was a difficulty at bedtime, because Mowgli would not sleep under anything that looked so like a panther-trap as that hut, and when they shut the door he went through the window. 'Give him his will,' said Messua's husband. 'Remember he can never till now have slept on a bed. If he is indeed sent in the place of our son he will not run away.'

So Mowgli stretched himself in some long, clean grass at the edge of the field, but before he had closed his eyes a soft gray nosed poked him under the chin.

'Phew!' said Gray Brother (he was the eldest of Mother Wolf's cubs). 'This is a poor reward for following thee twenty miles. Thou smellest of wood-smoke and cattle—altogether like a man already. Wake, Little Brother; I bring news.'

'Are all well in the jungle?' said Mowgli, hugging him.

'All except the wolves that were burned with the Red

Flower. Now, listen. Shere Khan has gone away to hunt far off till his coat grows again, for he is badly singed. When he returns he swears that he will lay thy bones in the Waingunga.'

'There are two words to that. I also have made a little promise. But news is always good. I am tired to-night,—very tired with new things, Gray Brother,—but bring me the news always.'

'Thou wilt not forget that thou art a wolf? Men will not make thee forget?' said Gray Brother anxiously.

'Never. I will always remember that I love thee and all in our cave; but also I will always remember that I have been cast out of the Pack.'

'And that thou mayest be cast out of another pack. Men are only men, Little Brother, and their talk is like the talk of frogs in a pond. When I come down here again, I will wait for thee in the bamboos at the edge of the grazing-ground.'

For three months after that night Mowgli hardly ever left the village gate, he was so busy learning the ways and customs of men. First he had to wear a cloth round him, which annoyed him horribly; and then he had to learn about money which he did not in the least understand, and about ploughing, of which he did not see the use. Then the little children in the village made him very angry. Luckily, the Law of the Jungle had taught him to keep his temper, for in the jungle life and food depend on keeping your temper; but when they made fun of him because he would not play games or fly kites, or because he mispronounced some word, only the knowledge that it was unsportsman-like to kill little naked cubs kept him from picking them up and breaking them in two.

He did not know his own strength in the least. In the jungle he knew he was weak compared with the beasts, but in the village people said that he was as strong as a bull.

And Mowgli had not the faintest idea of the difference that caste* makes between man and man. When the potter's donkey slipped in the clay-pit, Mowgli hauled it out by the tail, and helped to stack the pots for their journey to the market at Khanhiwara. That was very shocking, too, for the potter is a low-caste* man, and his donkey is worse. When the priest scolded him, Mowgli threatened to put him on the donkey, too, and the priest told Messua's husband that Mowgli had better be set to work as soon as possible;* and the village head-man told Mowgli that he would have to go out with the buffaloes next day, and herd them while they grazed. No one was more pleased than Mowgli; and that night, because he had been appointed a servant of the village, as it were, he went off to a circle that met every evening on a masonry platform under a great fig-tree. It was the village club, and the head-man and the watchman and the barber (who knew all the gossip of the village), and old Buldeo,* the village hunter, who had a Tower musket,* met and smoked. The monkeys sat and talked in the upper branches, and there was a hole under the platform where a cobra lived, and he had his little platter of milk every night because he was sacred; and the old men sat around the tree and talked, and pulled at the big *huqas* (the water-pipes), till far into the night. They told wonderful tales of gods and men and ghosts; and Buldeo told even more wonderful ones of the ways of beasts in the jungle, till the eyes of the children sitting outside the circle bulged out of their heads. Most of the tales were about animals, for the jungle was always at their door. The deer and the wild pig grubbed up their crops, and now and again the tiger carried off a man at twilight, within sight of the village gates.

Mowgli, who naturally knew something about what they were talking of, had to cover his face not to show that he was laughing, while Buldeo, the Tower musket across his knees, climbed on from one wonderful story to another, and Mowgli's shoulders shook.

Buldeo was explaining how the tiger that had carried away Messua's son was a ghost-tiger, and his body was inhabited by the ghost of a wicked old money-lender, who had died some years ago. 'And I know that this is true,' he said, 'because Purun Dass always limped from the blow that he got in a riot when his account-books were burned, and the tiger that I speak of *he* limps, too, for the tracks of his pads are unequal.'

'True, true; that must be the truth,' said the graybeards, nodding together.

'Are all these tales such cobwebs and moontalk?' said Mowgli. 'That tiger limps because he was born lame, as every one knows. To talk of the soul of a money-lender in a beast that never had the courage of a jackal is child's talk.'

Buldeo was speechless with surprise for a moment and the head-man stared.

'Oho! It is the jungle brat, is it?' said Buldeo. 'If thou are so wise, better bring his hide to Khanhiwara,* for the Government has set a hundred rupees* on his life. Better still, do not talk when thy elders speak.'

Mowgli rose to go. 'All the evening I have lain here listening,' he called back over his shoulder, 'and, except once or twice, Buldeo has not said one word of truth concerning the jungle, which is at his very doors. How, then, shall I believe the tales of ghosts and gods and goblins which he says he has seen?'

'It is full time that boy went to herding,' said the head-man, while Buldeo puffed and snorted at Mowgli's impertinence.

The custom of most Indian villages is for a few boys to take the cattle and buffaloes out to graze in the early morning, and bring them back at night; and the very cattle that would trample a white man to death allow themselves to be banged and bullied and shouted at by children that hardly come up to their noses. So long as the boys keep with the herds they are safe, for not even the tiger will charge a mob of cattle. But if they straggle to pick flowers or hunt lizards, they are sometimes carried off. Mowgli went through the village street in the dawn, sitting on the back of Rama,* the great herd bull; and the slaty-blue buffaloes, with their long, backward-sweeping horns and savage eyes, rose out of their byres, one by one, and followed him, and Mowgli made it very clear to the children with him that he was the master. He beat the buffaloes with a long, polished bamboo, and told Kamya, one of the boys, to graze the cattle by themselves, while he went on with the buffaloes, and to be very careful not to stray away from the herd.

An Indian grazing-ground is all rocks and scrub and tussocks and little ravines, among which the herds scatter and disappear. The buffaloes generally keep to the pools and muddy places, where they lie wallowing or basking in the warm mud for hours. Mowgli drove them on to the edge of the plain where the Waingunga River came out of the jungle; then he dropped from Rama's neck, trotted off to a bamboo clump, and found Gray Brother. 'Ah,' said Gray Brother, 'I have waited here very many days. What is the meaning of this cattle-herding work?'

'It is an order,' said Mowgli. 'I am a village herd for a while. What news of Shere Khan?'

'He has come back to this country, and has waited here a long time for thee. Now he has gone off again, for the game is scarce. But he means to kill thee.'

'Very good,' said Mowgli. 'So long as he is away do thou or one of the four brothers sit on that rock, so that I can see thee as I come out of the village. When he comes back wait for me in the ravine by the *dhâk*-tree* in the centre of the plain. We need not walk into Shere Khan's mouth.'

Then Mowgli picked out a shady place, and lay down and slept while the buffaloes grazed round him. Herding in India is one of the laziest things in the world. The cattle move and crunch, and lie down, and move on again, and they do not even low. They only grunt, and the buffaloes very seldom say anything, but get down into the muddy pools one after another, and work their way into the mud till only their noses and staring china-blue eyes show above the surface, and there they lie like logs. The sun makes the rocks dance in the heat, and the herd-children hear one kite (never any more) whistling almost out of sight overhead, and they know that if they died, or a cow died, that kite would sweep down, and the next kite miles away would see him drop and follow, and the next, and the next, and almost before they were dead there would be a score of hungry kites come out of nowhere. Then they sleep and wake and sleep again, and weave little baskets of dried grass and put grasshoppers in them; or catch two praying-mantises and make them fight; or string a necklace of red and black jungle-nuts; or watch a lizard basking on a rock, or a snake hunting a frog near the wallows. Then they sing long, long songs with odd native quavers at the end of them, and the day seems longer than most people's whole lives, and perhaps they make a mud castle with mud figures of men and horses and buffaloes, and put reeds into the men's hands, and pretend that they are kings and the figures are their armies, or that they are gods to be worshipped. Then evening comes, and the children call, and the buffaloes lumber up out of the sticky mud with noises like gunshots going off one after the other, and they all string across the gray plain back to the twinkling village lights.

Day after day Mowgli would lead the buffaloes out to their wallows, and day after day he would see Gray Brother's back a mile and a half away across the plain (so he knew that Shere Khan had not come back), and day after day he would lie on the grass listening to the noise round him, and dreaming of old days in the jungle. If Shere Khan had made a false step with his lame paw up in the jungles by the Waingunga, Mowgli would have heard him in those long, still mornings.

At last a day came when he did not see Gray Brother at the signal-place, and he laughed and headed the buffaloes for the ravine by the *dhâk*-tree, which was all covered with golden-red flowers. There sat Gray Brother, every bristle on his back lifted.

'He has hidden for a month to throw thee off thy guard. He crossed the ranges last night with Tabaqui, hot-foot on thy trail,' said the wolf, panting.

Mowgli frowned. 'I am not afraid of Shere Khan, but Tabaqui is very cunning.'

'Have no fear,' said Gray Brother, licking his lips a little. 'I met Tabaqui in the dawn. Now he is telling all his wisdom to the kites, but he told *me* everything before I broke his back. Shere Khan's plan is to wait for thee at the village gate this evening—for thee and for no one else. He is lying up now in the big dry ravine of the Waingunga.'

'Has he eaten to-day, or does he hunt empty?' said Mowgli, for the answer meant life or death to him.

'He killed at dawn,—a pig,—and he has drunk too. Remember, Shere Khan could never fast, even for the sake of revenge.'

'Oh! Fool, fool! What a cub's cub it is! Eaten and drunk too, and he thinks that I shall wait till he has slept! Now, where does he lie up? If there were but ten of us we might pull him down as he lies. These buffaloes will not charge unless they wind him, and I cannot speak their language. Can we get behind his track so that they may smell it?'

'He swam far down the Waingunga to cut that off,' said Gray Brother.

'Tabaqui told him that, I know. He would never have thought of it alone.' Mowgli stood with his finger in his mouth, thinking. 'The big ravine of the Waingunga. That opens out on the plain not half a mile from here. I can take the herd round through the jungle to the head of the ravine and then sweep down—but he would slink out at the foot. We must block that end. Gray Brother, canst thou cut the herd in two for me?'

'Not I, perhaps—but I have brought a wise helper.' Gray Brother trotted off and dropped into a hole. Then there lifted up a huge gray head that Mowgli knew well, and the hot air was filled with the most desolate cry of all the jungle—the hunting-howl of a wolf at mid-day.

'Akela! Akela!' said Mowgli, clapping his hands. 'I might have known that thou wouldst not forget me. We have a big work in hand. Cut the herd in two, Akela. Keep the cows and calves together, and the bulls and the plough-buffaloes by themselves.'

The two wolves ran, ladies'-chain fashion,* in and out of the herd, which snorted and threw up its head, and separated into two clumps. In one the cow-buffaloes stood, with their calves in the centre, and glared and pawed, ready, if a wolf would only stay still, to charge down and trample the life out of him. In the other the bulls and the young bulls snorted and stamped; but, though they looked more imposing, they were much less dangerous, for they had no calves to protect. No six men could have divided the herd so neatly.

'What orders?' panted Akela. 'They are trying to join again.'

Mowgli slipped on to Rama's back. 'Drive the bulls away to the left, Akela. Gray Brother, when we are gone, hold the cows together, and drive them into the foot of the ravine.'

'How far?' said Gray Brother, panting and snapping.

'Till the sides are higher than Shere Khan can jump,' shouted Mowgli. 'Keep them there till we come down.' The bulls swept off as Akela bayed, and Gray Brother stopped in front of the cows. They charged down on him, and he ran just before them to the foot of the ravine, as Akela drove the bulls far to the left.

'Well done! Another charge and they are fairly started. Careful, now—careful, Akela. A snap too much, and the bulls will charge. *Hujah!* This is wilder work than driving black-buck. Didst thou think these creatures could move so swiftly?' Mowgli called.

'I have—have hunted these too in my time,' gasped Akela in the dust. 'Shall I turn them into the jungle?'

'Ay, turn! Swiftly turn them! Rama is mad with rage. Oh, if I could only tell him what I need of him to-day!'

The bulls were turned to the right this time, and crashed into the standing thicket. The other herd-children, watching with the cattle half a mile away, hurried to the village as fast as their legs could carry them, crying that the buffaloes had gone mad and run away.

But Mowgli's plan was simple enough. All he wanted to do was to make a big circle uphill and get at the head of the ravine, and then take the bulls down it and catch Shere Khan between the bulls and the cows; for he knew that after a meal and a full drink Shere Khan would not be in any condition to fight or to clamber up the sides of the ravine. He was soothing the buffaloes now by voice, and

Akela had dropped far to the rear, only whimpering once
or twice to hurry the rear-guard. It was a long, long circle,
for they did not wish to get too near the ravine and give
Shere Khan warning. At last Mowgli rounded up the
bewildered herd at the head of the ravine on a grassy patch
that sloped steeply down to the ravine itself. From that
height you could see across the tops of the trees down to
the plain below; but what Mowgli looked at was the sides
of the ravine, and he saw with a great deal of satisfaction
that they ran nearly straight up and down, while the vines
and creepers that hung over them would give no foothold
to a tiger who wanted to get out.

'Let them breathe, Akela,' he said, holding up his hand.
'They have not winded him yet. Let them breathe. I must
tell Shere Khan who comes. We have him in the trap.'

He put his hands to his mouth and shouted down the
ravine,—it was almost like shouting down a tunnel,—and
the echoes jumped from rock to rock.

After a long time there came back the drawling, sleepy
snarl of a full-fed tiger just wakened.

'Who calls?' said Shere Khan, and a splendid peacock
fluttered up out of the ravine screeching.

'I, Mowgli. Cattle thief, it is time to come to the Council
Rock! Down—hurry them down, Akela! Down, Rama,
down!'

The herd paused for an instant at the edge of the slope,
but Akela gave tongue in the full hunting-yell, and they
pitched over one after the other, just as steamers shoot
rapids, the sand and stones spurting up round them. Once
started, there was no chance of stopping, and before they
were fairly in the bed of the ravine Rama winded Shere
Khan and bellowed.

'Ha! Ha!' said Mowgli, on his back. 'Now thou knowest!' and the torrent of black horns, foaming muzzles, and
staring eyes whirled down the ravine like boulders in
flood-time; the weaker buffaloes being shouldered out to
the sides of the ravine, where they tore through the
creepers. They knew what the business was before them—
the terrible charge of the buffalo-herd, against which no

tiger can hope to stand. Shere Khan heard the thunder of
their hoofs, picked himself up, and lumbered down the
ravine, looking from side to side for some way of escape;
but the walls of the ravine were straight, and he had to
keep on, heavy with his dinner and his drink, willing to do
anything rather than fight. The herd splashed through the
pool he had just left, bellowing till the narrow cut rang.
Mowgli heard an answering bellow from the foot of the
ravine, saw Shere Khan turn (the tiger knew if the worst
came to the worst it was better to meet the bulls than the
cows with their calves), and then Rama tripped, stumbled,
and went on again over something soft, and, with the bulls
at his heels, crashed full into the other herd, while the
weaker buffaloes were lifted clean off their feet by the
shock of the meeting. That charge carried both herds out
into the plain, goring and stamping and snorting. Mowgli
watched his time, and slipped off Rama's neck, laying
about him right and left with his stick.

'Quick, Akela! Break them up. Scatter them, or they will
be fighting one another. Drive them away, Akela. *Hai*,
Rama! *Hai! hai! hai!* my children. Softly now, softly! It is
all over.'

Akela and Gray Brother ran to and fro nipping the
buffaloes' legs, and though the herd wheeled once to
charge up the ravine again, Mowgli managed to turn
Rama, and the others followed him to the wallows.

Shere Khan needed no more trampling. He was dead,
and the kites were coming for him already.

'Brothers, that was a dog's death,' said Mowgli, feeling
for the knife he always carried in a sheath round his neck
now that he lived with men. 'But he would never have
shown fight. His hide will look well on the Council Rock.
We must get to work swiftly.'

A boy trained among men would never have dreamed of
skinning a ten-foot tiger alone, but Mowgli knew better
than any one else how an animal's skin is fitted on, and
how it can be taken off. But it was hard work, and Mowgli
slashed and tore and grunted for an hour, while the wolves

lolled out their tongues, or came forward and tugged as he ordered them.

Presently a hand fell on his shoulder, and looking up he saw Buldeo with the Tower musket. The children had told the village about the buffalo stampede, and Buldeo went out angrily, only too anxious to correct Mowgli for not taking better care of the herd. The wolves dropped out of sight as soon as they saw the man coming.

'What is this folly?' said Buldeo angrily. 'To think that thou canst skin a tiger! Where did the buffaloes kill him? It is the Lame Tiger, too, and there is a hundred rupees on his head. Well, well, we will overlook thy letting the herd run off, and perhaps I will give thee one of the rupees of the reward when I have taken the skin to Khanhiwara.' He fumbled in his waist-cloth for flint and steel, and stooped down to singe Shere Khan's whiskers. Most native hunters singe a tiger's whiskers to prevent his ghost haunting them.

'Hum!' said Mowgli, half to himself as he ripped back the skin of a fore-paw. 'So thou wilt take the hide to Khanhiwara for the reward, and perhaps give me one rupee? Now it is in my mind that I need the skin for my own use. Heh! old man, take away that fire!'

'What talk is this to the chief hunter of the village? Thy luck and the stupidity of thy buffaloes have helped thee to this kill. The tiger has just fed, or he would have gone twenty miles by this time. Thou canst not even skin him properly, little beggar-brat, and forsooth I, Buldeo, must be told not to singe his whiskers. Mowgli, I will not give thee one anna of the reward, but only a very big beating. Leave the carcass!'

'By the Bull that bought me,' said Mowgli, who was trying to get at the shoulder, 'must I stay babbling to an old ape all noon? Here, Akela, this man plagues me.'

Buldeo, who was still stooping over Shere Khan's head, found himself sprawling on the grass, with a gray wolf standing over him, while Mowgli went on skinning as though he were alone in all India.

'Ye-es,' he said, between his teeth. 'Thou art altogether

right, Buldeo. Thou wilt never give me one anna of the reward. There is an old war between this lame tiger and myself—a very old war, and—I have won.'

To do Buldeo justice, if he had been ten years younger he would have taken his chance with Akela had he met the wolf in the woods; but a wolf who obeyed the orders of this boy who had private wars with man-eating tigers was not a common animal. It was sorcery, magic of the worst kind, thought Buldeo, and he wondered whether the amulet round his neck would protect him. He lay as still as still, expecting every minute to see Mowgli turn into a tiger, too.

'Maharaj! Great King,' he said at last, in a husky whisper.

'Yes,' said Mowgli, without turning his head, chuckling a little.

'I am an old man. I did not know that thou wast anything more than a herd-boy. May I rise up and go away, or will thy servant tear me to pieces?'

'Go, and peace go with thee. Only, another time do not meddle with my game. Let him go, Akela.'

Buldeo hobbled away to the village as fast as he could, looking back over his shoulder in case Mowgli should change into something terrible. When he got to the village he told a tale of magic and enchantment and sorcery that made the priest look very grave.

Mowgli went on with his work, but it was nearly twilight before he and the wolves had drawn the great gay skin clear of the body.

'Now we must hide this and take the buffaloes home! Help me to herd them, Akela.'

The herd rounded up in the misty twilight, and when they got near the village Mowgli saw lights, and heard the conches and bells in the temple blowing and banging. Half the village seemed to be waiting for him by the gate. 'That is because I have killed Shere Khan,' he said to himself; but a shower of stones whistled about his ears, and the villagers shouted: 'Sorcerer! Wolf's brat! Jungle-demon!

Go away! Get hence quickly, or the priest will turn thee into a wolf again. Shoot, Buldeo, shoot!'

The old Tower musket went off with a bang, and a young buffalo bellowed in pain.

'More sorcery!' shouted the villagers. 'He can turn bullets. Buldeo, that was *thy* buffalo.'

'Now what is this?' said Mowgli, bewildered, as the stones flew thicker.

'They are not unlike the Pack, these brothers of thine,' said Akela, sitting down composedly. 'It is in my head that, if bullets mean anything, they would cast thee out.'

'Wolf! Wolf's cub! Go away!' shouted the priest, waving a sprig of the sacred *tulsi** plant.

'Again? Last time it was because I was a man. This time it is because I am a wolf. Let us go, Akela.'

A woman—it was Messua—ran across to the herd, and cried: 'Oh, my son, my son! They say thou art a sorcerer who can turn himself into a beast at will. I do not believe, but go away or they will kill thee. Buldeo says thou art a wizard, but I know thou hast avenged Nathoo's death.'

'Come back, Messua!' shouted the crowd. 'Come back, or we will stone thee.'

Mowgli laughed a little short ugly laugh, for a stone had hit him in the mouth. 'Run back, Messua. This is one of the foolish tales they tell under the big tree at dusk. I have at least paid for thy son's life. Farewell; and run quickly, for I shall send the herd in more swiftly than their brickbats. I am no wizard, Messua. Farewell!'

'Now, once more, Akela,' he cried. 'Bring the herd in.'

The buffaloes were anxious enough to get to the village. They hardly needed Akela's yell, but charged through the gate like a whirlwind, scattering the crowd right and left.

'Keep count!' shouted Mowgli scornfully. 'It may be that I have stolen one of them. Keep count, for I will do your herding no more. Fare you well, children of men, and thank Messua that I do not come in with my wolves and hunt you up and down your street.'

He turned on his heel and walked away with the Lone Wolf; and as he looked up at the stars he felt happy. 'No more sleeping in traps for me, Akela. Let us get Shere Khan's skin and go away. No; we will not hurt the village, for Messua was kind to me.'

When the moon rose over the plain, making it look all milky, the horrified villagers saw Mowgli, with two wolves at his heels and a bundle on his head, trotting across at the steady wolf's trot that eats up the long miles like fire. Then they banged the temple bells and blew the conches louder than ever; and Messua cried, and Buldeo embroidered the story of his adventures in the jungle, till he ended by saying that Akela stood up on his hind legs and talked like a man.

The moon was just going down when Mowgli and the two wolves came to the hill of the Council Rock, and they stopped at Mother Wolf's cave.

'They have cast me out from the Man-Pack, Mother,' shouted Mowgli, 'but I come with the hide of Shere Khan to keep my word.' Mother Wolf walked stiffly from the cave with the cubs behind her, and her eyes glowed as she saw the skin.

'I told him on that day, when he crammed his head and shoulders into this cave, hunting for thy life, Little Frog— I told him that the hunter would be the hunted. It is well done.'

'Little Brother, it is well done,' said a deep voice in the thicket. 'We were lonely in the jungle without thee,' and Bagheera came running to Mowgli's bare feet. They clambered up the Council Rock together, and Mowgli spread the skin out on the flat stone where Akela used to sit, and pegged it down with four slivers of bamboo, and Akela lay down upon it, and called the old call to the Council, 'Look—look well, O Wolves!' exactly as he had called when Mowgli was first brought there.

Ever since Akela had been deposed, the Pack had been without a leader, hunting and fighting at their own plea-sure. But they answered the call from habit, and some of them were lame from the traps they had fallen into, and some limped from shot-wounds, and some were mangy from eating bad food, and many were missing; but they

came to the Council Rock, all that were left of them, and
saw Shere Khan's striped hide on the rock, and the huge
claws dangling at the end of the empty, dangling feet. It
was then that Mowgli made up a song without any rhymes,
a song that came up into his throat all by itself, and he
shouted it aloud, leaping up and down on the rattling skin,
and beating time with his heels till he had no more breath
left, while Gray Brother and Akela howled between the
verses.

'Look well, O Wolves. Have I kept my word?' said
Mowgli when he had finished; and the wolves bayed,
'Yes,' and one tattered wolf howled:

'Lead us again, O Akela. Lead us again, O Man-cub, for
we be sick of this lawlessness, and we would be the Free
People once more.'

'Nay,' purred Bagheera, 'that may not be. When ye are
full-fed, the madness may come upon ye again. Not for
nothing are ye called the Free People. Ye fought for
freedom, and it is yours. Eat it, O Wolves.'

'Man-Pack and Wolf-Pack have cast me out,' said
Mowgli. 'Now I will hunt alone in the jungle.'

'And we will hunt with thee,' said the four cubs.

So Mowgli went away and hunted with the four cubs in
the jungle from that day on. But he was not always alone,
because years afterward he became a man and married.

But that is a story for grown-ups.*

Mowgli's Song

THAT HE SANG AT THE COUNCIL ROCK WHEN HE
DANCED ON SHERE KHAN'S HIDE

THE Song of Mowgli—I, Mowgli, am singing. Let the
jungle listen to the things I have done.

Shere Khan said he would kill—would kill! At the gates in
the twilight he would kill Mowgli, the Frog!

He ate and he drank. Drink deep, Shere Khan, for when
wilt thou drink again? Sleep and dream of the kill.

I am alone on the grazing-grounds. Gray Brother, come to
me! Come to me, Lone Wolf, for there is big game
afoot.

Bring up the great bull-buffaloes, the blue-skinned herd-
bulls with the angry eyes. Drive them to and fro as I
order.

Sleepest thou still, Shere Khan? Wake, oh wake! Here
come I, and the bulls are behind.

Rama, the King of the Buffaloes, stamped with his foot.
Waters of the Waingunga, whither went Shere Khan?

He is not Ikki to dig holes, nor Mao, the Peacock, that he
should fly. He is not Mang, the Bat, to hang in the
branches. Little bamboos that creak together, tell me
where he ran?

Ow! He is there. *Ahoo!* He is there. Under the feet of
Rama lies the Lame One! Up, Shere Khan!

Up and kill! Here is meat; break the necks of the bulls!

Hsh! He is asleep. We will not wake him, for his strength is
very great. The kites have come down to see it. The
black ants have come up to know it. There is a great
assembly in his honour.

Alala! I have no cloth to wrap me. The kites will see that I
am naked. I am ashamed to meet all these people.

Lend me thy coat, Shere Khan. Lend my thy gay striped
coat that I may go to the Council Rock.

By the Bull that bought me, I have made a promise—a
little promise. Only thy coat is lacking before I keep
my word.

With the knife—with the knife that men use—with the knife of the hunter, the man, I will stoop down for my gift.

Waters of the Waingunga, bear witness that Shere Khan gives me his coat for the love that he bears me. Pull, Gray Brother! Pull, Akela! Heavy is the hide of Shere Khan.

The Man-Pack are angry. They throw stones and talk child's talk. My mouth is bleeding. Let us run away.

Through the night, through the hot night, run swiftly with me, my brothers. We will leave the lights of the village and go to the low moon.

Waters of the Waingunga, the Man-Pack have cast me out. I did them no harm, but they were afraid of me. Why?

Wolf-Pack, ye have cast me out too. The jungle is shut to me and the village gates are shut. Why?

As Mang flies between the beasts and the birds, so fly I between the village and the jungle. Why?

I dance on the hide of Shere Khan, but my heart is very heavy. My mouth is cut and wounded with the stones from the village, but my heart is very light because I have come back to the jungle. Why?

These two things fight together in me as the snakes fight in the spring.

The water comes out of my eyes; yet I laugh while it falls. Why?

I am two Mowglis, but the hide of Shere Khan is under my feet.

All the jungle knows that I have killed Shere Khan. Look—look well, O Wolves!

Ahae! My heart is heavy with the things that I do not understand.

The White Seal

Oh! hush thee, my baby, the night is behind us,*
    And black are the waters that sparkled so green.
The moon, o'er the combers, looks downward to find us
    At rest in the hollows that rustle between.
Where billow meets billow, there soft be thy pillow;
    Ah, weary wee flipperling, curl at thy ease!
The storm shall not wake thee, nor shark overtake thee,
    Asleep in the arms of the slow-swinging seas.

Seal Lullaby

ALL these things happened several years ago at a place called Novastoshnah,* or North East Point, on the Island of St Paul, away and away in the Bering Sea. Limmershin,* the Winter Wren, told me the tale when he was blown on to the rigging of a steamer going to Japan, and I took him down into my cabin and warmed and fed him for a couple of days till he was fit to fly back to St Paul's again. Limmershin is a very odd little bird, but he knows how to tell the truth.

Nobody comes to Novastoshnah except on business, and the only people who have regular business there are the seals. They come in the summer months by hundreds and hundreds of thousands out of the cold gray sea; for Novastoshnah Beach has the finest accommodation for seals of any place in all the world.

Sea Catch* knew that, and every spring would swim from whatever place he happened to be in—would swim like a torpedo-boat straight for Novastoshnah, and spend a month fighting with his companions for a good place on the rocks as close to the sea as possible. Sea Catch was fifteen years old, a huge gray fur-seal with almost a mane on his shoulders, and long, wicked dog-teeth. When he heaved himself up on his front flippers he stood more than four feet clear of the ground, and his weight, if any one had been bold enough to weigh him, was nearly seven hundred pounds. He was scarred all over with the marks of savage fights, but he was always ready for just one fight more. He would put his head on one side, as though he were afraid to look his enemy in the face; then he would shoot it out like lightning, and when the big teeth were firmly fixed on the other seal's neck, the other seal might get away if he could, but Sea Catch would not help him.

Yet Sea Catch never chased a beaten seal, for that was against the Rules of the Beach. He only wanted room by the sea for his nursery; but as there were forty or fifty thousand other seals hunting for the same thing each spring, the whistling, bellowing, roaring, and blowing on the beach were something frightful.

From a little hill called Hutchinson's Hill you could look over three and a half miles of ground covered with fighting seals; and the surf was dotted all over with the heads of seals hurrying to land and begin their share of the fighting. They fought in the breakers, they fought in the sand, and they fought on the smooth-worn basalt rocks of the nurseries; for they were just as stupid and unaccommodating as men. Their wives never came to the island until late in May or early in June, for they did not care to be torn to pieces; and the young two-, three-, and four-year-old seals who had not begun housekeeping went inland about half a mile through the ranks of the fighters and played about on the sand-dunes in droves and legions, and rubbed off every single green thing that grew. They were called the holluschickie,*—the bachelors,—and there were perhaps two or three hundred thousand of them at Novastoshnah alone.

Sea Catch had just finished his forty-fifth fight one spring when Matkah,* his soft, sleek, gentle-eyed wife, came up out of the sea, and he caught her by the scruff of the neck and dumped her down on his reservation, saying gruffly: 'Late, as usual. Where *have* you been?'

It was not the fashion for Sea Catch to eat anything during the four months he stayed on the beaches, and so his temper was generally bad. Matkah knew better than to answer back. She looked round and cooed: 'How thoughtful of you! You've taken the old place again.'

'I should think I had,' said Sea Catch. 'Look at me!'

He was scratched and bleeding in twenty places; one eye was almost blind, and his sides were torn to ribbons.

'Oh, you men, you men!' Matkah said, fanning herself with her hind flipper. 'Why can't you be sensible and settle your places quietly? You look as though you had been fighting with the Killer Whale.'*

'I haven't been doing anything *but* fight since the middle of May. The beach is disgracefully crowded this season. I've met at least a hundred seals from Lukannon* Beach, house-hunting. Why can't people stay where they belong?'

'I've often thought we should be much happier if we hauled out at Otter Island instead of this crowded place,' said Matkah.

'Bah! Only the holluschickie go to Otter Island. If we went there they would say we were afraid. We must preserve appearances, my dear.'

Sea Catch sunk his head proudly between his fat shoulders and pretended to go to sleep for a few minutes, but all the time he was keeping a sharp look-out for a fight. Now that all the seals and their wives were on the land, you could hear their clamour miles out to sea above the loudest gales. At the lowest counting there were over a million seals on the beach,—old seals, mother seals, tiny babies, and holluschickie, fighting, scuffling, bleating, crawling, and playing together,—going down to the sea and coming up from it in gangs and regiments, lying over every foot of ground as far as the eye could reach, and skirmishing about in brigades through the fog. It is nearly always foggy at Novastoshnah, except when the sun comes out and makes everything look all pearly and rainbow-coloured for a little while.

Kotick,* Matkah's baby, was born in the middle of that confusion, and he was all head and shoulders, with pale, watery-blue eyes, as tiny seals must be; but there was something about his coat that made his mother look at him very closely.

'Sea Catch,' she said at last, 'our baby's going to be white!'

'Empty clam-shells and dry seaweed!' snorted Sea

Catch. 'There never has been such a thing in the world as a white seal.'

'I can't help that,' said Matkah; 'there's going to be now'; and she sang the low, crooning seal-song that all the mother seals sing to their babies:

> You mustn't swim till you're six weeks old,
>   Or your head will be sunk by your heels;
> And summer gales and Killer Whales
>   Are bad for baby seals.
>
> Are bad for baby seals, dear rat,
>   As bad as bad can be;
> But splash and grow strong,
> And you can't be wrong,
>   Child of the Open Sea!

Of course the little fellow did not understand the words at first. He paddled and scrambled about by his mother's side, and learned to scuffle out of the way when his father was fighting with another seal, and the two rolled and roared up and down the slippery rocks. Matkah used to go to sea to get things to eat, and the baby was fed only once in two days; but then he ate all he could, and throve upon it.

The first thing he did was to crawl inland, and there he met tens of thousands of babies of his own age, and they played together like puppies, went to sleep on the clean sand, and played again. The old people in the nurseries took no notice of them, and the holluschickie kept to their own grounds, so the babies had a beautiful playtime.

When Matkah came back from her deep-sea fishing she would go straight to their play-ground and call as a sheep calls for a lamb, and wait until she heard Kotick bleat. Then she would take the straightest of straight lines in his direction, striking out with her fore flippers and knocking the youngsters head over heels right and left. There were always a few hundred mothers hunting for their children through the playgrounds, and the babies were kept lively; but, as Matkah told Kotick, 'So long as you don't lie in muddy water and get mange, or rub the hard sand into a cut or scratch, and so long as you never go swimming when there is a heavy sea, nothing will hurt you here.'

Little seals can no more swim than little children, but they are unhappy till they learn. The first time that Kotick went down to the sea a wave carried him out beyond his depth, and his big head sank and his little hind flippers flew up exactly as his mother had told him in the song, and if the next wave had not thrown him back again he would have drowned.

After that he learned to lie in a beach-pool and let the wash of the waves just cover him and lift him up while he paddled, but he always kept his eye open for big waves that might hurt. He was two weeks learning to use his flippers; and all that while he floundered in and out of the water, and coughed and grunted and crawled up the beach and took cat-naps on the sand, and went back again, until at last he found that he truly belonged to the water.

Then you can imagine the times that he had with his companions, ducking under the rollers; or coming in on top of a comber and landing with a swash and a splutter as the big wave went whirling far up the beach; or standing up on his tail and scratching his head as the old people did; or playing 'I'm the King of the Castle' on slippery, weedy rocks that just stuck out of the wash. Now and then he would see a thin fin, like a big shark's fin, drifting along close to shore, and he knew that that was the Killer Whale, the Grampus, who eats young seals when he can get them; and Kotick would head for the beach like an arrow, and the fin would jig off slowly, as if it were looking for nothing at all.

Late in October the seals began to leave St. Paul's for the deep sea, by families and tribes, and there was no more fighting over the nurseries, and the holluschickie played anywhere they liked. 'Next year,' said Matkah to Kotick, 'you will be a holluschickie; but this year you must learn how to catch fish.'

They set out together across the Pacific, and Matkah showed Kotick how to sleep on his back with his flippers tucked down by his side* and his little nose just out of the water. No cradle is so comfortable as the long, rocking swell of the Pacific. When Kotick felt his skin tingle all over, Matkah told him he was learning the 'feel of the water,' and that tingly, prickly feelings meant bad weather coming, and he must swim hard and get away.

'In a little time,' she said, 'you'll know where to swim to, but just now we'll follow Sea Pig, the Porpoise, for he is very wise.' A school of porpoises were ducking and tearing through the water, and little Kotick followed them as fast as he could. 'How do you know where to go to?' he panted. The leader of the school rolled his white eyes, and ducked under. 'My tail tingles, youngster,' he said. 'That means there's a gale behind me. Come along! When you're south of the Sticky Water [he meant the Equator], and your tail tingles, that means there's a gale in front of you and you must head north. Come along! The water feels bad here.'

This was one of the very many things that Kotick learned, and he was always learning. Matkah taught him to follow the cod and the halibut along the under-sea banks, and wrench the rockling out of his hole among the weeds; how to skirt the wrecks lying a hundred fathoms below water, and dart like a rifle-bullet in at one port-hole and out at another as the fishes ran; how to dance on the top of the waves when the lightning was racing all over the sky, and wave his flipper politely to the stumpy-tailed Alba-tross and the Man-of-war Hawk as they went down the wind; how to jump three or four feet clear of the water, like a dolphin, flippers close to the side and tail curved; to leave the flying-fish alone because they are all bony; to take the shoulder-piece out of a cod at full speed ten fathoms deep; and never to stop and look at a boat or a ship, but particularly a row-boat. At the end of six months, what Kotick did not know about deep-sea fishing was not worth the knowing, and all that time he never set flipper on dry ground.

One day, however, as he was lying half asleep in the warm water somewhere off the Island of Juan Fernandez, he felt faint and lazy all over, just as human people do when the spring is in their legs, and he remembered the good firm beaches of Novastoshnah seven thousand miles away, the games his companions played, the smell of the sea-weed, the seal roar, and the fighting. That very minute he turned north, swimming steadily, and as he went on he met scores of his mates, all bound for the same place, and they said: 'Greeting, Kotick! This year we are all hollus-chickie, and we can dance the Fire-dance in the breakers off Lukannon and play on the new grass. But where did you get that coat?'

Kotick's fur was almost pure white now, and though he felt very proud of it, he only said: 'Swim quickly! My bones are aching for the land.' And so they all came to the beaches where they had been born, and heard the old seals, their fathers, fighting in the rolling mist.

That night Kotick danced the Fire-dance with the yearling seals. The sea is full of fire on summer nights all the way down from Novastoshnah to Lukannon, and each seal leaves a wake like burning oil behind him, and a flaming flash when he jumps, and the waves break in great phosphorescent streaks and swirls. Then they went inland to the holluschickie grounds, and rolled up and down in the new wild wheat, and told stories of what they had done while they had been at sea. They talked about the Pacific as boys would talk about a wood that they had been nutting in, and if any one had understood them, he could have gone away and made such a chart of that ocean as never was. The three- and four-year-old holluschickie romped down from Hutchinson's Hill, crying: 'Out of the way, youngsters! The sea is deep, and you don't know all that's in it yet. Wait till you've rounded the Horn. Hi, you yearling, where did you get that white coat?'

'I didn't get it,' said Kotick; 'it grew.' And just as he was going to roll the speaker over, a couple of black-haired men with flat red faces came from behind a sand-dune, and Kotick, who had never seen a man before, coughed and lowered his head. The holluschickie just bundled off a few yards and sat staring stupidly. The men were no less than Kerick Booterin, the chief of the seal-hunters on the island, and Patalamon, his son. They came from the little village not half a mile from the seal-nurseries, and they were deciding what seals they would drive up to the killing-pens (for seals were driven just like sheep), to be turned into sealskin jackets later on.

'Ho!' said Patalamon. 'Look! There's a white seal!'

Kerick Booterin turned nearly white under his oil and smoke, for he was an Aleut, and Aleuts are not clean people. Then he began to mutter a prayer. 'Don't touch him, Patalamon. There has never been a white seal since— since I was born. Perhaps it is old Zaharrof's ghost. He was lost last year in the big gale.'

'I'm not going near him,' said Patalamon. 'He's unlucky. Do you really think he is old Zaharrof come back? I owe him for some gulls' eggs.'

'Don't look at him,' said Kerick. 'Head off that drove of four-year-olds. The men ought to skin two hundred to-day, but it's the beginning of the season, and they are new to the work. A hundred will do. Quick!'

Patalamon rattled a pair of seal's shoulder-bones in front of a herd of holluschickie, and they stopped dead, puffing and blowing. Then he stepped near, and the seals began to move, and Kerick headed them inland, and they never tried to get back to their companions. Hundreds and hundreds of thousands of seals watched them being driven, but they went on playing just the same. Kotick was the only one who asked questions, and none of his companions could tell him anything, except that the men always drove seals in that way for six weeks or two months of every year.

'I am going to follow,' he said, and his eyes nearly popped out of his head as he shuffled along in the wake of the herd.

'The while seal is coming after us,' cried Patalamon. 'That's the first time a seal has ever come to the killing-grounds alone.'

'Hsh! Don't look behind you,' said Kerick. 'It *is* Zaharrof's ghost! I must speak to the priest about this.'

The distance to the killing-grounds was only half a mile,

but it took an hour to cover, because if the seals went too fast Kerick knew that they would get heated and then their fur would come off in patches when they were skinned. So they went on very slowly, past Sea-Lion's* Neck, past Webster House, till they came to the Salt House just beyond the sight of the seals on the beach. Kotick followed, panting and wondering. He thought that he was at the world's end, but the roar of the seal-nurseries behind him sounded as loud as the roar of a train in a tunnel. Then Kerick sat down on the moss and pulled out a heavy pewter watch and let the drove cool off for thirty minutes, and Kotick could hear the fog-dew dripping from the brim of his cap. Then ten or twelve men, each with an iron-bound club three or four feet long, came up, and Kerick pointed out one or two of the drove that were bitten by their companions or were too hot, and the men kicked those aside with their heavy boots made of the skin of a walrus's throat, and then Kerick said: 'Let go!' and then the men clubbed the seals on the head as fast as they could.

Ten minutes later little Kotick did not recognize his friends any more, for their skins were ripped off from the nose to the hind flippers—whipped off and thrown down on the ground in a pile.

That was enough for Kotick. He turned and galloped (a seal can gallop very swiftly for a short time) back to the sea, his little new moustache bristling with horror. At Sea-Lion's Neck, where the great sea-lions sit on the edge of the surf, he flung himself flipper overhead into the cool water, and rocked there, gasping miserably. 'What's here?' said a sea-lion gruffly; for as a rule the sea-lions keep themselves to themselves.

'*Scoochnie! Ochen scoochnie!*' ('I'm lonesome, very lonesome!') said Kotick. 'They're killing *all* the holluschickie on *all* the beaches!'

The sea-lion turned his head inshore. 'Nonsense!' he said; 'your friends are making as much noise as ever. You must have seen old Kerick polishing off a drove. He's done that for thirty years.'

'It's horrible,' said Kotick, backing water as a wave

went over him, and steadying himself with a screw-stroke of his flippers that brought him up all standing within three inches of a jagged edge of rock.

'Well done for a yearling!' said the sea-lion, who could appreciate good swimming. 'I suppose it *is* rather awful from your way of looking at it; but if you seals will come here year after year, of course the men get to know of it, and unless you can find an island where no men ever come, you will always be driven.'

'Isn't there any such island?' began Kotick.

'I've followed the *poltoos* [the halibut] for twenty years, and I can't say I've found it yet. But look here—you seem to have a fondness for talking to your betters; suppose you go to Walrus Islet and talk to Sea Vitch.* He may know something. Don't flounce off like that. It's a six-mile swim, and if I were you I should haul out and take a nap first, little one.'

Kotick thought that that was good advice, so he swam round to his own beach, hauled out, and slept for half an hour, twitching all over, as seals will. Then he headed straight for Walrus Islet, a little low sheet of rocky island almost due northeast from Novastoshnah, all ledges of rock and gulls' nests, where the walrus herded by themselves.

He landed close to old Sea Vitch—the big, ugly, bloated, pimpled, fat-necked, long-tusked walrus of the North Pacific, who has no manners except when he is asleep—as he was then, with his hind flippers half in and half out of the surf.

'Wake up!' barked Kotick, for the gulls were making a great noise.

'Hah! Ho! Humph! What's that?' said Sea Vitch, and he struck the next walrus a blow with his tusks and waked him up, and the next struck the next, and so on till they were all awake and staring in every direction but the right one.

'Hi! It's me,' said Kotick, bobbing in the surf and looking like a little white slug.

'Well! May I be——skinned!' said Sea Vitch, and they all

looked at Kotick as you can fancy a club full of drowsy old gentlemen would look at a little boy. Kotick did not care to hear any more about skinning just then; he had seen enough of it; so he called out: 'Isn't there any place for seals to go where men don't ever come?'

'Go and find out,' said Sea Vitch, shutting his eyes. 'Run away. We're busy here.'

Kotick made his dolphin-jump in the air and shouted as loud as he could: 'Clam-eater! Clam-eater!' He knew that Sea Vitch never caught a fish in his life, but always rooted for clams and sea-weeds, though he pretended to be a very terrible person. Naturally the Chickies and the Goove-rooskies and the Epatkas, the Burgomaster Gulls and the Kittiwakes and the Puffins, who are always looking for a chance to be rude, took up the cry, and—so Limmershin told me—for nearly five minutes you could not have heard a gun fired on Walrus Islet. All the population was yelling and screaming: 'Clam-eater! *Stareek* [old man]!' while Sea Vitch rolled from side to side grunting and coughing.

'*Now* will you tell?' said Kotick, all out of breath.

'Go and ask Sea Cow,' said Sea Vitch. 'If he is living still, he'll be able to tell you.'

'How shall I know Sea Cow when I meet him?' said Kotick, sheering off.

'He's the only thing in the sea uglier than Sea Vitch,' screamed a burgomaster gull, wheeling under Sea Vitch's nose. 'Uglier, and with worse manners! *Stareek!*'

Kotick swam back to Novastoshnah, leaving the gulls to scream. There he found that no one sympathised with him in his little attempts to discover a quiet place for the seals. They told him that men had always driven the hollus-chickie—it was part of the day's work—and that if he did not like to see ugly things he should not have gone to the killing-grounds. But none of the other seals had seen the killing, and that made the difference between him and his friends. Besides, Kotick was a white seal.

'What you must do,' said old Sea Catch, after he had heard his son's adventures, 'is to grow up and be a big seal like your father, and have a nursery on the beach, and then

they will leave you alone. In another five years you ought
to be able to fight for yourself.' Even gentle Matkah, his
mother, said: 'You will never be able to stop the killing.
Go and play in the sea, Kotick.' And Kotick went off and
danced the Fire-dance with a very heavy little heart.

That autumn he left the beach as soon as he could, and
set off alone because of a notion in his bullet-head. He was
going to find Sea Cow,* if there was such a person in the
sea, and he was going to find a quiet island with good firm
beaches for seals to live on, where men could not get at
them. So he explored and explored by himself from the
North to the South Pacific, swimming as much as three
hundred miles in a day and a night. He met with more
adventures than can be told, and narrowly escaped being
caught by the Basking Shark, and the Spotted Shark, and
the Hammerhead, and he met all the untrustworthy ruf-
fians that loaf up and down the seas, and the heavy polite
fish, and the scarlet-spotted scallops that are moored in
one place for hundreds of years, and grow very proud of it;
but he never met Sea Cow, and he never found an island
that he could fancy.

If the beach was good and hard, with a slope behind it
for seals to play on, there was always the smoke of a whaler
on the horizon, boiling down blubber, and Kotick knew
what *that* meant. Or else he could see that seals had once
visited the island and been killed off, and Kotick knew that
where men had come once they would come again.

He picked up with an old stumpy-tailed albatross, who
told him that Kerguelen Island was the very place for
peace and quiet, and when Kotick went down there he was
all but smashed to pieces against some wicked black cliffs
in a heavy sleet-storm with lighting and thunder. Yet as he
pulled out against the gale he could see that even there had
once been a seal-nursery. And it was so in all the other
islands that he visited.

Limmershin gave a long list of them, for he said that
Kotick spent five seasons exploring, with a four months'
rest each year at Novastoshnah, when the holluschickie
used to make fun of him and his imaginary islands. He

went to the Gallapagos,* a horrid dry place on the Equator, where he was nearly baked to death; he went to the Georgia Islands, the Orkneys, Emerald Island, Little Nightingale Island, Gough's Island, Bouvet's Island, the Crossets, and even to a little speck of an island south of the Cape of Good Hope. But everywhere the People of the Sea told him the same things. Seals had come to those islands once upon a time, but men had killed them all off. Even when he swam thousands of miles out of the Pacific, and got to a place called Cape Corrientes (that was when he was coming back from Gough's Island), he found a few hundred mangy seals on a rock, and they told him that men came there too.

That nearly broke his heart, and he headed round the Horn back to his own beaches; and on his way north he hauled out on an island full of green trees, where he found an old, old seal who was dying, and Kotick caught fish for him, and told him all his sorrows. 'Now,' said Kotick, 'I am going back to Novastoshnah, and if I am driven to the killing-pens with the holluschickie I shall not care.'

The old seal said: 'Try once more. I am the last of the Lost Rookery of Masafuera, and in the days when men killed us by the hundred thousand there was a story on the beaches that some day a white seal would come out of the north and lead the seal people to a quiet place. I am old and I shall never live to see that day, but others will. Try once more.'

And Kotick curled up his moustache (it was a beauty), and said: 'I am the only white seal that has ever been born on the beaches, and I am the only seal, black or white, who ever thought of looking for new islands.'

That cheered him immensely; and when he came back to Novastoshnah that summer, Matkah, his mother, begged him to marry and settle down, for he was no longer a holluschick, but a full-grown sea-catch, with a curly white mane on his shoulders, as heavy, as big, and as fierce as his father. 'Give me another season,' he said. 'Remember, Mother, it is always the seventh wave that goes farthest up the beach.'

Curiously enough, there was another seal who thought that she would put off marrying till the next year, and Kotick danced the Fire-dance with her all down Lukannon Beach the night before he set off on his last exploration.

This time he went westward, because he had fallen on the trail of a great shoal of halibut, and he needed at least one hundred pounds of fish a day to keep him in good condition. He chased them till he was tired, and then he curled himself up and went to sleep on the hollows of the ground-swell that sets in to Copper Island. He knew the coast perfectly well, so about midnight, when he felt himself gently bumped on a weed-bed, he said, 'Hm, tide's running strong tonight,' and turning over under water opened his eyes slowly and stretched. Then he jumped like a cat, for he saw huge things nosing about in the shoal water and browsing on the heavy fringes of the weeds.

'By the Great Combers of Magellan!'* he said, beneath his moustache. 'Who in the Deep Sea are these people?'

They were like no walrus, sea-lion, seal, bear, whale, shark, fish, squid, or scallop that Kotick had ever seen before. They were between twenty and thirty feet long, and they had no hind flippers, but a shovel-like tail that looked as if it had been whittled out of wet leather. Their heads were the most foolish-looking things you ever saw, and they balanced on the ends of their tails in deep water when they weren't grazing, bowing solemnly to one another and waving their front flippers as a fat man waves his arm.

'Ahem!' said Kotick. 'Good sport, gentlemen?' The big things answered by bowing and waving their flippers like the Frog-Footman.* When they began feeding again Kotick saw that their upper lip was split into two pieces that they could twitch apart about a foot and bring together again with a whole bushel of seaweed between the splits. They tucked the stuff into their mouths and chumped solemnly.

'Messy style of feeding, that,' said Kotick. They bowed again, and Kotick began to lose his temper. 'Very good,' he said. 'If you do happen to have an extra joint in your front flipper you needn't show off so. I see you bow gracefully, but I should like to know your names.' The split lips moved and twitched, and the glassy green eyes stared; but they did not speak.

'Well!' said Kotick, 'you're the only people I've ever met uglier than Sea Vitch—and with worse manners.'

Then he remembered in a flash what the Burgomaster Gull had screamed to him when he was a little yearling at Walrus Islet, and he tumbled backward in the water, for he knew that he had found Sea Cow at last.

The sea cows went on schlooping and grazing and chumping in the weed, and Kotick asked them questions in every language that he had picked up in his travels: and the Sea People talk nearly as many languages as human beings. But the Sea Cow did not answer, because Sea Cow cannot talk. He has only six bones in his neck where he ought to have seven, and they say under the sea that that prevents him from speaking even to his companions; but, as you know, he has an extra joint in his fore flipper, and by waving it up and down and about he makes what answers to a sort of clumsy telegraphic code.

By daylight Kotick's mane was standing on end and his temper was gone where the dead crabs go. Then the Sea Cow began to travel northward very slowly, stopping to hold absurd bowing councils from time to time, and Kotick followed them, saying to himself: 'People who are such idiots as these are would have been killed long ago if they hadn't found out some safe island; and what is good enough for the Sea Cow is good enough for the Sea Catch. All the same, I wish they'd hurry.'

It was weary work for Kotick. The herd never went more than forty or fifty miles a day, and stopped to feed at night, and kept close to the shore all the time; while Kotick swam round them, and over them, and under them, but he could not hurry them up one half-mile. As they went farther north they held a bowing council every few hours, and Kotick nearly bit off his moustache with impatience

till he saw that they were following up a warm current of
water, and then he respected them more.

One night they sank through the shiny water—sank like
stones—and, for the first time since he had known them,
began to swim quickly. Kotick followed, and the pace
astonished him, for he never dreamed that Sea Cow was
anything of a swimmer. They headed for a cliff by the
shore—a cliff that ran down into deep water, and plunged
into a dark hole at the foot of it, twenty fathoms under the
sea. It was a long, long swim, and Kotick badly wanted
fresh air before he was out of the dark tunnel they led him
through.

'My wig!'* he said, when he rose, gasping and puffing,
into open water at the farther end. 'It was a long dive, but
it was worth it.'

The sea cows had separated, and were browsing lazily
along the edges of the finest beaches that Kotick had ever
seen. There were long stretches of smooth-worn rock
running for miles, exactly fitted to make seal-nurseries,
and there were play-grounds of hard sand sloping inland
behind them, and there were rollers for seals to dance in,
and long grass to roll in, and sand-dunes to climb up and
down; and, best of all, Kotick knew by the feel of the
water, which never deceives a true Sea Catch, that no men
had ever come there.

The first thing he did was to assure himself that the
fishing was good, and then he swam along the beaches and
counted up the delightful low sandy islands half hidden in
the beautiful rolling fog. Away to the northward out to sea
ran a line of bars and shoals and rocks that would never let
a ship come within six miles of the beach; and between the
islands and the mainland was a stretch of deep water that
ran up to the perpendicular cliffs, and somewhere below
the cliffs was the mouth of the tunnel.

'It's Novastoshnah over again, but ten times better,'
said Kotick. 'Sea Cow must be wiser than I thought. Men
can't come down the cliffs, even if there were any men; and
the shoals to seaward would knock a ship to splinters. If
any place in the sea is safe, this is it.'

He began to think of the seal he had left behind him, but though he was in a hurry to go back to Novastoshnah, he thoroughly explored the new country, so that he would be able to answer all questions.

Then he dived and made sure of the mouth of the tunnel, and raced through to the southward. No one but a sea cow or a seal would have dreamed of there being such a place, and when he looked back at the cliffs even Kotick could hardly believe that he had been under them.

He was six days going home, though he was not swimming slowly; and when he hauled out just above Sea-Lion's Neck the first person he met was the seal who had been waiting for him, and she saw by the look in his eyes that he had found his island at last.

But the holluschickie and Sea Catch, his father, and all the other seals, laughed at him when he told them what he had discovered, and a young seal about his own age said: 'This is all very well, Kotick, but you can't come from no one knows where and order us off like this. Remember we've been fighting for our nurseries, and that's a thing you never did. You preferred prowling about in the sea.'

The other seals laughed at this, and the young seal began twisting his head from side to side. He had just married that year, and was making a great fuss about it.

'I've no nursery to fight for,' said Kotick. 'I want only to show you all a place where you will be safe. What's the use of fighting?'

'Oh, if you're trying to back out, of course I've no more to say,' said the young seal, with an ugly chuckle.

'Will you come with me if I win?' said Kotick; and a green light came into his eyes, for he was very angry at having to fight at all.

'Very good,' said the young seal carelessly. '*If* you win, I'll come.'

He had no time to change his mind, for Kotick's head darted out and his teeth sunk in the blubber of the young seal's neck. Then he threw himself back on his haunches and hauled his enemy down the beach, shook him, and knocked him over. Then Kotick roared to the seals: 'I've done my best for you these five seasons past. I've found you the island where you'll be safe, but unless your heads are dragged off your silly necks you won't believe. I'm going to teach you now. Look out for yourselves!'

Limmershin told me that never in his life—and Limmershin sees ten thousand big seals fighting every year—never in all his little life did he see anything like Kotick's charge into the nurseries. He flung himself at the biggest sea-catch he could find, caught him by the throat, choked him and bumped him and banged him till he grunted for mercy, and then threw him aside and attacked the next. You see, Kotick had never fasted for four months as the big seals did every year, and his deep-sea swimming-trips kept him in perfect condition, and, best of all, he had never fought before. His curly white mane stood up with rage, and his eyes flamed, and his big dog-teeth glistened, and he was splendid to look at.

Old Sea Catch, his father, saw him tearing past, hauling the grizzled old seals about as though they had been halibut, and upsetting the young bachelors in all directions; and Sea Catch gave one roar and shouted: 'He may be a fool, but he is the best fighter on the Beaches. Don't tackle your father, my son! He's with you!'

Kotick roared in answer, and old Sea Catch waddled in, his moustache on end, blowing like a locomotive, while Matkah and the seal that was going to marry Kotick cowered down and admired their men-folk. It was a gorgeous fight, for the two fought as long as there was a seal that dared lift up his head, and then they paraded grandly up and down the beach side by side, bellowing.

At night, just as the Northern Lights* were winking and flashing through the fog, Kotick climbed a bare rock and looked down on the scattered nurseries and the torn and bleeding seals. 'Now,' he said, 'I've taught you your lesson.'

'My wig!' said old Sea Catch, boosting himself up stiffly, for he was fearfully mauled. 'The Killer Whale himself could not have cut them up worse. Son, I'm proud of you, and what's more, *I'll* come with you to your island—if there is such a place.'

'Here you, fat pigs of the sea! Who comes with me to the Sea Cow's tunnel? Answer, or I shall teach you again,' roared Kotick.

There was a murmur like the ripple of the tide all up and down the beaches. 'We will come,' said thousands of tired voices. 'We will follow Kotick, the White Seal.'

Then Kotick dropped his head between his shoulders and shut his eyes proudly. He was not a white seal any more, but red from head to tail. All the same, he would have scorned to look at or touch one of his wounds.

A week later he and his army (nearly ten thousand holluschickie and old seals) went away north to the Sea Cow's tunnel, Kotick leading them, and the seals that stayed at Novastoshnah called them idiots. But next spring, when they all met off the fishing-banks of the Pacific, Kotick's seals told such tales of the new beaches beyond Sea Cow's tunnel that more and more seals left Novastoshnah.

Of course it was not all done at once, for the seals need a long time to turn things over in their minds, but year by year more seals went away from Novastoshnah, and Lukannon, and the other nurseries, to the quiet, sheltered beaches where Kotick sits all the summer through, getting bigger and fatter and stronger each year, while the holluschickie play round him, in that sea where no man comes.

Lukannon

This is the great deep-sea song that all the St. Paul seals sing when they are heading back to their beaches in the summer. It is a sort of very sad seal National Anthem.

I MET my mates in the morning (and oh, but I am old!)
Where roaring on the ledges the summer ground-swell
    rolled;
I heard them lift the chorus that dropped the breakers'
    song—
The beaches of Lukannon—two million voices strong!

The song of pleasant stations beside the salt lagoons,
The song of blowing squadrons that shuffled down the dunes.
The song of midnight dances that churned the sea to flame—
The beaches of Lukannon—before the sealers came!

I met my mates in the morning (I'll never meet them
    more!);
They came and went in legions that darkened all the shore.
And through the foam-flecked offing as far as voice could
    reach
We hailed the landing-parties and we sang them up the
    beach.

The beaches of Lukannon—the winter-wheat so tall—
The dripping, crinkled lichens, and the sea-fog drenching all!
The platforms of our playground, all shining smooth and
    worn!
The beaches of Lukannon—the home where we were born!

I meet my mates in the morning, a broken, scattered band.
Men shoot us in the water and club us on the land;
Men drive us to the Salt House like silly sheep and tame,
And still we sing Lukannon—before the sealers came.

Wheel down, wheel down to southward; oh, Gooverooska go!
And tell the Deep-Sea Viceroys the story of our woe;
Ere, empty as the shark's egg* the tempest flings ashore,
The beaches of Lukannon shall know their sons no more!

'Rikki-Tikki-Tavi'*

At the hole where he went in
Red-Eye called to Wrinkle-Skin.
Hear what little Red-Eye saith:
'Nag, come up and dance with death!'

Eye to eye and head to head,
  (*Keep the measure, Nag.*)
This shall end when one is dead;
  (*At thy pleasure, Nag.*)
Turn for turn and twist for twist—
  (*Run and hide thee, Nag.*)
Hah! The hooded Death has missed!
  (*Woe betide thee, Nag!*)

THIS is the story of the great war that Rikki-tikki-tavi fought single-handed, through the bath-rooms of the big bungalow in Segowlee cantonment. Darzee,* the tailor-bird, helped him, and Chuchundra,* the musk-rat,* who never comes out into the middle of the floor, but always creeps round by the wall, gave him advice; but Rikki-tikki did the real fighting.

He was a mongoose,* rather like a little cat in his fur and his tail, but quite like a weasel in his head and his habits. His eyes and the end of his restless nose were pink; he could scratch himself anywhere he pleased, with any leg, front or back, that he chose to use; he could fluff up his tail till it looked like a bottle-brush, and his war-cry, as he scuttled through the long grass, was: '*Rikk-tikk-tikki-tikki-tchk!*'

One day, a high summer flood washed him out of the burrow where he lived with his father and mother, and carried him, kicking and clucking, down a roadside ditch. He found a little wisp of grass floating there, and clung to it till he lost his senses. When he revived, he was lying in the hot sun on the middle of a garden path, very draggled indeed, and a small boy was saying: 'Here's a dead mongoose. Let's have a funeral.'

'No,' said his mother; 'let's take him in and dry him. Perhaps he isn't really dead.'

They took him into the house, and a big man picked him up between his finger and thumb, and said he was not dead but half choked; so they wrapped him in cotton-wool, and warmed him, and he opened his eyes and sneezed.

'Now,' said the big man (he was an Englishman who had just moved into the bungalow); don't frighten him, and we'll see what he'll do.'

It is the hardest thing in the world to frighten a mongoose, because he is eaten up from nose to tail with curiosity. The motto of all the mongoose family is, 'Run and find out'; and Rikki-tikki was a true mongoose. He looked at the cotton-wool, decided that it was not good to eat, ran all round the table, sat up and put his fur in order, scratched himself, and jumped on the small boy's shoulder.

'Don't be frightened, Teddy,' said his father. 'That's his way of making friends.'

'Ouch! He's tickling under my chin,' said Teddy.

Rikki-tikki looked down between the boy's collar and neck, snuffed at his ear, and climbed down to the floor, where he sat rubbing his nose.

'Good gracious,' said Teddy's mother, 'and that's a wild creature! I suppose he's so tame because we've been kind to him.'

'All mongooses are like that,' said her husband. 'If Teddy doesn't pick him up by the tail, or try to put him in a cage, he'll run in and out of the house all day long. Let's give him something to eat.'

They gave him a little piece of raw meat. Rikki-tikki liked it immensely, and when it was finished he went out into the verandah and sat in the sunshine and fluffed up his fur to make it dry to the roots. Then he felt better.

'There are more things to find out about in this house,' he said to himself, 'than all my family could find out in all their lives. I shall certainly stay and find out.'

He spent all that day roaming over the house. He nearly drowned himself in the bath-tubs, put his nose into the ink on a writing-table, and burnt it on the end of the big man's cigar, for he climbed up in the big man's lap to see how writing was done. At nightfall he ran into Teddy's nursery to watch how kerosene-lamps* were lighted, and when Teddy went to bed Rikki-tikki climbed up too; but he was a restless companion, because he had to get up and attend to every noise all through the night, and find out what made it. Teddy's mother and father came in, the last thing, to look at their boy, and Rikki-tikki was awake on the pillow. 'I don't like that,' said Teddy's mother; 'he may bite the child.' 'He'll do no such thing,' said the father. 'Teddy's safer with that little beast than if he had a bloodhound to watch him. If a snake came into the nursery now——'

But Teddy's mother wouldn't think of anything so awful.

Early in the morning Rikki-tikki came to early breakfast in the verandah riding on Teddy's shoulder, and they gave him banana and some boiled egg; and he sat on all their laps one after the other, because every well-brought-up mongoose always hopes to be a house-mongoose some day and have rooms to run about in, and Rikki-tikki's mother (she used to live in the General's house at Segowlee) had carefully told Rikki what to do if ever he came across white men.

Then Rikki-tikki went out into the garden to see what was to be seen. It was a large garden, only half cultivated, with bushes as big as summer-houses of Marshal Niel* roses, lime and orange trees, clumps of bamboos, and thickets of high grass. Rikki-tikki licked his lips. 'This is a splendid hunting-ground,' he said, and his tail grew bottle-brushy at the thought of it, and he scuttled up and down the garden, snuffing here and there till he heard very sorrowful voices in a thorn-bush.

It was Darzee, the tailor-bird, and his wife. They had made a beautiful nest by pulling two big leaves together and stitching them up the edges with fibres, and had filled the hollow with cotton and downy fluff. The nest swayed to and fro, as they sat on the rim and cried.

'What is the matter?' asked Rikki-tikki.

'We are very miserable,' said Darzee. 'One of our babies fell out of the nest yesterday, and Nag ate him.'

'H'm!' said Rikki-tikki, 'that is very sad—but I am a stranger here. Who is Nag?'

Darzee and his wife only cowered down in the nest without answering, for from the thick grass at the foot of the bush there came a low hiss—a horrid cold sound that made Rikki-tikki jump back two clear feet. Then inch by inch out of the grass rose up the head and spread hood of Nag,* the big black cobra, and he was five feet long from tongue to tail. When he had lifted one-third of himself clear of the ground, he stayed balancing to and fro exactly as a dandelion-tuft balances in the wind, and he looked at Rikki-tikki with the wicked snake's eyes that never change their expression, whatever the snake may be think-ing of.

'Who is Nag?' said he. '*I* am Nag. The great god Brahm* put his mark upon all our people when the first cobra spread his hood to keep the sun off Brahm as he slept. Look, and be afraid!'

He spread out his hood more than ever, and Rikki-tikki saw the spectacle-mark on the back of it that looks exactly like the eye part of a hook-and-eye fastening. He was afraid for the minute; but it is impossible for a mongoose to stay frightened for any length of time, and though Rikki-tikki had never met a live cobra before, his mother had fed him on dead ones, and he knew that all a grown mongoose's business in life was to fight and eat snakes. Nag knew that too, and at the bottom of his cold heart he was afraid.

'Well,' said Rikki-tikki, and his tail began to fluff up again, 'marks or no marks, do you think it is right for you to eat fledglings out of a nest?'

Nag was thinking to himself, and watching the least little movement in the grass behind Rikki-tikki. He knew that mongooses in the garden meant death sooner or later for him and his family, but he wanted to get Rikki-tikki off his guard. So he dropped his head a little, and put it on one side.

'Let us talk,' he said. 'You eat eggs. Why should not I eat birds?'

'Behind you! Look behind you!' sang Darzee.

Rikki-tikki knew better than to waste time in staring. He jumped up in the air as high as he could go, and just under him whizzed by the head of Nagaina,* Nag's wicked wife. She had crept up behind him as he was talking, to make an end of him; and he heard her savage hiss as the stroke missed. He came down almost across her back, and if he had been an old mongoose he would have known that then was the time to break her back with one bite; but he was afraid of the terrible lashing return-stroke of the cobra. He bit, indeed, but did not bite long enough, and he jumped clear of the whisking tail, leaving Nagaina torn and angry.

'Wicked, wicked Darzee!' said Nag, lashing up as high as he could reach toward the nest in the thorn-bush; but Darzee had built it out of reach of snakes, and it only swayed to and fro.

Rikki-tikki felt his eyes growing red and hot (when a mongoose's eyes grow red, he is angry),* and he sat back on his tail and hind legs like a little kangaroo, and looked all round him, and chattered with rage. But Nag and Nagaina had disappeared into the grass. When a snake misses its stroke, it never says anything or gives any sign of what it means to do next. Rikki-tikki did not care to follow them, for he did not feel sure that he could manage two snakes at once. So he trotted off to the gravel path near the house, and sat down to think. It was a serious matter for him.

If you read the old books of natural history, you will find they say that when the mongoose fights the snake and happens to get bitten, he runs off and eats some herb that cures him. That is not true. The victory is only a matter of quickness of eye and quickness of foot,—snake's blow against mongoose's jump,—and as no eye can follow the motion of a snake's head when it strikes, that makes things much more wonderful than any magic herb. Rikki-tikki knew he was a young mongoose, and it made him all the more pleased to think that he had managed to escape a blow from behind. It gave him confidence in himself, and when Teddy came running down the path, Rikki-tikki was ready to be petted.

But just as Teddy was stooping, something flinched a little in the dust, and a tiny voice said: 'Be careful. I am death!' It was Karait,* the dusty brown snakeling that lies for choice on the dusty earth; and his bite is as dangerous as the cobra's. But he is so small that nobody thinks of him, and so he does the more harm to people.

Rikki-tikki's eyes grew red again, and he danced up to Karait with the peculiar rocking, swaying motion that he had inherited from his family. It looks very funny, but it is so perfectly balanced a gait that you can fly off from it at any angle you please; and in dealing with snakes this is an advantage. If Rikki-tikki had only known, he was doing a much more dangerous thing than fighting Nag, for Karait is so small, and can turn so quickly, that unless Rikki bit him close to the back of the head, he would get the return-stroke in his eye or lip. But Rikki did not know: his eyes were all red, and he rocked back and forth, looking for a good place to hold. Karait struck out. Rikki jumped sideways and tried to run in, but the wicked little dusty gray head lashed within a fraction of his shoulder, and he had to jump over the body, and the head followed his heels close.

Teddy shouted to the house: 'Oh, look here! Our mongoose is killing a snake'; and Rikki-tikki heard a scream from Teddy's mother. His father ran out with a stick, but by the time he came up, Karait had lunged out once too far, and Rikki-tikki had sprung, jumped on the snake's back, dropped his head far between his fore-legs, bitten as high up the back as he could get hold, and rolled away. That bite paralysed Karait, and Rikki-tikki was just going to eat him up from the tail, after the custom of his family at dinner, when he remembered that a full meal makes a slow mongoose, and if he wanted all his strength and quickness ready, he must keep himself thin.

He went away for a dust-bath under the castor-oil bushes, while Teddy's father beat the dead Karait. 'What is the use of that?' thought Rikki-tikki. 'I have settle it all'; and then Teddy's mother picked him up from the dust and hugged him, crying that he had saved Teddy from death, and Teddy's father said that he was a providence, and Teddy looked on with big scared eyes. Rikki-tikki was rather amused at all the fuss, which, of course, he did not understand. Teddy's mother might just as well have petted Teddy for playing in the dust. Rikki was thoroughly enjoying himself.

That night, at dinner, walking to and fro among the wine-glasses on the table, he could have stuffed himself three times over with nice things; but he remembered Nag and Nagaina, and though it was very pleasant to be patted and petted by Teddy's mother, and to sit on Teddy's shoulder, his eyes would get red from time to time, and he would go off into is long war-cry of '*Rikk-tikk-tikki-tikki-tchk!*'

Teddy carried him off to bed, and insisted on Rikki-tikki sleeping under his chin. Rikki-tikki was too well bred to bite or scratch, but as soon as Teddy was asleep he went off for his nightly walk round the house, and in the dark he ran up against Chuchundra, the musk-rat, creeping round by the wall. Chuchundra is a broken-hearted little beast. He whimpers and cheeps all the night, trying to make up his mind to run into the middle of the room, but he never gets there.

'Don't kill me,' said Chuchundra, almost weeping. 'Rikki-tikki, don't kill me.'

'Do you think a snake-killer kills musk-rats?' said Rikki-tikki scornfully.

'Those who kill snakes get killed by snakes,' said Chuchundra, more sorrowfully than ever. 'And how am I to be sure that Nag won't mistake me for you some dark night?'

'There's not the least danger,' said Rikki-tikki; 'but Nag is in the garden, and I know you don't go there.'

'My cousin Chua,* the rat, told me——' said Chuchundra, and then he stopped.

'Told you what?'

'H'sh! Nag is everywhere, Rikki-tikki. You should have talked to Chua in the garden.'

'I didn't—so you must tell me. Quick, Chuchundra, or I'll bite you!'

Chuchundra sat down and cried till the tears rolled off his whiskers. 'I am a very poor man,' he sobbed. 'I never had spirit enough to run out into the middle of the room. H'sh! I mustn't tell you anything. Can't you *hear*, Rikki-tikki?'

Rikki-tikki listened. The house was as still as still, but he thought he could just catch the faintest *scratch-scratch* in the world,—a noise as faint as that of a wasp walking on a window-pane,—the dry scratch of a snake's scales on brick-work.

'That's Nag or Nagaina,' he said to himself; 'and he is crawling into the bath-room sluice. You're right, Chuchundra; I should have talked to Chua.'

He stole off to Teddy's bath-room, but there was nothing there, and then to Teddy's mother's bath-room. At the bottom of the smooth plaster wall there was a brick pulled out to make a sluice for the bath-water, and as Rikki-tikki stole in by the masonry curb where the bath is put, he heard Nag and Nagaina whispering together outside in the moonlight.

'When the house is emptied of people,' said Nagaina to her husband, '*he* will have to go away, and then the garden will be our own again. Go in quietly, and remember that the big man who killed Karait is the first one to bite. Then come out and tell me, and we will hunt for Rikki-tikki together.'

'But are you sure that there is anything to be gained by killing the people?' said Nag.

'Everything. When there were no people in the bungalow, did we have any mongoose in the garden? So long as the bungalow is empty, we are king and queen of the garden; and remember that as soon as our eggs in the melon-bed hatch (as they may to-morrow), our children will need room and quiet.'

'I had not thought of that,' said Nag. 'I will go, but there is no need that we should hunt for Rikki-tikki afterward. I will kill the big man and his wife, and the child if I can, and come away quietly. Then the bungalow will be empty, and Rikki-tikki will go.'

Rikki-tikki tingled all over with rage and hatred at this, and then Nag's head came through the sluice, and his five feet of cold body followed it. Angry as he was, Rikki-tikki was very frightened as he saw the size of the big cobra. Nag coiled himself up, raised his head, and looked into the bath-room in the dark, and Rikki could see his eyes glitter.

'Now, if I kill him here, Nagaina will know; and if I fight him on the open floor, the odds are in his favour. What am I to do?' said Rikki-tikki-tavi.

Nag waved to and fro, and then Rikki-tikki heard him drinking from the biggest water-jar that was used to fill the bath. 'That is good,' said the snake. 'Now, when Karait was killed, the big man had a stick. He may have that stick still, but when he comes in to bathe in the morning he will not have a stick. I shall wait here till he comes. Nagaina—do you hear me?—I shall wait here in the cool till daytime.'

There was no answer from outside, so Rikki-tikki knew Nagaina had gone away. Nag coiled himself down coil by coil, round the bulge at the bottom of the water-jar, and Rikki-tikki stayed still as death. After an hour he began to move, muscle by muscle, toward the jar. Nag was asleep, and Rikki-tikki looked at his big back, wondering which would be the best place for a good hold. 'If I don't break his back at the first jump,' said Rikki, 'he can still fight; and if he fights—O Rikki!' He looked at the thickness of the neck below the hood, but that was too much for him; and a bite near the tail would only make Nag savage.

'It must be the head,' he said at last; the head above the hood; and when I am once there, I must not let go.'

Then he jumped. The head was lying a little clear of the water-jar, under the curve of it; and, as his teeth met, Rikki braced his back against the bulge of the red earthenware to hold down the head. This gave him just one second's purchase, and he made the most of it. Then he was battered to and fro as a rat is shaken by a dog—to and fro on the floor, up and down, and round in great circles; but his eyes were red, and he held on as the body cart-whipped over the floor, upsetting the tin dipper and the soap-dish and the flesh-brush, and banged against the tin side of the bath. As he held he closed his jaws tighter and tighter, for he made sure he would be banged to death, and, for the honour of his family, he preferred to be found with his teeth locked. He was dizzy, aching, and felt shaken to pieces when something went off like a thunder-clap just behind him; a hot wind knocked him senseless, and red fire singed his fur. The big man had been wakened by the noise, and had fired both barrels of a shot-gun into Nag just behind the hood.

Rikki-tikki held on with his eyes shut, for now he was quite sure he was dead; but the head did not move, and the big man picked him up and said: 'It's the mongoose again, Alice; the little chap has saved *our* lives now.' Then Teddy's mother came in with a very white face, and saw what was left of Nag, and Rikki-tikki dragged himself to Teddy's bedroom and spent half the rest of the night shaking himself tenderly to find out whether he really was broken into forty pieces, as he fancied.

When morning came he was very stiff, but well pleased with his doings. 'Now I have Nagaina to settle with, and she will be worse than five Nags, and there's no knowing when the eggs she spoke of will hatch. Goodness! I must go and see Darzee,' he said.

Without waiting for breakfast, Rikki-tikki ran to the thorn-bush where Darzee was singing a song of triumph at the top of his voice. The news of Nag's death was all over the garden, for the sweeper had thrown the body on the rubbish-heap.

'Oh, you stupid tuft of feathers!' said Rikki-tikki angrily. 'Is this the time to sing?'

'Nag is dead—is dead—is dead!' sang Darzee. 'The valiant Rikki-tikki caught him by the head and held fast. The big man brought the bang-stick, and Nag fell in two pieces! He will never eat my babies again.'

'All that's true enough; but where's Nagaina?' said Rikki-tikki, looking carefully round him.

'Nagaina came to the bath-room sluice and called for Nag,' Darzee went on; 'and Nag came out on the end of a stick—the sweeper picked him up on the end of a stick and threw him upon the rubbish-heap. Let us sing about the great, the red-eyed Rikki-tikki!' and Darzee filled his throat and sang.

'If I could get up to your nest, I'd roll all your babies out!' said Rikki-tikki. 'You don't know when to do the right thing at the right time. You're safe enough in your nest there, but it's war for me down here. Stop singing a minute, Darzee.'

'For the great, the beautiful Rikki-tikki's sake I will stop,' said Darzee. 'What is it, O Killer of the terrible Nag?'

'Where is Nagaina, for the third time?'

'On the rubbish-heap by the stables, mourning for Nag. Great is Rikki-tikki with the white teeth.'

'Bother my white teeth! Have you ever heard where she keeps her eggs?'

'In the melon-bed, on the end nearest the wall, where the sun strikes nearly all day. She hid them there weeks ago.'

'And you never thought it worth while to tell me? The end nearest the wall, you said?'

'Rikki-tikki, you are not going to eat her eggs?'

'Not eat exactly; no. Darzee, if you have a grain of sense you will fly off to the stables and pretend that your wing is broken, and let Nagaina chase you away to this bush? I must get to the melon-bed, and if I went there now she'd see me.'

Darzee was a feather-brained little fellow who could never hold more than one idea at a time in his head; and just because he knew that Nagaina's children were born in eggs like his own, he didn't think at first that it was fair to kill them. But his wife was a sensible bird, and she knew that cobra's eggs meant young cobras later on; so she flew off from the nest, and left Darzee to keep the babies warm, and continue his song about the death of Nag. Darzee was very like a man in some ways.

She fluttered in front of Nagaina by the rubbish-heap, and cried out, 'Oh, my wing is broken! The boy in the house threw a stone at me and broke it.' Then she fluttered more desperately than ever.

Nagaina lifted up her head and hissed, 'You warned Rikki-tikki when I would have killed him. Indeed and truly, you've chosen a bad place to be lame in.' And she moved toward Darzee's wife, slipping along over the dust.

'The boy broke it with a stone!' shrieked Darzee's wife.

'Well! It may be some consolation to you when you're dead to know that I shall settle accounts with the boy. My husband lies on the rubbish-heap this morning, but before night the boy in the house will lie very still. What is the use of running away? I am sure to catch you. Little fool, look at me!'

Darzee's wife knew better than to do *that*, for a bird who looks at a snake's eyes gets so frightened that she cannot move. Darzee's wife fluttered on, piping sorrowfully, and never leaving the ground, and Nagaina quickened her pace.

Rikki-tikki heard them going up the path from the stables, and he raced for the end of the melon-patch near the wall. There, in the warm litter about the melons, very cunningly hidden, he found twenty-five eggs, about the size of a bantam's eggs, but with whitish skin instead of shell.

'I was not a day too soon,' he said; for he could see the baby cobras curled up inside the skin, and he knew that the minute they were hatched they could each kill a man or a mongoose. He bit off the tops of the eggs as fast as he could, taking care to crush the young cobras, and turned over the litter from time to time to see whether he had missed any. At last there were only three eggs left, and Rikki-tikki began to chuckle to himself, when he heard Darzee's wife screaming:

'Rikki-tikki, I led Nagaina toward the house, and she

has gone into the verandah, and—oh, come quickly—she means killing!'

Rikki-tikki smashed two eggs, and tumbled backward down the melon-bed with the third egg in his mouth, and scuttled to the verandah as hard as he could put foot to the ground. Teddy and his mother and father were there at early breakfast; but Rikki-tikki saw that they were not eating anything. They sat stone-still, and their faces were white. Nagaina was coiled up on the matting by Teddy's chair, within easy striking-distance of Teddy's bare leg, and she was swaying to and fro singing a song of triumph.

'Son of the big man that killed Nag,' she hissed, 'stay still. I am not ready yet. Wait a little. Keep very still, all you three. If you move I strike, and if you do not move I strike. Oh, foolish people, who killed my Nag!'

Teddy's eyes were fixed on his father, and all his father could do was to whisper, 'Sit still, Teddy. You mustn't move. Teddy, keep still.'

Then Rikki-tikki came up and cried: 'Turn round, Nagaina; turn and fight!'

'All in good time,' said she, without moving her eyes. 'I will settle my account with *you* presently. Look at your friends, Rikki-tikki. They are still and white; they are afraid. They dare not move, and if you come a step nearer I strike.'

'Look at your eggs,' said Rikki-tikki, 'in the melon-bed near the wall. Go and look, Nagaina.'

The big snake turned half round, and saw the egg on the verandah. 'Ah-h! Give it to me,' she said.

Rikki-tikki put his paws one on each side of the egg, and his eyes were blood-red. 'What price for a snake's egg? For a young cobra? For a young king-cobra? For the last—the very last of the brood? The ants are eating all the others down by the melon-bed.'

Nagaina spun clear round, forgetting everything for the sake of the one egg; and Rikki-tikki saw Teddy's father shoot out a big hand, catch Teddy by the shoulder, and drag him across the little table with the tea-cups, safe and out of reach of Nagaina.

'Tricked! Tricked! Tricked! *Rikk-tck-tck!*' chuckled Rikki-tikki. 'The boy is safe, and it was I—I—I that caught Nag by the hood last night in the bath-room.' Then he began to jump up and down, all four feet together, his head close to the floor. 'He threw me to and fro, but he could not shake me off. He was dead before the big man blew him in two. I did it. *Rikki-tikki-tck-tck!* Come then, Nagaina. Come and fight with me. You shall not be a widow long.'

Nagaina saw that she had lost her chance of killing Teddy, and the egg lay between Rikki-tikki's paws. 'Give me the egg, Rikki-tikki. Give me the last of my eggs, and I will go away and never come back,' she said, lowering her hood.

'Yes, you will go away, and you will never come back; for you will go to the rubbish-heap with Nag. Fight, widow! The big man has gone for his gun! Fight!'

Rikki-tikki was bounding all round Nagaina, keeping just out of reach of her stroke, his little eyes like hot coals. Nagaina gathered herself together, and flung out at him. Rikki-tikki jumped up and backward. Again and again and again she struck, and each time her head came with a whack on the matting of the verandah, and she gathered herself together like a watch-spring. Then Rikki-tikki danced in a circle to get behind her, and Nagaina spun round to keep her head to his head, so that the rustle of her tail on the matting sounded like dry leaves blown along by the wind.

He had forgotten the egg. It still lay on the verandah, and Nagaina came nearer and nearer to it, till at last, while Rikki-tikki was drawing breath, she caught it in her mouth, turned to the verandah steps, and flew like an arrow down the path, with Rikki-tikki behind her. When the cobra runs for her life, she goes like a whip-lash flicked across a horse's neck.

Rikki-tikki knew that he must catch her, or all the trouble would begin again. She headed straight for the long grass by the thorn-bush, and as he was running Rikki-tikki heard Darzee still singing his foolish little song of triumph. But Darzee's wife was wiser. She flew off her nest as Nagaina came along, and flapped her wings about Nagaina's head. If Darzee had helped they might have turned her; but Nagaina only lowered her hood and went on. Still, the instant's delay brought Rikki-tikki up to her, and as she plunged into the rat-hole where she and Nag used to live, his little white teeth were clenched on her tail, and he went down with her—and very few mongooses, however wise and old they may be, care to follow a cobra into its hole. It was dark in the hole; and Rikki-tikki never knew when it might open out and give Nagaina room to turn and strike at him. He held on savagely, and struck out his feet to act as brakes on the dark slope of the hot, moist earth.

Then the grass by the mouth of the hole stopped waving, and Darzee said: 'It is all over with Rikki-tikki! We must sing his death-song. Valiant Rikki-tikki is dead! For Nagaina will surely kill him underground.'

So he sang a very mournful song that he made up on the spur of the minute, and just as he got to the most touching part the grass quivered again, and Rikki-tikki covered with dirt, dragged himself out of the hole leg by leg, licking his whiskers. Darzee stopped with a little shout. Rikki-tikki shook some of the dust out of his fur and sneezed. 'It is all over,' he said. 'The widow will never come out again.' And the red ants that live between the grass stems heard him, and began to troop down one after another to see if he had spoken the truth.

Rikki-tikki curled himself up in the grass and slept where he was—slept and slept till it was late in the afternoon, for he had done a hard day's work.

'Now,' he said, when he awoke, 'I will go back to the house. Tell the Coppersmith, Darzee, and he will tell the garden that Nagaina is dead.'

The Coppersmith is a bird who makes a noise exactly like the beating of a little hammer on a copper pot; and the reason he is always making it is because he is the town-crier to every Indian garden, and tells all the news to everybody who cares to listen. As Rikki-tikki went up the path, he heard his 'attention' notes like a tiny dinner-gong; and then the steady '*Ding-dong-tock*! Nag is dead—*dong*! Nagaina is dead! *Ding-dong-tock!*' That set all the birds in the garden singing, and the frogs croaking; for Nag and Nagaina used to eat frogs as well as little birds.

When Rikki got to the house, Teddy and Teddy's mother (she looked very white still, for she had been fainting) and Teddy's father came out and almost cried over him; and that night he ate all that was given him till he could eat no more, and went to bed on Teddy's shoulder, where Teddy's mother saw him when she came to look late at night.

'He saved our lives and Teddy's life,' she said to her husband. 'Just think, he saved all our lives.'

Rikki-tikki woke up with a jump, for all the mongooses are light sleepers.

'Oh, it's you,' said he. 'What are you bothering for? All the cobras are dead; and if they weren't, I'm here.'

Rikki-tikki had a right to be proud of himself; but he did not grow too proud, and he kept that garden as a mongoose should keep it, with tooth and jump and spring and bite, till never a cobra dared show its head inside the walls.

Darzee's Chaunt

(SUNG IN HONOUR OF RIKKI-TIKKI-TAVI)

SINGER and tailor am I—
　　Doubled the joys that I know—
Proud of my lilt through the sky,
　　Proud of the house that I sew—
Over and under, so weave I my music—so weave I the
　　house that I sew.

Sing to your fledglings again,
　　Mother, oh lift up your head!
Evil that plagued us is slain,
　　Death in the garden lies dead.
Terror that hid in the roses is impotent—flung on the
　　dung-hill and dead!

Who hath delivered us, who?
　　Tell me his nest and his name.
Rikki, the valiant, the true,
　　Tikki, with eyeballs of flame,
Riki-tikki-tikki, the ivory-fangéd, the hunter with
　　eyeballs of flame.

Give him the Thanks of the Birds,
　　Bowing with tail-feathers spread!
Praise him with nightingale words—
　　Nay, I will praise him instead.
Hear! I will sing you the praise of the bottle-tailed
　　Rikki, with eyeballs of red!

(*Here Rikki-tikki interrupted, and the rest of the song is
lost.*)

Toomai of the Elephants

I will remember what I was, I am sick of rope and chain—
  I will remember my old strength and all my forest affairs.
I will not sell my back to man for a bundle of sugar-cane,
  I will go out to my own kind, and the wood-folk in their lairs.

I will go out until the day, until the morning break,
  Out to the winds' untainted kiss, the waters' clean caress:
I will forget my ankle-ring and snap my picket-stake.
  I will revisit my lost loves, and playmates masterless!

KALA NAG,* which means Black Snake, had served the
Indian Government in every way that an elephant* could
serve it for forty-seven years, and as he was fully twenty
years old when he was caught, that makes him nearly
seventy—a ripe age for an elephant. He remembered
pushing, with a big leather pad on his forehead, at a gun
stuck in deep mud, and that was before the Afghan War of
1842, and he had not then come to his full strength. His
mother, Radha Pyari,—Radha the darling,—who had
been caught in the same drive with Kala Nag, told him,
before his little milk tusks had dropped out, that elephants
who were afraid always got hurt; and Kala Nag knew that
that advice was good, for the first time that he saw a shell
burst he backed, screaming, into a stand of piled rifles, and
the bayonets pricked him in all his softest places. So before
he was twenty-five he gave up being afraid, and so he was
the best-loved and the best-looked-after elephant in the
service of the Government of India. He had carried tents,
twelve hundred pounds' weight of tents, on the march in
Upper India; he had been hoisted into a ship at the end of
a steam-crane and taken for days across the water, and
made to carry a mortar on his back in a strange and rocky
country very far from India, and had seen the Emperor
Theodore* lying dead in Magdala, and had come back
again in the steamer, entitled, so the soldiers said, to the
Abyssinian War medal. He had seen his fellow-elephants
die of cold and epilepsy and starvation and sunstroke up at

a placed called Ali Musjid, ten years later; and afterward he had been sent down thousands of miles south to haul and pile big baulks of teak in the timber-yards at Moulmein.* There he had half killed an insubordinate young elephant who was shirking his fair share of the work.

After that he was taken off timber-hauling, and employed, with a few score other elephants who were trained to the business, in helping to catch wild elephants among the Garo hills. Elephants are very strictly preserved by the Indian Government. There is one whole department which does nothing else but hunt them, and catch them, and break them in, and send them up and down the country as they are needed for work.

Kala Nag stood ten fair feet at the shoulders, and his tusks had been cut off short at five feet, and bound round the ends, to prevent them splitting, with bands of copper; but he could do more with those stumps than any untrained elephant could do with the real sharpened ones.

When, after weeks and weeks of cautious driving of scattered elephants across the hills, the forty or fifty wild monsters were driven into the last stockade,* and the big drop-gate, made of tree-trunks lashed together, jarred down behind them, Kala Nag, at the word of command, would go into that flaring, trumpeting pandemonium (generally at night, when the flicker of the torches made it difficult to judge distances), and, picking out the biggest and wildest tusker of the mob would hammer him and hustle him into quiet while the men on the backs of the other elephants roped and tied the smaller ones.

There was nothing in the way of fighting that Kala Nag, the old wise Black Snake, did not know, for he had stood up more than once in his time to the charge of the wounded tiger, and, curling up his soft trunk to be out of harm's way, had knocked the springing brute sideways in mid-air with a quick sickle-cut of his head, that he had invented all by himself; had knocked him over, and kneeled upon him with his huge knees till the life went out with a gasp and a howl, and there was only a fluffy striped thing on the ground for Kala Nag to pull by the tail.

'Yes,' said Big Toomai, his driver, the son of Black Toomai who had taken him to Abyssinia, and grandson of Toomai of the Elephants who had seen him caught, 'there is nothing that the Black Snake fears except me. He has seen three generations of us feed him and groom him, and he will live to see four.'

'He is afraid of *me* also,' said Little Toomai, standing up to his full height of four feet, with only one rag upon him. He was ten years old, the eldest son of Big Toomai, and, according to custom, he would take his father's place on Kala Nag's neck when he grew up, and would handle the heavy iron *ankus*, the elephant-goad that had been worn smooth by his father, and his grandfather, and his great-grandfather. He knew what he was talking of; for he had been born under Kala Nag's shadow, had played with the end of his trunk before he could walk, had taken him down to water as soon as he could walk, and Kala Nag would no more have dreamed of disobeying his shrill little orders than he would have dreamed of killing him on that day when Big Toomai carried the little brown baby under Kala Nag's tusks, and told him to salute his master that was to be.

'Yes,' said Little Toomai, 'he is afraid of *me*,' and he took long strides up to Kala Nag, called him a fat old pig, and made him lift up his feet one after the other.

'Wah!' said Little Toomai, 'thou art a big elephant,' and he wagged his fluffy head, quoting his father. 'The Government may pay for elephants, but they belong to us mahouts. When thou art old, Kala Nag, there will come some rich Rajah, and he will buy thee from the Government, on account of thy size and thy manners, and then thou wilt have nothing to do but to carry gold earings in thy ears, and a gold howdah on thy back, and a red cloth covered with gold on thy sides, and walk at the head of the processions of the King. Then I shall sit on thy neck, O Kala Nag, with a silver *ankus*, and men will run before us with golden sticks, crying, "Room for the King's elephant!" That will be good, Kala Nag, but not so good as this hunting in the jungles.'

'Umph!' said Big Toomai. 'Thou art a boy, and as wild as a buffalo-calf. This running up and down among the hills is not the best Government service. I am getting old, and I do not love wild elephants. Give me brick elephant-lines, one stall to each elephant, and big stumps to tie them to safely, and flat broad roads to exercise upon, instead of this come-and-go camping. Aha, the Cawnpore barracks were good. There was a bazaar close by, and only three hours' work a day.'

Little Toomai remembered the Cawnpore elephant-lines and said nothing. He very much preferred the camp life, and hated those broad, flat roads, with the daily grubbing for grass in the forage-reserve, and the long hours when there was nothing to do except to watch Kala Nag fidgeting in his pickets.

What Little Toomai liked was to scramble up bridle-paths that only an elephant could take; the dip into the valley below; the glimpses of the wild elephants browsing miles away; the rush of the frightened pig and peacock under Kala Nag's feet; the blinding warm rains, when all the hills and valleys smoked; the beautiful misty mornings when nobody knew where they would camp that night; the steady, cautious drive of the wild elephants, and the mad rush and blaze and hullabaloo of the last night's drive, when the elephants poured into the stockade like boulders in a landslide, found that they could not get out, and flung themselves at the heavy posts only to be driven back by yells and flaring torches and volleys of blank cartridge.

Even a little boy could be of use there, and Toomai was as useful as three boys. He would get his torch and wave it, and yell with the best. But the really good time came when the driving out began, and the Keddah—that is, the stockade—looked like a picture of the end of the world, and men had to make signs to one another, because they could not hear themselves speak. Then Little Toomai would climb up to the top of one of the quivering stockade-posts, his sun-bleached brown hair flying loose all over his shoulders, and he looking like a goblin in the torch-light; and as soon as there was a lull you could hear his high-pitched yells of encouragement to Kala Nag, above the trumpeting and crashing, and snapping of ropes, and groans of the tethered elephants. '*Maîl, maîl, Kala Nag!* (Go on, go on, Black Snake!) *Dant do!* (Give him the tusk!) *Somalo! Somalo!* (Careful, careful!) *Maro! Mar!* (Hit him, hit him!) Mind the post! *Arre! Arre! Hai! Yai! Kya-a-ah!*' he would shout, and the big fight between Kala Nag and the wild elephant would sway to and fro across the Keddah, and the old elephant-catchers would wipe the sweat out of their eyes, and find time to nod to Little Toomai wriggling with joy on the top of the posts.

He did more than wriggle. One night he slid down from the post and slipped in between the elephants, and threw up the loose end of a rope, which had dropped, to a driver who was trying to get a purchase on the leg of a kicking young calf (calves always give more trouble than full-grown animals). Kala Nag saw him, caught him in his trunk, and handed him up to Big Toomai, who slapped him then and there, and put him back on the post.

Next morning he gave him a scolding, and said: 'Are not good brick elephant-lines and a little tent-carrying enough, that thou must needs go elephant-catching on thy own account, little worthless? Now those foolish hunters, whose pay is less than my pay, have spoken to Petersen Sahib of the matter.' Little Toomai was frightened. He did not know much of white men, but Petersen Sahib was the greatest white man in the world to him. He was the head of all the Keddah operations—the man who caught all the elephants for the Government of India, and who knew more about the ways of elephants than any living man.

'What—what will happen?' said little Toomai.

'Happen! the worst than can happen. Petersen Sahib is a madman. Else why should he go hunting these wild devils? He may even require thee to be an elephant-catcher, to sleep anywhere in these fever-filled jungles, and at last to be trampled to death in the Keddah. It is well that this nonsense ends safely. Next week the catching is over, and we of the plains are sent back to our stations. Then we will march on smooth roads, and forget all this hunting. But, son, I am angry that thou shouldst meddle in the business that belongs to these dirty Assamese jungle-folk. Kala Nag will obey none but me, so I must go with him into the Keddah; but he is only a fighting elephant, and he does not help to rope them. So I sit at my ease, as befits a mahout,*—not a mere hunter,—a mahout, I say, and a man who gets a pension at the end of his service. Is the family of Toomai of the Elephants to be trodden underfoot in the dirt of a Keddah? Bad one! Wicked one! Worthless son! Go and wash Kala Nag and attend to his ears, and see that there are no thorns in his feet; or else Petersen Sahib will surely catch thee and make thee a wild hunter—a follower of elephants' foot-tracks, a jungle-bear. Bah! Shame! Go!'

Little Toomai went off without saying a word, but he told Kala Nag all his grievances while he was examining his feet. 'No matter,' said Little Toomai, turning up the fringe of Kala Nag's huge right ear. 'They have said my name to Petersen Sahib, and perhaps—and perhaps—and perhaps—who knows? Hai! That is a big thorn that I have pulled out!'

The next few days were spent in getting the elephants together, in walking the newly caught wild elephants up and down between a couple of tame ones, to prevent them from giving too much trouble on the downward march to the plains, and in taking stock of the blankets and ropes and things that had been worn out or lost in the forest.

Petersen Sahib came in on his clever she-elephant Pudmini; he had been paying off other camps among the hills, for the season was coming to an end, and there was a native clerk sitting at a table under a tree to pay the drivers their wages. As each man was paid he went back to his elephant, and joined the line that stood ready to start. The catchers, and hunters, and beaters, the men of the regular Keddah, who stayed in the jungle year in and year out, sat on the backs of the elephants that belonged to Petersen Sahib's permanent force, or leaned against the trees with their guns across their arms, and made fun of the drivers who were going away, and laughed when the newly caught elephants broke the line and ran about.

Big Toomai went up to the clerk with Little Toomai behind him, and Machua Appa, the head-tracker, said in an undertone to a friend of his, 'There goes one piece of good elephant-stuff at least. 'Tis a pity to send that young jungle-cock to moult in the plains.'

Now Petersen Sahib had ears all over him, as a man must have who listens to the most silent of all living things—the wild elephant. He turned where he was lying all along on Pudmini's back, and said, 'What is that? I did not know of a man among the plains-drivers who had wit enough to rope even a dead elephant.'

'This is not a man, but a boy. He went into the Keddah at the last drive, and threw Barmao there the rope when we were trying to get that young calf with the blotch on his shoulder away from his mother.'

Machua Appa pointed at Little Toomai, and Petersen Sahib looked, and Little Toomai bowed to the earth.

'He throw a rope? He is smaller than a picket-pin. Little one, what is thy name?' said Petersen Sahib.

Little Toomai was too frightened to speak, but Kala Nag was behind him, and Toomai made a sign with his hand, and the elephant caught him up in his trunk and held him level with Pudmini's forehead, in front of the great Petersen Sahib. Then Little Toomai covered his face with his hands, for he was only a child, and except where elephants were concerned, he was just as bashful as a child could be.

'Oho!' said Petersen Sahib, smiling underneath his moustache, 'and why didst thou teach thy elephant *that* trick? Was it to help thee steal green corn from the roofs of the houses when the ears are put out to dry?'

'Not green corn, Protector of the Poor,—melons,' said Little Toomai, and all the men sitting about broke into a roar of laughter. Most of them had taught their elephants that trick when they were boys. Little Toomai was hanging eight feet up in the air, and he wished very much that he were eight feet under ground.

'He is Toomai, my son, Sahib,' said Big Toomai, scowling. 'He is a very bad boy, and he will end in a jail, Sahib.'

'Of that I have my doubts,' said Petersen Sahib. 'A boy who can face a full Keddah at his age does not end in jails. See, little one, here are four annas to spend in sweetmeats because thou hast a little head under that great thatch of hair. In time thou mayest become a hunter too.' Big Toomai scowled more than ever. 'Remember, though, that Keddahs are not good for children to play in,' Petersen Sahib went on.

'Must I never go there, Sahib?' asked Little Toomai, with a big gasp.

'Yes,' Petersen Sahib smiled again. 'When thou hast seen the elephants dance. That is the proper time. Come to me when thou hast seen the elephants dance, and then I will let thee go into all the Keddahs.'

There was another roar of laughter, for that is an old joke among elephant-catchers, and it means just never. There are great cleared flat places hidden away in the forests that are called elephants' ball-rooms,* but even these are only found by accident, and no man has ever seen the elephants dance. When a driver boasts of his skill and bravery the other drivers say, 'And when didst *thou* see the elephants dance?'

Kala Nag put Little Toomai down, and he bowed to the earth again and went away with his father, and gave the silver four-anna piece to his mother, who was nursing his baby-brother, and they all were put up on Kala Nag's back, and the line of grunting, squealing elephants rolled down the hill-path to the plains. It was a very lively march on account of the new elephants, who gave trouble at every ford, and who needed coaxing or beating every other minute.

Big Toomai prodded Kala Nag spitefully, for he was very angry, but Little Toomai was too happy to speak. Petersen Sahib had noticed him, and given him money, so he felt as a private soldier would feel if he had been called out of the ranks and praised by his commander-in-chief.

'What did Petersen Sahib mean by the elephant-dance?' he said, at last, softly to his mother.

Big Toomai heard him and grunted. 'That thou shouldst never be one of these hill-buffaloes of trackers. *That* was what he meant. Oh you in front, what is blocking the way?'

An Assamese driver, two or three elephants ahead, turned round angrily, crying: 'Bring up Kala Nag, and knock this youngster of mine into good behaviour. Why should Petersen Sahib have chosen *me* to go down with you donkeys of the rice-fields? Lay your beast alongside, Toomai and let him prod with his tusks. By all the Gods of the Hills, these new elephants are possessed, or else they can smell their companions in the jungle.'

Kala Nag hit the new elephant in the ribs and knocked the wind out of him, as Big Toomai said, 'We have swept the hills of wild elephants at the last catch. It is only your carelessness in driving. Must I keep order along the whole line?'

'Hear him!' said the other driver. '*We* have swept the hills! Ho! ho! You are very wise, you plains-people. Any one but a mud-head who never saw the jungle would know that *they* know that the drives are ended for the season. Therefore all the wild elephants to-night will——but why should I waste wisdom on a river-turtle?'

'What will they do?' Little Toomai called out.

'*Ohé*, little one. Art thou there? Well, I will tell thee, for thou hast a cool head. They will dance, and it behooves thy father, who has swept *all* the hills of *all* the elephants, to double-chain his pickets to-night.'

'What talk is this?' said Big Toomai. 'For forty years, father and son, we have tended elephants, and we have never heard such moonshine about dances.'

'Yes; but a plains-man who lives in a hut knows only the four walls of his hut. Well, leave thy elephants unshackled to-night and see what comes; as for their dancing, I have seen the place where——*Bapree-Bap!** how many windings has the Dihang River?* Here is another ford, and we must swim the calves. Stop still, you behind there.'

And in this way, talking and wrangling and splashing through the rivers, they made their first march to a sort of receiving-camp for the new elephants; but they lost their tempers long before they got there.

Then the elephants were chained by their hind legs to their big stumps of pickets, and extra ropes were fitted to the new elephants, and the fodder was piled before them, and the hill-drivers went back to Petersen Sahib through the afternoon light, telling the plains-drivers to be extra careful that night, and laughing when the plains-drivers asked the reason.

Little Toomai attended to Kala Nag's supper, and as evening fell wandered through the camp, unspeakably happy, in search of a tom-tom. When an Indian child's heart is full, he does not run about and make a noise in an irregular fashion. He sits down to a sort of revel all by himself. And Little Toomai had been spoken to by Petersen Sahib! If he had not found what he wanted I believe he would have burst. But the sweetmeat-seller in the camp lent him a little tom-tom*—a drum beaten with the flat of the hand—and he sat down, cross-legged, before Kala Nag as the stars began to come out, the tom-tom in his lap, and he thumped and he thumped and he thumped, and the more he thought of the great honour that had been done to him, the more he thumped, all alone among the elephant-fodder. There was no tune and no words, but the thumping made him happy.

The new elephants strained at their ropes, and squealed and trumpeted from time to time, and he could hear his mother in the camp hut putting his small brother to sleep with an old, old song about the great God Shiv,* who once told all the animals what they should eat. It is a very soothing lullaby, and the first verse says:

Shiv, who poured the harvest and made the winds to blow,
Sitting at the doorways of a day of long ago,
Gave to each his portion, food and toil and fate,
From the King upon the *guddee** to the Beggar at the gate.
    All things made he—Shiva the Preserver.

Mahadeo! Mahadeo! he made all,—
Thorn for the camel, fodder for the kine,
And mother's heart for sleepy head, O little son of mine!

Little Toomai came in with a joyous *tunk-a-tunk* at the end of each verse, till he felt sleepy and stretched himself on the fodder at Kala Nag's side.

At last the elephants began to lie down one after another, as is their custom, till only Kala Nag at the right of the line was left standing up; and he rocked slowly from side to side, his ears put forward to listen to the night wind as it blew very slowly across the hills. The air was full of all the night noises that, taken together, make one big silence—the click of one bamboo-stem against the other, the rustle of something alive in the undergrowth, the scratch and squawk of a half-waked bird (birds are awake in the night much more often than we imagine), and the fall of water ever so far away. Little Toomai slept for some time, and when he waked it was brilliant moonlight and Kala Nag was still standing up with his ears cocked. Little Toomai turned, rustling in the fodder, and watched the curve of his big back against half the stars in heaven; and while he watched he heard, so far away that it sounded no more than a pinhole of noise pricked through the stillness, the 'hoot-toot' of a wild elephant.

All the elephants in the lines jumped up as if they had been shot, and their grunts at last waked the sleeping mahouts, and they came out and drove in the picket-pegs with big mallets, and tightened this rope and knotted that till all was quiet. One new elephant had nearly grubbed up his picket, and Big Toomai took off Kala Nag's leg-chain and shackled that elephant fore-foot to hind-foot, but slipped a loop of grass-string round Kala Nag's leg, and told him to remember that he was tied fast. He knew that he and his father and his grandfather had done the very same thing hundreds of times before. Kala Nag did not answer to the order by gurgling, as he usually did. He stood still, looking out across the moonlight, his head a little raised, and his ears spread like fans, up to the great folds of the Garo hills.

'Look to him if he grows restless in the night,' said Big Toomai to Little Toomai, and he went into the hut and slept. Little Toomai was just going to sleep, too, when he heard the coir* string snap with a little 'tang', and Kala Nag rolled out of his pickets as slowly and as silently as a cloud rolls out of the mouth of a valley. Little Toomai pattered after him, barefooted, down the road in the moonlight, calling under his breath, 'Kala Nag! Kala Nag! Take me with you, O Kala Nag!' The elephant turned without a sound, took three strides back to the boy in the moonlight, put down his trunk, swung him up to his neck, and almost before Little Toomai had settled his knees slipped into the forest.

There was one blast of furious trumpeting from the lines, and then the silence shut down on everything, and Kala Nag began to move. Sometimes a tuft of high grass washed along his sides as a wave washes along the sides of a ship, and sometimes a cluster of wild-pepper vines would scrape along his back, or a bamboo would creak where his shoulder touched it; but between those times he moved absolutely without any sound, drifting through the thick Garo forest as though it had been smoke. He was going uphill, but though Little Toomai watched the stars in the rifts of the trees, he could not tell in what direction.

Then Kala Nag reached the crest of the ascent and stopped for a minute, and Little Toomai could see the tops of the trees lying all speckled and furry under the moonlight for miles and miles, and the blue-white mist over the river in the hollow. Toomai leaned forward and looked, and he felt that the forest was awake below him—awake and alive and crowded. A big brown fruit-eating bat brushed past his ear; a porcupine's quills rattled in the thicket; and in the darkness between the tree-stems he heard a hog-boar* digging hard in the moist, warm earth, and snuffing as it digged.

Then the branches closed over his head again, and Kala Nag began to go down into the valley—not quietly this time, but as a runaway gun goes down a steep bank—in one rush. The huge limbs moved as steadily as pistons, eight feet to each stride, and the wrinkled skin of the elbow-points rustled. The undergrowth on either side of him ripped with a noise like torn canvas, and the saplings that he heaved away right and left with his shoulders sprang back again, and banged him on the flank, and great trails of creepers, all matted together, hung from his tusks as he threw his head from side to side and ploughed out his pathway. Then Little Toomai laid himself down close to the great neck, lest a swinging bough should sweep him to the ground, and he wished that he were back in the lines again.

The grass began to get squashy, and Kala Nag's feet sucked and squelched as he put them down, and the night mist at the bottom of the valley chilled Little Toomai. There was a splash and a trample, and the rush of running water, and Kala Nag strode through the bed of a river, feeling his way at each step. Above the noise of the water, as it swirled round the elephant's legs, Little Toomai could hear more splashing and some trumpeting both up stream and down—great grunts and angry snortings, and all the mist about him seemed to be full of rolling, wavy shadows.

'*Ai!*' he said, half aloud, his teeth chattering. 'The elephant-folk are out to-night. It *is* the dance, then.'

Kala Nag swashed* out of the water, blew his trunk clear, and began another climb; but this time he was not alone, and he had not to make his path. That was made already, six feet wide, in front of him, where the bent jungle-grass was trying to recover itself and stand up. Many elephants must have gone that way only a few minutes before. Little Toomai looked back, and behind him a great wild tusker, with his little pig's eyes glowing like hot coals, was just lifting himself out of the misty river. Then the trees closed up again, and they went on and up, with trumpetings and crashings, and the sound of breaking branches on every side of them.

At last Kala Nag stood still between two tree-trunks at

the very top of the hill. They were part of a circle of trees that grew round an irregular space of some three or four acres, and in all that space, as Little Toomai could see, the ground had been trampled down as hard as a brick floor. Some trees grew in the centre of the clearing, but their bark was rubbed away, and the white wood beneath showed all shiny and polished in the patches of moonlight. There were creepers hanging from the upper branches, and the bells of the flowers of the creepers, great waxy white things like convolvuluses, hung down fast asleep; but within the limits of the clearing there was not a single blade of green—nothing but the trampled earth.

The moonlight showed it all iron-gray, except where some elephants stood upon it, and their shadows were inky black. Little Toomai looked, holding his breath, with his eyes starting out of his head, and as he looked, more and more and more elephants swung out into the open from between the tree-trunks. Little Toomai could count only up to ten, and he counted again and again on his fingers till he lost count of the tens, and his head began to swim. Outside the clearing he could hear them crashing in the undergrowth as they worked their way up the hillside; but as soon as they were within the circle of the tree-trunks they moved like ghosts.

There were white-tusked wild males, with fallen leaves and nuts and twigs lying in the wrinkles of their necks and the folds of their ears; fat, slow-footed she-elephants, with restless little pinky-black calves only three or four feet high running under their stomachs; young elephants with their tusks just beginning to show, and very proud of them; lanky, scraggy old-maid elephants, with their hollow anxious faces, and trunks like rough bark; savage old bull-elephants, scarred from shoulder to flank with great weals and cuts of bygone fights, and the caked dirt of their solitary mud-baths dropping from their shoulders; and there was one with a broken tusk and the marks of the full-stroke, the terrible drawing scrape, of a tiger's claws on his side.

They were standing head to head, or walking to and fro

across the ground in couples, or rocking and swaying all by themselves—scores and scores of elephants.

Toomai knew that so long as he lay still on Kala Nag's neck nothing would happen to him; for even in the rush and scramble of a Keddah-drive a wild elephant does not reach up with his trunk and drag a man off the neck of a tame elephant; and these elephants were not thinking of men that night. Once they started and put their ears forward when they heard the chinking of a leg-iron in the forest, but it was Pudmini, Petersen Sahib's pet elephant, her chain snapped short off, grunting, snuffling up the hillside. She must have broken her pickets, and come straight from Petersen Sahib's camp; and Little Toomai saw another elephant, one that he did not know, with deep rope-galls on his back and breast. He, too, must have run away from some camp in the hills about.

At last there was no sound of any more elephants moving in the forest, and Kala Nag rolled out from his station between the trees and went into the middle of the crowd, clucking and gurgling, and all the elephants began to talk in their own tongue, and to move about.

Still lying down, Little Toomai looked down upon scores and scores of broad backs, and wagging ears, and tossing trunks, and little rolling eyes. He heard the click of tusks as they crossed other tusks by accident, and the dry rustle of trunks twined together, and the chafing of enormous sides and shoulders in the crowd, and the incessant flick and *hissh* of the great tails. Then a cloud came over the moon, and he sat in black darkness; but the quiet, steady hustling and pushing and gurgling went on just the same. He knew that there were elephants all round Kala Nag, and that there was no chance of backing him out of the assembly; so he set his teeth and shivered. In a Keddah at least there was torch-light and shouting, but here he was all alone in the dark, and once a trunk came up and touched him on the knee.

Then an elephant trumpeted, and they all took it up for five or ten terrible seconds. The dew from the trees above spattered down like rain on the unseen backs, and a dull booming noise began, not very loud at first, and Little Toomai could not tell what it was; but it grew and grew, and Kala Nag lifted up one fore foot and then the other, and brought them down on the ground—one-two, one-two, as steadily as trip-hammers.* The elephants were stamping all together now, and it sounded like a war-drum beaten at the mouth of a cave. The dew fell from the trees till there was no more left to fall, and the booming went on, and the ground rocked and shivered, and Little Toomai put his hands up to his ears to shut out the sound. But it was all one gigantic jar that ran through him—this stamp of hundreds of heavy feet on the raw earth. Once or twice he could feel Kala Nag and all the others surge forward a few strides, and the thumping would change to the crushing sound of juicy green things being bruised, but in a minute or two the boom of feet on hard earth began again. A tree was creaking and groaning somewhere near him. He put out his arm and felt the bark, but Kala Nag moved forward, still tramping, and he could not tell where he was in the clearing. There was no sound from the elephants, except once, when two or three little calves squeaked together. Then he heard a thump and a shuffle, and the booming went on. It must have lasted fully two hours, and Little Toomai ached in every nerve; but he knew by the smell of the night air that the dawn was coming.

The morning broke in one sheet of pale yellow behind the green hills, and the booming stopped with the first ray, as though the light had been an order. Before Little Toomai had got the ringing out of his head, before even he had shifted his position, there was not an elephant in sight except Kala Nag, Pudmini, and the elephant with the rope-galls, and there was neither sign nor rustle nor whisper down the hillsides to show where the others had gone.

Little Toomai stared again and again. The clearing, as he remembered it, had grown in the night. More trees stood in the middle of it, but the undergrowth and the jungle-grass at the sides had been rolled back. Little

Toomai stared once more. Now he understood the trampling. The elephants had stamped out more room—had stamped the thick grass and juicy cane to trash, the trash into slivers, the slivers into tiny fibres, and the fibres into hard earth.

'Wah!' said Little Toomai, and his eyes were very heavy. 'Kala Nag, my lord, let us keep by Pudmini and go to Petersen Sahib's camp, or I shall drop from thy neck.'

The third elephant watched the two go away, snorted, wheeled round, and took his own path. He may have belonged to some little native king's establishment, fifty or sixty or a hundred miles away.

Two hours later, as Petersen Sahib was eating early breakfast, the elephants who had been double-chained that night, began to trumpet, and Pudmini, mired to the shoulders, with Kala Nag, very foot-sore, shambled into the camp.

Little Toomai's face was gray and pinched, and his hair was full of leaves and drenched with dew; but he tried to salute Petersen Sahib, and cried faintly: 'The dance—the elephant-dance! I have seen it, and I—I die!' As Kala Nag sat down, he slid off his neck in a dead faint.

But, since native children have no nerves worth speaking of, in two hours he was lying very contentedly in Petersen Sahib's hammock with Petersen Sahib's shooting-coat under his head, and a glass of warm milk, a little brandy, with a dash of quinine inside of him; and while the old hairy, scarred hunters of the jungles sat three-deep before him, looking at him as though he were a spirit, he told his tale in short words, as a child will, and wound up with:

'Now, if I lie in one word, send men to see, and they will find that the elephant-folk have trampled down more room in their dance-room, and they will find ten and ten, and many times ten, tracks leading to that dance-room. They made more room with their feet. I have seen it. Kala Nag took me, and I saw. Also Kala Nag is very leg-weary!'

Little Toomai lay back and slept all through the long afternoon and into the twilight, and while he slept

Petersen Sahib and Machua Appa followed the track of the two elephants for fifteen miles across the hills. Petersen Sahib had spent eighteen years in catching elephants, and he had only once before found such a dance-place. Machua Appa had no need to look twice at the clearing to see what had been done there, or to scratch with his toe in the packed, rammed earth.

'The child speaks truth,' said he. 'All this was done last night, and I have counted seventy tracks crossing the river. See, Sahib, where Pudmini's leg-iron cut the bark off that tree! Yes; she was there too.'*

They looked at each other, and up and down, and they wondered; for the ways of elephants are beyond the wit of any man, black or white, to fathom.

'Forty years and five,' said Machua Appa, 'have I followed my lord, the elephant, but never have I heard that any child of man had seen what this child has seen. By all the Gods of the Hills, it is—what can we say?' and he shook his head.

When they got back to camp it was time for the evening meal. Petersen Sahib ate alone in his tent, but he gave orders that the camp should have two sheep and some fowls, as well as a double ration of flour and rice and salt, for he knew that there would be a feast.

Big Toomai had come up hot-foot from the camp in the plains to search for his son and his elephant, and now that he had found them he looked at them as though he were afraid of them both. And there was a feast by the blazing camp-fires in front of the lines of picketed elephants, and Little Toomai was the hero of it all; and the big brown elephant-catchers, the trackers and drivers and ropers, and the men who know all the secrets of breaking the wildest elephants, passed him from one to the other, and they marked his forehead with blood from the breast of a newly killed jungle-cock, to show that he was a forester, initiated and free of all the jungles.

And at last, when the flames died down, and the red light of the logs made the elephants look as though they had been dipped in blood too, Machua Appa, the head of all the drivers of all the Keddahs,—Machua Appa, Petersen Sahib's other self, who had never seen a made road in forty years: Machua Appa, who was so great that he had no other name than Machua Appa,—leaped to his feet, with Little Toomai held high in the air above his head, and shouted: 'Listen, my brothers. Listen, too, you my lords in the lines there, for I, Machua Appa, am speaking! This little one shall no more be called Little Toomai, but Toomai of the Elephants, as his great-grandfather was called before him. What never man has seen he has seen through the long night, and the favour of the elephant-folk and of the Gods of the Jungles is with him. He shall become a great tracker; he shall become greater than I, even I—Machua Appa! He shall follow the new trail, and the stale trail, and the mixed trail, with a clear eye! He shall take no harm in the Keddah when he runs under their bellies to rope the wild tuskers; and if he slips before the feet of the charging bull-elephant, that bull-elephant shall know who he is and shall not crush him. *Aihai!* my lords in the chains,'—he whirled up the line of pickets,— 'here is the little one that has seen your dances in your hidden places—the sight that never man saw! Give him honour, my lords! *Salaam karo*, my children. Make your salute to Toomai of the Elephants! Gunga* Pershad, ahaa! Hira Guj,* Birchi Guj,* Kuttar Guj,* ahaa! Pudmini,— thou hast seen him at the dance, and thou too, Kala Nag, my pearl among elephants!—ahaa! Together! To Toomai of the Elephants. *Barrao!*'

And at that last wild yell the whole line flung up their trunks till the tips touched their foreheads, and broke out into the full salute—the crashing trumpet-peal that only the viceroy of India hears, the Salaamut of the Keddah.

But it was all for the sake of Little Toomai, who had seen what never man had seen before—the dance of the elephants at night and alone in the heart of the Garo hills!

Shiv and the Grasshopper

SHIV, who poured the harvest and made the winds to
    blow,
Sitting at the doorways of a day of long ago,
Gave to each his portion, food and toil and fate,
From the King upon the *guddee* to the Beggar at the gate.
   All things made he—Shiva the Preserver.
   Mahadeo! Mahadeo! he made all,—
   Thorn for the camel, fodder for the kine,
   And mother's heart for sleepy head, O little son of mine!

Wheat he gave to rich folk, millet to the poor,
Broken scraps for holy men that beg from door to door;
Cattle to the tiger, carrion to the kite,
And rags and bones to wicked wolves without the wall at
    night.
Naught he found too lofty, none he saw too low—
Parbati beside him watched them come and go;
Thought to cheat her husband, turning Shiv to jest—
Stole the little grasshopper and hid it in her breast.
   So she tricked him, Shiva the Preserver.
   Mahadeo! Mahadeo! turn and see.
   Tall are the camels, heavy are the kine,
   But this was least of little things, O little son of mine!

When the dole was ended, laughingly she said,
'Master, of a million mouths is not one unfed?'
Laughing, Shiv made answer, 'All have had their part,
Even he, the little one, hidden 'neath thy heart.'
From her breast she plucked it, Parbati the thief,
Saw the Least of Little Things gnawed a new-grown leaf!
Saw and feared and wondered, making prayer to Shiv,
Who hath surely given meat to all that live.

All things made he—Shiva the Preserver
Mahadeo! Mahadeo! he made all,—
Thorn for the camel, fodder for the kine,
And mother's heart for sleepy head, O little son of mine!

Her Majesty's Servants

You can work it out by Fractions or by simple Rule of Three,*
But the way of Tweedle-dum is not the way of Tweedle-dee.*
You can twist it, you can turn it, you can plait it till you drop,
But the way of Pilly-Winky's not the way of Winkie-Pop!*

IT had been raining heavily for one whole month—raining on a camp of thirty thousand men, thousands of camels,* elephants, horses, bullocks, and mules, all gathered together at a place called Rawal Pindi,* to be reviewed by the Viceroy of India. He was receiving a visit from the Amir of Afghanistan—a wild king of a very wild country; and the Amir had brought with him for a bodyguard eight hundred men and horses who had never seen a camp or a locomotive before in their lives—savage men and savage horses from somewhere at the back of Central Asia. Every night a mob of these horses would be sure to break their heel-ropes, and stampede up and down the camp through the mud in the dark, or the camels would break loose and run about and fall over the ropes of the tents, and you can imagine how pleasant that was for men trying to go to sleep. My tent lay far away from the camel lines, and I thought it was safe; but one night a man popped his head in and shouted, 'Get out, quick! They're coming! My tent's gone!'

I knew who 'they' were; so I put on my boots and waterproof and scuttled out into the slush. Little Vixen, my fox-terrier, went out through the other side; and then there was a roaring and a grunting and bubbling, and I saw the tent cave in, as the pole snapped, and begin to dance about like a mad ghost. A camel had blundered into it, and wet and angry as I was, I could not help laughing. Then I ran on, because I did not know how many camels might have got loose, and before long I was out of sight of the camp, ploughing my way through the mud.

At last I fell over the tail-end of a gun, and by that knew I was somewhere near the Artillery lines where the cannon were stacked* at night. As I did not want to plowter* about any more in the drizzle and the dark, I put my waterproof over the muzzle of one gun, and made a sort of wigwam with two or three rammers* that I found, and lay along the tail of another gun, wondering where Vixen had got to, and where I might be.

Just as I was getting ready to sleep I heard a jingle of harness and a grunt, and a mule passed me shaking his wet ears. He belonged to a screw-gun battery, for I could hear the rattle of the straps and rings and chains and things on his saddle-pad. The screw-guns are tiny little cannon made in two pieces that are screwed together when the time comes to use them. They are taken up mountains, anywhere that a mule can find a road, and they are very useful for fighting in rocky country.

Behind the mule there was a camel, with his big soft feet squelching and slipping in the mud, and his neck bobbing to and fro like a strayed hen's. Luckily, I knew enough of beast language—not wild-beast language, but camp-beast language, of course—from the natives to know what he was saying.

He must have been the one that flopped into my tent, for he called to the mule, 'What shall I do? Where shall I go? I have fought with a white thing that waved, and it took a stick and hit me on the neck.' (That was my broken tent-pole, and I was very glad to know it.) 'Shall we run on?'

'Oh, it was you,' said the mule, 'you and your friends, that have been disturbing the camp? All right. You'll be beaten for this in the morning; but I may as well give you something on account now.'

I heard the harness jingle as the mule backed and caught the camel two kicks in the ribs that rang like a drum. 'Another time,' he said, 'you'll know better than to run through a mule-battery at night, shouting "Thieves and fire!" Sit down, and keep your silly neck quiet.'

The camel doubled up camel-fashion, like a two-foot rule, and sat down whimpering. There was a regular beat of hoofs in the darkness, and a big troop-horse cantered up as steadily as though he was on parade, jumped a gun-tail and landed close to the mule.

'It's disgraceful,' he said, blowing out his nostrils. 'Those camels have racketed through our lines again—the third time this week. How's a horse to keep his condition if he isn't allowed to sleep. Who's here?'

'I'm the breech-piece mule of number two gun of the First Screw Battery,'* said the mule, 'and the other's one of your friends. He's waked me up too. Who are you?'

'Number Fifteen, E Troop, Ninth Lancers—Dick Cunliffe's horse. Stand over a little, there.'

'Oh, beg your pardon,' said the mule. 'It's too dark to see much. Aren't these camels too sickening for anything? I walked out of my lines to get a little peace and quiet here.'

'My lords,' said the camel humbly, 'we dreamed bad dreams in the night, and we were very much afraid. I am only a baggage-camel of the 39th Native Infantry, and I am not so brave as you are, my lords.'

'Then why the pickets didn't you stay and carry baggage for the 39th Native Infantry, instead of running all round the camp?' said the mule.

'They were such very bad dreams,' said the camel. 'I am sorry. Listen! What is that? Shall we run on again?'

'Sit down,' said the mule, 'or you'll snap your long legs between the guns.' He cocked one ear and listened. 'Bullocks!' he said; 'gun-bullocks. On my word, you and your friends have waked the camp very thoroughly. It takes a good deal of prodding to put up a gun-bullock.'

I heard a chain dragging along the ground, and a yoke of the great sulky white bullocks that drag the heavy siege-guns when the elephants won't go any nearer to the firing, came shouldering along together; and almost stepping on the chain was another battery-mule, calling wildly for 'Billy.'

'That's one of our recruits,' said the old mule to the troop-horse. 'He's calling for me. Here, youngster, stop squealing; the dark never hurt anybody yet.'

The gun-bullocks lay down together and began chewing the cud, but the young mule huddled close to Billy.

'Things!' he said; 'fearful and horrible Billy! They came into our lines while we were asleep. D'you think they'll kill us?'

'I've a very great mind to give you a number-one* kicking,' said Billy. 'The idea of a fourteen-hand mule with your training disgracing the battery before this gentleman!'

'Gently, gently!' said the troop-horse. 'Remember they are always like this to begin with. The first time I ever saw a man (it was in Australia when I was a three-year-old) I ran for half a day, and if I'd seen a camel I should have been running still.'

Nearly all our horses for the English cavalry are brought to India from Australia, and are broken in by the troopers themselves.

'True enough,' said Billy. 'Stop shaking, youngster. The first time they put the full harness with all its chains on my back, I stood on my fore legs and kicked every bit of it off. I hadn't learned the real science of kicking then, but the battery said they had never seen anything like it.'

'But this wasn't harness or anything that jingled,' said the young mule. 'You know I don't mind that now, Billy. It was Things like trees, and they fell up and down the lines and bubbled; and my head-rope broke, and I couldn't find my driver, and I couldn't find you, Billy, so I ran off with—with these gentlemen.'

'H'm!' said Billy. 'As soon as I heard the camels were loose I came away on my own account, quietly. When a battery—a screw-gun mule calls gun-bullocks gentlemen, he must be very badly shaken up. Who are you fellows on the ground there?'

The gun-bullocks rolled their cuds, and answered both together: 'The seventh yoke* of the first gun of the Big Gun Battery. We were asleep when the camels came, but when we were trampled on we got up and walked away. It is better to lie quiet in the mud than to be disturbed on good bedding. We told your friend here that there was nothing to be afraid of, but he knew so much that he thought otherwise. Wah!'

They went on chewing.

'That comes of being afraid,' said Billy. 'You get laughed at by gun-bullocks. I hope you like it, young un.'

The young mule's teeth snapped, and I heard him say something about not being afraid of any beefy old bullock in the world; but the bullocks only clicked their horns together and went on chewing.

'Now, don't be angry *after* you've been afraid. That's the worst kind of cowardice,' said the troop-horse. 'Anybody can be forgiven for being scared in the night, *I* think, if they see things they don't understand. We've broken out of our pickets, again and again, four hundred and fifty of us, just because a new recruit got to telling tales of whipsnakes at home in Australia till we were scared to death of the loose ends of our head-ropes.'

'That's all very well in camp,' said Billy 'I'm not above stampeding myself, for the fun of the thing, when I haven't been out for a day or two; but what do you do on active service?'

'Oh, that's quite another set of new shoes,' said the troop-horse. 'Dick Cunliffe's on my back then, and drives his knees into me, and all I have to do is to watch where I am putting my feet, and to keep my hind legs well under me, and be bridle-wise.'

'What's bridle-wise?' said the young mule.

'By the Blue Gums of the Black Blocks,' snorted the troop-horse, 'do you mean to say that you aren't taught to be bridle-wise in your business? How can you do anything, unless you can spin round at once when the rein is pressed on your neck? It means life or death to your man, and of course that's life or death to you. Get round with your hind legs under you the instant you feel the rein on your neck. If you haven't room to swing round, rear up a little and come round on your hind legs. That's being bridle-wise.'

'We aren't taught that way,' said Billy the mule stiffly. 'We're taught to obey the man at our head: step off when

he says so, and step in when he says so. I suppose it comes
to the same thing. Now, with all this fine fancy business
and rearing, which must be very bad for your hocks,* what
do you *do*?'

'That depends,' said the troop-horse. 'Generally I have
to go in among a lot of yelling, hairy men with knives,—
long shiny knives, worse than the farrier's knives,—and I
have to take care that Dick's boot is just touching the next
man's boot without crushing it. I can see Dick's lance to
the right of my right eye, and I know I'm safe. I shouldn't
care to be the man or horse that stood up to Dick and me
when we're in a hurry.'

'Don't the knives hurt?' said the young mule.

'Well, I got one cut across the chest once, but that
wasn't Dick's fault——'

'A lot I should have cared whose fault it was, if it hurt!'
said the young mule.

'You must,' said the troop-horse. 'If you don't trust
your man, you may as well run away at once. That's what
some of our horses do, and I don't blame them. As I was
saying, it wasn't Dick's fault. The man was lying on the
ground, and I stretched myself not to tread on him, and he
slashed up at me. Next time I have to go over a man lying
down I shall step on him—hard.'

'H'm!' said Billy; 'it sounds very foolish. Knives are
dirty things at any time. The proper thing to do is to climb
up a mountain with a well-balanced saddle, hang on by all
four feet and your ears too, and creep and crawl and
wriggle along, till you come out hundreds of feet above
any one else, on a ledge where there's just room enough for
your hoofs. Then you stand still and keep quiet,—never
ask a man to hold your head, young un,—keep quiet while
the guns are being put together, and then you watch the
little poppy shells drop down into the tree-tops ever so far
below.'

'Don't you ever trip?' said the troop-horse.

'They say that when a mule trips you can split a hen's
ear,'* said Billy. 'Now and again *per-haps* a badly-packed
saddle will upset a mule, but it's very seldom. I wish I

could show you our business. It's beautiful. Why it took me three years to find out what the men were driving at. The science of the thing is never to show up against the sky-line, because, if you do, you may get fired at. Remember that, young un. Always keep hidden as much as possible, even if you have to go a mile out of your way. I lead the battery when it comes to that sort of climbing.'

'Fired at without the chance of running into the people who are firing!' said the troop-horse, thinking hard. 'I couldn't stand that. I should want to charge, with Dick.'

'Oh no, you wouldn't; you know that as soon as the guns are in position *they'll* do all the charging. That's scientific and neat; but knives—pah!'

The baggage-camel had been bobbing his head to and fro for some time past, anxious to get a word in edgeways. Then I heard him say, as he cleared his throat, nervously:

'I—I—I have fought a little, but not in that climbing way or that running way.'

'No. Now you mention it,' said Billy, 'you don't look as though you were made for climbing or running—much. Well, how was it, old Hay-bales?'

'The proper way,' said the camel. 'We all sat down——'

'Oh, my crupper* and breastplate*!' said the troop-horse under his breath. 'Sat down?'

'We sat down—a hundred of us,' the camel went on, 'in a big square, and the men piled our packs and saddles outside the square, and they fired over our backs, the men did, on all sides of the square.

'What sort of men? Any men that came along?' said the troop-horse. 'They teach us in riding-school to lie down and let our masters fire across us, but Dick Cunliffe is the only man I'd trust to do that. I tickles my girths, and besides, I can't see with my head on the ground.'

'What does it matter who fires across you?' said the camel. 'There are plenty of men and plenty of other camels close by, and a great many clouds of smoke. I am not frightened then. I sit still and wait.'

'And yet,' said Billy, 'you dream bad dreams and upset the camp at night. Well! well! Before I'd lie down, not to speak of sitting down, and let a man fire across me, my heels and his head would have something to say to each other. Did you ever hear anything so awful as that?'

There was a long silence, and then one of the gun-bullocks lifted up his big head and said, 'This is very foolish indeed. There is only one way of fighting.'

'Oh, go on,' said Billy. '*Please* don't mind me. I suppose you fellows fight standing on your tails?'

'Only one way,' said the two together. (They must have been twins.) 'This is that way. To put all twenty yoke* of us to the big gun as soon as Two Tails trumpets.' ('Two Tails' is camp slang for the elephant.)

'What does Two Tails trumpet for?' said the young mule.

'To show that he is not going any nearer to the smoke on the other side. Two Tails is a great coward. Then we tug the big gun all together—*Heya—Hullah! Heeyah! Hullah! We* do not climb like cats nor run like calves. We go across the level plain, twenty yoke of us, till we are unyoked again, and we graze while the big guns talk across the plain to some town with mud walls, and pieces of the wall fall out, and the dust goes up as though many cattle were coming home.'

'Oh! And you choose that time for grazing, do you?' said the young mule.

'That time or any other. Eating is always good. We eat till we are yoked up again and tug the gun back to where Two Tails is waiting for it. Sometimes there are big guns in the city that speak back, and some of us are killed, and then there is all the more grazing for those that are left. This is Fate—nothing but Fate. None the less, Two Tails is a great coward. That is the proper way to fight. We are brothers from Hapur.* Our father was a sacred bull of Shiva. We have spoken.'

'Well, I've certainly learned something to-night,' said the troop-horse. 'Do you gentlemen of the screw-gun battery feel inclined to eat when you are being fired at with big guns, and Two Tails is behind you?'

'About as much as we feel inclined to sit down and let

men sprawl all over us, or run into people with knives. I never heard such stuff. A mountain ledge, a well-balanced load, a driver you can trust to let you pick your own way, and I'm your mule; but the other things—no!' said Billy, with a stamp of his foot.

'Of course,' said the troop-horse, 'every one is not made in the same way, and I can quite see that your family, on your father's side, would fail to understand a great many things.'

'Never you mind my family on my father's side,' said Billy angrily; for every mule* hates to be reminded that his father was a donkey. 'My father was a Southern gentleman, and he could pull down and bite and kick into rags every horse he came across. Remember that, you big brown Brumby!'*

Brumby means wild horse without any breeding. Imagine the feelings of Sunol* if a car-horse* called her a 'skate,'* and you can imagine how the Australian horse felt. I saw the white of his eye glitter in the dark.

'See here, you son of an imported Malaga* jackass,' he said between his teeth, 'I'd have you know that I'm related on my mother's side to Carbine,* winner of the Melbourne Cup; and where *I* come from we aren't accustomed to being ridden over roughshod by any parrot-mouthed, pig-headed mule in a pop-gun pea-shooter battery. Are you ready?'

'On your hind legs!' squealed Billy. They both reared up facing each other, and I was expecting a furious fight, when a gurgly, rumbly voice called out of the darkness to the right: 'Children, what are you fighting about there? Be quiet.'

Both beasts dropped down with a snort of disgust, for neither horse nor mule can bear to listen to an elephant's voice.

'It's Two Tails!' said the troop-horse. 'I can't stand him. A tail at each end isn't fair!'

'My feelings exactly,' said Billy, crowding into the troop-horse for company. 'We're very alike in some things.'

'I suppose we've inherited them from our mothers,' said the troop-horse. 'It's not worth quarrelling about. Hi! Two Tails, are you tied up?'

'Yes,' said Two Tails, with a laugh all up his trunk. 'I'm picketed for the night. I've heard what you fellows have been saying. But don't be afraid. I'm not coming over.'

The bullocks and the camel said, half aloud: 'Afraid of Two Tails—what nonsense!' And the bullocks went on: 'We are sorry that you heard, but it is true. Two Tails, why are you afraid of the guns when they fire?'

'Well,' said Two Tails, rubbing one hind leg against the other, exactly like a little boy saying a poem, 'I don't quite know whether you'd understand.'

'We don't, but we have to pull the guns,' said the bullocks.

'I know it, and I know you are a good deal braver than you think you are. But it's different with me My battery captain called me a Pachydermatous* Anachronism the other day.'

'That's another way of fighting, I suppose?' said Billy, who was recovering his spirits.

'*You* don't know what that means, of course, but I do. It means betwixt and between, and that is just where I am. I can see inside my head what will happen when a shell bursts; and you bullocks can't.'

'I can,' said the troop-horse. 'At least a little bit. I try not to think about it.'

'I can see more than you, and I *do* think about it. I know there's a great deal of me to take care of, and I know that nobody knows how to cure me when I'm sick. All they can do is to stop my driver's pay till I get well, and I can't trust my driver.'

'Ah!' said the troop-horse. 'That explains it. I can trust Dick.'

'You could put a whole regiment of Dicks on my back without making me feel any better. I know just enough to be uncomfortable, and not enough to go on in spite of it.'

'We do not understand,' said the bullocks.

'I know you don't. I'm not talking to you. You don't know what blood is.'

'We do,' said the bullocks. 'It is red stuff that soaks into the ground and smells.'

The troop-horse gave a kick and a bound and a snort.

'Don't talk of it,' he said. 'I can smell it now, just thinking of it. It makes me want to run—when I haven't Dick on my back.'

'But it is not here,' said the camel and the bullocks. 'Why are you so stupid?'

'It's vile stuff,' said Billy. 'I don't want to run, but I don't want to talk about it.'

'There you are!' said Two Tails, waving his tail to explain.

'Surely. Yes, we have been here all night,' said the bullocks.

Two Tails stamped his foot till the iron ring on it jingled. 'Oh, I'm not talking to *you*. You can't see inside your heads.'

'No. We see out of our four eyes,' said the bullocks. 'We see straight in front of us.'

'If I could do that and nothing else you wouldn't be needed to pull the big guns at all. If I was like my captain—he can see things inside his head before the firing begins, and he shakes all over, but he knows too much to run away—if I was like him I could pull the guns. But if I were as wise as all that I should never be here. I should be a king in the forest, as I used to be, sleeping half the day and bathing when I liked. I haven't had a good bath for a month.'

'That's all very fine,' said Billy; 'but giving a thing a long name doesn't make it any better.'

'H'sh!' said the troop-horse. 'I think I understand what Two Tails means.'

'You'll understand better in a minute,' said Two Tails angrily. 'Now, just you explain to me why you don't like *this!*'

He began trumpeting furiously at the top of his trumpet.

'Stop that!' said Billy and the troop-horse together, and I could hear them stamp and shiver. An elephant's trumpeting is always nasty, especially on a dark night.

'I shan't stop,' said Two Tails. 'Won't you explain that, please? *Hhrrmph! Rrrt! Rrrmph! Rrrhha!*' Then he stopped suddenly, and I heard a little whimper in the dark, and knew that Vixen had found me at last. She knew as well as I did that if there is one thing in the world the elephant is more afraid of than another, it is a little barking dog;* so she stopped to bully Two Tails in his pickets, and yapped round his big feet. Two Tails shuffled and squeaked. 'Go away, little dog!' he said. 'Don't snuff at my ankles, or I'll kick at you. Good little dog—nice little doggie, then! Go home, you yelping little beast! Oh, why doesn't some one take her away? She'll bite me in a minute.'

'Seems to me,' said Billy to the troop-horse, 'that our friend Two Tails is afraid of most things. Now, if I had a full meal for every dog I've kicked across the parade-ground, I should be as fat as Two Tails nearly.'

I whistled, and Vixen ran up to me, muddy all over, and licked my nose, and told me a long tale about hunting for me all through the camp. I never let her know that I understood beast talk, or she would have taken all sorts of liberties. So I buttoned her into the breast of my overcoat, and Two Tails shuffled and stamped and growled to himself.

'Extraordinary! Most extraordinary!' he said. 'It runs in our family. Now, where has that nasty little beast gone to?'

I heard him feeling about with his trunk.

'We all seem to be affected in various ways,' he went on, blowing his nose. 'Now, you gentlemen were alarmed, I believe, when I trumpeted.'

'Not alarmed, exactly,' said the troop-horse, 'but it made me feel as though I had hornets where my saddle ought to be. Don't begin again.'

'I'm frightened of a little dog, and the camel here is frightened by bad dreams in the night.'

'It is very lucky for us that we haven't all got to fight in the same way,' said the troop-horse.

'What I want to know,' said the young mule, who had been quiet for a long time—'what *I* want to know is, why we have to fight at all.'

'Because we're told to,' said the troop-horse, with a snort of contempt.

'Orders,' said Billy the mule; and his teeth snapped.

'*Hukm hai!*' (It is an order), said the camel with a gurgle; and Two Tails and the bullocks repeated, '*Hukm hai!*'

'Yes, but who gives the orders?' said the recruit-mule.

'The man who walks at your head—Or sits on your back—Or holds the nose-rope—Or twists your tail,' said Billy and the troop-horse and the camel and the bullocks one after the other.

'But who gives them the orders?'

'Now you want to know too much, young un,' said Billy, 'and that is one way of getting kicked. All you have to do is to obey the man at your head and ask no questions.'

'He's quite right,' said Two Tails. 'I can't always obey, because I'm betwixt and between; but Billy's right. Obey the man next to you who gives the order, or you'll stop all the battery, besides getting a thrashing.'

The gun-bullocks got up to go. 'Morning is coming,' they said. 'We will go back to our lines. It is true that we see only out of our eyes, and we are not very clever; but still, we are the only people to-night who have not been afraid. Good-night, you brave people.'

Nobody answered, and the troop-horse said, to change the conversation, 'Where's that little dog? A dog means a man somewhere about.'

'Here I am,' yapped Vixen, 'under the gun-tail with my man. You big, blundering beast of a camel you, you upset our tent. My man's very angry.'

'Phew!' said the bullocks. 'He must be white?'

'Of course he is,' said Vixen. 'Do you suppose I'm looked after by a black bullock-driver?'

'*Huah! Ouach! Ugh!*' said the bullocks 'Let us get away quickly.'

They plunged forward in the mud, and managed somehow to run their yoke on the pole of an ammunition-waggon, where it jammed.

'Now you *have* done it,' said Billy calmly. 'Don't struggle. You're hung up till daylight. What on earth's the matter?'

The bullocks went off into the long, hissing snorts that Indian cattle give, and pushed and crowded and slued and stamped and slipped and nearly fell down in the mud, grunting savagely.

'You'll break your necks in a minute,' said the troop-horse. 'What's the matter with white men? I live with 'em.'

'They—eat—us! Pull!' said the near bullock: the yoke snapped with a twang, and they lumbered off together.

I never knew before what made Indian cattle so scared of Englishmen. We eat beef*—a thing that no cattle-driver touches—and of course the cattle do not like it.

'May I be flogged with my own pad-chains! Who'd have thought of two big lumps like those losing their heads?' said Billy.

'Never mind. I'm going to look at this man. Most of the white men, I know, have things in their pockets,' said the troop-horse.

'I'll leave you, then. I can't say I'm over-fond of 'em myself. Besides, white men who haven't a place to sleep in are more than likely to be thieves, and I've a good deal of Government property on my back. Come along, young un, and we'll go back to our lines. Good-night, Australia! See you on parade to-morrow, I suppose. Good-night, old Hay-bale!—try to control your feelings, won't you? Good-night, Two Tails! If you pass us on the ground to-morrow, don't trumpet. It spoils our formation.'

Billy the mule stumped off with the swaggering limp of an old campaigner, as the troop-horse's head came nuzzling into my breast, and I gave him biscuits; while Vixen, who is a most conceited little dog, told him fibs about the scores of horses that she and I kept.

'I'm coming to the parade to-morrow in my dog-cart,' she said. 'Where will you be?'

'On the left hand of the second squadron. I set the time for all my troop, little lady,' he said politely. 'Now I must go back to Dick. My tail's all muddy, and he'll have two hours' hard work dressing me for parade.'

The big parade of all the thirty thousand men was held that afternoon, and Vixen and I had a good place close to the Viceroy and the Amir of Afghanistan, with his high, big black hat of astrakhan wool and the great diamond star in the centre. The first part of the review was all sunshine, and the regiments went by in wave upon wave of legs all moving together, and guns all in a line, till our eyes grew dizzy. Then the cavalry came up, to the beautiful cavalry canter of 'Bonnie Dundee,'* and Vixen cocked her ear where she sat on the dog-cart.* The second squadron of the Lancers shot by, and there was the troop-horse, with his tail like spun silk, his head pulled into his breast, one ear forward and one back, setting the time for all his squadron, his legs going as smoothly as waltz-music. Then the big guns came by, and I saw Two Tails and two other elephants harnessed in line to a forty-pounder siege-gun, while twenty yoke of oxen walked behind. The seventh pair had a new yoke, and they looked rather stiff and tired. Last came the screw-guns, and Billy the mule carried himself as though he commanded all the troops, and his harness was oiled and polished till it winked. I gave a cheer all by myself for Billy the mule, but he never looked right or left.

The rain began to fall again, and for a while it was too misty to see what the troops were doing. They had made a big half-circle across the plain, and were spreading out into a line. That line grew and grew and grew till it was three-quarters of a mile long from wing to wing—one solid wall of men, horses, and guns. Then it came on straight toward the Viceroy and the Amir, and as it got nearer the ground began to shake, like the deck of a steamer when the engines are going fast.

Unless you have been there you cannot imagine what a frightening effect this steady come-down of troops has on the spectators, even when they know it is only a review. I looked at the Amir. Up till then he had not shown the shadow of a sign of astonishment or anything else; but now his eyes began to get bigger and bigger, and he picked up the reins on his horse's neck and looked behind him. For a minute it seemed as though he were going to draw his sword and slash his way out through the English men and women in the carriages at the back. Then the advance stopped dead, the ground stood still, the whole line saluted, and thirty bands began to play all together. That was the end of the review, and the regiments went off to their camps in the rain; and an infantry band struck up with—

> The animal's went in two by two,*
>   Hurrah!
> The animals went in two by two,
> The elephant and the battery mu-
> l', and they all got into the Ark
> For to get out of the rain!

Then I heard an old grizzled, long-haired Central Asian chief, who had come down with the Amir, asking questions of a native officer.

'Now,' said he, 'in what manner was this wonderful thing done?'

And the officer answered, 'There was an order, and they obeyed.'

'But are the beasts as wise as the men?' said the chief.

'They obey, as the men do. Mule, horse, elephant, or bullock, he obeys his driver, and the driver his sergeant, and the sergeant his lieutenant, and the lieutenant his captain, and the captain his major, and the major his colonel, and the colonel his brigadier commanding three regiments, and the brigadier his general, who obeys the

Viceroy, who is the servant of the Empress. Thus it is done.'

'Would it were so in Afghanistan!' said the chief; 'for there we obey only our own wills.'

'And for that reason,' said the native officer, twirling his moustache, 'your Amir whom you do not obey must come here and take orders from our Viceroy.'

Parade-Song of the Camp-Animals

ELEPHANTS OF THE GUN-TEAMS*

WE lent to Alexander the strength of Hercules,
The wisdom of our foreheads, the cunning of our knees;
We bowed our necks to service; they ne'er were loosed
     again,—
Make way there, way for the ten-foot teams
     Of the Forty-Pounder train!

GUN-BULLOCKS*

Those heroes in their harnesses avoid a cannon-ball,
And what they know of powder upsets them one and all;
Then *we* come into action and tug the guns again,—
Make way there, way for the twenty yoke
     Of the Forty-Pounder train!

CAVALRY HORSES*

By the brand on my withers, the finest of tunes
Is played by the Lancers, Hussars, and Dragoons,
And it's sweeter than 'Stables' or 'Water' to me,
The Cavalry Canter of 'Bonnie Dundee'!

Then feed us and break us and handle and groom,
And give us good riders and plenty of room,

And launch us in column of squadrons and see
The way of the war-horse to 'Bonnie Dundee'!

SCREW-GUN MULES*

As me and my companions were scrambling up a hill,
The path was lost in rolling stones, but we went forward
        still;
For we can wriggle and climb, my lads, and turn up
        everywhere,
And it's our delight on a mountain height, with a leg or
        two to spare!

Good luck to every sergeant, then, that lets us pick our
        road;
Bad luck to all the driver-men that cannot pack a load:
For we can wriggle and climb, my lads, and turn up
        everywhere,
 And it's our delight on a mountain height, with a leg or
        two to spare!

COMMISSARIAT CAMELS

We haven't a camelty tune of our own
To help us trollop along,
But every neck is a hairy trombone
(*Rtt-ta-ta-ta!* is a hairy trombone!)
And this is our marching-song:
Can't! Don't! Shan't! Won't!
Pass it along the line!
Somebody's pack has slid from his back,
'Wish it were only mine!
Somebody's load has tipped off in the road—
Cheer for a halt and a row!
Urr! Yarrh! Grr! Arrh!
Somebody's catching it now!

ALL THE BEASTS TOGETHER

Children of the Camp are we,
Serving each in his degree;
Children of the yoke and goad,
Pack and harness, pad and load.
See our line across the plain,
Like a heel-rope bent again,
Reaching, writhing, rolling far,
Sweeping all away to war!
While the men that walk beside,
Dusty, silent, heavy-eyed,
Cannot tell why we or they
March and suffer day by day.
  Children of the Camp are we,
  Serving each in his degree;
  Children of the yoke and goad,
  Pack and harness, pad and load.

The Second Jungle Book

CONTENTS

How Fear Came

The stream is shrunk—the pool is dry,
And we be comrades, thou and I;
With fevered jowl and dusty flank
Each jostling each along the bank;
And by one drouthy fear made still,
Foregoing thought of quest or kill.
Now 'neath his dam the fawn may see,
The lean Pack-wolf as cowed as he,
And the tall buck, unflinching, note
The fangs that tore his father's throat.
The pools are shrunk—the streams are dry,
And we be playmates, thou and I,
Till yonder cloud—Good Hunting!—loose
The rain that breaks our Water Truce.

THE Law of the Jungle—which is by far the oldest law in the world—has arranged for almost every kind of accident that may befall the Jungle People, till now its code is as perfect as time and custom can make it. If you have read about Mowgli,* you will remember that he spent a great part of his life in the Seeonee Wolf-Pack, learning the Law from Baloo,* the Brown Bear; and it was Baloo who told him, when the boy grew impatient at the constant orders, that the Law was like the Giant Creeper, because it dropped across every one's back and no one could escape. 'When thou hast lived as long as I have, Little Brother, thou wilt see how all the Jungle obeys at least one Law. And that will be no pleasant sight,' said Baloo.

This talk went in at one ear and out at the other, for a boy who spends his life eating and sleeping does not worry about anything till it actually stares him in the face. But, one year, Baloo's words came true, and Mowgli saw all the Jungle working under the Law.

It began when the winter Rains failed almost entirely, and Ikki,* the Porcupine, meeting Mowgli in a bamboo-thicket, told him that the wild yams were drying up. Now everybody knows that Ikki is ridiculously fastidious in his choice of food, and will eat nothing but the very best and ripest. So Mowgli laughed and said, 'What is that to me?'

'Not much *now*,' said Ikki, rattling his quills in a stiff, uncomfortable way, 'but later we shall see. Is there any more diving into the deep rock-pool below the Bee-Rocks, Little Brother?'

'No. The foolish water is going all away, and I do not wish to break my head,' said Mowgli, who, in those days, was quite sure that he knew as much as any five of the Jungle People put together.

'That is thy loss. A small crack might let in some wisdom.' Ikki ducked quickly to prevent Mowgli from pulling his nose-bristles, and Mowgli told Baloo what Ikki had said. Baloo looked very grave, and mumbled half to himself: 'If I were alone I would change my hunting-grounds now, before the others began to think. And yet— hunting among strangers ends in fighting; and they might hurt the Man-cub. We must wait and see how the *mohwa** blooms.'

That spring the *mohwa* tree, that Baloo was so fond of, never flowered. The greeny, cream-coloured, waxy blossoms were heat-killed before they were born, and only a few bad-smelling petals came down when he stood on his hind legs and shook the tree. Then, inch by inch, the untempered heat crept into the heart of the Jungle, turning it yellow, brown, and at last black. The green growths in the sides of the ravines burned up to broken wires and curled films of dead stuff; the hidden pools sank down and caked over, keeping the last least footmark on their edges as if it had been cast in iron; the juicy-stemmed creepers fell away from the trees they clung to and died at their feet; the bamboos withered, clanking when the hot winds blew, and the moss peeled off the rocks deep in the Jungle, till they were as bare and as hot as the quivering blue boulders in the bed of the stream.

The birds and the monkey-people went north early in the year, for they knew what was coming; and the deer and the wild pig broke far away to the perished fields of the villages, dying sometimes before the eyes of men too weak to kill them. Chil,* the Kite, stayed and grew fat, for there was a great deal of carrion, and evening after evening he brought the news to the beasts, too weak to force their way to fresh hunting-grounds, that the sun was killing the Jungle for three days' flight in every direction.

Mowgli, who had never known what real hunger meant, fell back on stale honey, three years old, scraped out of deserted rock-hives—honey black as a sloe, and dusty with dried sugar. He hunted, too, for deep-boring grubs under the bark of the trees, and robbed the wasps of their new broods. All the game in the Jungle was no more than skin and bone, and Bagheera could kill thrice in a night, and hardly get a full meal. But the want of water was the worst, for though the Jungle People drink seldom they must drink deep.

And the heat went on and on, and sucked up all the moisture, till at last the main channel of the Waingunga* was the only stream that carried a trickle of water between its dead banks; and when Hathi,* the wild elephant, who lives for a hundred years and more, saw a long, lean blue ridge of rock show dry in the very centre of the stream, he knew that he was looking at the Peace Rock, and then and there he lifted up his trunk and proclaimed the Water Truce, as his father before him had proclaimed it fifty years ago. The deer, wild pig, and buffalo took up the cry hoarsely; and Chil, the Kite, flew in great circles far and wide, whistling and shrieking the warning.

By the Law of the Jungle it is death to kill at the drinking-places when once the Water Truce has been declared. The reason of this is that drinking comes before eating. Every one in the Jungle can scramble along somehow when only game is scarce; but water is water, and when there is but one source of supply, all hunting stops while the Jungle People go there for their needs. In good seasons, when water was plentiful, those who came down to drink at the Waingunga—or anywhere else, for that matter—did so at the risk of their lives, and that risk made no small part of the fascination of the night's doings. To move down so cunningly that never a leaf stirred; to wade knee-deep in the roaring shallows that drown all noise from behind; to drink, looking backward over one shoulder, every muscle ready for the first desperate bound of keen terror; to roll on the sandy margin, and return, wet-muzzled and well plumped out, to the admiring herd, was a thing that all tall-antlered young bucks took a delight in, precisely because they knew that at any moment Bagheera* or Shere Khan* might leap upon them and bear them down. But now all that life-and-death fun was ended, and the Jungle People came up, starved and weary, to the shrunken river,—tiger, bear, deer, buffalo, and pig, all together,—drank the fouled waters, and hung above them, too exhausted to move off.

The deer and the pig had tramped all day in search of something better than dried bark and withered leaves. The buffaloes had found no wallows to be cool in, and no green crops to steal. The snakes had left the Jungle and come down to the river in the hope of finding a stray frog. They curled round wet stones, and never offered to strike when the nose of a rooting pig dislodged them. The river-turtles had long ago been killed by Bagheera, cleverest of hunters, and the fish had buried themselves deep in the dry mud. Only the Peace Rock lay across the shallows like a long snake, and the little tired ripples hissed as they dried on its hot side.

It was here that Mowgli came nightly for the cool and the companionship. The most hungry of his enemies would hardly have cared for the boy then. His naked hide made him seem more lean and wretched than any of his fellows. His hair was bleached to tow colour by the sun; his ribs stood out like the ribs of a basket, and the lumps on his knees and elbows, where he used to track on all fours, gave his shrunken limbs the look of knotted grass-stems. But his eye, under his matted forelock, was cool and quiet, for Bagheera was his adviser in this time of trouble, and told him to go quietly, hunt slowly, and never, on any account, lose his temper.

'It is an evil time,' said the Black Panther, one furnace-hot evening, 'but it will go if we can live till the end. Is thy stomach full, Man-cub?'

'There is stuff in my stomach, but I get no good of it. Think you, Bagheera, the Rains have forgotten us and will never come again?'

'Not I! We shall see the *mohwa* in blossom yet, and the little fawns all fat with new grass. Come down to the Peace Rock and hear the news. On my back, Little Brother.'

'This is no time to carry weight. I can still stand alone, but—indeed we be no fatted bullocks, we two.'

Bagheera looked along his ragged, dusty flank and whispered: 'Last night I killed a bullock under the yoke. So low was I brought that I think I should not have dared to spring if he had been loose. *Wou!*'

Mowgli laughed. 'Yes, we be great hunters now,' said he. 'I am very bold—to eat grubs,' and the two came down together through the crackling undergrowth to the river-bank and the lace-work of shoals that ran out from it in every direction.

'The water cannot live long,' said Baloo, joining them. 'Look across. Yonder are trails like the roads of Man.'

On the level plain of the farther bank the stiff jungle-grass had died standing, and, dying, had mummied. The beaten tracks of the deer and the pig, all heading toward the river, had striped that colourless plain with dusty gullies driven through the ten-foot grass, and, early as it was, each long avenue was full of first-comers hastening to the water. You could hear the does and fawns coughing in the snuff-like dust.

Up-stream, at the bend of the sluggish pool round the Peace Rock, and Warden of the Water Truce, stood Hathi, the wild elephant, with his sons, gaunt and gray in the moonlight, rocking to and fro—always rocking. Below him a little were the vanguard of the deer; below these, again, the pig and the wild buffalo; and on the opposite bank, where the tall trees came down to the water's edge, was the place set apart for the Eaters of Flesh—the tiger, the wolves, the panther, the bear, and the others.

'We are under one Law, indeed,' said Bagheera, wading

into the water and looking across at the lines of clicking horns and starting eyes where the deer and the pig pushed each other to and fro. 'Good hunting, all you of my blood,' he added, lying down at full length, one flank thrust out of the shallows; and then, between his teeth, 'But for that which is the Law it would be *very* good hunting.'

The quick-spread ears of the deer caught the last sentence, and a frightened whisper ran along the ranks. 'The Truce! Remember the Truce!'

'Peace there, peace!' gurgled Hathi, the wild elephant. 'The Truce holds, Bagheera. This is no time to talk of hunting.'

'Who should know better than I?' Bagheera answered, rolling his yellow eyes up-stream. 'I am an eater of turtles—a fisher of frogs. *Ngaayah!* Would I could get good from chewing branches!'

'*We* wish so, very greatly,' bleated a young fawn, who had only been born that spring, and did not at all like it. Wretched as the Jungle People were, even Hathi could not help chuckling; while Mowgli, lying on his elbows in the warm water, laughed aloud, and beat up the scum with his feet.

'Well spoken, little bud-horn,' Bagheera purred. 'When the Truce ends that shall be remembered in thy favour,' and he looked keenly through the darkness to make sure of recognising the fawn again.

Gradually the talking spread up and down the drinking-places. One could hear the scuffling, snorting pig asking for more room; the buffaloes grunting among themselves as they lurched out across the sand-bars, and the deer telling pitiful stories of their long foot-sore wanderings in quest of food. Now and again they asked some question of the Eaters of Flesh across the river, but all the news was bad, and the roaring hot wind of the Jungle came and went between the rocks and the rattling branches, and scattered twigs and dust on the water.

'The men-folk, too, they die beside their ploughs,' said a young sambhur. 'I passed three between sunset and night. They lay still, and their Bullocks with them. We also shall lie still in a little.'

'The river has fallen since last night,' said Baloo. 'O Hathi, hast thou ever seen the like of this drought?'

'It will pass, it will pass,' said Hathi, squirting water along his back and sides.

'We have one here that cannot endure long,' said Baloo; and he looked toward the boy he loved.

'I?' said Mowgli indignantly, sitting up in the water. 'I have no long fur to cover my bones, but—but if *thy* hide were taken off, Baloo——'

Hathi shook all over at the idea, and Baloo said severely:

'Man-cub, that is not seemly to tell a Teacher of the Law. *Never* have I been seen without my hide.'

'Nay, I meant no harm, Baloo; but only that thou art, as it were, like the cocoanut in the husk, and I am the same cocoanut all naked. Now that brown husk of thine——' Mowgli was sitting cross-legged, and explaining things with his forefinger in his usual way, when Bagheera put out a paddy paw* and pulled him over backward into the water.

'Worse and worse,' said the Black Panther, as the boy rose spluttering. 'First Baloo is to be skinned, and now he is a cocoanut. Be careful that he does not do what the ripe cocoanuts do.'

'And what is that?' said Mowgli, off his guard for the minute, though that is one of the oldest catches in the Jungle.

'Break thy head,' said Bagheera quietly, pulling him under again.

'It is not good to make a jest of thy teacher,' said the bear, when Mowgli had been ducked for the third time.

'Not good! What would ye have? That naked thing running to and fro makes a monkey-jest of those who have once been good hunters, and pulls the best of us by the whiskers for sport.' This was Shere Khan, the Lame Tiger, limping down to the water. He waited a little to enjoy the sensation he made among the deer on the opposite bank; then he dropped his square, frilled head and began to lap, growling: 'The Jungle has become a whelping-ground for naked cubs now. Look at me, Man-cub!'*

Mowgli looked—stared, rather—as insolently as he knew how, and in a minute Shere Khan turned away uneasily. 'Man-cub this, and Man-cub that,' he rumbled, going on with his drink, 'the cub is neither man nor cub, or he would have been afraid. Next season I shall have to beg his leave for a drink. *Augrh!*'

'That may come too,' said Bagheera, looking him steadily between the eyes. 'That may come, too—Faugh, Shere Khan!—what new shame hast thou brought here?'

The Lame Tiger had dipped his chin and jowl in the water, and dark, oily streaks were floating from it downstream.

'Man!' said Shere Khan coolly, 'I killed an hour since.' He went on purring and growling to himself.

The line of beasts shook and wavered to and fro, and a whisper went up that grew to a cry: 'Man! Man! He has killed Man!' Then all looked towards Hathi, the wild elephant, but he seemed not to hear. Hathi never does anything till the time comes, and that is one of the reasons why he lives so long.

'At such a season as this to kill Man! Was no other game afoot?' said Bagheera scornfully, drawing himself out of the tainted water, and shaking each paw, cat-fashion, as he did so.

'I killed for choice—not for food.' The horrified whisper began again, and Hathi's watchful little white eye cocked itself in Shere Khan's direction. 'For choice,' Shere Khan drawled. 'Now come I to drink and make me clean again. Is there any to forbid?'

Bagheera's back began to curve like a bamboo in a high wind, but Hathi lifted up his trunk and spoke quietly.

'Thy kill was from choice?' he asked; and when Hathi asks a question it is best to answer.

'Even so. It was my right and my Night. Thou knowest, O Hathi.' Shere Khan spoke almost courteously.

'Yes, I know,' Hathi answered; and, after a little silence, 'Hast thou drunk thy fill?'

'For to-night, yes.'

'Go then. The river is to drink, and not to defile. None but the Lame Tiger would so have boasted of his right at this season when—when we suffer together—Man and Jungle People alike. Clean or unclean, get to thy lair, Shere Khan!'

The last words rang out like silver trumpets, and Hathi's three sons rolled forward half a pace, though there was no need. Shere Khan slunk away, not daring to growl, for he knew—what every one else knows—that when the last comes to the last, Hathi is the Master of the Jungle.

'What is this right Shere Khan speaks of?' Mowgli whispered in Bagheera's ear. 'To kill man is *always* shameful. The Law says so. And yet Hathi says——'

'Ask him. I do not know, Little Brother. Right or no right, if Hathi had not spoken I would have taught that lame butcher his lesson. To come to the Peace Rock fresh from a kill of Man—and to boast of it—is a jackal's trick. Besides, he tainted the good water.'

Mowgli waited for a minute to pick up his courage, because no one cared to address Hathi directly, and then he cried: 'What is Shere Khan's right, O Hathi?' Both banks echoed his words, for all the People of the Jungle are intensely curious, and they had just seen something that none, except Baloo, who looked very thoughtful, seemed to understand.

'It is an old tale,' said Hathi; 'a tale older than the Jungle. Keep silence along the banks, and I will tell that tale.'

There was a minute or two of pushing and shouldering among the pigs and the buffalo, and then the leaders of the herds grunted, one after another, 'We wait,' and Hathi strode forward till he was nearly knee-deep in the pool by the Peace Rock. Lean and wrinkled and yellow-tusked though he was, he looked what the Jungle knew him to be—their master.

'Ye know, children,' he began, 'that of all things ye most fear Man'; and there was a mutter of agreement.

'This tale touches thee, Little Brother,' said Bagheera to Mowgli.

'I? I am of the Pack—a hunter of the Free People,' Mowgli answered. 'What have I to do with Man?'

'And ye do not know why ye fear Man?' Hathi went on. 'This is the reason. In the beginning of the Jungle, and none know when that was, we of the Jungle walked together having no fear of one another. In those days there was no drought, and leaves and flowers and fruit grew on the same tree, and we ate nothing at all except leaves and flowers and grass and fruit and bark.'

'I am glad I was not born in those days,' said Bagheera. 'Bark is only good to sharpen claws.'

'And the Lord of the Jungle was Tha,* the First of the Elephants. He drew the Jungle out of deep waters with his trunk; and where he made furrows in the ground with his tusks, there the rivers ran; and where he struck with his foot, there rose ponds of good waters; and when he blew through his trunk,—thus,—the trees fell. That was the manner in which the Jungle was made by Tha; and so the tale was told to me.'

'It has not lost fat in the telling,' Bagheera whispered, and Mowgli laughed behind his hand.

'In those days there was no corn or melons or pepper or sugar-cane, nor were there any little huts such as ye have all seen; and the Jungle People knew nothing of Man, but lived in the Jungle together, making one people. But presently they began to dispute over their food, though there was grazing enough for all. They were lazy. Each wished to eat where he lay, as sometimes we can do now when the spring rains are good. Tha, the First of the Elephants, was busy making new jungles and leading the rivers in their beds. He could not walk in all places; therefore he made the First of the Tigers the master and the judge of the Jungle, to whom the Jungle People should bring their disputes. In those days the First of the Tigers ate fruit and grass with the others. He was as large as I am, and he was very beautiful, in colour all over like the blossom of the yellow creeper. There was never stripe nor bar upon his hide in those good days when this Jungle was new. All the Jungle People came before him without fear, and his word was the Law of all the Jungle. We were then, remember ye, one people.

'Yet upon a night there was a dispute between two bucks—a grazing-quarrel such as ye now settle with the horns and the fore-feet—and it is said that as the two spoke together before the First of the Tigers lying among the flowers, a buck pushed him with his horns, and the First of the Tigers forgot that he was the master and judge of the Jungle, and, leaping upon that buck, broke his neck.

'Till that night never one of us had died, and the First of the Tigers, seeing what he had done, and being made foolish by the scent of the blood, ran away into the marshes of the North, and we of the Jungle, left without a judge, fell to fighting among ourselves; and Tha heard the noise of it and came back. Then some of us said this and some of us said that, but he saw the dead buck among the flowers, and asked who had killed, and we of the Jungle would not tell because the smell of the blood made us foolish. We ran to and fro in circles, capering and crying out and shaking our heads. Then Tha gave an order to the trees that hang low, and to the trailing creepers of the Jungle, that they should mark the killer of the buck so that he should know him again, and he said, "Who will now be master of the Jungle People?" Then up leaped the Gray Ape who lives in the branches, and said, "I will now be master of the Jungle." At this Tha laughed, and said, "So be it," and went away very angry.

'Children, ye know the Gray Ape. He was then as he is now. At the first he made a wise face for himself, but in a little while he began to scratch and to leap up and down, and when Tha came back he found the Gray Ape hanging, head down, from a bough, mocking those who stood below; and they mocked him again. And so there was no Law in the Jungle—only foolish talk and senseless words.

'Then Tha called us all together and said: "The first of

your masters has brought Death into the Jungle, and the second Shame. Now it is time there was a Law, and a Law that ye must not break. Now ye shall know Fear, and when ye have found him ye shall know that he is your master, and the rest shall follow." Then we of the Jungle said, "What is Fear?" And Tha said "Seek till ye find." So we went up and down the Jungle seeking for Fear, and presently the buffaloes——'

'Ugh!' said Mysa,* the leader of the buffaloes, from their sand-bank.

'Yes, Mysa, it was the buffaloes. They came back with the news that in a cave in the Jungle sat Fear, and that he had no hair, and went upon his hind legs. Then we of the Jungle followed the herd till we came to that cave, and Fear stood at the mouth of it, and he was, as the buffaloes had said, hairless, and he walked upon his hinder legs. When he saw us he cried out, and his voice filled us with the fear that we have now of that voice when we hear it, and we ran away, tramping upon and tearing each other because we were afraid. That night, so it was told to me, we of the Jungle did not lie down together as used to be our custom, but each tribe drew off by itself—the pig with the pig, the deer with the deer; horn to horn, hoof to hoof,—like keeping to like and so lay shaking in the Jungle.

'Only the First of the Tigers was not with us, for he was still hidden in the marshes of the North, and when word was brought to him of the Thing we had seen in the cave, he said: "I will go to this Thing and break his neck." So he ran all the night till he came to the cave; but the trees and the creepers on his path, remembering the order that Tha had given, let down their branches and marked him as he ran, drawing their fingers across his back, his flank, his forehead, and his jowl. Wherever they touched him there was a mark and a stripe upon his yellow hide. *And those stripes do his children wear to this day!* When he came to the cave, Fear, the Hairless One, put out his hand and called him "The Striped One that comes by night," and the First of the Tigers was afraid of the Hairless One, and ran back to the swamps howling.'

Mowgli chuckled quietly here, his chin in the water.

'So loud did he howl that Tha heard him and said, "What is the sorrow?" And the First of the Tigers, lifting up his muzzle to the new-made sky, which is now so old, said: "Give me back my power, O Tha. I am made ashamed before all the Jungle, and I have run away from a Hairless One, and he has called me a shameful name." "And why?" said Tha. "Because I am smeared with the mud of the marshes," said the First of the Tigers. "Swim, then, and roll on the wet grass, and if it be mud it will wash away," said Tha; and the First of the Tigers swam, and rolled and rolled upon the grass, till the Jungle ran round and round before his eyes, but not one little bar upon all his hide was changed, and Tha, watching him, laughed. Then the First of the Tigers said, "What have I done that this comes to me?" Tha said, "Thou has killed the buck, and thou hast let Death loose in the Jungle, and with Death has come Fear, so that the people of the Jungle are afraid one of the other, as thou art afraid of the Hairless One." The First of the Tigers said, "They will never fear me, for I knew them since the beginning." Tha said, "Go and see." And the First of the Tigers ran to and fro, calling aloud to the deer and the pig and the sambhur and the porcupine and all the Jungle Peoples, and they all ran away from him who had been their judge, because they were afraid.

'Then the First of the Tigers came back, and his pride was broken in him, and, beating his head upon the ground, he tore up the earth with all his feet and said: "Remember that I was once the Master of the Jungle. Do not forget me, O Tha! Let my children remember that I was once without shame or fear!" And Tha said: "This much I will do, because thou and I together saw the Jungle made. For one night in each year it shall be as it was before the buck was killed—for thee and for thy children. In that one night, if ye meet the Hairless One—and his name is Man— ye shall not be afraid of him, but he shall be afraid of you, as though ye were judges of the Jungle and masters of all things. Show him mercy in that night of his fear, for thou hast known what Fear is."

'Then the First of the Tigers answered, "I am content"; but when next he drank he saw the black stripes upon his flank and his side, and he remembered the name that the Hairless One had given him, and he was angry. For a year he lived in the marshes, waiting till Tha should keep his promise. And upon a night when the Jackal of the Moon [the Evening Star] stood clear of the Jungle, he felt that his Night was upon him, and he went to that cave to meet the Hairless One. Then it happened as Tha promised, for the Hairless One fell down before him and lay along the ground, and the First of the Tigers struck him and broke his back, for he thought that there was but one such Thing in the Jungle, and that he had killed Fear. Then, nosing above the kill, he heard Tha coming down from the woods of the North, and presently the voice of the First of the Elephants, which is the voice that we hear now——'

The thunder was rolling up and down the dry, scarred hills, but it brought no rain—only heat-lightning that flickered along the ridges—and Hathi went on: '*That* was the voice he heard, and it said: "Is this thy mercy?" The First of the Tigers licked his lips and said: "What matter? I have killed Fear." And Tha said: "O blind and foolish! Thou hast untied the feet of Death, and he will follow thy trail till thou diest. Thou hast taught Man to kill!"'

'The First of the Tigers, standing stiffly to his kill, said: "He is as the buck was. There is no Fear. Now I will judge the Jungle Peoples once more."'

'And Tha said: "Never again shall the Jungle People come to thee. They shall never cross they trail, nor sleep near thee, nor follow after thee, nor browse by thy lair. Only Fear shall follow thee, and with a blow that thou canst not see he shall bid thee wait his pleasure. He shall make the ground to open under thy feet, and the creeper to twist about thy neck, and the tree-trunks to grow together about thee higher than thou canst leap, and at the last he shall take thy hide to wrap his cubs when they are cold.

Thou has shown him no mercy, and none will he show thee.''

'The First of the Tigers was very bold, for his Night was still on him, and he said: "The Promise of Tha is the Promise of Tha. He will not take away my Night?" And Tha said: "The one Night is thine, as I have said, but there is a price to pay. Thou hast taught Man to kill, and he is no slow learner.''

'The First of the Tigers said: "He is here under my foot, and his back is broken. Let the Jungle know I have killed Fear.''

'Then Tha laughed, and said: "Thou hast killed one of many, but thou thyself shalt tell the Jungle—for thy Night is ended.''

'So the day came; and from the mouth of the cave went out another Hairless One, and he saw the kill in the path, and the First of the Tigers above it, and he took a pointed stick——'

'They throw a thing that cuts now,' said Ikki, rustling down the bank; for Ikki was considered uncommonly good eating by Gonds*—they called him Ho-Igoo—and he knew something of the wicked little Gondee axe that whirls across a clearing like a dragon-fly.

'It was a pointed stick, such as they put in the foot of a pit-trap,' said Hathi, 'and throwing it, he struck the First of the Tigers deep in the flank. Thus it happened as Tha said, for the First of the Tigers ran howling up and down the Jungle till he tore out the stick, and all the Jungle knew that the Hairless One could strike from far off, and they feared more than before. So it came about that the First of the Tigers taught the Hairless One to kill—and ye know what harm that has since done to all our peoples—through the noose, and the pitfall, and the hidden trap, and the flying stick, and the stinging fly that comes out of white smoke [Hathi meant the rifle], and the Red Flower* that drives us into the open. Yet for one night in the year the Hairless One fears the Tiger, as Tha promised, and never has the Tiger given him cause to be less afraid. Where he finds him, there he kills him, remembering how the First of the Tigers was made ashamed. For the rest, Fear walks up and down the Jungle by day and by night.'

'*Ahi! Aoo!*' said the deer, thinking of what it all meant to them.

'And only when there is one great Fear over all, as there is now, can we of the Jungle lay aside our little fears, and meet together in one place as we do now.'

'For one night only does Man fear the Tiger?' said Mowgli.

'For one night only,' said Hathi.

'But I—but we—but all the Jungle knows that Shere Khan kills Man twice and thrice in a moon.'

'Even so. *Then* he springs from behind and turns his head aside as he strikes, for he is full of fear. If Man looked at him* he would run. But on his one Night he goes openly down to the village. He walks between the houses and thrusts his head into the doorway, and the men fall on their faces, and there he does his kill. One kill in that Night.'

'Oh!' said Mowgli to himself, rolling over in the water. '*Now* I see why it was Shere Khan bade me look at him! He got no good of it, for he could not hold his eyes steady, and—and I certainly did not fall down at his feet. But then I am not a man, being of the Free People.'

'Umm!' said Bagheera deep in his furry throat. 'Does the Tiger know his Night?'

'Never till the Jackal of the Moon stands clear of the evening mist. Sometimes it falls in the dry summer and sometimes in the wet rains—this one Night of the Tiger. But for the First of the Tigers, this would never have been, nor would any of us have known fear.'

The deer grunted sorrowfully, and Bagheera's lips curled in a wicked smile. 'Do men know this—tale?' said he.

'None know it except the tigers, and we, the elephants— the children of Tha. Now ye by the pools have heard it, and I have spoken.'

'Hathi dipped his trunk into the water as a sign that he did not wish to talk.

'But—but—but,' said Mowgli, turning to Baloo, 'why did not the First of the Tigers continue to eat grass and leaves and trees? He did but break the buck's neck. He did not *eat*. What led him to the hot meat?'

'The trees and the creepers marked him, Little Brother, and made him the striped thing that we see. Never again would he eat their fruit; but from that day he revenged himself upon the deer, and the others, the Eaters of Grass,' said Baloo.

'Then *thou* knowest the tale. Heh? Why have I never heard?'

'Because the Jungle is full of such tales. If I made a beginning there would never be an end to them. Let go my ear, Little Brother.'

The Law of the Jungle

JUST to give you an idea of the immense variety of the Jungle Law, I have translated into verse (Baloo always recited them in a sort of sing-song) a few of the laws that apply to the wolves. There are, of course, hundreds and hundreds more, but these will do for specimens of the simpler rulings.

Now this is the Law of the Jungle—as old and as true as the sky;
And the Wolf that shall keep it may prosper, but the Wolf that shall
    break it must die.

As the creeper that girdles the tree-trunk the Law runneth forward
    and back—
For the strength of the Pack is the Wolf, and the strength of the Wolf
    is the Pack.

Wash daily from nose-tip to tail-tip; drink deeply, but never too
    deep;
And remember the night is for hunting, and forget not the day is
    for sleep.

The Jackal may follow the Tiger, but, Cub, when thy whiskers
    are grown,

Remember the Wolf is a hunter—go forth and get food of thine
   own.

Keep peace with the Lords of the Jungle—the Tiger, the
   Panther, the Bear;
And trouble not Hathi the Silent, and mock not the Boar in his
   lair.

When Pack meets with Pack in the Jungle, and neither will go
   from the trail.
Lie down till the leaders have spoken—it may be fair words shall
   prevail.

When ye fight with a Wolf of the Pack, ye must fight him alone
   and afar,
Lest others take part in the quarrel, and the Pack be diminished
   by war.

The Lair of the Wolf is his refuge, and where he has made him
   his home,
Not even the Head Wolf may enter, not even the Council may
   come.

The Lair of the Wolf is his refuge, but where he has digged it too
   plain,
The Council shall send him a message, and so he shall change it
   again.

If ye kill before midnight, be silent, and wake not the woods with
   your bay,
Lest ye frighten the deer from the crops, and the brothers go
   empty away.

Ye may kill for yourselves, and your mates, and your cubs as they
   need, and ye can;
But kill not for pleasure of killing, and *seven times never kill Man.*

If ye plunder his Kill from a weaker, devour not all in thy pride;
Pack-Right is the right of the meanest; so leave him the head and
   the hide.

The Kill of the Pack is the meat of the Pack. Ye must eat where it
  lies;
And no one may carry away of that meat to his lair, or he dies.

The Kill of the Wolf is the meat of the Wolf. He may do what he
  will,
But, till he has given permission, the Pack may not eat of that
  Kill.

Cub-Right is the right of the Yearling. From all of his Pack he
  may claim
Full-gorge when the killer has eaten; and none may refuse him
  the same.

Lair-Right is the right of the Mother. From all of her year she
  may claim.
One haunch of each kill for her litter, and none may deny her the
  same.

Cave-Right is the right of the Father—to hunt by himself for his
  own:
He is freed of all calls to the Pack; he is judged by the Council
  alone.

Because of his age and his cunning, because of his gripe and his
  paw,
In all that the Law leaveth open the word of the Head Wolf is
  Law.

*Now these are the Laws of the Jungle, and many and mighty are
  they;*
*But the head and the hoof of the Law and the haunch and the hump
  is—Obey!*

The Miracle of Purun Bhagat*

The night we felt the earth would move,
  We stole and plucked him by the hand,
Because we loved him with the love
  That knows but cannot understand.

And when the roaring hillside broke,
  And all our world fell down in rain,
We saved him, we the Little Folk;
  But lo! he does not come again!

Mourn now, we saved him for the sake
  Of such poor love as wild ones may.
Mourn ye! Our brother will not wake,
  And his own kind drive us away!
                          *Dirge of the Langurs**

THERE was once a man in India who was Prime Minister of one of the semi-independent native States in the north-western part of the country. He was a Brahmin,* so high-caste that caste ceased to have any particular meaning for him; and his father had been an important official in the gay-coloured tag-rag and bobtail of an old-fashioned Hindu Court. But as Purun Dass grew up he felt that the old order of things was changing, and that if any one wished to get on in the world he must stand well with the English, and imitate all that the English believed to be good. At the same time a native official must keep his own master's favour. This was a difficult game, but the quiet, close-mouthed young Brahmin, helped by a good English education at a Bombay University, played it coolly, and rose, step by step, to be Prime Minister of the kingdom. That is to say, he held more real power than his master, the Maharajah.

When the old king—who was suspicious of the English, their railways and telegraphs—died, Purun Dass stood high with his young successor, who had been tutored by an Englishman; and between them, though he always took care that his master should have the credit, they established schools for little girls, made roads, and started State dispensaries and shows of agricultural implements, and published a yearly blue-book on the 'Moral and Material Progress of the State,' and the Foreign Office and the Government of India were delighted. Very few native States take up English progress altogether, for they will not believe, as Purun Dass showed he did, that what was good for the Englishman must be twice as good for the Asiatic. The Prime Minister became the honoured friend of Viceroys, and Governors, and Lieutenant-Governors, and medical missionaries, and common missionaries, and hard-riding English officers who came to shoot in the State preserves, as well as of whole hosts of tourists who travelled up and down India in the cold weather, showing how things ought to be managed. In his spare time he would endow scholarships for the study of medicine and manufactures on strictly English lines, and write letters to the *Pioneer*,* the greatest Indian daily paper, explaining his master's aims and objects.

At last he went to England on a visit, and had to pay enormous sums to the priests when he came back; for even so high-caste a Brahmin as Purun Dass lost caste by crossing the black sea. In London he met and talked with every one worth knowing—men whose names go all over the world—and saw a great deal more than he said. He was given honorary degrees by learned universities, and he made speeches and talked of Hindu social reform to English ladies in evening dress, till all London cried, 'This is the most fascinating man we have ever met at dinner since cloths were first laid.'

When he returned to India there was a blaze of glory, for the Viceroy himself made a special visit to confer upon the Maharajah the Grand Cross of the Star of India*—all diamonds and ribbons and enamel; and at the same ceremony, while the cannon boomed, Purun Dass was made a Knight Commander of the Order of the Indian Empire; so that his name stood Sir Purun Dass, K.C.I.E.

That evening, at dinner in the big Viceregal tent, he stood up with the badge and the collar of the Order on his breast, and replying to the toast of his master's health, made a speech few Englishmen could have bettered.

Next month, when the city had returned to its sun-baked quiet, he did a thing no Englishman would have dreamed of doing; for, so far as the world's affairs went, he died. The jewelled order of his knighthood went back to the Indian Government, and a new Prime Minister was appointed to the charge of affairs, and a great game of General Post* began in all the subordinate appointments. The priests knew what had happened, and the people guessed; but India is the one place in the world where a man can do as he pleases and nobody asks why; and the fact that Dewan* Sir Purun Dass, K.C.I.E., had resigned position, palace, and power, and taken up the begging-bowl and ochre-coloured dress of a Sunnyasi, or holy man, was considered nothing extraordinary. He had been, as the Old Law recommends, twenty years a youth, twenty years a fighter,—though he had never carried a weapon in his life,—and twenty years head of a household. He had used his wealth and his power for what he knew both to be worth; he had taken honour when it came his way; he had seen men and cities far and near, and men and cities had stood up and honoured him. Now he would let these things go, as a man drops the cloak he no longer needs.

Behind him, as he walked through the city gates, an antelope skin and brass-handled crutch under his arm, and a begging-bowl of polished brown *coco-de-mer** in his hand, barefoot, alone, with eyes cast on the ground— behind him they were firing salutes from the bastions in honour of his happy successor. Purun Dass nodded. All that life was ended; and he bore it no more ill-will or good-will than a man bears to a colourless dream of the night. He was a Sunnyasi—a houseless, wandering mendicant, depending on his neighbours for his daily bread; and so long as there is a morsel to divide in India, neither priest nor beggar starves. He had never in his life tasted meat, and very seldom eaten even fish. A five-pound note would have covered his personal expenses for food through any one of the many years in which he had been absolute

master of millions of money. Even when he was being
lionised in London he had held before him his dream of
peace and quiet—the long, white, dusty Indian road,
printed all over with bare feet, the incessant, slow-moving
traffic, and the sharp-smelling wood smoke curling up
under the fig-trees in the twilight, where the wayfarers sit
at their evening meal.

When the time came to make that dream true the Prime
Minister took the proper steps, and in three days you
might more easily have found a bubble in the trough of the
long Atlantic seas than Purun Dass among the roving,
gathering, separating millions of India.

At night his antelope skin was spread where the darkness overtook him—sometimes in a Sunnyasi monastery by
the roadside; sometimes by a mud-pillar shrine of Kala
Pir,* where the Jogis,* who are another misty division of
holy men, would receive him as they do those who know
what castes and divisions are worth; sometimes on the
outskirts of a little Hindu village, where the children
would steal up with the food their parents had prepared;
and sometimes on the pitch of the bare grazing-grounds,
where the flame of his stick fire waked the drowsy camels.
It was all one to Purun Dass—or Purun Bhagat, as he
called himself now. Earth, people, and food were all one.
But unconsciously his feet drew him away northward and
eastward; from the south to Rohtak; from Rohtak to
Kurnool; from Kurnool to ruined Samanah, and then up-
stream along the dried bed of the Gugger river that fills
only when the rain falls in the hills, till one day he saw the
far line of the great Himalayas.

Then Purun Bhagat smiled, for he remembered that his
mother was of Rajput Brahmin birth, from Kulu* way—a
Hill-woman, always home-sick for the snows—and that
the least touch of Hill blood* draws a man in the end back
to where he belongs.

'Yonder,' said Purun Bhagat, breasting the lower slopes
of the Sewaliks, where the cacti stand up like seven-
branched candlesticks—'yonder I shall sit down and get
knowledge'; and the cool wind of the Himalayas whistled
about his ears as he trod the road that led to Simla.*

The last time he had come that way it had been in state, with a clattering cavalry escort, to visit the gentlest and most affable of Viceroys; and the two had talked for an hour together about mutual friends in London, and what the Indian common folk really thought of things. This time Purun Bhagat paid no calls, but leaned on the rail of the Mall, watching that glorious view of the Plains spread out forty miles below, till a native Mohammedan police-man told him he was obstructing traffic; and Purun Bhagat salaamed reverently to the Law, because he knew the value of it, and was seeking for a Law of his own. Then he moved on, and slept that night in an empty hut at Chota Simla,* which looks like the very last end of the earth, but it was only the beginning of his journey.

He followed the Himalaya-Thibet road, the little ten-foot track that is blasted out of solid rock, or strutted out on timbers over gulfs a thousand feet deep; that dips into warm, wet, shut-in valleys, and climbs out across bare, grassy hill-shoulders where the sun strikes like a burning-glass; or turns through dripping, dark forests where the tree-ferns dress the trunks from head to heel, and the pheasant calls to his mate. And he met Thibetan herdsmen with their dogs and flocks of sheep, each sheep with a little bag of borax* on his back, and wandering wood-cutters, and cloaked and blanketed Lamas from Thibet, coming into India on pilgrimage, and envoys of little solitary Hill-states, posting furiously on ring-streaked and piebald ponies, or the cavalcade of a Rajah paying a visit; or else for a long, clear day he would see nothing more than a black bear grunting and rooting below in the valley. When he first started, the roar of the world he had left still rang in his ears, as the roar of a tunnel rings long after the train has passed through; but when he had put the Mutteeanee Pass behind him that was all done, and Purun Bhagat was alone with himself, walking, wondering, and thinking, his eyes on the ground, and his thoughts with the clouds.

One evening he crossed the highest pass he had met till then—it had been a two-days' climb—and came out on a line of snow-peaks that banded all the horizon—

mountains from fifteen to twenty thousand feet high, looking almost near enough to hit with a stone, though they were fifty or sixty miles away. The pass was crowned with dense, dark forest—deodar, walnut, wild cherry, wild olive, and wild pear, but mostly deodar, which is the Himalayan cedar; and under the shadow of the deodars stood a deserted shrine to Kali*—who is Durga, who is Sitala, who is sometimes worshipped against the smallpox.

Purun Dass swept the stone floor clear, smiled at the grinning statue, made himself a little mud fireplace at the back of the shrine, spread his antelope skin on a bed of fresh pine-needles, tucked his *bairagi*—his brass-handled crutch—under his armpit, and sat down to rest.

Immediately below him the hillside fell away, clean and cleared for fifteen hundred feet, where a little village of stone-walled houses, with roofs of beaten earth, clung to the steep tilt. All round it the tiny terraced fields lay out like aprons of patchwork on the knees of the mountain, and cows no bigger than beetles grazed between the smooth stone circles of the threshing-floors. Looking across the valley, the eye was deceived by the size of things, and could not at first realise that what seemed to be low scrub, on the opposite mountain-flank, was in truth a forest of hundred-foot pines. Purun Bhagat saw an eagle swoop across the gigantic hollow, but the great bird dwindled to a dot ere it was half-way over. A few bands of scattered clouds strung up and down the valley, catching on a shoulder of the hills, or rising up and dying out when they were level with the head of the pass. And 'Here shall I find peace,' said Purun Bhagat.

Now, a Hill-man makes nothing of a few hundred feet up or down, and as soon as the villagers saw the smoke in the deserted shrine, the village priest climbed up the terraced hillside to welcome the stranger.

When he met Purun Bhagat's eyes—the eyes of a man used to control thousands—he bowed to the earth, took the begging-bowl without a word, and returned to the village saying, 'We have at last a holy man. Never have I seen such a man. He is of the Plains—but pale-coloured—

a Brahmin of the Brahmins.' Then all the housewives of the village said, 'Think you he will stay with us?' and each did her best to cook the most savoury meal for the Bhagat. Hill-food is very simple, but with buckwheat and Indian corn, and rice and red pepper, and little fish out of the stream in the valley, and honey from the flue-like hives built in the stone walls, and dried apricots, and turmeric,* and wild ginger, and bannocks* of flour, a devout woman can make good things, and it was a full bowl that the priest carried to the Bhagat. Was he going to stay? asked the priest. Would he need a *chela*—a disciple—to beg for him? Had he a blanket against the cold weather? Was the food good?

Purun Bhagat ate, and thanked the giver. It was in his mind to stay. That was sufficient, said the priest. Let the begging-bowl be placed outside the shrine, in the hollow made by those two twisted roots, and daily should the Bhagat be fed; for the village felt honoured that such a man—he looked timidly into the Bhagat's face—should tarry among them.

That day saw the end of Purun Bhagat's wanderings. He had come to the place appointed for him—the silence and the space. After this, time stopped, and he, sitting at the mouth of the shrine, could not tell whether he were alive or dead; a man with control of his limbs, or a part of the hills, and the clouds, and the shifting rain and sunlight. He would repeat a Name* softly to himself a hundred hundred times, till, at each repetition, he seemed to move more and more out of his body, sweeping up to the doors of some tremendous discovery; but, just as the door was opening, his body would drag him back, and, with grief, he felt he was locked up again in the flesh and bones of Purun Bhagat.

Every morning the filled begging-bowl was laid silently in the crutch of the roots outside the shrine. Sometimes the priest brought it; sometimes a Ladakhi* trader, lodging in the village, and anxious to get merit, trudged up the path; but, more often, it was the woman who had cooked the meal overnight; and she would murmur, hardly above her breath: 'Speak for me before the gods, Bhagat. Speak for such a one, the wife of so-and-so!' Now and then some bold child would be allowed the honour, and Purun Bhagat would hear him drop the bowl and run as fast as his little legs could carry him, but the Bhagat never came down to the village. It was laid out like a map at his feet. He could see the evening gatherings, held on the circle of the threshing-floors, because that was the only level ground; could see the wonderful unnamed green of the young rice, the indigo blues of the Indian corn, the dock-like patches of buckwheat, and, in its season, the red bloom of the amaranth, whose tiny seeds, being neither grain nor pulse, make a food that can be lawfully eaten by Hindus in time of fasts.

When the year turned, the roofs of the huts were all little squares of purest gold, for it was on the roofs that they laid out their cobs of the corn to dry. Hiving and harvest, rice-sowing and husking, passed before his eyes, all embroidered down there on the many-sided plots of fields, and he thought of them all, and wondered what they all led to at the long last.

Even in populated India a man cannot a day sit still before the wild things run over him as though he were a rock; and in that wilderness very soon the wild things, who knew Kali's Shrine well, came back to look at the intruder. The *langurs*, the big gray-whiskered monkeys of the Himalayas, were, naturally, the first, for they are alive with curiosity; and when they had upset the begging-bowl, and rolled it round the floor, and tried their teeth on the brass-handled crutch, and made faces at the antelope skin, they decided that the human being who sat so still was harmless. At evening, they would leap down from the pines, and beg with their hands for things to eat, and then swing off in graceful curves. They liked the warmth of the fire, too, and huddled round it till Purun Bhagat had to push them aside to throw on more fuel; and in the morning, as often as not, he would find a furry ape sharing his blanket.* All day long, one or other of the tribe would sit by his side, staring out at the snows, crooning and looking unspeakably wise and sorrowful.

After the monkeys came the *barasingh*,* that big deer which is like our red deer, but stronger. He wished to rub off the velvet of his horns against the cold stones of Kali's statue, and stamped his feet when he saw the man at the shrine. But Purun Bhagat never moved, and, little by little, the royal stag edged up and nuzzled his shoulder. Purun Bhagat slid one cool hand along the hot antlers, and the touch soothed the fretted beast, who bowed his head, and Purun Bhagat very softly rubbed and ravelled off the velvet. Afterward, the *barasingh* brought his doe and fawn—gentle things that mumbled on the holy man's blanket—or would come alone at night, his eyes green in the fire-flicker, to take his share of fresh walnuts. At last, the musk-deer, the shyest and almost the smallest of the deerlets, came, too, her big rabbity ears erect; even brindled, silent *mushick-nabha*,* must needs find out what the light in the shrine meant, and drop out her moose-like nose into Purun Bhagat's lap, coming and going with the shadows of the fire. Purun Bhagat called them all 'my brothers,' and his low call of '*Bhai! Bhai!*'* would draw them from the forest at noon if they were within earshot. The Himalayan black bear, moody and suspicious—Sona, who has the V-shaped white mark under his chin—passed that way more than once; and since the Bhagat showed no fear, Sona showed no anger, but watched him, and came closer, and begged a share of the caresses, and a dole of bread or wild berries. Often, in the still dawns, when the Bhagat would climb to the very crest of the pass to watch the red day walking along the peaks of the snows, he would find Sona shuffling and grunting at his heels, thrusting a curious fore-paw under fallen trunks, and bringing it away with a *whoof* of impatience; or his early steps would wake Sona where he lay curled up, and the great brute, rising erect, would think to fight, till he heard the Bhagat's voice and knew his best friend.

Nearly all hermits and holy men who live apart from the big cities have the reputation of being able to work miracles with the wild things, but all the miracle lies in keeping still, in never making a hasty movement, and, for a long time, at least, in never looking directly at a visitor. The villagers saw the outline of the *barasingh* stalking like a shadow through the dark forest behind the shrine; saw the *minaul*, the Himalayan pheasant, blazing in her best colours before Kali's statue; and the *langurs* on their haunches, inside, playing with the walnut shells. Some of the children, too, had heard Sona singing to himself, bear-fashion, behind the fallen rocks, and the Bhagat's reputation as miracle-worker stood firm.

Yet nothing was farther from his mind than miracles. He believed that all things were one big Miracle, and when a man knows that much he knows something to go upon. He knew for a certainty that there was nothing great and nothing little in this world: and day and night he strove to think out his way into the heart of things, back to the place whence his soul had come.

So thinking, his untrimmed hair fell down about his shoulders, the stone slab at the side of the antelope skin was dented into a little hole by the foot of his brass-handled crutch, and the place between the tree-trunks, where the begging-bowl rested day after day, sunk and wore into a hollow almost as smooth as the brown shell itself; and each beast knew his exact place at the fire. The fields changed their colours with the seasons; the threshing floors filled and emptied, and filled again and again; and again and again, when winter came, the *langurs* frisked among the branches feathered with light snow, till the mother-monkeys brought their sad-eyed little babies up from the warmer valleys with the spring. There were few changes in the village. The priest was older, and many of the little children who used to come with the begging-dish sent their own children now; and when you asked of the villagers how long their holy man had lived in Kali's Shrine at the head of the pass, they answered, 'Always.'

Then came such summer rains as had not been known in the Hills for many seasons. Through three good months the valley was wrapped in cloud and soaking mist—steady, unrelenting downfall, breaking off into thunder-shower after thunder-shower. Kali's Shrine stood above the clouds, for the most part, and there was a whole month in which the Bhagat never caught a glimpse of his village. It was packed away under a white floor of cloud that swayed and shifted and rolled on itself and bulged upward, but never broke from its piers—the streaming flanks of the valley.

All that time he heard nothing but the sound of a million little waters, overhead from the trees, and underfoot along the gound, soaking through the pine-needles, dripping from the tongues of draggled fern, and spouting in newly-torn muddy channels down the slopes. Then the sun came out, and drew forth the good incense of the deodars and the rhododendrons, and that far-off, clean smell which the Hill people call 'the smell of the snows.' The hot sunshine lasted for a week, and then the rains gathered together for their last downpour, and the water fell in sheets that flayed off the skin of the ground and leaped back in mud. Purun Bhagat heaped his fire high that night, for he was sure his brothers would need warmth; but never a beast came to the shrine, though he called and called till he dropped asleep, wondering what had happened in the woods.

It was in the black heart of the night, the rain drumming like a thousand drums, that he was roused by a plucking at his blanket, and, stretching out, felt the little hand of a *langur*. 'It is better here than in the trees,' he said sleepily, loosening a fold of blanket; 'take it and be warm.' The monkey caught his hand and pulled hard. 'Is it food, then?' said Purun Bhagat. 'Wait awhile, and I will prepare some.' As he kneeled to throw fuel on the fire the *langur* ran to the door of the shrine, crooned, and ran back again, plucking at the man's knee.

'What is it? What is thy trouble, Brother?' said Purun Bhagat, for the *langur's* eyes were full of things that he could not tell. 'Unless one of thy caste be in a trap—and none set traps here—I will not go into that weather. Look, Brother, even the *barasingh* comes for shelter!'

The deer's antlers clashed as he strode into the shrine,

clashed against the grinning statue of Kali. He lowered them in Purun Bhagat's direction and stamped uneasily, hissing through his half-shut nostrils.

'Hai! Hai! Hai!' said the Bhagat, snapping his fingers. 'Is *this* payment for a night's lodging!' But the deer pushed him toward the door, and as he did so Purun Bhagat heard the sound of something opening with a sigh, and saw two slabs of the floor draw away from each other, while the sticky earth below smacked its lips.

'Now I see,' said Purun Bhagat. 'No blame to my brothers that they did not sit by the fire to-night. The mountain is falling. And yet—why should I go?' His eye fell on the empty begging-bowl, and his face changed. 'They have given me good food daily since—since I came, and, if I am not swift, to-morrow there will not be one mouth in the valley. Indeed, I must go and warn them below. Back there, Brother! Let me get to the fire.'

The *barasingh* backed unwillingly as Purun Bhagat drove a pine torch deep into the flame, twirling it till it was well lit. 'Ah! ye came to warn me,' he said, rising. 'Better than that we shall do; better than that. Out, now, and lend me thy neck, Brother, for I have but two feet.'

He clutched the bristling withers of the *barasingh* with his right hand, held the torch away with his left, and stepped out of the shrine into the desperate night. There was no breath of wind, but the rain nearly drowned the flare as the great deer hurried down the slope, sliding on his haunches. As soon as they were clear of the forest more of the Bhagat's brothers joined them. He heard, though he could not see, the *langurs* pressing about him, and behind them the *uhh! uhh!* of Sona. The rain matted his long white hair into ropes; the water splashed beneath his bare feet, and his yellow robe clung to his frail old body, but he stepped down steadily, leaning against the *barasingh*. He was no longer a holy man, but Sir Purun Dass, K.C.I.E., Prime Minister of no small State, a man accustomed to command, going out to save life. Down the steep, plashy path they poured all together, the Bhagat and his brothers, down and down till the deer's feet clicked and stumbled on the wall of a threshing-floor, and he snorted because he smelt Man. Now they were at the head of the one crooked village street, and the Bhagat beat with his crutch on the barred windows of the blacksmith's house, as his torch blazed up in the shelter of the eaves. 'Up and out!' cried Purun Bhagat; and he did not know his own voice, for it was years since he had spoken aloud to a man. 'The hill falls! The hill is falling! Up and out, oh, you within!'

'It is our Bhagat,' said the blacksmith's wife. 'He stands among his beasts. Gather the little ones and give the call.'

It ran from house to house, while the beasts, cramped in the narrow way, surged and huddled round the Bhagat, and Sona puffed impatiently.

The people hurried into the street—they were no more than seventy souls all told—and in the glare of the torches they saw their Bhagat holding back the terrified *barasingh*, while the monkeys plucked piteously at his skirts, and Sona sat on his haunches and roared.

'Across the valley and up the next hill!' shouted Purun Bhagat. 'Leave none behind! We follow!'

Then the people ran as only Hill folk can run, for they knew that in a landslip you must climb for the highest ground across the valley. They fled, splashing through the little river at the bottom, and panted up the terraced fields on the far side, while the Bhagat and his brethren followed. Up and up the opposite mountain they climbed, calling to each other by name—the roll-call of the village—and at their heels toiled the big *barasingh*, weighted by the failing strength of Purun Bhagat. At last the deer stopped in the shadow of a deep pine-wood, five hundred feet up the hillside. His instinct, that had warned him of the coming slide, told him he would be safe here.

Purun Bhagat dropped fainting by his side, for the chill of the rain and that fierce climb were killing him; but first he called to the scattered torches ahead, 'Stay and count your numbers'; then, whispering to the deer as he saw the lights gather in a cluster: 'Stay with me, Brother. Stay—till—I—go!'

There was a sigh in the air that grew to a mutter, and a

mutter that grew to a roar, and a roar that passed all sense of hearing, and the hillside on which the villagers stood was hit in the darkness, and rocked to the blow. Then a note as steady, deep, and true as the deep C of the organ drowned everything for perhaps five minutes, while the very roots of the pines quivered to it. It died away, and the sound of the rain falling on miles of hard ground and grass changed to the muffled drum of water on soft earth. That told its own tale.

Never a villager—not even the priest—was bold enough to speak to the Bhagat who had saved their lives. They crouched under the pines and waited till the day. When it came they looked across the valley and saw that what had been forest, and terraced field, and track-threaded grazing-ground was one raw, red, fan-shaped smear, with a few trees flung head-down on the scarp.* That red ran high up the hill of their refuge, damming back the little river, which had begun to spread into a brick-coloured lake. Of the village, of the road to the shrine, of the shrine itself, and the forest behind, there was no trace. For one mile in width and two thousand feet in sheer depth the mountain-side had come away bodily, planed clean from head to heel.

And the villagers, one by one, crept through the wood to pray before their Bhagat. They saw the *barasingh* standing over him, who fled when they came near, and they heard the *langurs* wailing in the branches, and Sona moaning up the hill; but their Bhagat was dead, sitting cross-legged,* his back against a tree, his crutch under his armpit, and his face turned to the north-east.

The priest said: 'Behold a miracle after a miracle, for in this very attitude must all Sunnyasis be buried! Therefore where he now is we will build the temple to our holy man.'

They built the temple before a year was ended—a little stone-and-earth shrine—and they called the hill the Bhagat's Hill, and they worship there with lights and flowers and offerings to this day. But they do not know that the saint of their worship is the late Sir Purun Dass, K.C.I.E., D.C.L.,* Ph.D.,* etc., once Prime Minister of the progressive and enlightened State of Mohiniwala,* and honorary or corresponding member of more learned and scientific societies than will ever do any good in this world or the next.*

A Song of Kabir*

OH, light was the world that he weighed in his hands!
Oh, heavy the tale of his fiefs and his lands!
He has gone from the *guddee** and put on the shroud,
And departed in guise of *bairagi** avowed!

Now the white road to Delhi is mat for his feet,
The *sal** and the *kikar** must guard him from heat;
His home is the camp, and the waste, and the crowd—
He is seeking the Way* as *bairagi* avowed!

He has looked upon Man, and his eyeballs are clear
(There was One; there is One, and but One, saith Kabir);
The Red Mist of Doing has thinned to a cloud—
He has taken the Path for *bairagi* avowed!

To learn and discern of his brother the clod,
Of his brother the brute, and his brother the God.
He has gone from the council and put on the shroud
('Can ye hear?' saith Kabir), a *bairagi* avowed!

Letting in the Jungle

Veil them, cover them, wall them round—
  Blossom, and creeper, and weed—
Let us forget the sight and the sound,
  The smell and the touch of the breed!

Fat black ash by the altar-stone,
  Here is the white-foot rain,
And the does bring forth in the fields unsown,
  And none shall affright them again;
And the blind walls crumble, unknown, o'erthrown,
  And none shall inhabit again!

YOU will remember, if you have read the tales in the first Jungle Book, that after Mowgli had pinned Shere Khan's hide to the Council Rock, he told as many as were left of the Seeonee Pack that henceforward he would hunt in the Jungle alone; and the four children of Mother and Father Wolf said that they would hunt with him. But it is not easy to change one's life all in a minute—particularly in the Jungle. The first thing Mowgli did, when the disorderly Pack had slunk off, was to go to the home-cave, and sleep for a day and a night. Then he told Mother Wolf and Father Wolf as much as they could understand of his adventures among men; and when he made the morning sun flicker up and down the blade of his skinning-knife,— the same he had skinned Shere Khan with,—they said he had learned something. Then Akela* and Gray Brother had to explain their share of the great buffalo-drive in the ravine, and Baloo toiled up the hill to hear all about it, and Bagheera scratched himself all over with pure delight at the way in which Mowgli had managed his war.

It was long after sunrise, but no one dreamed of going to sleep, and from time to time, during the talk, Mother Wolf would throw up her head, and sniff a deep snuff of satisfaction as the wind brought her the smell of the tiger-skin on the Council Rock.

'But for Akela and Gray Brother here,' Mowgli said, at

the end, 'I could have done nothing. Oh, mother, mother! if thou hadst seen the black herd-bulls pour down the ravine, or hurry through the gates when the Man-Pack flung stones at me!'

'I am glad I did not see that last,' said Mother Wolf stiffly. 'It is not *my* custom to suffer my cubs to be driven to and fro like jackals. *I* would have taken a price from the Man-Pack; but I would have spared the woman who gave thee the milk. Yes, I would have spared her alone.'

'Peace, peace, Raksha!'* said Father Wolf, lazily, 'Our Frog has come back again—so wise that his own father must lick his feet; and what is a cut, more or less, on the head? Leave Men alone.' Baloo and Bagheera both echoed: 'Leave Men alone.'

Mowgli, his head on Mother Wolf's side, smiled contentedly, and said that, for his own part, he never wished to see, or hear, or smell Man again.

'But what,' said Akela, cocking one ear—'but what if men do not leave thee alone, Little Brother?'

'We be *five*,' said Gray Brother, looking round at the company, and snapping his jaws on the last word.

'We also might attend to that hunting,' said Bagheera, with a little *switch-switch* of his tail, looking at Baloo. 'But why think of men now, Akela?'

'For this reason,' the Lone Wolf answered: 'when that yellow thief's hide was hung up on the rock, I went back along our trail to the village, stepping in my tracks, turning aside, and lying down, to make a mixed trail in case one should follow us. But when I had fouled the trail so that I myself hardly knew it again, Mang,* the Bat, came hawking* between the trees, and hung up above me. Said Mang, "The village of the Man-Pack, where they cast out the Man-cub, hums like a hornet's nest."'

'It was a big stone that I threw,' chuckled Mowgli, who had often amused himself by throwing ripe paw-paws into a hornet's nest, and racing off to the nearest pool before the hornets caught him.

'I asked of Mang what he had seen. He said that the Red Flower blossomed at the gate of the village, and men sat about it carrying guns. Now *I* know, for I have good cause,'—Akela looked down at the old dry scars on his flank and side,—'that men do not carry guns for pleasure. Presently, Little Brother, a man with a gun follows our trail—if, indeed, he be not already on it.'

'But why should he? Men have cast me out. What more do they need?' said Mowgli angrily.

'Thou art a man, Little Brother,' Akela returned. 'It is not for *us*, the Free Hunters, to tell thee what thy brethren do, or why.'

He had just time to snatch up his paw as the skinning-knife cut deep into the ground below. Mowgli struck quicker than an average human eye could follow, but Akela was a wolf; and even a dog, who is very far removed from the wild wolf, his ancestor, can be waked out of deep sleep by a cart-wheel touching his flank, and can spring away unharmed before that wheel comes on.

'Another time,' Mowgli said quietly, returning the knife to its sheath, 'speak of the Man-Pack and of Mowgli in *two* breaths—not one.'

'Phff! That is a sharp tooth,' said Akela, snuffing at the blade's cut in the earth, 'but living with the Man-Pack has spoiled thine eye, Little Brother. I could have killed a buck while thou wast striking.'

Bagheera sprang to his feet, thrust up his head as far as he could, sniffed, and stiffened through every curve in his body. Gray Brother followed his example quickly, keeping a little to his left to get the wind that was blowing from the right, while Akela bounded fifty yards up wind, and, half-crouching, stiffened too. Mowgli looked on enviously. He could smell things as very few human beings could, but he had never reached the hair-trigger-like sensitiveness of a Jungle nose; and his three months in the smoky village had set him back sadly. However, he dampened his finger, rubbed it on his nose, and stood erect to catch the upper scent, which, though it is the faintest, is the truest.

'Man!' Akela growled, dropping on his haunches.

'Buldeo!'* said Mowgli, sitting down. 'He follows our trail, and yonder is the sunlight on his gun. Look!'

It was no more than a splash of sunlight, for a fraction of a second, on the brass champs of the old Tower musket, but nothing in the Jungle winks with just that flash, except when the clouds race over the sky. Then a piece of mica, or a little pool, or even a highly-polished leaf will flash like a heliograph. But that day was cloudless and still.

'I knew men would follow,' said Akela triumphantly. 'Not for nothing have I led the Pack.'

The four cubs said nothing, but ran down hill on their bellies, melting into the thorn and under-brush as a mole melts into a lawn.

'Where go ye, and without word?' Mowgli called.

'H'sh! We roll his skull here before mid-day!' Gray Brother answered.

'Back! Back and wait! Man does not eat Man!' Mowgli shrieked.

'Who was a wolf but now? Who drove the knife at me for thinking he might be Man?' said Akela, as the four wolves turned back sullenly and dropped to heel.

'Am I to give reason for all I choose to do?' said Mowgli furiously.

'That is Man! There speaks Man!' Bagheera muttered under his whiskers. 'Even so did men talk round the King's cages* at Oodeypore. We of the Jungle know that Man is wisest of all. If we trusted our ears we should know that of all things he is most foolish.' Raising his voice, he added, 'The Man-cub is right in this. Men hunt in packs. To kill one, unless we know what the others will do, is bad hunting. Come, let us see what this Man means toward us.'

'We will not come,' Gray Brother growled. 'Hunt alone, Little Brother. *We* know our own minds. The skull would have been ready to bring by now.'

Mowgli had been looking from one to the other of his friends, his chest heaving and his eyes full of tears. He strode forward to the wolves, and, dropping on one knee, said: 'Do I not know my mind? Look at me!'

They looked uneasily, and when their eyes wandered, he called them back again and again, till their hair stood up all over their bodies, and they trembled in every limb, while Mowgli stared and stared.

'Now,' said he, 'of us five, which is leader?'

'Thou art leader, Little Brother,' said Gray Brother, and he licked Mowgli's foot.

'Follow, then,' said Mowgli, and the four followed at his heels with their tails between their legs.

'This comes of living with the Man-Pack,' said Bagheera, slipping down after them. 'There is more in the Jungle now than Jungle Law, Baloo.'

The old bear said nothing, but he thought many things.

Mowgli cut across noiselessly through the Jungle, at right angles to Buldeo's path, till, parting the undergrowth, he saw the old man, his musket on his shoulder, running up the trail of overnight at a dog-trot.

You will remember that Mowgli had left the village with the heavy weight of Shere Khan's raw hide on his shoulders, while Akela and Gray Brother trotted behind, so that the triple trail was very clearly marked. Presently Buldeo came to where Akela, as you know, had gone back and mixed it all up. Then he sat down, and coughed and grunted, and made little casts round and about into the Jungle to pick it up again, and all the time he could have thrown a stone over those who were watching him. No one can be so silent as a wolf when he does not care to be heard; and Mowgli, though the wolves thought he moved very clumsily, could come and go like a shadow. They ringed the old man as a school of porpoises ring a steamer at full speed, and as they ringed him they talked unconcernedly, for their speech began below the lowest end of the scale that untrained human beings can hear. (The other end is bounded by the high squeak of Mang, the Bat, which very many people cannot catch at all. From that note all the bird and bat and insect talk takes on.)

'This is better than any kill,' said Gray Brother, as Buldeo stooped and peered and puffed. 'He looks like a lost pig in the Jungles by the river. What does he say?' Buldeo was muttering savagely.

Mowgli translated. 'He says that packs of wolves must

have danced round me. He says that he never saw such a trail in his life. He says he is tired.'

'He will be rested before he picks it up again,' said Bagheera coolly, as he slipped round a tree-trunk, in the game of blindman's-buff that they were playing. '*Now*, what does the lean thing do?'

'Eat or blow smoke out of his mouth. Men always play with their mouths,' said Mowgli; and the silent trailers saw the old man fill and light and puff at a water-pipe, and they took good note of the smell of the tobacco, so as to be sure of Buldeo in the darkest night, if necessary.

Then a little knot of charcoal-burners came down the path, and naturally halted to speak to Buldeo, whose fame as a hunter reached for at least twenty miles round. They all sat down and smoked, and Bagheera and the others came up and watched while Buldeo began to tell the story of Mowgli, the Devil-child, from one end to another, with additions and inventions. How he himself had really killed Shere Khan; and how Mowgli had turned himself into a wolf, and fought with him all the afternoon, and changed into a boy again and bewitched Buldeo's rifle, so that the bullet turned the corner, when he pointed it at Mowgli, and killed one of Buldeo's own buffaloes; and how the village, knowing him to be the bravest hunter in Seeonee, had sent him out to kill this Devil-child. But meantime the village had got hold of Messua* and her husband, who were undoubtedly the father and mother of this Devil-child, and had barricaded them in their own hut, and presently would torture them to make them confess they were witch and wizard, and then they would be burned to death.

'When?' said the charcoal-burners, because they would very much like to be present at the ceremony.

Buldeo said that nothing would be done till he returned, because the village wished him to kill the Jungle Boy first. After that they would dispose of Messua and her husband, and divide their lands and buffaloes among the village. Messua's husband had some remarkably fine buffaloes, too. It was an excellent thing to destroy wizards, Buldeo thought; and the people who entertained Wolf-children out of the Jungle were clearly the worst kind of witches.

But, said the charcoal-burners, what would happen if the English heard of it? The English, they had heard, were a perfectly mad people, who would not let honest farmers kill witches in peace.

Why, said Buldeo, the head-man of the village would report that Messua and her husband had died of snake-bite. *That* was all arranged, and the only thing now was to kill the Wolf-child. They did not happen to have seen anything of such a creature?

The charcoal-burners looked round cautiously, and thanked their stars they had not; but they had no doubt that so brave a man as Buldeo would find him if any one could. The sun was getting rather low, and they had an idea that they would push on to Buldeo's village and see that wicked witch. Buldeo said that, though it was his duty to kill the Devil-child, he could not think of letting a party of unarmed men go through the Jungle, which might produce the Wolf-demon at any minute, without his escort. He, therefore, would accompany them, and if the sorcerer's child appeared—well, he would show them how the best hunter in Seeonee dealt with such things. The Brahmin, he said, had given him a charm against the creature that made everything perfectly safe.

'What says he? What says he? What says he?' the wolves repeated every few minutes; and Mowgli translated until he came to the witch part of the story, which was a little beyond him, and then he said that the man and woman who had been so kind to him were trapped.

'Does Man trap Man?' said Bagheera.

'So he says. I cannot understand the talk. They are all mad together. What have Messua and her man to do with me that they should be put in a trap; and what is all this talk about the Red Flower? I must look to this. Whatever they would do to Messua they will not do till Buldeo returns. And so——' Mowgli thought hard, with his fingers playing round the haft of the skinning-knife, while

Buldeo and the charcoal-burners went off very valiantly in single file.

'I go hot-foot back to the Man-Pack,' Mowgli said at last.

'And those?' said Gray Brother, looking hungrily after the brown backs of the charcoal-burners.

'Sing them home,' said Mowgli, with a grin; 'I do not wish them to be at the village gates till it is dark. Can ye hold them?'

Gray Brother bared his white teeth in contempt. 'We can head them round and round in circles like tethered goats—if I know Man.'

'That I do not need. Sing to them a little, lest they be lonely on the road, and, Gray Brother, the song need not be of the sweetest. Go with them, Bagheera, and help make that song. When night is shut down, meet me by the village—Gray Brother knows the place.'

'It is no light hunting to work for a Man-cub. When shall I sleep?' said Bagheera, yawning, though his eyes showed that he was delighted with the amusement. 'Me to sing to naked men! But let us try.'

He lowered his head so that the sound would travel, and cried a long, long, 'Good hunting'—a midnight call in the afternoon, which was quite awful enough to begin with. Mowgli heard it rumble, and rise, and fall, and die off in a creepy sort of whine behind him, and laughed to himself as he ran through the Jungle. He could see the charcoal-burners huddled in a knot; old Buldeo's gun-barrel waving, like a banana-leaf, to every point of the compass at once. Then Gray Brother gave the *Ya-la-hi! Yalaha!* call for the buck-driving, when the Pack drives the nilghai,* the big blue cow, before them, and it seemed to come from the very ends of the earth, nearer, and nearer, and nearer, till it ended in a shriek snapped off short. The other three answered, till even Mowgli could have vowed that the full Pack was in full cry, and then they all broke into the magnificent Morning-song in the Jungle, with every turn, and flourish, and grace-note that a deep-mouthed wolf of the Pack knows. This is a rough rendering of the song, but

you must imagine what it sounds like when it breaks the
afternoon hush of the Jungle:–

> One moment past our bodies cast
>   No shadow on the plain;
> Now clear and black they stride our track,
>   And we run home again.
> In the morning hush, each rock and bush
>   Stands hard, and high, and raw:
> Then give the Call: '*Good rest to all*
>   *That keep the Jungle Law!*'
>
> Now horn and pelt our peoples melt
>   In covert to abide;
> Now, crouched and still, to cave and hill
>   Our Jungle Barons glide.
> Now, stark and plain, Man's oxen strain,
>   That draw the new-yoked plough;
> Now, stripped and dread, the dawn is red
>   Above the lit *talao*.*
>
> Ho! Get to lair! The sun's aflare
>   Behind the breathing grass:
> And creaking through the young bamboo
>   The warning whispers pass.
> By day made strange, the woods we range
>   With blinking eyes we scan;
> While down the skies the wild duck cries
>   '*The Day—The Day to Man!*'
>
> The dew is dried that drenched our hide
>   Or washed about our way;
> And where we drank, the puddled bank
>   Is crisping into clay.
> The traitor Dark gives up each mark
>   Of stretched or hooded claw;
> Then hear the Call: '*Good rest to all*
>   *That keep the Jungle Law!*'

But no translation can give the effect of it, or the yelping
scorn the Four threw into every word of it, as they heard
the trees crash when the men hastily climbed up into the

branches, and Buldeo began repeating incantations and charms. Then they lay down and slept, for, like all who live by their own exertions, they were of a methodical cast of mind; and no one can work well without sleep.

Meantime, Mowgli was putting the miles behind him, nine to the hour, swinging on, delighted to find himself so fit after all his cramped months among men. The one idea in his head was to get Messua and her husband out of the trap, whatever it was; for he had a natural mistrust of traps. Later on, he promised himself, he would pay his debts to the village at large.

It was at twilight when he saw the well-remembered grazing-grounds, and the *dhâk*-tree* where Gray Brother had waited for him on the morning that he killed Shere Khan. Angry as he was at the whole breed and community of Man, something jumped up in his throat and made him catch his breath when he looked at the village roofs. He noticed that every one had come in from the fields unusually early, and that, instead of getting to their evening cooking, they gathered in a crowd under the village tree, and chattered, and shouted.

'Men must always be making traps for men, or they are not content,' said Mowgli. 'Last night it was Mowgli—but that night seems many Rains ago. To-night it is Messua and her man. Tomorrow, and for very many nights after, it will be Mowgli's turn again.'

He crept along outside the wall till he came to Messua's hut, and looked through the window into the room. There lay Messua, gagged, and bound hand and foot, breathing hard, and groaning: her husband was tied to the gaily-painted bedstead. The door of the hut that opened into the street was shut fast, and three or four people were sitting with their backs to it.

Mowgli knew the manners and customs of the villagers very fairly. He argued that so long as they could eat, and talk, and smoke, they would not do anything else; but as soon as they had fed they would begin to be dangerous. Buldeo would be coming in before long, and if his escort had done its duty, Buldeo would have a very interesting tale to tell. So he went in through the window, and, stooping over the man and the woman, cut their thongs, pulling out the gags, and looked round the hut for some milk.

Messua was half wild with pain and fear (she had been beaten and stoned all the morning), and Mowgli put his hand over her mouth just in time to stop a scream. Her husband was only bewildered and angry, and sat picking dust and things out of his torn beard.

'I knew—I knew he would come,' Messua sobbed at last. 'Now do I *know* that he is my son!' and she hugged Mowgli to her heart. Up to that time Mowgli had been perfectly steady, but now he began to tremble all over, and that surprised him immensely.

'Why are these thongs? Why have they tied thee?' he asked, after a pause.

'To be put to the death for making a son of thee—what else?' said the man sullenly, 'Look! I bleed.'

Messua said nothing, but it was at *her* wounds that Mowgli looked, and they heard him grit his teeth when he saw the blood.

'Whose work is this?' said he. 'There is a price to pay.'

'The work of all the village. I was too rich. I had too many cattle. *Therefore* she and I are witches, because we gave thee shelter.'

'I do not understand. Let Messua tell the tale.'

'I gave thee milk, Nathoo; dost thou remember?' Messua said timidly. 'Because thou wast my son, whom the tiger took, and because I loved thee very dearly. They said that I was thy mother, the mother of a devil, and therefore worthy of death.'

'And what is a devil?' said Mowgli. 'Death I have seen.'

The man looked up gloomily, but Messua laughed. 'See!' she said to her husband, 'I knew—I said that he was no sorcerer. He is my son—my son!'

'Son or sorcerer, what good will that do us?' the man answered. 'We be as dead already.'

'Yonder is the road to the Jungle'—Mowgli pointed

through the window. 'Your hands and feet are free. Go now.'

'We do not know the Jungle, my son, as—as thou knowest,' Messua began. 'I do not think that I could walk far.'

'And the men and women would be upon our backs and drag us here again,' said the husband.

'H'm!' said Mowgli, and he tickled the palm of his hand with the tip of his skinning-knife; 'I have no wish to do harm to any one of this village—*yet*. But I do not think they will stay thee. In a little while they will have much else to think upon. Ah!' he lifted his head and listened to shouting and trampling outside. 'So they have let Buldeo come home at last?'

'He was sent out this morning to kill thee,' Messua cried. 'Didst thou meet him?'

'Yes—we—I met him. He has a tale to tell; and while he is telling it there is time to do much. But first I will learn what they mean. Think where ye would go, and tell me when I come back.'

He bounded through the window and ran along again outside the wall of the village till he came within ear-shot of the crowd round the peepul-tree.* Buldeo was lying on the ground, coughing and groaning, and every one was asking him questions. His hair had fallen about his shoulders; his hands and legs were skinned from climbing up trees, and he could hardly speak, but he felt the importance of his position keenly. From time to time he said something about devils and singing devils, and magic enchantment, just to give the crowd a taste of what was coming. Then he called for water.

'Bah!' said Mowgli. 'Chatter—chatter! Talk, talk! Men are blood-brothers of the *Bandar-log*.* Now he must wash his mouth with water; now he must blow smoke; and when all that is done he has still his story to tell. They are very wise people—men. They will leave no one to guard Messua till their ears are stuffed with Buldeo's tales. And—I grow as lazy as they!'

He shook himself and glided back to the hut. Just as he was at the window he felt a touch on his foot.

'Mother,' said he, for he knew that tongue well, 'what dost *thou* here?'

'I heard my children singing through the woods, and I followed the one I loved best. Little Frog, I have a desire to see that woman who gave thee milk,' said Mother Wolf, all wet with the dew.

'They have bound and mean to kill her. I have cut those ties, and she goes with her man through the Jungle.'

'I also will follow. I am old, but not yet toothless.' Mother Wolf reared herself up on end, and looked through the window into the dark of the hut.

In a minute she dropped noiselessly, and all she said was: 'I gave thee thy first milk; but Bagheera speaks truth: Man goes to Man at the last.

'Maybe,' said Mowgli, with a very unpleasant look on his face; 'but to-night I am very far from that trail. Wait here, but do not let her see.'

'*Thou* wast never afraid of *me*, Little Frog,' said Mother Wolf, backing into the high grass, and blotting herself out, as she knew how.

'And now,' said Mowgli cheerfully, as he swung into the hut again, 'they are all sitting round Buldeo, who is saying that which did not happen. When his talk is finished, they say they will assuredly come here with the Red—with fire and burn you both. And then?'

'I have spoken to my man,' said Messua. 'Khanhiwara* is thirty miles from here, but at Khanhiwara we may find the English——'

'And what Pack are they?' said Mowgli.

'I do not know. They be white, and it is said that they govern all the land, and do not suffer people to burn or beat each other without witnesses. If we can get thither to-night, we live. Otherwise we die.'

'Live, then. No man passes the gates to-night. But what does *he* do?' Messua's husband was on his hands and knees digging up the earth in one corner of the hut.

'It is his little money,' said Messua. 'We can take nothing else.'

'Ah, yes. The stuff that passes from hand to hand and never grows warmer. Do they need it outside this place also?' said Mowgli.

The man stared angrily. 'He is a fool, and no devil,' he muttered. 'With the money I can buy a horse. We are too bruised to walk far, and the village will follow us in an hour.'

'I say they will *not* follow till I choose; but a horse is well thought of, for Messua is tired.' Her husband stood up and knotted the last of the rupees into his waist-cloth. Mowgli helped Messua through the window, and the cool night air revived her, but the Jungle in the starlight looked very dark and terrible.

'Ye know the trail to Khanhiwara?' Mowgli whispered. They nodded.

'Good. Remember, now, not to be afraid. And there is no need to go quickly. Only—only there may be some small singing in the Jungle behind you and before.'

'Think you we would have risked a night in the Jungle through anything less than the fear of burning? It is better to be killed by beasts than by men,' said Messua's husband; but Messua looked at Mowgli and smiled.

'I say,' Mowgli went on, just as though he were Baloo repeating an old Jungle Law for the hundredth time to a foolish cub—'I say that not a tooth in the Jungle is bared against you; not a foot in the Jungle is lifted against you. Neither man nor beast shall stay you till you come within eye-shot of Khanhiwara. There will be a watch about you.' He turned quickly to Messua, saying, '*He* does not believe, but thou wilt believe?'

'Aye, surely, my son. Man, ghost, or wolf of the Jungle, I believe.'

'*He* will be afraid when he hears my people singing. Thou wilt know and understand. Go now, and slowly, for there is no need of any haste. The gates are shut.'

Messua flung herself sobbing at Mowgli's feet, but he lifted her very quickly with a shiver. Then she hung about

his neck and called him every name of blessing she could
think of, but her husband looked enviously across his
fields, and said: '*If* we reach Khanhiwara, and I get the ear
of the English, I will bring such a lawsuit against the
Brahmin and old Buldeo and the others as shall eat the
village to the bone. They shall pay me twice over for my
crops untilled and my buffaloes unfed. I will have a great
justice.'

Mowgli laughed. 'I do not know what justice is, but—
come next Rains and see what is left.'

They went off toward the Jungle, and Mother Wolf
leaped from her place of hiding.

'Follow!' said Mowgli; 'and look to it that all the Jungle
knows these two are safe. Give tongue a little. I would call
Bagheera.'

The long, low howl rose and fell, and Mowgli saw
Messua's husband flinch and turn, half minded to run
back to the hut.

'Go on,' Mowgli called cheerfully. 'I said there might be
singing. That call will follow up to Khanhiwara. It is
Favour of the Jungle.'

Messua urged her husband forward, and the darkness
shut down on them and Mother Wolf as Bagheera rose up
almost under Mowgli's feet, trembling with delight of the
night that drives the Jungle People wild.

'I am ashamed of my brethren,' he said, purring.

'What? Did they not sing sweetly to Buldeo?' said
Mowgli.

'Too well! Too well! They made even *me* forget my
pride, and, by the Broken Lock that freed me, I went
singing through the Jungle as though I were out wooing in
the spring! Didst thou not hear us?'

'I had other game afoot. Ask Buldeo if he liked the song.
But where are the Four? I do not wish one of the Man-
Pack to leave the gates to-night.'

'What need of the Four, then?' said Bagheera, shifting
from foot to foot, his eyes ablaze, and purring louder than
ever. 'I can hold them, Little Brother. Is it killing at last?
The singing and the sight of the men climbing up the trees

have made me very ready. Who is Man that we should care for him—the naked brown digger, the hairless and toothless, the eater of earth? I have followed him all day—at noon—in the white sunlight. I herded him as the wolves herd buck. I am Bagheera! Bagheera! Bagheera! As I dance with my shadow, so danced I with those men. Look!' The great panther leaped as a kitten leaps at a dead leaf whirling overhead, struck left and right into the empty air, that sang under the strokes, landed noiselessly, and leaped again and again, while the half purr, half growl gathered head as steam rumbles in a boiler. 'I am Bagheera—in the Jungle—in the night, and my strength is in me. Who shall stay my stroke? Man-cub, with one blow of my paw I could beat thy head flat as a dead frog in the summer!'

'Strike, then!' said Mowgli, in the dialect of the village, *not* the talk of the Jungle, and the human words brought Bagheera to a full stop, flung back on haunches that quivered under him, his head just at the level of Mowgli's. Once more Mowgli stared,* as he had stared at the rebellious cubs, full into the beryl-green eyes till the red glare behind their green went out like the light of a lighthouse shut off twenty miles across the sea; till the eyed dropped, and the big head with them—dropped lower and lower, and the red rasp of a tongue grated on Mowgli's instep.

'Brother—Brother—Brother!' the boy whispered, stroking steadily and lightly from the neck along the heaving back: 'Be still, be still! It is the fault of the night, and no fault of thine.'

'It was the smells of the night,' said Bagheera penitently. 'This air cries aloud to me. But how dost *thou* know!'

Of course the air round an Indian village is full of all kinds of smells, and to any creature who does nearly all his thinking through his nose, smells are as maddening as music and drugs are to human beings. Mowgli gentled* the panther for a few minutes longer, and he lay down like a cat before a fire, his paws tucked under his breast, and his eyes half shut.

'Thou are of the Jungle and *not* of the Jungle,' he said at last. 'And I am only a black panther. But I love thee, Little Brother.'

'They are very long at their talk under the tree,' Mowgli said, without noticing the last sentence. 'Buldeo must have told many tales. They should come soon to drag the woman and her man out of the trap and put them into the Red Flower. They will find that trap sprung. Ho! ho!'

'Nay, listen,' said Bagheera. 'The fever is out of my blood now. Let them find *me* there! Few would leave their houses after meeting me. It is not the first time I have been in a cage; and I do not think they will tie *me* with cords.'

'Be wise, then,' said Mowgli, laughing; for he was beginning to feel as reckless as the panther, who had glided into the hut.

'Pah!' Bagheera grunted. 'This place is rank with Man, but here is just such a bed as they gave me to lie upon in the King's cages at Oodeypore. Now I lie down.' Mowgli heard the strings of the cot crack under the great brute's weight. 'By the Broken Lock that freed me, they will think they have caught big game! Come and sit beside me, Little Brother; we will give them "good hunting" together!'

'No; I have another thought in my stomach. The Man-Pack shall not know what share I have in the sport. Make thine own hunt. I do not wish to see them.'

'Be it so,' said Bagheera. 'Ah, now they come!'

The conference under the peepul-tree had been growing noisier and noisier, at the far end of the village. It broke in wild yells, and a rush up the street of men and women, waving clubs and bamboos and sickles and knives. Buldeo and the Brahmin were at the head of it, but the mob was close at their heels, and they cried, 'The witch and the wizard! Let us see if hot coins will make them confess! Burn the hut over their heads! We will teach them to shelter wolf-devils! Nay, beat them first! Torches! More torches! Buldeo, heat the gun-barrels!'

Here was some little difficulty with the catch of the door. It had been very firmly fastened, but the crowd tore it away bodily, and the light of the torches streamed into the room where, stretched at full length on the bed, his paws crossed and lightly hung down over one end, black as the Pit, and terrible as a demon, was Bagheera. There was one half-minute of desperate silence, as the front ranks of the crowd clawed and tore their way back from the threshold, and in that minute Bagheera raised his head and yawned—elaborately, carefully, and ostentatiously—as he would yawn when he wished to insult an equal. The fringed lips drew back and up; the red tongue curled; the lower jaw dropped and dropped till you could see half-way down the hot gullet; and the gigantic dog-teeth stood clear to the pit of the gums till they rang together, upper and under, with the snick of steel-faced wards shooting home round the edges of a safe. Next instant the street was empty; Bagheera had leaped back through the window, and stood at Mowgli's side, while a yelling, screaming torrent scrambled and tumbled one over another in their panic haste to get to their own huts.

'They will not stir till day comes,' said Bagheera quietly. 'And now?'

The silence of the afternoon sleep seemed to have overtaken the village; but, as they listened, they could hear the sound of heavy grain-boxes being dragged over earthen floors and set down against doors. Bagheera was quite right; the village would not stir till daylight. Mowgli sat still, and thought, and his face grew darker and darker.

'What have I done?' said Bagheera, at last, coming to his feet, fawning.

'Nothing but great good. Watch them now till the day. I sleep.' Mowgli ran off into the Jungle, and dropped like a dead man across a rock, and slept and slept the day round, and the night back again.

When he waked, Bagheera was at his side, and there was a newly-killed buck at his feet. Bagheera watched curiously while Mowgli went to work with his skinning-knife, ate and drank, and turned over with his chin in his hands.

'The man and the woman are come safe within eye-shot of Khanhiwara,' Bagheera said. 'Thy lair mother sent the word back by Chil, the Kite. They found a horse before midnight of the night they were freed, and went very quickly. Is not that well?'

'That is well,' said Mowgli.

'And thy Man-Pack in the village did not stir till the sun was high this morning. Then they ate their food and ran back quickly to their houses.'

'Did they, by chance, see thee?'

'It may have been. I was rolling in the dust before the gate at dawn, and I may have made also some small song to myself. Now, Little Brother, there is nothing more to do. Come hunting with me and Baloo. He has new hives that he wishes to show, and we all desire thee back again as of old. Take off that look which makes even me afraid! The man and woman will not be put into the Red Flower, and all goes well in the Jungle. Is it not true? Let us forget the Man-Pack.'

'They shall be forgotten in a little while. Where does Hathi feed to-night?'

'Where he chooses. Who can answer for the Silent One? But why? What is there Hathi can do which we cannot?'

'Bid him and his three sons come here to me.'

'But, indeed, and truly, Little Brother, it is not—it is not seemly to say "Come," and "Go," to Hathi. Remember, he is the Master of the Jungle, and before the Man-Pack changed the look on thy face, he taught thee the Master-words of the Jungle.'

'That is all one. I have a Master-word for him now. Bid him come to Mowgli, the Frog; and if he does not hear at first, bid him come because of the Sack of the Fields of Bhurtpore.'*

'The Sack of the Fields of Bhurtpore,' Bagheera repeated two or three times to make sure. 'I go. Hathi can but be angry at the worst, and I would give a moon's hunting to hear a Master-word that compels the Silent One.'

He went away, leaving Mowgli stabbing furiously with his skinning-knife into the earth. Mowgli had never seen human blood in his life before till he had seen, and—what meant much more to him—smelled Messua's blood on the thongs that bound her. And Messua had been kind to him, and, so far as he knew anything about love, he loved Messua as completely as he hated the rest of mankind. But deeply as he loathed them, their talk, their cruelty, and their cowardice, not for anything the Jungle had to offer could he bring himself to take a human life, and have that terrible scent of blood back again in his nostrils. His plan was simpler, but much more thorough; and he laughed to himself when he thought that it was one of old Buldeo's tales told under the peepul-tree in the evening that had put the idea into his head.

'It *was* a Master-word,' Bagheera whispered in his ear. 'They were feeding by the river, and they obeyed as though they were bullocks. Look, where they come now!'

Hathi and his three sons had arrived in their usual way, without a sound. The mud of the river was still fresh on their flanks, and Hathi was thoughtfully chewing the green stem of a young plantain-tree that he had gouged up with his tusks. But every line in his vast body showed to Bagheera, who could see things when he came across them, that it was not the Master of the Jungle speaking to a Man-cub, but one who was afraid coming before one who was not. His three sons rolled side by side, behind their father.

Mowgli hardly lifted his head at Hathi gave him 'Good hunting.' He kept him swinging and rocking, and shifting from one foot to another, for a long time before he spoke; and when he opened his mouth it was to Bagheera, not to the elephants.

'I will tell a tale that was told to me by the hunter ye hunted to-day,' said Mowgli. 'It concerns an elephant, old and wise, who fell into a trap, and the sharpened stake in the pit scarred him from a little above his heel to the crest of his shoulder, leaving a white mark.' Mowgli threw out his hand, and as Hathi wheeled the moonlight showed a long white scar on his slaty side, as though he had been struck with a red-hot whip. 'Men came to take him from the trap,' Mowgli continued, 'but he broke his ropes, for he was strong, and went away till his wound was healed.

Then came he, angry, by night to the fields of those hunters. And I remember now that he had three sons. These things happened many, many Rains ago, and very far away—among the fields of Bhurtpore. What came to those fields at the next reaping, Hathi?'

'They were reaped by me and by my three sons,' said Hathi.

'And to the ploughing that follows the reaping?' said Mowgli.

'There was no ploughing,' said Hathi.

'And to the men that live by the green crops on the ground?' said Mowgli.

'They went away.'

'And to the huts in which the men slept?' said Mowgli.

'We tore the roofs to pieces, and the Jungle swallowed up the walls,' said Hathi.

'And what more?' said Mowgli.

'As much good ground as I can walk over in two nights from the east to the west, and from the north to the south as much as I can walk over in three nights, the Jungle took. We let in the Jungle upon five villages; and in those villages, and in their lands, the grazing-ground and the soft crop-grounds, there is not one man to-day who takes his food from the ground. That was the Sack of the Fields of Bhurtpore, which I and my three sons did; and now I ask, Man-cub, how the news of it came to thee?' said Hathi.

'A man told me, and now I see even Buldeo can speak truth. It was well done, Hathi with the white mark; but the second time it shall be done better, for the reason that there is a man to direct. Thou knowest the village of the Man-Pack that cast me out? They are idle, senseless, and cruel; they play with their mouths, and they do not kill the weaker for food, but for sport. When they are full-fed they would throw their own breed into the Red Flower. This I have seen. It is not well that they should live here any more. I hate them!'

'Kill, then,' said the youngest of Hathi's three sons, picking up a tuft of grass, dusting it against his fore-legs, and throwing it away, while his little red eyes glanced furtively from side to side.

'What good are white bones to me?' Mowgli answered angrily. 'Am I the cub of a wolf to play in the sun with a raw head? I have killed Shere Khan, and his hide rots on the Council Rock; but—but I do not know whither Shere Khan is gone, and my stomach is still empty. Now I will take that which I can see and touch. Let in the Jungle upon that village, Hathi!'

Bagheera shivered, and cowered down. He could understand, if the worst came to the worst, a quick rush down the village street, and a right and left blow into a crowd, or a crafty killing of men as they ploughed in the twilight; but this scheme for deliberately blotting out an entire village from the eyes of man and beast frightened him. Now he saw why Mowgli had sent for Hathi. No one but the long-lived elephant could plan and carry through such a war.

'Let them run as the men ran from the fields of Bhurtpore, till we have the rain-water for the only plough, and the noise of the rain on the thick leaves for the pattering of their spindles—till Bagheera and I lair in the house of the Brahmin, and the buck drink at the tank behind the temple! Let in the Jungle, Hathi!'

'But I—but we have no quarrel with them, and it needs the red rage of great pain ere we tear down the places where men sleep,' said Hathi doubtfully.

'Are ye the only eaters of grass in the Jungle? Drive in your peoples. Let the deer and the pig and the nilghai look to it. Ye need never show a hand's breadth of hide till the fields are naked. Let in the Jungle, Hathi!'

'There will be no killing? My tusks were red at the Sack of the Fields of Bhurtpore, and I would not wake that smell again.'

'Nor I. I do not wish even their bones to lie on the clean earth. Let them go and find a fresh lair. They cannot stay here. I have seen and smelled the blood of the woman that gave me food—the woman whom they would have killed but for me. Only the smell of the new grass on their door-steps can take away that smell. It burns in my mouth. Let in the Jungle, Hathi!'

'Ah!' said Hathi. 'So did the scar of the stake burn on my hide till we watched the villages die under in the spring growth. Now I see. Thy war shall be our war. We will let in the Jungle!'

Mowgli had hardly time to catch his breath—he was shaking all over with rage and hate—before the place where the elephants had stood was empty, and Bagheera was looking at him with terror.

'By the Broken Lock that freed me!' said the Black Panther at last. 'Art *thou* the naked thing I spoke for in the Pack when all was young? Master of the Jungle, when my strength goes, speak for me—speak for Baloo—speak for us all! We are cubs before thee! Snapped twigs under foot! Fawns that have lost their doe!'

The idea of Bagheera being a stray fawn upset Mowgli altogether, and he laughed and caught his breath, and sobbed and laughed again, till he had to jump into a pool to make himself stop. Then he swam round and round, ducking in and out of the bars of the moonlight like the frog, his namesake.

By this time Hathi and his three sons had turned, each to one point of the compass, and were striding silently down the valleys a mile away. They went on and on for two days' march—that is to say, a long sixty miles—through the Jungle; and every step they took, and every wave of their trunks, was known and noted and talked over by Mang and Chil and the Monkey People and all the birds. Then they began to feed, and fed quietly for a week or so. Hathi and his sons are like Kaa,* the Rock Python. They never hurry till they have to.

At the end of that time—and none knew who had started it—a rumour went through the Jungle that there was better food and water to be found in such and such a valley. The pig—who, of course, will go to the ends of the earth for a full meal—moved first by companies, scuffling over the rocks, and the deer followed, with the small wild foxes that live on the dead and dying of the herds; and the heavy-shouldered nilghai moved parallel with the deer, and the wild buffaloes of the swamps came after the nilghai. The least little thing would have turned the scattered, straggling droves that grazed and sauntered and drank and grazed again; but whenever there was an alarm some one would rise up and soothe them. At one time it would be Sahi the Porcupine, full of news of good feed just a little farther on; at another Mang would cry cheerily and flap down a glade to show it was all empty; or Baloo, his mouth full of roots, would shamble alongside a wavering line and half frighten, half romp it clumsily back to the proper road. Very many creatures broke back or ran away or lost interest, but very many were left to go forward. At the end of another ten days or so the situation was this. The deer and the pig and the nilghai were milling round and round in a circle of eight or ten miles radius, while the Eaters of Flesh skirmished round its edge. And the centre of that circle was the village, and round the village the crops were ripening, and in the crops sat men on what they call *machans*—platforms like pigeon-perches, made of sticks at the top of four poles—to scare away birds and other stealers. Then the deer were coaxed no more. The Eaters of Flesh were close behind them, and forced them forward and inward.

It was a dark night when Hathi and his three sons slipped down from the Jungle, and broke off the poles of the *machans* with their trunks; they fell as a snapped stalk of hemlock in bloom falls, and the men that tumbled from them heard the deep gurgling of the elephants in their ears. Then the vanguard of the bewildered armies of the deer broke down and flooded into the village grazing-grounds and the ploughed fields; and the sharp-hoofed, rooting wild pig came with them, and what the deer left the pig spoiled, and from time to time an alarm of wolves would shake the herds, and they would rush to and fro desperately, treading down the young barley, and cutting flat the banks of the irrigating channels. Before the dawn broke the pressure on the outside of the circle gave way at one point. The Eaters of Flesh had fallen back and left an open path to the south, and drove upon drove of buck fled along it. Others, who were bolder, lay up in the thickets to finish their meal next night.

But the work was practically done. When the villagers looked in the morning they saw their crops were lost. And that meant death if they did not get away, for they lived year in and year out as near to starvation as the Jungle was near to them. When the buffaloes were sent to graze the hungry brutes found that the deer had cleared the grazing-grounds, and so wandered into the Jungle and drifted off with their wild mates; and when twilight fell the three or four ponies that belonged to the village lay in their stables with their heads beaten in. Only Bagheera could have given those strokes, and only Bagheera would have thought of insolently dragging the last carcass to the open street.

The villagers had no heart to make fires in the fields that night, so Hathi and his three sons went gleaning among what was left; and where Hathi gleans there is no need to follow. The men decided to live on their stored seed-corn until the rains had fallen, and then to take work as servants till they could catch up with the lost year; but as the grain-dealer was thinking of his well-filled crates of corn, and the prices he would levy at the sale of it, Hathi's sharp tusks were picking out the corner of his mud-house, and smashing open the big wicker-chest, leeped* with cow-dung, where the precious stuff lay.

When that last loss was discovered, it was the Brahmin's turn to speak. He had prayed to his own Gods without answer. It might be, he said, that, unconsciously, the village had offended some one of the Gods of the Jungle, for, beyond doubt, the Jungle was against them. So they sent for the head-man of the nearest tribe of wandering Gonds—little, wise, and very black hunters, living in the deep Jungle, whose fathers came of the oldest race in India—the aboriginal owners of the land. They made the Gond welcome with what they had, and he stood on one leg, his bow in his hand, and two or three poisoned arrows stuck through his top-knot, looking half afraid and half contemptuously at the anxious villagers and their ruined fields. They wished to know whether his Gods—the Old Gods—were angry with them, and what sacrifices should be offered. The Gond said nothing, but picked up a trail of the *Karela*,* the vine that bears the bitter wild gourd, and laced it to and fro across the temple door in the face of the staring red Hindu image. Then he pushed with his hand in the open air along the road to Khanhiwara, and went back to his Jungle, and watched the Jungle People drifting through it. He knew that when the Jungle moves only white men can hope to turn it aside.

There was no need to ask his meaning. The wild gourd would grow where they had worshipped their God, and the sooner they saved themselves the better.

But it is hard to tear a village from its moorings. They stayed on as long as any summer food was left to them, and they tried to gather nuts in the Jungle, but shadows with glaring eyes watched them, and rolled before them even at mid-day; and when they ran back afraid to their walls, on the tree-trunks they had passed not five minutes before the bark would be stripped and chiselled with the stroke of some great taloned paw. The more they kept to their village, the bolder grew the wild things that gambolled and bellowed on the grazing-grounds by the Waingunga. They had no time to patch and plaster the rear walls of the empty byres that backed on to the Jungle; the wild pig trampled them down, and the knotty-rooted vines hurried after and threw their elbows over the new-won ground, and the coarse grass bristled behind the vines like the lances of a goblin army following a retreat. The unmarried men ran away first, and carried the news far and near that the village was doomed. Who could fight, they said, against the Jungle, or the Gods of the Jungle, when the very village cobra had left his hole in the platform under the peepul-tree? So their little commerce with the outside world shrunk as the trodden paths across the open grew fewer and fainter. At last the nightly trumpetings of Hathi and his three sons ceased to trouble them; for they had no more to be robbed of. The crop on the ground and the seed in the ground had been taken. The outlying fields were already losing their shape, and it was time to throw themselves on the charity of the English at Khanhiwara.

Native fashion, they delayed their departure from one day to another till the first Rains caught them and the unmended roofs let in a flood, and the grazing-ground stood ankle deep, and all life came on with a rush after the heat of the summer. Then they waded out—men, women, and children—through the blinding hot rain of the morning, but turned naturally for one farewell look at their homes.

They heard, as the last burdened family filed through the gate, a crash of falling beams and thatch behind the walls. They saw a shiny, snaky black trunk lifted for an instant, scattering sodden thatch. It disappeared, and there was another crash, followed by a squeal. Hathi had been plucking off the roofs of the huts as you pluck water-lilies, and a rebounding beam had pricked him. He needed only this to unchain his full strength, for of all things in the Jungle the wild elephant enraged is the most wantonly destructive.* He kicked backward at a mud wall that crumbled at the stroke, and, crumbling, melted to yellow mud under the torrent of rain. Then he wheeled and squealed, and tore through the narrow streets, leaning against the huts right and left, shivering the crazy doors, and crumpling up the eaves; while his three sons raged behind as they had raged at the Sack of the Fields of Bhurtpore.

'The Jungle will swallow these shells,' said a quiet voice in the wreckage. 'It is the outer wall that must lie down,' and Mowgli, with the rain sluicing over his bare shoulders and arms, leaped back from a wall that was settling like a tired buffalo.

'All in good time,' panted Hathi. 'Oh, but my tusks were red at Bhurtpore! To the outer wall, children! With the head! Together! Now!'

The four pushed side by side; the outer wall bulged, split, and fell, and the villagers, dumb with horror, saw the savage, clay-streaked heads of the wreckers in the ragged gap. Then they fled, houseless and foodless, down the valley, as their village, shredded and tossed and trampled, melted behind them.

A month later the place was a dimpled mound, covered with soft, green young stuff; and by the end of the Rains there was the roaring Jungle in full blast on the spot that had been under plough not six months before.

Mowgli's Song Against People

I WILL let loose against you the fleet-footed vines—
I will call in the Jungle to stamp out your lines!
    The roofs shall fade before it,
      The house-beams shall fall,
    And the *Karela*, the bitter *Karela*,
      Shall cover it all!

In the gates of these your councils my people shall sing,
In the doors of these your garners the Bat-folk shall cling;
    And the snake shall be your watchman,
      By a hearthstone unswept;
    For the *Karela*, the bitter *Karela*,
      Shall fruit where ye slept!

Ye shall not see my strikers; ye shall hear them and guess;
By night, before the moon-rise, I will send for my cess,
    And the wolf shall be your herdsman
      By a landmark removed,
    For the *Karela*, the bitter *Karela*,
      Shall seed where ye loved!

I will reap your fields before you at the hands of a host;
Ye shall glean behind my reapers, for the bread that is lost;
    And the deer shall be your oxen
      By a headland untilled,
    For the *Karela*, the bitter *Karela*,
      Shall leaf where ye build!

I have untied against you the club-footed vines,
I have sent in the Jungle to swamp out your lines!
    The trees—the trees are on you!
      The house-beams shall fall,
    And the *Karela*, the bitter *Karela*,
      Shall cover you all!

The Undertakers

When ye say to Tabaqui, 'My Brother!' when ye call the
  Hyena to meat,
Ye may cry the Full Truce with Jacala—the Belly that runs
  on four feet.

Jungle Law

'RESPECT the aged!'

It was a thick voice—a muddy voice that would have
made you shudder—a voice like something soft breaking
in two. There was a quaver in it, a croak and a whine.

'Respect the aged! O Companions of the River—respect
the aged!'

Nothing could be seen on the broad reach of the river
except a little fleet of square-sailed, wooden-pinned
barges, loaded with building-stone, that had just come
under the railway bridge, and were driving down-stream.
They put their clumsy helms over to avoid the sand-bar
made by the scour* of the bridge-piers, and as they passed,
three abreast, the horrible voice began again:

'O Brahmins* of the River—respect the aged and infirm!'

A boatman turned where he sat on the gunwale, lifted
up his hand, said something that was not a blessing, and
the boats creaked on through the twilight. The broad
Indian river, that looked more like a chain of little lakes
than a stream, was as smooth as glass, reflecting the sandy-
red sky in mid-channel, but splashed with patches of
yellow and dusky purple near and under the low banks.
Little creeks ran into the river in the wet season, but now
their dry mouths hung clear above water-line. On the left
shore, and almost under the railway bridge, stood a mud-
and-brick and thatch-and-stick village, whose main street,
full of cattle going back to their byres, ran straight to the
river, and ended in a sort of rude brick pier-head, where
people who wanted to wash could wade in step by step.
That was the Ghaut of the village of Mugger-Ghaut.*

Night was falling fast over the fields of lentils and rice and cotton in the low-lying ground yearly flooded by the river; over the reeds that fringed the elbow of the bend, and the tangled jungle of the grazing-grounds behind the still reeds. The parrots and crows, who had been chattering and shouting over their evening drink, had flown inland to roost, crossing the out-going battalions of the flying-foxes;* and cloud upon cloud of water-birds came whistling and 'honking' to the cover of the reed-beds. There were geese, barrel-headed and black-backed, teal, widgeon, mallard, and sheldrake, with curlews, and here and there a flamingo.

A lumbering Adjutant-crane brought up the rear, flying as though each slow stroke would be his last.

'Respect the aged! Brahmins of the River—respect the aged!'

The Adjutant half turned his head, sheered a little in the direction of the voice, and landed stiffly on the sand-bar below the bridge. Then you saw what a ruffianly brute he really was. His back view was immensely respectable, for he stood nearly six feet high, and looked rather like a very proper bald-headed parson. In front it was different, for his Ally Sloper*-like head and neck had not a feather to them, and there was a horrible raw-skin pouch on his neck under his chin—a hold-all for the things his pick-axe beak might steal. His legs were long and thin and skinny, but he moved them delicately, and looked at them with pride as he preened down his ashy-grey tail-feathers, glanced over the smooth of his shoulder, and stiffened into 'Stand at attention.'

A mangy little Jackal, who had been yapping hungrily on a low bluff, cocked up his ears and tail, and scuttered across the shallows to join the Adjutant.

He was the lowest of his caste—not that the best of jackals were good for much, but this one was peculiarly low, being half a begger, half a criminal—a cleaner-up of village rubbish-heaps, desperately timid or wildly bold, everlastingly hungry, and full of cunning that never did him any good.

'Ugh!' he said, shaking himself dolefully as he landed. 'May the red mange destroy the dogs of this village! I have three bites for each flea upon me, and all because I looked—only looked, mark you—at an old shoe in a cowbyre. Can I eat mud?' He scratched himself under his left ear.

'I heard,' said the Adjutant, in a voice like a blunt saw going through a thick board—'I *heard* there was a newborn puppy in that same shoe.'

'To hear is one thing; to know is another,' said the Jackal, who had a very fair knowledge of proverbs, picked up by listening to men round the village fires of an evening.

'Quite true. So, to make sure, I took care of that puppy while the dogs were busy elsewhere.'

'They were *very* busy,' said the Jackal. 'Well, I must not go to the village hunting for scraps yet awhile. And so there truly was a blind puppy in that shoe?'

'It is here,' said the Adjutant, squinting over his beak at his full pouch. 'A small thing, but acceptable now that charity is dead in the world.'

'Ahai! The world is iron in these days,' wailed the Jackal. Then his restless eye caught the least possible ripple on the water, and he went on quickly: 'Life is hard for us all, and I doubt not that even our excellent master, the Pride of the Ghaut and the Envy of the River——'

'A liar, a flatterer, and a Jackal were all hatched out of the same egg,' said the Adjutant to nobody in particular; for he was rather a fine sort of a liar on his own account when he took the trouble.

'Yes, the Envy of the River,' the Jackal repeated, raising his voice. 'Even he, I doubt not, finds that since the bridge has been built good food is more scarce. But on the other hand, though I would by no means say this to his noble face, he is so wise and so virtuous—as I, alas! am not——'

'When the Jackal owns he is gray, how black must the Jackal be!' muttered the Adjutant. He could not see what was coming.

'That *his* food never fails, and in consequence——'

There was a soft grating sound, as though a boat had just touched in shoal water. The Jackal spun round quickly and faced (it is always best to face) the creature he had been talking about. It was a twenty-four-foot crocodile, cased in what looked like treble-riveted boiler-plate, studded and keeled and crested; the yellow points of his upper teeth just overhanging his beautifully fluted lower jaw. It was the blunt-nosed Mugger of Mugger-Ghaut, older than any man in the village, who had given his name to the village; the demon of the ford before the railway bridge came—murderer, man-eater, and local fetish in one. He lay with his chin in the shallows, keeping his place by an almost invisible rippling of his tail, and well the Jackal knew that one stroke of that same tail in the water would carry the Mugger up the bank with the rush of a steam-engine.

'Auspiciously met, Protector of the Poor!' he fawned, backing at every word. 'A delectable voice was heard, and we came in the hopes of sweet conversation. My tailless presumption, while waiting here, led me, indeed, to speak of thee. It is my hope that nothing was overheard.'

Now the Jackal had spoken just to be listened to, for he knew flattery was the best way of getting things to eat, and the Mugger knew that the Jackal had spoken for this end, and the Jackal knew that the Mugger knew, and the Mugger knew that the Jackal knew that the Mugger knew, and so they were all very contented together.

The old brute pushed and panted and grunted up the bank, mumbling, 'Respect the aged and infirm!' and all the time his little eyes burned like coals under the heavy, horny eyelids on the top of his triangular head, as he shoved his bloated barrel-body along between his crutched legs. Then he settled down, and, accustomed as the Jackal was to his ways, he could not help starting, for the hundredth time, when he saw how exactly the Mugger imitated a log adrift on the bar. He had even taken pains to lie at the exact angle a naturally stranded log would make with the water, having regard to the current of the season at the time and place. All this was only a matter of habit, of course, because the Mugger had come ashore for pleasure; but a crocodile is never quite full, and if the Jackal had been deceived by the likeness he would not have lived to philosophise over it.

'My child, I heard nothing,' said the Mugger, shutting one eye. 'The water was in my ears, and also I was faint with hunger. Since the railway bridge was built my people at my village have ceased to love me; and that is breaking my heart.'

'Ah, shame!' said the Jackal. 'So noble a heart, too! But men are all alike, to my mind.'

'Nay, there are very great differences indeed,' the Mugger answered gently, 'Some are as lean as boat-poles. Others again are fat as young ja—dogs. Never would I causelessly revile men. They are of all fashions, but the long years have shown me that, one with another, they are very good. Men, women, and children—I have no fault to find with them. And remember, child, he who rebukes the World is rebuked by the World.'

'Flattery is worse than an empty tin can in the belly. But that which we have just heard is wisdom,' said the Adjutant, bringing down one foot.

'Consider, though, their ingratitude to this excellent one,' began the Jackal tenderly.

'Nay, nay, not ingratitude!' the Mugger said. 'They do not think for others; that is all. But I have noticed, lying at my station below the ford, that the stairs of the new bridge are cruelly hard to climb, both for old people and young children. The old, indeed, are not so worthy of consideration, but I am grieved—I am truly grieved—on account of the fat children. Still, I think, in a little while, when the newness of the bridge has worn away, we shall see my people's bare brown legs bravely splashing through the ford as before. Then the old Mugger will be honoured again.'

'But surely I saw marigold wreaths floating off the edge of the Ghaut only this noon,' said the Adjutant.

Marigold wreaths are a sign of reverence all India over.

'An error—an error. It was the wife of the sweetmeat-seller. She loses her eyesight year by year, and cannot tell a log from me—the Mugger of the Ghaut. I saw the mistake when she threw the garland, for I was lying at the very foot of the Ghaut, and had she taken another step I might have shown her some little difference. Yet she meant well, and we must consider the spirit of the offering.'

'What good are marigold wreaths when one is on the rubbish-heap?' said the Jackal, hunting for fleas, but keeping one wary eye on his Protector of the Poor.

'True, but they have not yet begun to make the rubbish-heap that shall carry *me*. Five times have I seen the river draw back from the village and make new land at the foot of the street. Five times have I seen the village rebuilt on the banks, and I shall see it built yet five times more. I am no faithless, fish-hunting Gavial,* I, at Kasi to-day and Prayag to-morrow, as the saying is, but the true and constant watcher of the ford. It is not for nothing, child, that the village bears my name, and "he who watches long," as the saying is, "shall at last have his reward."'

'*I* have watched long—very long—nearly all my life, and my reward has been bites and blows,' said the Jackal.

'Ho! ho! ho!' roared the Adjutant.

> 'In August was the Jackal born;
> The Rains fell in September;
> "Now such a fearful flood as this,"
> Says he, "I can't remember!"'

There is one very unpleasant peculiarity about the Adjutant. At uncertain times he suffers from acute attacks of the fidgets or cramp in his legs, and though he is more virtuous to behold than any of the cranes, who are all immensely respectable, he flies off into wild, cripple-stilt war-dances, half opening his wings and bobbing his bald head up and down; while for reasons best known to himself he is very careful to time his worst attacks with his nastiest remarks. At the last word of his song he came to attention again, ten times adjutaunter than before.

The Jackal winced, though he was full three seasons old,

but you cannot resent an insult from a person with a beak a yard long, and the power of driving it like a javelin. The Adjutant was a most notorious coward, but the Jackal was worse.

'We must live before we can learn,' said the Mugger, 'and there is this to say: Little jackals are very common, child, but such a mugger as I am is not common. For all that, I am not proud, since pride is destruction; but take notice, it is Fate, and against his Fate no one who swims or walks or runs should say anything at all. I am well contented with Fate. With good luck, a keen eye, and the custom of considering whether a creek or a backwater has an outlet to it ere you ascend, much may be done.'

'Once I heard that even the Protector of the Poor made a mistake,' said the Jackal viciously.

'True; but there my Fate helped me. It was before I had come to my full growth—before the last famine but three (by the Right and Left of Gunga, how full used the streams to be in those days!). Yes, I was young and unthinking, and when the flood came, who so pleased as I? A little made me very happy then. The village was deep in flood, and I swam above the Ghaut and went far inland, up to the rice-fields, and they were deep in good mud. I remember also a pair of bracelets (glass they were, and troubled me not a little) that I found that evening. Yes, glass bracelets; and, if my memory serves me well, a shoe. I should have shaken off both shoes, but I was hungry. I learned better later. Yes. And so I fed and rested me; but when I was ready to go to the river again the flood had fallen, and I walked through the mud of the main street. Who but I? Came out all my people, priests and women and children, and I looked upon them with benevolence. The mud is not a good place to fight in. Said a boatman, "Get axes and kill him, for he is the Mugger of the ford." "Not so," said the Brahmin. "Look, he is driving the flood before him! He is the godling of the village." Then they threw many flowers at me, and by happy thought one led a goat across the road.'

'How good—how very good is goat!' said the Jackal.

'Hairy—too hairy, and when found in the water more than likely to hide a cross-shaped hook. But the goat I accepted, and went down to the Ghaut in great honour. Later, my Fate sent me the boatman who had desired to cut off my tail with an axe. His boat grounded upon an old shoal which you would not remember.'

'We are not *all* jackals here,' said the Adjutant. 'Was it the shoal made where the stone-boats sank in the year of the great drouth—a long shoal that lasted three floods?'

'There were two,' said the Mugger; 'an upper and a lower shoal.'

'Ay, I forgot. A channel divided them, and later dried up again,' said the Adjutant, who prided himself on his memory.

'On the lower shoal my well-wisher's craft grounded. He was sleeping in the bows, and, half awake, leaped over to his waist—no, it was no more than to his knees—to push off. His empty boat went on and touched again below the next reach, as the river ran then. I followed, because I knew men would come out to drag it ashore.'

'And did they do so?' said the Jackal, a little awe-stricken. This was hunting on a scale that impressed him.

'There and lower down they did. I went no farther, but that gave me three in one day—well-fed *manjis* (boatmen) all, and, except in the case of the last (then I was careless), never a cry to warn those on the bank.'

'Ah, noble sport! But what cleverness and great judgment it requires!' said the Jackal.

'Not cleverness, child, but only thought. A little thought in life is like salt upon rice, as the boatmen say, and I have thought deeply always. The Gavial, my cousin, the fish-eater, has told me how hard it is for him to follow his fish, and how one fish differs from the other, and how he must know them all, both together and apart. I say that is wisdom; but, on the other hand, by cousin, the Gavial, lives among his people. *My* people do not swim in companies, with their mouths out of the water, as Rewa does; not do they constantly rise to the surface of the water, and turn over on their sides, like Mohoo and little

Chapta; nor do they gather in shoals after flood, like Batchua and Chilwa.'

'All are very good eating,' said the Adjutant, clattering his beak.

'So my cousin says, and makes a great to-do over hunting them, but they do not climb the banks to escape his sharp nose. *My* people are otherwise. Their life is on the land, in the houses, among the cattle. I must know what they do, and what they are about to do; and, adding the tail to the trunk, as the saying is, I make up the whole elephant. Is there a green branch and an iron ring hanging over the doorway? The old Mugger knows that a boy has been born in that house, and must some day come down to the Ghaut to play. Is a maiden to be married? The old Mugger knows, for he sees the men carry gifts back and forth; and she, too, comes down to the Ghaut to bathe before her wedding, and—he is there. Has the river changed its channel, and made new land where there was only sand before? The Mugger knows.'

'Now, of what use is that knowledge?' said the Jackal. 'The river has shifted even in my little life.' Indian rivers are nearly always moving about in their beds, and will shift, sometimes, as much as two or three miles in a season, drowning the fields on one bank, and spreading good silt on the other.

'There is no knowledge so useful,' said the Mugger, 'for new land means new quarrels. The Mugger knows. Oho! the Mugger knows. As soon as the water has drained off, he creeps up the little creeks that men think would not hide a dog, and there he waits. Presently comes a farmer saying he will plant cucumbers here, and melons there, in the new land that the river has given him. He feels the good mud with his bare toes. Anon comes another, saying he will put onions, and carrots, and sugar-cane in such and such places. They meet as boats adrift meet, and each rolls his eye at the other under the big blue turban. The old Mugger sees and hears. Each calls the other "Brother," and they go to mark out the boundaries of the new land. The Mugger hurries with them from point to point, shuffling very low through the mud. Now they begin to quarrel! Now they say hot words! Now they pull turbans! Now they lift up their *lathis** (clubs), and, at last, one falls backward into the mud, and the other runs away. When he comes back the dispute is settled, as the iron-bound bamboo of the loser witnesses. Yet they are not grateful to the Mugger. No, they cry "Murder!" and their families fight with sticks, twenty a-side. My people are good people—upland Jats*—Malwais* of the Bêt.* They do not give blows for sport, and, when the fight is done, the old Mugger waits far down the river, out of sight of the village, behind the *kikar*-scrub yonder. Then come they down, my broad-shouldered Jats—eight or nine together under the stars, bearing the dead man upon a bed. They are old men with gray beards, and voices as deep as mine. They light a little fire—ah! how well I know that fire!— and they drink tobacco, and they nod their heads together forward in a ring, or sideways toward the dead man upon the bank. They say the English Law will come with a rope for this matter, and that such a man's family will be ashamed, because such a man must be hanged in the great square of the Jail. Then say the friends of the dead, "Let him hang!" and the talk is all to do over again—once, twice, twenty times in the long night. Then says one, at last, "The fight was a fair fight. Let us take blood-money, a little more than is offered by the slayer, and we will say no more about it." Then do they haggle over the blood-money, for the dead was a strong man, leaving many sons. Yet before *amratvela* (sunrise) they put the fire to him a little, as the custom is, and the dead man comes to me, and *he* says no more about it. Aha! my children, the Mugger knows—the Mugger knows—and my Malwah Jats are a good people!'

'They are too close—too narrow in the hand for my crop,' croaked the Adjutant. 'They waste not the polish on the cow's horn, as the saying is; and, again, who can glean after a Malwah?'

'Ah, I—glean—*them*,' said the Mugger.

'Now, in Calcutta of the South, in the old days,' the

Adjutant went on, 'everything was thrown into the streets, and we picked and chose. Those were dainty seasons. But to-day they keep their streets as clean as the outside of an egg, and my people fly away. To be clean is one thing; to dust, sweep, and sprinkle seven times a day wearies the very Gods themselves.'

'There was a down-country jackal had it from a brother, who told me, that in Calcutta of the South all the jackals were as fat as otters in the Rains,' said the Jackal, his mouth watering at the bare thought of it.

'Ah, but the white-faces are there—the English, and they bring dogs from somewhere down the river in boats—big fat dogs—to keep those same jackals lean,' said the Adjutant.

'They are, then, as hard-hearted as these people? I might have known. Neither earth, sky, nor water shows charity to a jackal. I saw the tents of a white-face last season, after the Rains, and I also took a new yellow bridle to eat. The white-faces do not dress their leather in the proper way. It made me very sick.'

'That was better than my case,' said the Adjutant. 'When I was in my third season, a young and a bold bird, I went down to the river where the big boats come in. The boats of the English are thrice as big as this village.'

'He has been as far as Delhi, and says all the people there walk on their heads,' muttered the Jackal. The Mugger opened his left eye, and looked keenly at the Adjutant.

'It is true,' the big bird insisted. 'A liar only lies when he hopes to be believed. No one who had not seen those boats *could* believe this truth.'

'*That* is more reasonable,' said the Mugger. 'And then?'

'From the insides of this boat they were taking out great pieces of white stuff, which, in a little while, turned to water. Much split off, and fell about on the shore, and the rest they swiftly put into a house with thick walls. But a boatman, who laughed, took a piece no larger than a small dog, and threw it to me. I—all my people—swallow without reflection, and that piece I swallowed as is our custom. Immediately I was afflicted with an excessive cold which, beginning in my crop, ran down to the extreme end of my toes, and deprived me even of speech, while the boatmen laughed at me. Never have I felt such cold. I danced in my grief and amazement till I could recover my breath, and then I danced and cried out against the falseness of this world; and the boatmen derided me till they fell down. The chief wonder of the matter, setting aside that marvellous coldness, was that there was nothing at all in my crop when I had finished my lamentings!'

The Adjutant had done his very best to describe his feelings after swallowing a seven-pound lump of Wenham Lake* ice, off an American ice-ship, in the days before Calcutta made her ice by machinery; but as he did not know what ice was, and as the Mugger and the Jackal knew rather less, the tale missed fire.

'Anything,' said the Mugger, shutting his left eye again—'*anything* is possible that comes out of a boat thrice the size of Mugger-Ghaut. My village is not a small one.'

There was a whistle overhead on the bridge, and the Delhi Mail slid across, all the carriages gleaming with light, and the shadows faithfully following along the river. It clanked away into the dark again; but the Mugger and the Jackal were so well used to it that they never turned their heads.

'Is that anything less wonderful than a boat thrice the size of Mugger-Ghaut?' said the bird, looking up.

'I saw that built, child. Stone by stone I saw the bridge-piers rise, and when the men fell off (they were wondrous sure-footed for the most part—but *when* they fell) I was ready. After the first pier was made they never thought to look down the stream for the body to burn. There, again, I saved much trouble. There was nothing strange in the building of the bridge,' said the Mugger.

'But that which goes across, pulling the roofed carts! That is strange,' the Adjutant repeated.

'It is, past any doubt, a new breed of bullock. Some day it will not be able to keep its foothold up yonder, and will fall as the men did. The old Mugger will be ready.'

The Jackal looked at the Adjutant, and the Adjutant looked at the Jackal. If there was one thing they were more certain of than another, it was that the engine was everything in the wide world except a bullock. The Jackal had watched it time and again from the aloe hedges by the side of the line, and the Adjutant had seen engines since the first locomotive ran in India. But the Mugger had only looked up at the thing from below, where the brass dome seemed rather like a bullock's hump.

'M—yes, a new kind of bullock,' the Mugger repeated ponderously, to make himself quite sure in his own mind; and 'Certainly it is a bullock,' said the Jackal.

'And again it might be——' began the Mugger pettishly.

'Certainly—most certainly,' said the Jackal, without waiting for the other to finish.

'What?' said the Mugger angrily, for he could feel that the others knew more than he did. 'What might it be? *I* never finished my words. You said it was a bullock.'

'It is anything the Protector of the Poor pleases. I am *his* servant—not the servant of the thing that crosses the river.'

'Whatever it is, it is white-face work,' said the Adjutant; 'and for my own part, I would not lie out upon a place so near to it as this bar.'

'You do not know the English as I do,' said the Mugger. 'There was a white-face here when the bridge was built, and he would take a boat in the evenings and shuffle with his feet on the bottom-boards, and whisper: "Is he here? Is he there? Bring me my gun." I could hear him before I could see him—each sound that he made—creaking and puffing and rattling his gun, up and down the river. As surely as I had picked up one of his workmen, and thus saved great expense in wood for the burning, so surely would he come down to the Ghaut, and shout in a loud voice that he would hunt me, and rid the river of me—the Mugger of Mugger-Ghaut! *Me!* Children, I have swum under the bottom of his boat for hour after hour, and heard him fire his gun at logs; and when I was well sure he was wearied, I have risen by his side and snapped my jaws in his face. When the bridge was finished he went away. All the English hunt in that fashion, except when they are hunted.'

'Who hunts the white-faces?' yapped the Jackal excitedly.

'No one now, but I have hunted them in my time.'

'I remember a little of that Hunting. I was young then,' said the Adjutant, clattering his beak significantly.

'I was well established here. My village was being builded for the third time, as I remember, when my cousin, the Gavial, brought me word of rich waters above Benares. At first I would not go, for my cousin, who is a fish-eater, does not always know the good from the bad; but I heard my people talking in the evenings, and what they said made me certain.'

'And what did they say?' the Jackal asked.

'They said enough to make me, the Mugger of Mugger-Ghaut, leave water and take to my feet. I went by night, using the littlest streams as they served me; but it was the beginning of the hot weather, and all streams were low. I crossed dusty roads; I went through tall grass; I climbed hills in the moonlight. Even rocks did I climb, children— consider this well. I crossed the tail of Sirhind,* the waterless, before I could find the set of the little rivers that flow Gungaward. I was a month's journey from my own people and the river that I knew. That was very marvellous!'

'What food on the way?' said the Jackal, who kept his soul in his little stomach, and was not a bit impressed by the Mugger's land travels.

'That which I could find—*cousin*,' said the Mugger slowly, dragging each word.

Now you do not call a man a cousin in India unless you think you can establish some kind of blood-relationship, and as it is only in old fairytales that the Mugger ever marries a jackal, the Jackal knew for what reason he had been suddenly lifted into the Mugger's family circle. If they had been alone he would not have cared, but the Adjutant's eyes twinkled with mirth at the ugly jest.

'Assuredly, Father, I might have known,' said the Jackal. A mugger does not care to be called a father of jackals, and the Mugger of Mugger-Ghaut said as much— and a great deal more which there is no use in repeating here.

'The Protector of the Poor has claimed kinship. How can I remember the precise degree? Moreover, we eat the same food. He has said it,' was the Jackal's reply.

That made matters rather worse, for what the Jackal hinted at was that the Mugger must have eaten his food on that land-march fresh and fresh every day, instead of keeping it by him till it was in a fit and proper condition, as every self-respecting mugger and most wild beasts do when they can. Indeed, one of the worst terms of contempt along the River-bed is 'eater of fresh meat.' It is nearly as bad as calling a man a cannibal.

'That food was eaten thirty seasons ago,' said the Adjutant quietly. 'If we talk for thirty seasons more it will never come back. Tell us now, what happened when the good waters were reached after thy most wonderful land journey. If we listened to the howling of every jackal the business of the town would stop, as the saying is.'

The Mugger must have been grateful for the interruption, because he went on, with a rush:

'By the Right and Left of Gunga! when I came there never did I see such waters!'

'Were they better, then, than the big flood of last season?' said the Jackal.

'Better! That flood was no more than comes every five years—a handful of drowned strangers, some chickens, and a dead bullock in muddy water with cross-currents. But the season I think of, the river was low, smooth, and even, and, as the Gavial had warned me, the dead English came down, touching each other. I got my girth in that season—my girth and my depth. From Agra, by Etawah and the broad waters by Allahabad——'

'Oh, the eddy that set under the walls of the fort at

Allahabad!' said the Adjutant. 'They came in there like widgeon to the reeds, and round and round they swung—thus!'

He went off into his horrible dance again, while the Jackal looked on enviously. He naturally could not remember the terrible year of the Mutiny they were talking about. The Mugger continued:

'Yes, by Allahabad one lay still in the slack-water and let twenty go by to pick one; and, above all, the English were not cumbered with jewellery and nose-rings and anklets as my women are nowadays. To delight in ornaments is to end with a rope for necklace, as the saying is. All the muggers of all the rivers grew fat then, but it was my Fate to be fatter than them all. The news was that the English were being hunted into the rivers, and by the Right and Left of Gunga! we believed it was true. So far as I went south I believed it to be true; and I went down-stream beyond Monghyr and the tombs that look over the river.'

'I know that place,' said the Adjutant. 'Since those days Monghyr is a lost city. Very few live there now.'

'Thereafter I worked up-stream very slowly and lazily, and a little above Monghyr there came down a boatful of white-faces—alive! They were, as I remember, women, lying under a cloth spread over sticks, and crying aloud. There was never a gun fired at us, the watchers of the fords in those days. All the guns were busy elsewhere. We could hear them day and night inland, coming and going as the wind shifted. I rose up full before the boat, because I had never seen white-faces alive, though I knew them well—otherwise. A naked white child kneeled by the side of the boat, and, stooping over, must needs try to trail his hands in the river. It is a pretty thing to see how a child loves running water. I had fed that day, but there was yet a little unfilled space within me. Still, it was for sport and not for food that I rose at the child's hands. They were so clear a mark that I did not even look when I closed; but they were so small that though my jaws rang true—I am sure of that—the child drew them up swiftly, unhurt. They must have passed between tooth and tooth—those small white hands. I should have caught him cross-wise at the elbows; but, as I said, it was only for sport and desire to see new things that I rose at all. They cried out one after another in the boat, and presently I rose again to watch them. The boat was too heavy to push over. They were only women, but he who trusts a woman will walk on duckweed in a pool, as the saying is: and by the Right and Left of Gunga, that is truth!'

'Once a woman gave me some dried skin from a fish,' said the Jackal. 'I had hoped to get her baby, but horse-food is better than the kick of a horse, as the saying is. What did thy woman do?'

'She fired at me with a short gun of a kind I have never seen before or since. Five times, one after another' (the Mugger must have met with an old-fashioned revolver); 'and I stayed open-mouthed and gaping, my head in the smoke. Never did I see such a thing. Five times, as swiftly as I wave my tail—thus!'

The Jackal, who had been growing more and more interested in the story, had just time to leap back as the huge tail swung by like a scythe.

'Not before the fifth shot,' said the Mugger, as though he had never dreamed of stunning one of his listeners—'not before the fifth shot did I sink, and I rose in time to hear a boatman telling all those white women that I was most certainly dead. One bullet had gone under a neck-plate of mine. I know not if it is there still, for the reason I cannot turn my head. Look and see, child. It will show that my tale is true.'

'I?' said the Jackal. 'Shall an eater of old shoes, a bone-cracker, presume to doubt the word of the Envy of the River? May my tail be bitten off by blind puppies if the shadow of such a thought has crossed my humble mind! The Protector of the Poor has condescended to inform me, his slave, that once in his life he has been wounded by a woman. That is sufficient, and I will tell the tale to all my children, asking for no proof.'

'Over-much civility is sometimes no better than over-much discourtesy, for, as the saying is, one can choke a

guest with curds. I do *not* desire that any children of thine
should know that the Mugger of Mugger-Ghaut took his
only wound from a woman. They will have much else to
think of if they get their meat as miserably as does their
father.'

'It is forgotten long ago! It was never said! There never
was a white woman! There was no boat! Nothing whatever
happened at all.'

The Jackal waved his brush to show how completely
everything was wiped out of his memory, and sat down
with an air.

'Indeed, very many things happened,' said the Mugger,
beaten in his second attempt that night to get the better of
his friend. (Neither bore malice, however. Eat and be
eaten was fair law along the river, and the Jackal came in
for his share of plunder when the Mugger had finished a
meal.) 'I left that boat and went up-stream, and, when I
had reached Arrah and the back-waters behind it, there
were no more dead English. The river was empty for a
while. Then came one or two dead, in red coats, not
English, but of one kind all—Hindus and Purbeeahs*—
then five and six abreast, and at last, from Arrah to the
North beyond Agra, it was as though whole villages had
walked into the water. They came out of little creeks one
after another, as the logs come down in the Rains. When
the river rose they rose also in companies from the shoals
they had rested upon; and the falling flood dragged them
with it across the fields and through the Jungle by the long
hair. All night, too, going North, I heard the guns, and by
day the shod feet of men crossing fords, and that noise
which a heavy cart-wheel makes on sand under water; and
every ripple brought more dead. At last even I was afraid,
for I said: "If this thing happen to men, how shall the
Mugger of Mugger-Ghaut escape?" There were boats,
too, that came up behind me without sails, burning
continually, as the cotton-boats sometimes burn, but
never sinking.'

'Ah!' said the Adjutant. 'Boats like those come to

Calcutta of the South. They are tall and black, they beat up the water behind them with a tail, and they——'

'Are thrice as big as my village. *My* boats were low and white; they beat up the water on either side of them, and were no larger than the boats of one who speaks truth should be. They made me very afraid, and I left water and went back to this my river, hiding by day and walking by night, when I could not find little streams to help me. I came to my village again, but I did not hope to see any of my people there. Yet they were ploughing and sowing and reaping, and going to and fro in their fields, as quietly as their own cattle.'

'Was there still good food in the river?' said the Jackal.

'More than I had any desire for. Even I—and I do not eat mud—even I was tired, and, as I remember, a little frightened of this constant coming down of the silent ones. I heard my people say in my village that all the English were dead; but those that came, face down, with the current were *not* English, as my people saw. Then my people said that it was best to say nothing at all, but to pay the tax and plough the land. After a long time the river cleared, and those that came down it had been clearly drowned by the floods, as I could well see; and though it was not so easy then to get food, I was heartily glad of it. A little killing here and there is no bad thing—but even the Mugger is sometimes satisfied, as the saying is.'

'Marvellous! Most truly marvellous!' said the Jackal. 'I am become fat through merely hearing about so much good eating. And afterward what, if it be permitted to ask, did the Protector of the Poor do?'

'I said to myself—and by the Right and Left of Gunga! I locked my jaws on that vow—I said I would never go roving any more. So I lived by the Ghaut, very close to my own people, and I watched over them year after year; and they loved me so much that they threw marigold wreaths at my head whenever they saw it lift. Yes, and my Fate has been very kind to me, and the river is good enough to respect my poor and infirm presence; only——'

'No one is all happy from his beak to his tail,' said the

Adjutant sympathetically. 'What does the Mugger of Mugger-Ghaut need more?'

'That little white child which I did not get,' said the Mugger, with a deep sigh. 'He was very small, but I have not forgotten. I am old now, but before I die it is my desire to try one new thing. It is true they are a heavy-footed, noisy, and foolish people, and the sport would be small, but I remember the old days above Benares, and, if the child lives, he will remember still. It may be he goes up and down the bank of some river, telling how he once passed his hands between the teeth of the Mugger of Mugger-Ghaut, and lived to make a tale of it. My Fate has been very kind, but that plagues me sometimes in my dreams—the thought of the little white child in the bows of that boat.' He yawned, and closed his jaws. 'And now I will rest and think. Keep silent, my children, and respect the aged.'

He turned stiffly, and shuffled to the top of the sand-bar, while the Jackal drew back with the Adjutant to the shelter of a tree stranded on the end nearest the railway bridge.

'That was a pleasant and profitable life,' he grinned, looking up inquiringly at the bird who towered above him. 'And not once, mark you, did he think fit to tell me where a morsel might have been left along the banks. Yet I have told *him* a hundred times of good things wallowing downstream. How true is the saying, "All the world forgets the Jackal and the Barber when the news has been told!" Now he is going to sleep! *Arrh!*'

'How can a Jackal hunt with a Mugger?' said the Adjutant coolly. 'Big thief and little thief; it is easy to say who gets the pickings.'

The Jackal turned, whining impatiently, and was going to curl himself up under the tree-trunk, when suddenly he cowered, and looked up through the draggled branches at the bridge almost above his head.

'What now?' said the Adjutant, opening his wings uneasily.

'Wait till we see. The wind blows from us to them, but they are not looking for us—those two men.'

'Men, is it? My office protects me. All India knows I am holy.' The Adjutant, being a first-class scavenger, is allowed to go where he pleases, and so this one never flinched.

'I am not worth a blow from anything better than an old shoe,' said the Jackal, and listened again. 'Hark to that footfall!' he went on. 'That was no country leather, but the shod foot of a white-face. Listen again! Iron hits iron up there! It is a gun! Friend, those heavy-footed, foolish English are coming to speak with the Mugger.'

'Warn him, then. He was called Protector of the Poor by some one not unlike a starving Jackal but a little time ago.'

'Let my cousin protect his own hide. He has told me again and again there is nothing to fear from the white-faces. They must be white-faces. Not a villager of Mugger-Ghaut would dare to come after him. See, I said it was a gun! Now, with good luck, we shall feed before daylight. He cannot hear well out of water, and—this time it is not a woman!'

A shiny barrel glittered for a minute in the moonlight on the girders. The Mugger was lying on the sand-bar as still as his own shadow, his fore-foot spread out a little, his head dropped between them, snoring like a—mugger.

A voice on the bridge whispered: 'It's an odd shot—straight down almost—but as safe as houses. Better try behind the neck. Golly! what a brute! The villagers will be wild if he's shot, though. He's the *deota* [godling] of these parts.'

'Don't care a rap,' another voice answered; 'he took about fifteen of my best coolies while the bridge was building, and it's time he was put a stop to. I've been after him in a boat for weeks. Stand by with the Martini* as soon as I've given him both barrels of this.'

'Mind the kick, then. A double four-bore's* no joke.'

'That's for him to decide. Here goes!'

There was a roar like the sound of a small cannon (the biggest sort of elephant-rifle is not very different from some artillery), and a double streak of flame, followed by the stinging crack of a Martini, whose long bullet makes nothing of a crocodile's plates. But the explosive bullets did the work. One of them struck just behind the Mugger's neck, a hand's-breadth to the left of the backbone, while the other burst a little lower down, at the beginning of the tail. In ninety-nine cases out of a hundred a mortally-wounded crocodile can scramble to deep water and get away; but the Mugger of Mugger-Ghaut was literally broken into three pieces. He hardly moved his head before the life went out of him, and he lay as flat as the Jackal.

'Thunder and lightning! Lightning and thunder!' said that miserable little beast. 'Has the thing that pulls the covered carts over the bridge tumbled at last?'

'It is no more than a gun,' said the Adjutant, though his very tail-feathers quivered. 'Nothing more than a gun. He is certainly dead. Here come the white-faces.'

The two Englishmen had hurried down from the bridge and across to the sand-bar, where they stood admiring the length of the Mugger. Then a native with an axe cut off the big head, and four men dragged it across the spit.

'The last time that I had my hand in a Mugger's mouth,' said one of the Englishmen, stooping down (he was the man who had built the bridge), 'it was when I was about five years old—coming down the river by boat to Monghyr. I was a Mutiny baby, as they call it. Poor mother was in the boat, too, and she often told me how she fired dad's old pistol at the beast's head.'

'Well, you've certainly had your revenge on the chief of the clan—even if the gun has made your nose bleed. Hi, you boatmen! Haul that head up the bank, and we'll boil it for the skull. The skin's too knocked about to keep. Come along to bed now. This was worth sitting up all night for, wasn't it?'

Curiously enough, the Jackal and the Adjutant made the very same remark not three minutes after the men had left.

A Ripple Song*

Once a ripple came to land
  In the golden sunset burning—
Lapped against a maiden's hand,
  By the ford returning.

*Dainty foot and gentle breast—
Here, across, be glad and rest.
'Maiden, wait,' the ripple saith;
'Wait awhile, for I am Death!'*

'Where my lover calls I go—
  Shame it were to treat him coldly—
'Twas a fish that circled so,
  Turning over boldly.'

*Dainty foot and tender heart,
Wait the loaded ferry-cart.
'Wait, ah, wait!' the ripple saith;
'Maiden, wait, for I am Death!'*

'When my lover calls I haste—
  Dame Disdain was never wedded!'
Ripple-ripple round her waist,
  Clear the current eddied.

*Foolish heart and faithful hand,
Little feet that touched no land,
Far away the ripple sped,
Ripple—ripple—running red!*

The King's Ankus*

These are the Four that are never content, that have never
been filled since the Dews began—
Jacala's mouth, and the glut of the Kite, and the hands of
the Ape, and the Eyes of Man.

Jungle Saying

KAA, the big Rock Python, had changed his skin for
perhaps the two-hundredth* time since his birth; and
Mowgli, who never forgot that he owed his life to Kaa for
a night's work at Cold Lairs,* which you may perhaps
remember, went to congratulate him. Skin-changing
always makes a snake moody and depressed till the new
skin begins to shine and look beautiful. Kaa never made
fun of Mowgli any more, but accepted him, as the other
Jungle People did, for the Master of the Jungle, and
brought him all the news that a python of his size would
naturally hear. What Kaa did not know about the Middle
Jungle, as they call it,—the life that runs close to the earth
or under it, the boulder, burrow, and the tree-bole life,—
might have been written upon the smallest of his scales.

That afternoon Mowgli was sitting in the circle of Kaa's
great coils, fingering the flaked and broken old skin that
lay all looped and twisted among the rocks just as Kaa had
left it. Kaa had very courteously packed himself under
Mowgli's broad, bare shoulders, so that the boy was really
resting in a living arm-chair.

'Even to the scales of the eyes it is perfect,' said Mowgli,
under his breath, playing with the old skin. 'Strange to see
the covering of one's own head at one's own feet!'

'Ay, but I lack feet,' said Kaa; 'and since this is the
custom of all my people, I do not find it strange. Does thy
skin never feel old and harsh?'

'Then go I and wash, Flathead; but, it is true, in the
great heats I have wished I could slough my skin without
pain, and run skinless.'

'I wash, and *also* I take off my skin. How looks the new coat?'

Mowgli ran his hand down the diagonal checkerings of the immense back. 'The Turtle is harder-backed, but not so gay,' he said judgmatically. 'The Frog, my name-bearer, is more gay, but not so hard. It is very beautiful to see—like the mottling in the mouth of a lily.'

'It needs water. A new skin never comes to full colour before the first bath. Let us go bathe.'

'I will carry thee,' said Mowgli; and he stooped down, laughing, to lift the middle section of Kaa's great body, just where the barrel was thickest. A man might just as well have tried to heave up a two-foot water-main; and Kaa lay still, puffing with quiet amusement. Then the regular evening game began—the Boy in the flush of his great strength, and the Python in his sumptuous new skin, standing up one against the other for a wrestling match—a trial of eye and strength. Of course, Kaa could have crushed a dozen Mowglis if he had let himself go; but he played carefully, and never loosed one-tenth of his power. Ever since Mowgli was strong enough to endure a little rough handling, Kaa had taught him this game, and it suppled his limbs as nothing else could. Sometimes Mowgli would stand lapped almost to his throat in Kaa's shifting coils, striving to get one arm free and catch him by the throat. Then Kaa would give way limply, and Mowgli, with both quick-moving feet, would try to cramp the purchase of that huge tail as it flung backward feeling for a rock or a stump. They would rock to and fro, head to head, each waiting for his chance, till the beautiful, statue-like group melted in a whirl of black-and-yellow coils and struggling legs and arms, to rise up again and again. 'Now! now! now!' said Kaa, making feints with his head that even Mowgli's quick hand could not turn aside. 'Look! I touch thee here, Little Brother! Here, and here! Are thy hands numb? Here again!'

The game always ended in one way—with a straight, driving blow of the head that knocked the boy over and over. Mowgli could never learn the guard for that lightning lunge, and, as Kaa said, there was not the least use in trying.

'Good hunting!' Kaa grunted at last; and Mowgli, as usual, was shot away half a dozen yards, gasping and laughing. He rose with his fingers full of grass, and followed Kaa to the wise snake's pet bathing-place—a deep, pitchy-black pool surrounded with rocks, and made interesting by sunken tree-stumps. The boy slipped in, Jungle-fashion, without a sound, and dived across; rose, too, without a sound, and turned on his back, his arms behind his head, watching the moon rising above the rocks, and breaking up her reflection in the water with his toes. Kaa's diamond-shaped head cut the pool like a razor, and came out to rest on Mowgli's shoulder. They lay still, soaking luxuriously in the cool water.

'It is *very* good,' said Mowgli at last, sleepily. 'Now, in the Man-Pack, at this hour, as I remember, they laid them down upon hard pieces of wood in the inside of a mud-trap, and, having carefully shut out all the clean winds, drew foul cloth over their heavy heads and made evil songs through their noses. It is better in the Jungle.'

A hurrying cobra slipped down over a rock and drank, gave them 'Good hunting!' and went away.

'Sssh!' said Kaa, as though he had suddenly remembered something. 'So the Jungle gives thee all that thou hast ever desired, Little Brother?'

'Not all,' said Mowgli, laughing; 'else there would be a new and strong Shere Khan to kill once a moon. Now, I could kill with my own hands, asking no help of buffaloes.* And also I have wished the sun to shine in the middle of the Rains, and the Rains to cover the sun in the deep of summer; and also I have never gone empty but I wished that I had killed a goat; and also I have never killed a goat but I wished it had been buck; nor buck but I wished it had been nilghai. But thus do we feel, all of us.'

'Thou has no other desire?' the big snake demanded.

'What more can I wish? I have the Jungle, and the favour of the jungle! Is there more anywhere between sunrise and sunset?'

'Now, the Cobra said——' Kaa began.

'What cobra? He that went away just now said nothing. He was hunting.'

'It was another.'

'Hast thou many dealings with the Poison People? I give them their own path. They carry death in the fore-tooth, and that is not good—for they are so small. But what hood is this thou hast spoken with?'

Kaa rolled slowly in the water like a steamer in a beam sea. 'Three or four moons since,' said he, 'I hunted in Cold Lairs, which place thou hast not forgotten. And the thing I hunted fled shrieking past the tanks and to that house whose side I once broke for thy sake, and ran into the ground.'

'But the people of Cold Lairs do not live in burrows.' Mowgli knew that Kaa was talking of the Monkey People.

'This thing was not living, but seeking to live,' Kaa replied, with a quiver of his tongue. 'He ran into a burrow that led very far. I followed, and having killed, I slept. When I waked I went forward.'

'Under the earth?'

'Even so, coming at last upon a White Hood* [a white cobra], who spoke of things beyond my knowledge, and showed me many things I had never before seen.'

'New game? Was it good hunting?' Mowgli turned quickly on his side.

'It was no game, and would have broken all my teeth; but the White Hood said that a man—he spoke as one that knew the breed—that a man would give the breath under his ribs for only the sight of those things.'

'We will look,' said Mowgli. 'I now remember that I was once a man.'

'Slowly—slowly. It was haste killed the Yellow Snake that ate the sun. We two spoke together under the earth, and I spoke of thee, naming thee as a man. Said the White Hood (and he is indeed as old as the Jungle): "It is long since I have seen a man. Let him come, and he shall see all these things, for the least of which very many men would die."'

'That *must* be new game. And yet the Poison People do not tell us when game is afoot. They are an unfriendly folk.'

'It is *not* game. It is—it is—I cannot say what it is.'

'We will go there. I have never seen a White Hood, and I wish to see the other things. Did he kill them?'

'They are all dead things. He says he is the keeper of them all.'

'Ah! As a wolf stands above meat he has taken to his own lair. Let us go.'

Mowgli swam to bank, rolled on the grass to dry himself, and the two set off for Cold Lairs, the deserted city of which you may have heard. Mowgli was not the least afraid of the Monkey People in those days, but the Monkey People had the liveliest horror of Mowgli. Their tribes, however, were raiding in the Jungle, and so Cold Lairs stood empty and silent in the moonlight. Kaa led up to the ruins of the queen's pavilion that stood on the terrace, slipped over the rubbish, and dived down the half-choked staircase that went underground from the centre of the pavilion. Mowgli gave the snake-call,—'We be of one blood, ye and I,'—and followed on his hands and knees. They crawled a long distance down a sloping passage that turned and twisted several times, and at last came to where the root of some great tree, growing thirty feet overhead, had forced out a solid stone in the wall. They crept through the gap, and found themselves in a large vault, whose domed roof had been also broken away by tree-roots so that a few streaks of light dropped down into the darkness.

'A safe lair,' said Mowgli, rising to his firm feet, 'but over-far to visit daily. And now what do we see?'

'Am I nothing?' said a voice in the middle of the vault; and Mowgli saw something white move till, little by little, there stood up the hugest cobra he had ever set eyes on—a creature nearly eight feet long, and bleached by being in darkness to an old ivory-white. Even the spectacle-marks of his spread hood had faded to faint yellow. His eyes were as red as rubies, and altogether he was most wonderful.

'Good hunting!' said Mowgli, who carried his manners with his knife, and that never left him.

'What of the city?' said the White Cobra, without answering the greeting. 'What of the great, the walled city—the city of a hundred elephants and twenty thousand horses, and cattle past counting—the city of the King of Twenty Kings? I grow deaf here, and it is long since I heard their war-gongs.'

'The Jungle is above our heads,' said Mowgli. 'I know only Hathi and his sons among elephants. Bagheera has slain all the horses in one village, and—what is a King?'

'I told thee,' said Kaa softly to the Cobra,—'I told thee, four moons ago, that thy city was not.'

'The city—the great city of the forest whose gates are guarded by the King's towers—can never pass. They builded it before my father's father came from the egg, and it shall endure when my son's sons are as white as I! Salomdhi,* son of Chandrabija,* son of Viyeja,* son of Yegasuri,* made it in the days of Bappa Rawal.* Whose cattle are *ye*?'

'It is a lost trail,' said Mowgli, turning to Kaa. 'I know not his talk.'

'Nor I. He is very old. Father of Cobras, there is only the Jungle here, as it has been since the beginning.'

'Then who is *he*,' said the White Cobra, 'sitting down before me, unafraid, knowing not the name of the King, talking our talk through a man's lips? Who is he with the knife and the snake's tongue?'

'Mowgli they call me,' was the answer. 'I am of the Jungle. The wolves are my people, and Kaa here is my brother. Father of Cobras, who art thou?'

'I am the Warden of the King's Treasure. Kurrun Raja* builded the stone above me, in the days when my skin was dark, that I might teach death to those who came to steal. Then they let down the treasure through the stone, and I heard the song of the Brahmins my masters.'

'Umm!' said Mowgli to himself. 'I have dealt with one Brahmin already, in the Man-Pack, and—I know what I know. Evil comes here in a little.'

'Five times since I came here has the stone been lifted, but always to let down more, and never to take away. There are no riches like these riches—the treasures of a hundred kings. But it is long and long since the stone was last moved, and I think that my city has forgotten.'

'There is no city. Look up. Yonder are roots of the great trees tearing the stones apart. Trees and men do not grow together,' Kaa insisted.

'Twice and thrice have men found their way here,' the White Cobra answered savagely; 'but they never spoke till I came upon them groping in the dark, and then they cried only a little time. But *ye* come with lies, Man and Snake both, and would have me believe the city is not, and that my wardship ends. Little do men change in the years. But *I* change never! Till the stone is lifted, and the Brahmins come down singing the songs that I know, and feed me with warm milk, and take me to the light again, I—I—*I*, and no other, am the Warden of the King's Treasure! The city is dead, ye say, and here are the roots of the trees? Stoop down, then, and take what ye will. Earth has no treasure like to these. Man with the snake's tongue, if thou canst go alive by the way that thou hast entered at, the lesser Kings will be thy servants!'

'Again the trail is lost,' said Mowgli coolly. 'Can any jackal* have burrowed so deep and bitten this great White Hood? He is surely mad. Father of Cobras, I see nothing here to take away.'

'By the Gods of the Sun and Moon, it is the madness of death upon the boy!' hissed the Cobra. 'Before thine eyes close I will allow thee this favour. Look though, and see what man has never seen before!'

'They do not well in the Jungle who speak to Mowgli of favours,' said the boy, between his teeth; 'but the darkness changes all, as I know. I will look, if that please thee.'

He stared with puckered-up eyes round the vault, and then lifted up from the floor a handful of something that glittered.

'Oho!' said he, 'this is like the stuff they play with in the Man-Pack: only this is yellow and the other was brown.'

He let the gold pieces fall, and moved forward. The floor of the vault was buried some five or six feet deep in coined gold and silver that had burst from the sacks it had been originally stored in, and, in the long years, the metal had packed and settled as sand packs at low tide. On it and in it, and rising through it, as wrecks lift through the sand, were jewelled elephant-howdahs* of embossed silver, studded with plates of hammered gold, and adorned with carbuncles and turquoises. There were palanquins and litters for carrying queens, framed and braced with silver and enamel, with jade-handled poles and amber curtain-rings; there were golden candlesticks hung with pierced emeralds that quivered on the branches; there were studded images, five feet high, of forgotten gods, silver with jewelled eyes; there were coats of mail, gold inlaid on steel, and fringed with rotted and blackened seed-pearls; there were helmets, crested and beaded with pigeon's-blood rubies; there were shields of lacquer, of tortoise-shell and rhinoceros-hide, strapped and bossed with red gold and set with emeralds at the edge; there were sheaves of diamond-hilted swords, daggers, and hunting-knives; there were golden sacrificial bowls and ladles, and portable altars of a shape that never sees the light of day; there were jade cups and bracelets; there were incense-burners, combs, and pots for perfume, henna, and eye-powder, all in embossed gold; there were nose-rings, armlets, head-bands, finger-rings, and girdles past any counting; there were belts, seven fingers broad, of square-cut diamonds and rubies, and wooden boxes, trebly clamped with iron, from which the wood had fallen away in powder, showing the pile of uncut star-sapphires, opals, cat's-eyes, sapphires, rubies, diamonds, emeralds, and garnets within.

The White Cobra was right. No mere money would begin to pay the value of this treasure, the sifted pickings of centuries of war, plunder, trade, and taxation. The coins alone were priceless, leaving out of count all the precious stones; and the dead weight of the gold and silver alone might be two of three hundred tons. Every native ruler in India to-day, however poor, has a hoard to which he is always adding; and though, once in a long while, some enlightened prince may send off forty or fifty bullock-cart loads of silver to be exchanged for Government securities, the bulk of them keep their treasure and the knowledge of it very closely to themselves.

But Mowgli naturally did not understand what these things meant. The knives interested him a little, but they did not balance so well as his own, and so he dropped them. At last he found something really fascinating laid on the front of a howdah half buried in the coins. It was a three-foot ankus, or elephant-goad—something like a small boat-hook. The top was one round, shining ruby, and eight inches of the handle below it were studded with rough turquoises close together, giving a most satisfactory grip. Below them was a rim of jade with a flower-pattern running round it—only the leaves were emeralds, and the blossoms were rubies sunk in the cool, green stone. The rest of the handle was a shaft of pure ivory, while the point—the spike and hook—was gold-inlaid steel with pictures of elephant-catching; and the pictures attracted Mowgli, who saw that they had something to do with his friend Hathi the Silent.

The White Cobra had been following him closely.

'Is this not worth dying to behold?' he said. 'Have I not done thee a great favour?'

'I do not understand,' said Mowgli. 'The things are hard and cold, and by no means good to eat. But this'—he lifted the ankus—'I desire to take away, that I may see it in the sun. Thou sayest they are all thine? Wilt thou give it to me, and I will bring thee frogs to eat?'

The White Cobra fairly shook with evil delight. 'Assuredly I will give it,' he said. 'All that is here I will give thee—till thou goest away.'

'But I go now. This place is dark and cold, and I wish to take the thorn-pointed thing to the Jungle.'

'Look by thy foot! What is that there?'

Mowgli picked up something white and smooth. 'It is the bone of a man's head,' he said quietly. 'And here are two more.'

'They came to take the treasure away many years ago. I spoke to them in the dark, and they lay still.'

'But what do I need of this that is called treasure? If thou wilt give me the ankus to take away, it is good hunting. If not, it is good hunting none the less. I do not fight with the Poison People, and I was also taught the Master-word of thy tribe.'

'There is but one Master-word here. It is mine!'

Kaa flung himself forward with blazing eyes. 'Who bade me bring the Man?' he hissed.

'I surely,' the old Cobra lisped. 'It is long since I have seen Man, and this Man speaks our tongue.'

'But there was no talk of killing. How can I go to the Jungle and say that I have led him to his death?' said Kaa.

'I talk not of killing till the time. And as to thy going or not going, there is the hole in the wall. Peace, now, thou fat monkey-killer! I have but to touch thy neck, and the Jungle will know thee no longer. Never Man came here that went away with the breath under his ribs. I am the Warden of the Treasure of the King's City!'

'But, thou white worm of the dark, I tell thee there is neither king nor city! The Jungle is all about us!' cried Kaa.

'There is still the Treasure. But this can be done. Wait awhile, Kaa of the Rocks, and see the boy run. There is room for great sport here. Life is good. Run to and fro awhile, and make sport, boy!'

Mowgli put his hand on Kaa's head quietly.

'The white thing has dealt with men of the Man-Pack until now. He does not know me,' he whispered. 'He has asked for this hunting. Let him have it.' Mowgli had been standing with the ankus held point down. He flung it from him quickly, and it dropped crossways just behind the great snake's hood, pinning him to the floor. In a flash, Kaa's weight was upon the writhing body, paralysing it from hood to tail. The red eyes burned, and the six spare inches of the head struck furiously right and left.

'Kill!' said Kaa, as Mowgli's hand went to his knife.

'No,' he said, as he drew the blade; 'I will never kill

again save for food. But look you, Kaa!' He caught the snake behind the hood, forced the mouth open with the blade of the knife, and showed the terrible poison-fangs of the upper jaw lying black and withered in the gum. The White Cobra had outlived his poison, as a snake will.

'*Thuu*'* ('It is dried up'),[1] said Mowgli; and motioning Kaa away, he picked up the ankus, setting the White Cobra free.

'The King's Treasure needs a new Warden,' he said gravely. 'Thuu, thou hast not done well. Run to and fro and make sport, Thuu!'

'I am ashamed. Kill me!' hissed the White Cobra.

'There has been too much talk of killing. We will go now. I take the thorn-pointed thing, Thuu, because I have fought and worsted thee.'

'See, then, that the thing does not kill thee at last. It is Death! Remember, it is Death! There is enough in that thing to kill the men of all my city. Not long wilt thou hold it, Jungle Man, nor he who takes it from thee. They will kill, and kill, and kill for its sake! My strength is dried up, but the ankus will do my work. It is Death! It is Death! It is Death!'

Mowgli crawled out through the hole into the passage again, and the last that he saw was the White Cobra striking furiously with his harmless fangs at the stolid golden faces of the gods that lay on the floor, and hissing, 'It is Death!'

They were glad to get to the light of day once more; and when they were back in their own Jungle and Mowgli made the ankus glitter in the morning light, he was almost as pleased as though he had found a bunch of new flowers to stick in his hair.

'This is brighter than Bagheera's eyes,' he said delightedly, as he twirled the ruby. 'I will show it to him; but what did the Thuu mean when he talked of death?'

'I cannot say. I am sorrowful to my tail's tail that he felt not thy knife. There is always evil at Cold Lairs—above

---

[1] Literally, a rotted out tree-stump.

ground or below. But now I am hungry. Dost thou hunt with me this dawn?' said Kaa.

'No; Bagheera must see this thing. Good hunting!' Mowgli danced off, flourishing the great ankus, and stopping from time to time to admire it, till he came to that part of the Jungle Bagheera chiefly used, and found him drinking after a heavy kill. Mowgli told him all his adventures from beginning to end, and Bagheera sniffed at the ankus between whiles. When Mowgli came to the White Cobra's last words, the Panther purred approvingly.

'Then the White Hood spoke the thing which is?' Mowgli asked quickly.

'I was born in the King's cages at Oodeypore, and it is in my stomach that I know some little of Man. Very many men would kill thrice in a night for the sake of that one big red stone alone.'

'But the stone makes it heavy to the hand. My little bright knife is better; and—see! the red stone is not good to eat. Then *why* would they kill?'

'Mowgli, go thou and sleep. Thou hast lived among men, and——'

'I remember. Men kill because they are not hunting;—for idleness and pleasure. Wake again, Bagheera. For what use was this thorn-pointed thing made?'

Bagheera half opened his eyes—he was very sleepy—with a malicious twinkle.

'It was made by men to thrust into the head of the sons of Hathi, so that the blood should pour out. I have seen the like in the street of Oodeypore, before our cages. That thing has tasted the blood of many such as Hathi.'

'But why do they thrust into the heads of elephants?'

'To teach them Man's Law. Having neither claws nor teeth, men make these things—and worse.'

'Always more blood when I come near, even to the things the Man-Pack have made,' said Mowgli disgustedly. He was getting a little tired of the weight of the ankus. 'If I had known this, I would not have taken it. First it was Messua's blood on the thongs, and now it is Hathi's. I will use it no more. Look!'

The ankus flew sparkling, and buried itself point down thirty yards away, between the trees. 'So my hands are clean of Death,' said Mowgli, rubbing his palms on the fresh, moist earth. 'The Thuu said Death would follow me. He is old and white and mad.'

'White or black, or death or life, *I* am going to sleep, Little Brother. I cannot hunt all night and howl all day, as do some folk.'

Bagheera went off to a hunting-lair that he knew, about two miles off. Mowgli made an easy way for himself up a convenient tree, knotted three of four creepers together, and in less time than it takes to tell was swinging in a hammock fifty feet above the ground. Though he had no positive objection to strong daylight, Mowgli followed the custom of his friends, and used it as little as he could. When he waked among the very loud-voiced peoples that live in the trees, it was twilight once more, and he had been dreaming of the beautiful pebbles he had thrown away.

'At least I will look at the thing again,' he said, and slid down a creeper to the earth; but Bagheera was before him. Mowgli could hear him snuffing in the half light.

'Where is the thorn-pointed thing?' cried Mowgli.

'A man has taken it. Here is the trail.'

'Now we shall see whether the Thuu spoke truth. If the pointed thing is Death, that man will die. Let us follow.'

'Kill first,' said Bagheera. 'An empty stomach makes a careless eye. Men go very slowly, and the Jungle is wet enough to hold the lightest mark.'

They killed as soon as they could, but it was nearly three hours before they finished their meat and drink and buckled down to the trail. The Jungle People know that nothing makes up for being hurried over your meals.

'Think you the pointed thing will turn in the man's hand and kill him?' Mowgli asked. 'The Thuu said it was Death.'

'We shall see when we find,' said Bagheera, trotting with his head low. 'It is single-foot' (he meant that there was only one man), 'and the weight of the thing has pressed his heel far into the ground.'

'Hai! This is as clear as summer lightning,' Mowgli answered; and they fell into the quick, choppy trail-trot in and out through the checkers of the moonlight, following the marks of those two bare feet.

'Now he runs swiftly,' said Mowgli. 'The toes are spread apart.' They went on over some wet ground. 'Now why does he turn aside here?'

'Wait!' said Bagheera, and flung himself forward with one superb bound as far as ever he could. The first thing to do when a trail ceases to explain itself is to cast forward without leaving your own confusing foot-marks on the ground. Bagheera turned as he landed, and faced Mowgli, crying, 'Here comes another trail to meet him. It is a smaller foot, this second trail, and the toes turn inward.'

Then Mowgli ran up and looked. 'It is the foot of a Gond hunter,' he said. 'Look! Here he dragged his bow on the grass. That is why the first trail turned aside so quickly. Big Foot hid from Little Foot.'

'That is true,' said Bagheera. 'Now, lest by crossing each other's tracks we foul the signs, let each take one trail. I am Big Foot, Little Brother, and thou art Little Foot, the Gond.'

Bagheera leaped back to the original trail, leaving Mowgli stooping above the curious narrow track of the wild little man of the woods.

'Now,' said Bagheera, moving step by step along the chain of footprints, 'I, Big Foot, turn aside here. Now I hide me behind a rock and stand still, not daring to shift my feet. Cry thy trail, Little Brother.'

'Now, I, Little Foot, come to the rock,' said Mowgli, running up his trail. 'Now, I sit down under the rock, leaning upon my right hand, and resting my bow between my toes. I wait long, for the mark of my feet is deep here.'

'I also,' said Bagheera, hidden behind the rock. 'I wait, resting the end of the thorn-pointed thing upon a stone. It slips, for here is a scratch upon the stone. Cry thy trail, Little Brother.'

'One, two twigs and a big branch are broken here,' said Mowgli, in an undertone. 'Now, how shall I cry *that*? Ah!

It is plain now. I, Little Foot, go away making noises and tramplings so that Big Foot may hear me.' He moved away from the rock pace by pace among the trees, his voice rising in the distance as he approached a little cascade. 'I—go—far—away—to—where—the—noise—of—falling—water—covers—my—noise; and—here—I—wait. Cry thy trail, Bagheera, Big Foot!'

The panther had been casting in every direction to see how Big Foot's trail led away from behind the rock. Then he gave tongue:

'I come from behind the rock upon my knees, dragging the thorn-pointed thing. Seeing no one, I run. I, Big Foot, run swiftly. The trail is clear. Let each follow his own. I run!'

Bagheera swept on along the clearly-marked trail, and Mowgli followed the steps of the Gond. For some time there was silence in the Jungle.

'Where art thou, Little Foot?' cried Bagheera. Mowgli's voice answered him not fifty yards to the right.

'Um!' said the Panther, with a deep cough. 'The two run side by side, drawing nearer!'

They raced on another half-mile, always keeping about the same distance, till Mowgli, whose head was not so close to the ground as Bagheera's, cried: 'They have met. Good hunting—look! Here stood Little Foot, with his knee on a rock—and yonder is Big Foot indeed!'

Not ten yards in front of them, stretched across a pile of broken rocks, lay the body of a villager of the district, a long, small-feathered Gond arrow through his back and breast.

'Was the Thuu so old and so mad, Little Brother?' said Bagheera gently. 'Here is one death, at least.'

'Follow on. But where is the drinker of elephant's blood—the red-eyed thorn?'

'Little Foot has it—perhaps. It is single-foot again now.'

The single trail of a light man who had been running quickly and bearing a burden on his left shoulder held on round a long, low spur of dried grass, where each footfall seemed, to the sharp eyes of the trackers, marked in hot iron.

Neither spoke till the trail ran up to the ashes of a camp-fire hidden in a ravine.

'Again!' said Bagheera, checking as though he had been turned into stone.

The body of a little wizened Gond lay with its feet in the ashes, and Bagheera looked inquiringly at Mowgli.

'That was done with a bamboo,' said the boy, after one glance. 'I have used such a thing among the buffaloes when I served in the Man-Pack. The Father of Cobras—I am sorrowful that I made a jest of him—knew the breed well, as I might have known. Said I not that men kill for idleness?'

'Indeed, they killed for the sake of the red and blue stones,' Bagheera answered. 'Remember, I was in the King's cages at Oodeypore.'

'One, two, three, four tracks,' said Mowgli, stooping over the ashes. 'Four tracks of men with shod feet. They do not go so quickly as Gonds. Now, what evil had the little woodman done to them? See, they talked together, all five, standing up, before they killed him. Bagheera, let us go back. My stomach is heavy in me, and yet it heaves up and down like an oriole's nest at the end of a branch.'

'It is not good hunting to leave game afoot. Follow!' said the panther. 'Those eight shod feet have not gone far.'

No more was said for fully an hour, as they worked up the broad trail of the four men with shod feet.

It was clear, hot daylight now, and Bagheera said, 'I smell smoke.'

'Men are always more ready to eat than to run,' Mowgli answered, trotting in and out between the low scrub bushes of the new Jungle they were exploring. Bagheera, a little to his left, made an indescribable noise in his throat.

'Here is one that had done with feeding,' said he. A tumbled bundle of gay-coloured clothes lay under a bush, and round it was some split flour.

'That was done by the bamboo again,' said Mowgli.

'See! that white dust is what men eat. They have taken the kill from this one,—he carried their food,—and given him for a kill to Chil, the Kite.'

'It is the third,' said Bagheera.

'I will go with new, big frogs to the Father of Cobras, and feed him fat,' said Mowgli to himself. 'The drinker of elephant's blood is Death himself—but still I do not understand!'

'Follow!' said Bagheera.

They had not gone half a mile farther when they heard Ko, the Crow, singing the death-song in the top of a tamarisk under whose shade three men were lying. A half-dead fire smoked in the centre of the circle, under an iron plate which held a blackened and burned cake of unleavened bread. Close to the fire, and blazing in the sunshine, lay the ruby-and-turquoise ankus.

'The thing works quickly; all ends here,' said Bagheera. 'How did *these* die, Mowgli? There is no mark on any.'

A Jungle-dweller gets to learn by experience as much as many doctors know of poisonous plants and berries. Mowgli sniffed the smoke that came up from the fire, broke off a morsel of the blackened bread, tasted it, and spat it out again.

'Apple of Death,' he coughed. 'The first must have made it ready in the food for *these*, who killed him, having first killed the Gond.'

'Good hunting, indeed! The kills follow close,' said Bagheera.

'Apple of Death' is what the Jungle called thorn-apple or dhatura,* the readiest poison in all India.

'What now?' said the panther. 'Must thou and I kill each other for yonder red-eyed slayer?'

'Can it speak?' said Mowgli in a whisper. 'Did I do it a wrong when I threw it away? Between us two it can do no wrong, for we do not desire what men desire. If it be left here, it will assuredly continue to kill men one after another as fast as nuts fall in a high wind. I have no love to men, but even I would not have them die six in a night.'

'What matter? They are only men. They killed one

another, and were well pleased,' said Bagheera. 'That first little woodman hunted well.'

'They are cubs none the less; and a cub will drown himself to bite the moon's light on the water. The fault was mine,' said Mowgli, who spoke as though he knew all about everything. 'I will never again bring into the Jungle strange things—not though they be as beautiful as flowers. This'—he handled the ankus gingerly—'goes back to the Father of Cobras. But first we must sleep, and we cannot sleep near these sleepers. Also we must bury *him*, lest he run away and kill another six. Dig me a hole under that tree.'

'But, Little Brother,' said Bagheera, moving off to the spot, 'I tell thee it is no fault of the blood-drinker. The trouble is with the men.'

'All one,' said Mowgli. 'Dig the hole deep. When we wake I will take him up and carry him back.'

Two nights later, as the White Cobra sat mourning in the darkness of the vault, ashamed, and robbed, and alone, the turquoise ankus whirled through the hole in the wall, and clashed on the floor of golden coins.

'Father of Cobras,' said Mowgli (he was careful to keep the other side of the wall), 'get thee a young and ripe one of thine own people to help thee guard the King's Treasure, so that no man may come away alive any more.'

'Ah-ha! It returns, then. I said the thing was Death. How comes it that thou art still alive?' the old Cobra mumbled, twining lovingly round the ankus-haft.

'By the Bull that bought me, I do not know! That thing has killed six times in a night. Let him go out no more.'

The Song of the Little Hunter

ERE Mor the Peacock flutters, ere the Monkey People cry,
  Ere Chil the Kite swoops down a furlong sheer,
  Through the Jungle very softly flits a shadow and a sigh—
He is Fear, O Little Hunter, he is Fear!
Very softly down the glade runs a waiting, watching shade,
  And the whisper spreads and widens far and near;
And the sweat is on thy brow, for he passes even now—
  He is Fear, O Little Hunter, he is Fear!

Ere the moon has climbed the mountain, ere the rocks are
        ribbed with light,
  When the downward-dipping trails are dank and drear,
Comes a breathing hard behind thee—*snuffle-snuffle* through
        the night—
  It is Fear, O Little Hunter, it is Fear!
On thy knees and draw the bow; bid the shrilling arrow go;
  In the empty, mocking thicket plunge the spear;
But thy hands are loosed and weak, and the blood has left thy
        cheek—
  It is Fear, O Little Hunter, it is Fear!

When the heat-cloud sucks the tempest, when the slivered
        pine-trees fall,
  When the blinding, blaring raid-squalls lash and veer;
Through the war-gongs of the thunder rings a voice more loud
        than all—
  It is Fear, O Little Hunter, it is Fear!
Now the spates are banked and deep; now the footless
        boulders leap—
  Now the lightning shows each littlest leaf-rib clear—
But thy throat is shut and dried, and thy heart against thy side
  Hammers: Fear, O Little Hunter—this is Fear!

Quiquern*

The People of the Eastern Ice, they are melting like the
    snow—
They beg for coffee and sugar; they go where the white men
    go.
The people of the Western Ice, they learn to steal and fight;
They sell their fur to the trading-post: they sell their souls
    to the white.
The People of the Southern Ice, they trade with the whaler's
    crew;
Their women have many ribbons, but their tents are torn
    and few.
But the People of the Elder Ice, beyond the white man's
    ken—
Their spears are made of the narwhal-horn, and they are the
    last of the Men!

Translation

'He has opened his eyes. Look!'

'Put him in the skin again. He will be a strong dog. On the fourth month we will name him.'

'For whom?' said Amoraq.

Kadlu's eye rolled round the skin-lined snow-house till it fell on fourteen-year-old Kotuko sitting on the sleeping-bench, making a button out of walrus ivory. 'Name him for me,' said Kotuko, with a grin. 'I shall need him one day.'

Kadlu grinned back till his eyes were almost buried in the fat of his flat cheeks, and nodded to Amoraq, while the puppy's fierce mother whined to see her baby wriggling far out of reach in the little sealskin pouch hung above the warmth of the blubber-lamp. Kotuko went on with his carving, and Kadlu threw a rolled bundle of leather dog-harnesses into a tiny little room that opened from one side of the house, slipped off his heavy deerskin hunting-suit, put it into a whalebone-net that hung above another lamp, and dropped down on the sleeping-bench to whittle at a piece of frozen seal-meat till Amoraq, his wife, should bring the regular dinner of boiled meat and blood-soup.

He had been out since early dawn at the seal-holes, eight
miles away, and had come home with three big seal. Half-
way down the long, low snow passage or tunnel that led to
the inner door of the house you could hear snappings and
yelpings, as the dogs of his sleigh-team, released from the
day's work, scuffled for warm places.

When the yelpings grew too loud Kotuko lazily rolled
off the sleeping-bench, and picked up a whip with an
eighteen-inch handle of springy whalebone, and twenty-
five feet of heavy, plaited thong. He dived into the passage,
where it sounded as though all the dogs were eating him
alive; but that was no more than their regular grace before
meals. When he crawled out at the far end, half a dozen
furry heads followed him with their eyes as he went to a
sort of gallows of whale-jawbones, from which the dog's
meat was hung; split off the frozen stuff in big lumps with
a broad-headed spear; and stood, his whip in one hand and
the meat in the other. Each beast was called by name, the
weakest first, and woe betide any dog that moved out of his
turn; for the tapering lash would shoot out like thonged
lightning, and flick away an inch or so of hair and hide.
Each beast growled, snapped, choked once over his portion, and hurried back to the protection of the passage,
while the boy stood upon the snow under the blazing
Northern Lights* and dealt out justice. The last to be
served was the big black leader of the team, who kept order
when the dogs were harnessed; and to him Kotuko gave a
double allowance of meat as well as an extra crack of the
whip.

'Ah!' said Kotuko, coiling up the lash, 'I have a little one
over the lamp that will make a great many howlings.
Sarpok! Get in!'

He crawled back over the huddled dogs, dusted the dry
snow from his furs with the whalebone beater that
Amoraq kept by the door, tapped the skin-lined roof of the
house to shake off any icicles that might have fallen from
the dome of snow above, and curled up on the bench. The
dogs in the passage snored and whined in their sleep, the
boy-baby in Amoraq's deep fur hooded kicked and choked

and gurgled, and the mother of the newly-named puppy lay at Kotuko's side, her eyes fixed on the bundle of sealskin, warm and safe above the broad yellow flame of the lamp.

And all this happened far away to the north, beyond Labrador,* beyond Hudson's Strait, where the great tides heave the ice about, north of Melville Peninsula—north even of the narrow Fury and Hecla Straits—on the north shore of Baffin Land, where Bylot's Island stands above the ice of Lancaster Sound like a pudding-bowl wrong side up. North of Lancaster Sound there is little we know anything about, except North Devon and Ellesmere Land; but even there live a few scattered people, next door, as it were, to the very Pole.

Kadlu was an Inuit,*—what you call an Esquimau,*— and his tribe, some thirty persons all told, belonged to the Tununirmiut—'the country lying at the back of something.' In the maps that desolate coast is written Navy Board Inlet, but the Inuit name is best, because the country lies at the very back of everything in the world. For nine months of the year there is only ice and snow, and gale after gale, with a cold that no one can realise who has never seen the thermometer even at zero. For six months of those nine it is dark; and that is what makes it so horrible. In the three months of the summer it only freezes every other day and every night, and then the snow begins to weep off on the southerly slopes, and a few ground-willows put out their woolly buds, a tiny stonecrop or so makes believe to blossom, beaches of fine gravel and rounded stones run down to the open sea, and polished boulders and streaked rocks lift up above the granulated snow. But all that is gone in a few weeks, and the wild winter locks down again on the land; while at sea the ice tears up and down the offing,* jamming and ramming, and splitting and hitting, and pounding and grounding, till it all freezes together, ten feet thick, from the land outward to deep water.

In the winter Kadlu would follow the seal to the edge of this land-ice, and spear them as they came up to breathe at

their blow-holes. The seal must have open water to live
and catch fish in, and in the deep of winter the ice would
sometimes run eighty miles without a break from the
nearest shore. In the spring he and his people retreated
from the floes to the rocky mainland, where they put up
tents of skins, and snared the sea-birds, or speared the
young seal basking on the beaches. Later, they would go
south into Baffin Land after the reindeer, and to get their
year's store of salmon from the hundreds of streams and
lakes of the interior; coming back north in September or
October for the musk-ox* hunting and the regular winter
sealery. This travelling was done with dog-sleighs,*
twenty and thirty miles a day, or sometimes down the
coast in big skin 'woman-boats,' when the dogs and the
babies lay among the feet of the rowers, and the women
sang songs as they glided from cape to cape over the
glassy, cold waters. All the luxuries that the Tununirmiut
knew came from the south—driftwood for sleigh-runners,
rod-iron for harpoon-tips, steel knives, tin kettles that
cooked food much better than the old soap-stone affairs,
flint and steel, and even matches, as well as coloured
ribbons for the women's hair, little cheap mirrors, and red
cloth for the edging of deerskin dress-jackets. Kadlu
traded the rich, creamy, twisted narwhal* horn and musk-
ox teeth (these are just as valuable as pearls) to the
Southern Inuit, and they, in turn, traded with the whalers
and the missionary-posts of Exeter and Cumberland
Sounds; and so the chain went on, till a kettle picked up by
a ship's cook in the Bhendy Bazaar* might end its days
over a blubber-lamp somewhere on the cool side of the
Arctic Circle.

Kadlu, being a good hunter, was rich in iron harpoons,
snow-knives, bird-darts, and all the other things that make
life easy up there in the great cold; and he was the head of
his tribe, or, as they say, 'the man who knows all about it
by practice.' This did not give him any authority, except
now and then he could advise his friends to change their
hunting-grounds; but Kotuko used it to domineer a little,
in the lazy, fat Inuit fashion, over the other boys, when

they came out at night to play ball in the moonlight, or to sing the Child's Song to the Aurora Borealis.

But at fourteen an Inuit feels himself a man, and Kotuko was tired of making snares for wild-fowl and kit-foxes,* and most tired of all of helping the women to chew seal- and deer-skins (that supples them as nothing else can) the long day through, while the men were out hunting. He wanted to go into the *quaggi*, the Singing-House, when the hunters gathered there for their mysteries, and the *angekok*, the sorcerer, frightened them into the most delightful fits after the lamps were put out, and you could hear the Spirit of the Reindeer stamping on the roof; and when a spear was thrust out into the open black night it came back covered with hot blood. He wanted to throw his big boots into the net with the tired air of the head of a family, and to gamble with the hunters when they dropped in of an evening and played a sort of home-made roulette with a tin pot and a nail. There were hundreds of things that he wanted to do, but the grown men laughed at him and said, 'Wait till you have been in the buckle,* Kotuko. Hunting is not *all* catching.'

Now that his father had named a puppy for him, things looked brighter. An Inuit does not waste a good dog on his son till the boy knows something of dog-driving; and Kotuko was more than sure that he knew more than everything.

If the puppy had not had an iron constitution he would have died from over-stuffing and over-handling. Kotuko made him a tiny harness with a trace to it, and hauled him all over the house-floor shouting: 'Aua! Ja aua!' (Go to the right). 'Choiachoi! Ja choiachoi!' (Go to the left). 'Ohaha!' (Stop). The puppy did not like it at all, but being fished for in this way was pure happiness beside being put to the sleigh for the first time. He just sat down on the snow, and played with the seal-hide trace that ran from his harness to the *pitu*, the big thong in the bows of the sleigh. Then the team started, and the puppy found the heavy ten-foot sleigh running up his back, and dragging him along the snow, while Kotuko laughed till the tears ran down his

face. There followed days and days of the cruel whip that
hisses like the wind over ice, and his companions all bit
him because he did not know his work, and the harness
chafed him, and he was not allowed to sleep with Kotuko
any more, but had to take the coldest place in the passage.
It was a sad time for the puppy.

The boy learned, too, as fast as the dog; though a dog-
sleigh is a heart-breaking thing to manage. Each beast is
harnessed, the weakest nearest to the driver, by his own
separate trace, which runs under his left fore-leg to the
main thong, where it is fastened by a sort of button and
loop which can be slipped by a turn of the wrist, thus
freeing one dog at a time. This is very necessary, because
young dogs often get the trace between their hind
legs, where it cuts to the bone. And they one and all *will* go
visting their friends as they run, jumping in and out
among the traces. Then they fight, and the result is more
mixed than a wet fishing-line next morning. A great deal
of trouble can be avoided by scientific use of the whip.
Every Inuit boy prides himself as being a master of the
long lash; but it is easy to flick at a mark on the ground,
and difficult to lean forward and catch a shirking dog just
behind the shoulders when the sleigh is going at full speed.
If you call one dog's name for 'visiting,' and accidentally
lash another, the two will fight it out at once, and stop all
the others. Again, if you travel with a companion and
begin to talk, or by yourself and sing, the dogs will halt,
turn round, and sit down to hear what you have to say.
Kotuko was run away from once or twice through forgetting to block the sleigh when he stopped; and he broke
many lashings, and ruined a few thongs before he could be
trusted with a full team of eight and the light sleigh. Then
he felt himself a person of consequence, and on smooth,
black ice, with a bold heart and a quick elbow, he smoked
along over the levels as fast as a pack in full cry. He would
go ten miles to the seal-holes, and when he was on the
hunting-grounds he would twitch a trace loose from the
pitu, and free the big black leader, who was the cleverest
dog in the team. As soon as the dog had scented a

breathing-hole, Kotuko would reverse the sleigh, driving a
couple of sawed-off antlers, that stuck up like perambula-
tor-handles from the back-rest, deep into the snow, so that
the team could not get away. Then he would crawl forward
inch by inch, and wait till the seal came up to breathe.
Then he would stab down swiftly with his spear and
running-line, and presently would haul his seal up to the
lip of the ice, while the black leader came up and helped to
pull the carcass across the ice to the sleigh. That was the
time when the harnessed dogs yelled and foamed with
excitement, and Kotuko laid the long lash like a red-hot
bar across all their faces, till the carcass froze stiff. Going
home was the heavy work. The loaded sleigh had to be
humoured among the rough ice, and the dogs sat down
and looked hungrily at the seal instead of pulling. At last
they would strike the well-worn sleigh road to the village,
and toodle-kiyi* along the ringing ice, heads down and
tails up, while Kotuko struck up the 'An-gutivaun tai-na
tau-na-ne taina' (The Song of the Returning Hunter), and
voices hailed him from house to house under all that dim,
star-litten sky.

   When Kotuko the dog came to his full growth he
enjoyed himself too. He fought his way up the team
steadily, fight after fight, till one fine evening, over their
food, he tackled the big, black leader (Kotuko the boy saw
fair play), and made second dog of him, as they say. So he
was promoted to the long thong of the leading dog,
running five feet in advance of all the others: it was his
bounden duty to stop all fighting, in harness or out of it,
and he wore a collar of copper wire, very thick and heavy.
On special occasions he was fed with cooked food inside
the house, and sometimes was allowed to sleep on the
bench with Kotuko. He was a good seal-dog, and would
keep a musk-ox at bay by running round him and snapping at his heels. He would even—and this for a sleigh-dog
is the last proof of bravery—he would even stand up to the
gaunt Arctic wolf, whom all dogs of the North, as a rule,
fear beyond anything that walks the snow. He and his
master—they did not count the team of ordinary dogs as

company—hunted together, day after day and night after night, fur-wrapped boy and savage, long-haired, narrow-eyed, white-fanged, yellow brute. All an Inuit has to do is to get food and skins for himself and his family. The women-folk make the skins into clothing, and occasionally help in trapping small game; but the bulk of the food—and they eat enormously—must be found by the men. If the supply fails there is no one up there to buy or beg or borrow from. The people must die.

An Inuit does not think of the chances till he is forced to. Kadlu, Kotuko, Amoraq, and the boy-baby who kicked about in Amoraq's fur hood and chewed pieces of blubber all day, were as happy together as any family in the world. They came of a very gentle race—an Inuit seldom loses his temper, and almost never strikes a child—who did not know exactly what telling a real lie meant, still less how to steal. They were content to spear their living out of the heart of the bitter, hopeless cold; to smile oily smiles, and tell queer ghost and fairy tales of evenings, and eat till they could eat no more, and sing the endless woman's song: 'Amna aya, aya amna, ah! ah!' through the long lamp-lighted days as they mended their clothes and their hunting-gear.

But one terrible winter everything betrayed them. The Tununirmiut returned from the yearly salmon-fishing, and made their houses on the early ice to the north of Bylot's Island, ready to go after the seal as soon as the sea froze. But it was an early and savage autumn. All through September there were continuous gales that broke up the smooth seal-ice when it was only four or five feet thick, and forced it inland, and piled a great barrier, some twenty miles broad, of lumped and ragged and needly ice, over which it was impossible to draw the dog-sleighs. The edge of the floe off which the seal were used to fish in winter lay perhaps twenty miles beyond this barrier, and out of reach of the Tununirmiut. Even so, they might have managed to scrape through the winter on their stock of frozen salmon and stored blubber, and what the traps gave them, but in December one of their hunters came across a *tupik* (a skin-tent) of three women and a girl nearly dead, whose men had come down from the far North and been crushed in their little skin hunting-boats while they were out after the long-horned narwhal. Kadlu, of course, could only distribute the women among the huts of the winter village, for no Inuit dare refuse a meal to a stranger. He never knows when his own turn may come to beg. Amoraq took the girl, who was about fourteen, into her own house as a sort of servant. From the cut of her sharp-pointed hood, and the long diamond pattern of her white deer-skin leggings, they supposed she came from Ellesmere Land. She had never seen tin cooking-pots or wooden-shod sleighs before; but Kotuko the boy and Kotuko the dog were rather fond of her.

Then all the foxes went south, and even the wolverine,* that growling, blunt-headed little thief of the snow, did not take the trouble to follow the line of empty traps that Kotuko set. The tribe lost a couple of their best hunters, who were badly crippled in a fight with a musk-ox, and this threw more work on the others. Kotuko went out, day after day, with a light hunting-sleigh and six or seven of the strongest dogs, looking till his eyes ached for some patch of clear ice where a seal might perhaps have scratched a breathing-hole. Kotuko the dog ranged far and wide, and in the dead stillness of the ice-fields Kotuko the boy could hear his half-choked whine of excitement, above a seal-hold three miles away, as plainly as though he were at his elbow. When the dog found a hole the boy would build himself a little, low snow wall to keep off the worst of the bitter wind, and there he would wait ten, twelve, twenty hours for the seal to come up to breathe, his eyes glued to the tiny mark he had made above the hole to guide the downward thrust of his harpoon, a little seal-skin mat under his feet, and his legs tied together in the *tutareang* (the buckle that the old hunters had talked about). This helps to keep a man's legs from twitching as he waits and waits and waits for the quick-eared seal to rise. Though there is no excitement in it, you can easily believe that the sitting still in the buckle with the thermometer perhaps forty degrees below zero is the hardest work an Inuit knows. When a seal was caught, Kotuko the dog would bound forward, his trace trailing behind him, and help to pull the body to the sleigh, where the tired and hungry dogs lay sullenly under the lee of the broken ice.

A seal did not go very far, for each mouth in the little village had a right to be filled, and neither bone, hide, nor sinew was wasted. The dogs' meat was taken for human use, and Amoraq fed the team with pieces of old summer skin-tents raked out from under the sleeping-bench, and they howled and howled again, and waked to howl hungrily. One could tell by the soap-stone lamps in the huts that famine was near. In good seasons, when blubber was plentiful, the light in the boat-shaped lamps would be two feet high—cheerful, oily, and yellow. Now it was a bare six inches: Amoraq carefully pricked down the moss wick, when an unwatched flame brightened for a moment, and the eyes of all the family followed her hand. The horror of famine up there in the great cold is not so much dying, as dying in the dark. All the Inuit dread the dark that presses on them without a break for six months in each year; and when the lamps are low in the houses the minds of people begin to be shaken and confused.

But worse was to come.

The underfed dogs snapped and growled in the passages, glaring at the cold stars, and snuffing into the bitter wind, night after night. When they stopped howling the silence fell down again as solid and as heavy as a snowdrift against a door, and men could hear the beating of their blood in the thin passages of the ear, and the thumping of their own hearts, that sounded as loud as the noise of sorcerers' drums beaten across the snow. One night Kotuko the dog, who had been unusually sullen in harness, leaped up and pushed his head against Kotuko's knee. Kotuko patted him, but the dog still pushed blindly forward, fawning. Then Kadlu waked, and gripped the heavy wolf-like head, and stared into the glassy eyes. The dog whimpered and shivered between Kadlu's knees. The hair rose about his neck, and he growled as though a stranger were at the door; then he barked joyously, and rolled on the ground, and bit at Kotuko's boot like a puppy.

'What is it?' said Kotuko; for he was beginning to be afraid.

'The sickness,' Kadlu answered. 'It is the dog-sickness.' Kotuko the dog lifted his nose and howled and howled again.

'I have not seen this before. What will he do?' said Kotuko.

Kadlu shrugged one shoulder a little, and crossed the hut for his short stabbing-harpoon. The big dog look at him, howled again, and slunk away down the passage, while the other dogs drew aside right and left to give him ample room. When he was out on the snow he barked furiously, as though on the tail of a musk-ox, and, barking and leaping and frisking, passed out of sight. His trouble was not hydrophobia,* but simple, plain madness. The cold and the hunger, and, above all, the dark, had turned his head; and when the terrible dog-sickness once shows itself in a team, it spreads like wild-fire. Next hunting-day another dog sickened, and was killed then and there by Kotuko as he bit and struggled among the traces. Then the black second dog, who had been the leader in the old days, suddenly gave tongue on an imaginary reindeer-track, and when they slipped him from the *pitu* he flew at the throat of an ice-cliff, and ran away as his leader had done, his harness on his back. After that no one would take the dogs out again. They needed them for something else,* and the dogs knew it; and though they were tied down and fed by hand, their eyes were full of despair and fear. To make things worse, the old women began to tell ghost-tales, and to say that they had met the spirits of the dead hunters lost that autumn, who prophesied all sorts of horrible things.

Kotuko grieved more for the loss of his dog than anything else; for though an Inuit eats enormously he also knows how to starve. But the hunger, the darkness, the cold, and the exposure told on his strength, and he began to hear voices inside his head, and to see the people who were not there, out of the tail of his eye. One night—he had unbuckled himself after ten hours' waiting above a 'blind' seal-hole, and was staggering back to the village faint and dizzy—he halted to lean his back against a boulder which happened to be supported like a rocking-stone on a single jutting point of ice. His weight disturbed the balance of the thing, it rolled over ponderously, and as Kotuko sprang aside to avoid it, slid after him, squeaking and hissing on the ice-slope.

That was enough for Kotuko. He had been brought up to believe that every rock and boulder had its owner (its *inua*), who was generally a one-eyed kind of a Woman-Thing called a *tornaq*, and that when a *tornaq* meant to help a man she rolled after him inside her stone house, and asked him whether he would take her for a guardian spirit. (In summer thaws the ice-propped rocks and boulders roll and slip all over the face of the land, so you can easily see how the idea of live stones arose.) Kotuko heard the blood beating in his ears as he had heard it all day, and he thought that was the *tornaq* of the stone speaking to him. Before he reached home he was quite certain that he had held a long conversation with her, and as all his people believed that this was quite possible, no one contradicted him.

'She said to me, "I jump down, I jump down from my place on the snow,"' cried Kotuko, with hollow eyes, leaning forward in the half-lighted hut. 'She said, "I will be a guide." She says, "I will guide you to the good seal-holes." Tomorrow I go out, and the *tornaq* will guide me.'

Then the *angekok*, the village sorcerer, came in, and Kotuko told him the tale a second time. It lost nothing in the telling.

'Follow the *tornait* [the spirits of the stones], and they will bring us food again,' said the *angekok*.

Now the girl from the North had been lying near the lamp, eating very little and saying less for days past; but when Amoraq and Kadlu next morning packed and lashed a little hand-sleigh for Kotuko, and loaded it with his hunting-gear and as much blubber and frozen seal-meat as they could spare, she took the pulling-rope, and stepped out boldly at the boy's side.

'Your house is my house,' she said, as the little bone-shod sleigh squeaked and bumped behind them in the awful Arctic night.

'My house is your house,' said Kotuko; 'but *I* think that we shall both go to Sedna together.'

Now Sedna is the Mistress of the Underworld, and the Inuit believe that every one who dies must spend a year in her horrible country before going to Quadliparmiut, the Happy Place, where it never freezes and the fat reindeer trot up when you call.

Through the village people were shouting: 'The *tornait* have spoken to Kotuko. They will show him open ice. He will bring us the seal again!' Their voices were soon swallowed up by the cold, empty dark, and Kotuko and the girl shouldered close together as they strained on the pulling-rope or humoured the sleigh through the ice in the direction of the Polar Sea. Kotuko insisted that the *tornaq* of the stone had told him to go north, and north they went under Tuktuqdjung the Reindeer—those stars that we call the Great Bear.*

No European could have made five miles a day over the ice-rubbish and the sharp-edged drifts; but those two knew exactly the turn of the wrist that coaxes a sleigh round a hummock, the jerk that nearly lifts it out of an ice-crack, and the exact strength that goes to the few quiet strokes of the spear-head that make a path possible when everything looks hopeless.

The girl said nothing, but bowed her head, and the long wolverine-fur fringe of her ermine hood blew across her broad, dark face. The sky above them was an intense velvety black, changing to bands of Indian red on the horizon, where the great stars burned like street-lamps. From time to time a greenish wave of the Northern Lights would roll across the hollow of the high heavens, flick like a flag, and disappear; or a meteor would crackle from darkness to darkness, trailing a shower of sparks behind. Then they could see the ridged and furrowed surface of the floe tipped and laced with strange colours—red, copper, and bluish; but in the ordinary starlight everything turned to one frost-bitten gray. The floe, as you will remember, had been battered and tormented by the autumn gales till it was one frozen earthquake. There were gullies and ravines, and holes like gravel-pits, cut in ice; lumps and scattered pieces frozen down to the original floor of the floe; blotches of old black ice that had been thrust under the floe in some gale and heaved up again; roundish boulders of ice; saw-like edges of ice carved by the snow that flies before the wind; and sunken pits where thirty or forty acres lay below the level of the rest of the field. From a little distance you might have taken the lumps for seal or walrus, overturned sleighs or men on a hunting expedition, or even the great Ten-legged White Spirit-Bear himself; but in spite of these fantastic shapes, all on the very edge of starting into life, there was neither sound nor the least faint echo of sound. And through this silence and through this waste, where the sudden lights flapped and went out again, the sleigh and the two that pulled it crawled like things in a nightmare—a nightmare of the end of the world at the end of the world.

When they were tired Kotuko would make what the hunters call a 'half-house,' a very small snow hut, into which they would huddle with the travelling-lamp, and try to thaw out the frozen seal-meat. When they had slept, the march began again—thirty miles a day to get ten miles northward. The girl was always very silent, but Kotuko muttered to himself and broke out into songs he had learned in the Singing-House—summer songs, and reindeer and salmon songs—all horribly out of place at that season. He would declare that he heard the *tornaq* growling to him, and would run wildly up a hummock, tossing his arms and speaking in loud, threatening tones. To tell the truth, Kotuko was very nearly crazy for the time being; but the girl was sure that he was being guided by his guardian spirit, and that everything would come right. She was not surprised, therefore, when at the end of the fourth march Kotuko, whose eyes were burning like fire-balls in his head, told her that his *tornaq* was following them across the snow in the shape of a two-headed dog. The girl looked where Kotuko pointed, and something seemed to slip into a ravine. It was certainly not human, but everybody knew that the *tornait* preferred to appear in the shape of bear and seal, and such like.

It might have been the Ten-legged White Spirit-Bear himself, or it might have been anything, for Kotuko and the girl were so starved that their eyes were untrustworthy. They had trapped nothing, and seen no trace of game since they had left the village; their food would not hold out for another week, and there was a gale coming. A Polar storm can blow for ten days without a break, and all that while it is certain death to be abroad. Kotuko laid up a snow-house large enough to take in the hand-sleigh (never be separated from your meat), and while he was shaping the last irregular block of ice that makes the key-stone of the roof, he saw a Thing* looking at him from a little cliff of ice half a mile away. The air was hazy, and the Thing seemed to by forty feet long and ten feet high, with twenty feet of tail and a shape that quivered all along the outlines. The girl saw it too, but instead of crying aloud with terror, said quietly, 'That is Quiquern. What comes after?'

'He will speak to me,' said Kotuko; but the snow-knife trembled in his hand as he spoke, because however much a man may believe that he is a friend of strange and ugly spirits, he seldom likes to be taken quite at his word. Quiquern, too, is the phantom of a gigantic toothless dog without any hair, who is supposed to live in the far North, and to wander about the country just before things are going to happen. They may be pleasant or unpleasant things, but not even the sorcerers care to speak about Quiquern. He makes the dogs go mad. Like the Spirit-Bear, he has several extra pairs of legs,—six or eight,—and this Thing jumping up and down in the haze had more legs than any real dog needed. Kotuko and the girl huddled into their hut quickly. Of course if the Quiquern had wanted them, he could have torn it to pieces above their heads, but the sense of a foot-thick snow-wall between themselves and the wicked dark was great comfort. The gale broke with a shriek of wind like the shriek of a train, and for three days and three nights it held, never varying one point, and never lulling even for a minute. They fed the stone lamp between their knees, and nibbled at the half-warm seal-meat, and watched the black soot gather on the roof for seventy-two long hours. The girl counted up the food in the sleigh; there was not more than two days' supply, and Kotuko looked over the iron heads and the deer-sinew fastenings of his harpoon and his seal-lance and his bird-dart. There was nothing else to do.

'We shall go to Sedna soon—very soon,' the girl whispered. 'In three days we shall lie down and go. Will your *tornaq* do nothing? Sing her an *angekok's* song to make her come here.'

He began to sing in the high-pitched howl of the magic songs, and the gale went down slowly. In the middle of his song the girl started, laid her mittened hand and then her head to the ice floor of the hut. Kotuko followed her example, and the two kneeled, staring into each other's eyes, and listening with every nerve. He ripped a thin sliver of whalebone from the rim of a bird-snare that lay on the sleigh, and, after straightening, set it upright in a little hole in the ice, firming it down with his mitten. It was almost as delicately adjusted as a compass-needle, and now instead of listening they watched. The thin rod quivered a little—the least little jar in the world; then it vibrated steadily for a few seconds, came to rest, and vibrated again, this time nodding to another point of the compass.

'Too soon!' said Kotuko. 'Some big floe has broken far away outside.'

The girl pointed at the rod, and shook her head. 'It is the big breaking,' she said. 'Listen to the ground-ice. It knocks.'

When they kneeled this time they heard the most curious muffled grunts and knockings, apparently under their feet. Sometimes it sounded as though a blind puppy were squeaking above the lamp; then as if a stone were being ground on hard ice; and again, like muffled blows on a drum; but all dragged out and made small, as though they travelled through a little horn a weary distance away.

'We shall not go to Sedna lying down,' said Kotuko. 'It is the breaking. The *tornaq* has cheated us. We shall die.'

All this may sound absurd enough, but the two were face to face with a very real danger. The three days' gale had driven the deep water of Baffin's Bay southerly, and piled it on to the edge of the far-reaching land-ice that stretches from Bylot's Island to the west. Also, the strong current which sets east out of Lancaster Sound carried with it mile upon mile of what they call pack-ice—rough ice that has not frozen into fields; and this pack was bombarding the floe* at the same time that the swell and heave of the storm-worked sea was weakening and undermining it. What Kotuko and the girl had been listening to were the faint echoes of that fight thirty or forty miles away, and the little tell-tale rod quivered to the shock of it.

Now, as the Inuit say, when the ice once wakes after its long winter sleep, there is no knowing what may happen, for solid floe-ice changes shape almost as quickly as a cloud. The gale was evidently a spring gale sent out of time, and anything was possible.

Yet the two were happier in their minds than before. If the floe broke up there would be no more waiting and suffering. Spirits, goblins, and witch-people were moving about on the racking ice, and they might find themselves stepping into Sedna's country side by side with all sorts of wild Things, the flush of excitement still on them. When they left the hut after the gale, the noise on the horizon was steadily growing, and the tough ice moaned and buzzed all round them.

'It is still waiting,' said Kotuko.

On the top of a hummock sat or crouched the eight-legged Thing that they had seen three days before—and it howled horribly.

'Let us follow,' said the girl. 'It may know some way that does not lead to Sedna'; but she reeled from weakness as she took the pulling-rope. The Thing moved off slowly and clumsily across the ridges, heading always towards the westward and the land, and they followed, while the growling thunder at the edge of the floe rolled nearer and nearer. The floe's lip was split and cracked in every direction for three or four miles inland, and great pans of ten-foot-thick ice from a few yards to twenty acres square, were jolting and ducking and surging into one another, and into the yet unbroken floe, as the heavy swell took and shook and spouted between them. This battering-ram ice was, so to speak, the first army that the sea was flinging against the floe. The incessant crash and jar of these cakes almost drowned the ripping sound of sheets of pack-ice driven bodily under the floe as cards are hastily pushed under a tablecloth. Where the water was shallow these sheets would be piled one atop of the other till the bottommost touched mud fifty feet down, and the disco-loured sea banked behind the muddy ice till the increasing pressure drove all forward again. In addition to the floe and the pack-ice, the gale and the currents were bringing down true bergs, sailing mountains of ice, snapped off from the Greenland side of the water or the north shore of Melville Bay. They pounded in solemnly, the waves breaking white round them, and advanced on the floe like an old-time fleet under full sail. A berg that seemed ready to carry the world before it would ground helplessly in deep water, reel over, and wallow in a lather of foam and mud and flying frozen spray, while a much smaller and lower one would rip and ride into the flat floe, flinging tons of ice on either side, and cutting a track half a mile long before it was stopped. Some fell like swords, shearing a raw-edged canal; and others splintered into a shower of blocks, weighing scores of tons apiece, that whirled and skirled among the hummocks. Others, again, rose up bodily out of the water when they shoaled, twisted as though in pain, and fell solidly on their sides, while the sea threshed over their shoulders. This trampling and crowd-ing and bending and buckling and arching of the ice into every possible shape was going on as far as the eye could reach all along the north line of the floe. From where Kotuko and the girl were, the confusion looked no more than an uneasy, rippling, crawling movement under the horizon; but it came toward them each moment, and they could hear, far away to landward, a heavy booming, as it might have been the boom of artillery through a fog. That showed that the floe was being jammed home against the iron cliffs of Bylot's Island, the land to the southward behind them.

'This has never been before,' said Kotuko, staring stupidly. 'This is not the time. How can the floe break *now*?'

'Follow *that*!' the girl cried, pointing to the Thing half limping, half running distractedly before them. They followed, tugging at the hand-sleigh, while nearer and nearer came the roaring march of the ice. At last the fields round them cracked and starred in every direction, and the cracks opened and snapped like the teeth of wolves. But where the Thing rested, on a mound of old and scattered ice-blocks some fifty feet high, there was no motion. Kotuko leaped forward wildly, dragging the girl after him, and crawled to the bottom of the mound. The talking of the ice grew louder and louder around them, but the mound stayed fast, and, as the girl looked at him, he threw his right elbow upward and outward, making the Inuit sign for land in the shape of an island. And land it was that the eight-legged, limping Thing had led them to—some granite-tipped, sand-beached islet off the coast, shod and sheathed and masked with ice so that no man could have told it from the floe, but at the bottom solid earth, and not shifting ice! The smashing and rebound of the floes as they grounded and splintered marked the borders of it, and a friendly shoal ran out to the northward, and turned aside the rush of the heaviest ice, exactly as a ploughshare turns over loam. There was danger, of course, that some heavily squeezed ice-field might shoot up the beach, and plane off the top of the islet bodily; but that did not trouble Kotuko and the girl when they made their snow-house and began to eat, and heard the ice hammer and skid along the beach. The Thing had disappeared, and Kotuko was talking excitedly about his power over spirits as he crouched round the lamp. In the middle of his wild sayings the girl began to laugh, and rock herself backward and forward.

Behind her shoulder, crawling into the hut crawl by crawl, there were two heads, one yellow and one black, that belonged to two of the most sorrowful and ashamed dogs that ever you saw. Kotuko the dog was one, and the black leader was the other. Both were now fat, well-looking, and quite restored to their proper minds, but coupled to each other in an extraordinary fashion. When the black leader ran off, you remember, his harness was still on him. He must have met Kotuko the dog, and played or fought with him, for his shoulder-loop had caught in the plaited copper wire of Kotuko's collar, and had drawn tight, so that neither could get at the trace to gnaw it apart, but each was fastened sidelong to his neighbour's neck. That, with the freedom of hunting on their own account, must have helped to cure their madness. They were very sober.

The girl pushed the two shamefaced creatures towards Kotuko, and, sobbing with laughter, cried, 'That is Quiquern, who led us to safe ground. Look at his eight legs and double head!'

Kotuko cut them free, and they fell into his arms, yellow and black together, trying to explain how they had got their senses back again. Kotuko ran a hand down their ribs, which were round and well clothed. 'They have found food,' he said, with a grin. 'I do not think we shall go to Sedna so soon. My *tornaq* sent these. The sickness has left them.'

As soon as they had greeted Kotuko, these two, who had been forced to sleep and eat and hunt together for the past few weeks, flew at each other's throat, and there was a beautiful battle in the snow-house. 'Empty dogs do not fight,' Kotuko said. 'They have found the seal. Let us sleep. We shall find food.'

When they waked there was open water on the north beach of the island, and all the loosened ice had been driven landward. The first sound of the surf is one of the most delightful that the Inuit can hear, for it means that spring is on the road. Kotuko and the girl took hold of hands and smiled, for the clear, full roar of the surge among the ice reminded them of salmon and reindeer time and the smell of blossoming ground-willows. Even as they looked, the sea began to skim over between the floating cakes of ice, so intense was the cold; but on the horizon there was a vast red glare, and that was the light of the sunken sun. It was more like hearing him yawn in his sleep than seeing him rise, and the glare lasted for only a few minutes, but it marked the turn of the year. Nothing, they felt, could alter that.

Kotuko found the dogs fighting over a fresh-killed seal who was following the fish that a gale always disturbs. He was the first of some twenty of thirty seal that landed on the island in the course of the day, and till the sea froze hard there were hundreds of keen black heads rejoicing in the shallow free water and floating about with the floating ice.

It was good to eat seal-liver again; to fill the lamps recklessly with blubber, and watch the flame blaze three feet in the air; but as soon as the new sea-ice bore, Kotuko and the girl loaded the hand-sleigh, and made the two dogs pull as they had never pulled in their lives, for they feared what might have happened in their village. The weather was as pitiless as usual; but it is easier to draw a sleigh loaded with good food than to hunt starving. They left five-and-twenty seal carcasses buried in the ice of the beach, all ready for use, and hurried back to their people. The dogs showed them the way as soon as Kotuko told them what was expected, and though there was no sign of a landmark, in two days they were giving tongue outside Kadlu's house. Only three dogs answered them; the others had been eaten, and the houses were all dark. But when Kotuko shouted, 'Ojo!' (boiled meat),* weak voices replied, and when he called the muster of the village name by name, very distinctly, there were no gaps in it.

An hour later the lamps blazed in Kadlu's house; snow-water was heating; the pots were beginning to simmer, and the snow was dripping from the roof, as Amoraq made ready a meal for all the village, and the boy-baby in the hood chewed at a strip of rich nutty blubber, and the hunters slowly and methodically filled themselves to the very brim with seal-meat. Kotuko and the girl told their tale. The two dogs sat between them, and whenever their names came in, they cocked an ear apiece and looked most thoroughly ashamed of themselves. A dog who has once gone mad and recovered, the Inuit say, is safe against all further attacks.

'So the *tornaq* did not forget us,' said Kotuko. 'The storm blew, the ice broke, and the seal swam in behind the fish that were frightened by the storm. Now the new seal-holes are not two days distant. Let the good hunters go to-morrow and bring back the seal I have speared—twenty-five seal buried in the ice. When we have eaten those we will all follow the seal on the floe.'

'What do *you* do?' said the sorcerer in the same sort of voice as he used to Kadlu, richest of the Tununirmiut.

Kadlu looked at the girl from the North, and said quietly, '*We* build a house.' He pointed to the north-west side of Kadlu's house, for that is the side on which the married son or daughter always lives.

The girl turned her hands palm upward, with a little despairing shake of her head. She was a foreigner, picked up starving, and could bring nothing to the housekeeping.

Amoraq jumped from the bench where she sat, and began to sweep things into the girl's lap—stone lamps, iron skin-scrapers, tin kettles, deer-skins embroidered with musk-ox teeth, and real canvas-needles such as sailors use—the finest dowry that has ever been given on the far edge of the Arctic Circle, and the girl from the North bowed her head down to the very floor.

'Also these!' said Kotuko, laughing and signing to the dogs, who thrust their cold muzzles into the girl's face.

'Ah,' said the *angekok*, with an important cough, as though he had been thinking it all over. 'As soon as Kotuko left the village I went to the Singing-House and sang magic. I sang all the long nights, and called upon the Spirit of the Reindeer. *My* singing made the gale blow that broke the ice and drew the two dogs toward Kotuko when the ice would have crushed his bones. *My* song drew the seal in behind the broken ice. My body lay still in the *quaggi*, but my spirit ran about on the ice, and guided Kotuko and the dogs in all the things they did. I did it.'

Everybody was full and sleepy, so no one contradicted; and the *angekok*, by virtue of his office, helped himself to yet another lump of boiled meat, and lay down to sleep with the others in the warm, well-lighted, oil-smelling home.

Now Kotuko, who drew very well in the Inuit fashion, scratched pictures of all these adventures on a long, flat piece of ivory with a hole at one end. When he and the girl went north to Ellesmere Land in the year of the Wonderful Open Winter, he left the picture story with Kadlu, who lost it in the shingle when his dog-sleigh broke down one summer on the beach of Lake Netilling at Nikosiring, and there a Lake Inuit found it next spring and sold it to a man at Imigen who was interpreter on a Cumberland Sound whaler, and he sold it to Hans Olsen, who was afterward a quartermaster on board a big steamer that took tourists to the North Cape in Norway. When the tourist season was over, the steamer ran between London and Australia, stopping at Ceylon, and there Olsen sold the ivory to a Cingalese* jeweller for two imitation sapphires. I found it under some rubbish in a house at Colombo, and have translated it from one end to the other.

'Angutivaun Taina'

[This is a very free translation of the Song of the Returning
Hunter, as the men used to sing it after seal-spearing. The Inuit
always repeat things over and over again.]

OUR gloves are stiff with the frozen blood,
   Our furs with the drifted snow,
As we come in with the seal—the seal!
   In from the edge of the floe.

Au jana! Aua! Oha! Haq!
   And the yelping dog-teams go,
And the long whips crack, and the men come back,
   Back from the edge of the floe!

We tracked our seal to his secret place,
   We heard him scratch below,
We made our mark, and we watched beside,
   Out on the edge of the floe.

We raised our lance when he rose to breathe,
   We drove it downward—so!
And we played him thus, and we killed him thus,
   Out on the edge of the floe.

Our gloves are glued with the frozen blood,
   Our eyes with the drifting snow;
But we come back to our wives again,
   Back from the edge of the floe!

Au jana! Aua! Oha! Haq!
   And the loaded dog-teams go,
And the wives can hear their men come back,
   Back from the edge of the floe!

Red Dog

For our white and our excellent nights—for the nights of
    swift running,
      Fair ranging, far-seeing, good hunting, sure cunning!
For the smells of the dawning, untainted, ere dew has
    departed!
For the rush through the mist, and the quarry blind-started!
For the cry of our mates when the sambhur has wheeled and
    is standing at bay.
        For the risk and the riot of night!
        For the sleep at the lair-mouth by day,
          It is met, and we go to the fight.
             Bay! O Bay!

IT was after the letting in of the Jungle that the pleasantest
part of Mowgli's life began. He had the good conscience
that comes from paying debts;* all the Jungle was his
friend, and just a little afraid of him. The things that he
did and saw and heard when he was wandering from one
people to another, with or without his four companions,
would make many many stories, each as long as this one.
So you will never be told how he met the Mad Elephant of
Mandla who killed two-and-twenty bullocks drawing
eleven carts of coined silver to the Government Treasury,
and scattered the shiny rupees in the dust; how he fought
Jacala, the Crocodile, all one long night in the Marshes of
the North, and broke his skinning-knife on the brute's
back-plates; how he found a new and longer knife round
the neck of a man who had been killed by a wild boar, and
how he tracked that boar and killed him as a fair price for
the knife; how he was caught up once in the Great Famine,
by the moving of the deer, and nearly crushed to death in
the swaying hot herds; how he saved Hathi the Silent from
being once more trapped in a pit with a stake at the
bottom, and how, next day, he himself fell into a very
cunning leopard-trap, and how Hathi broke the thick
wooden bars to pieces above him; how he milked the wild
buffaloes in the swamp, and how——

But we must tell one tale at a time. Father and Mother Wolf died, and Mowgli rolled a big boulder against the mouth of their cave, and cried the Death Song over them; Baloo grew very old and stiff, and even Bagheera, whose nerves were steel and whose muscles were iron, was a shade slower on the kill than he had been. Akela turned from gray to milky white with pure age; his ribs stuck out, and he walked as though he had been made of wood, and Mowgli killed for him. But the young wolves, the children of the disbanded Seeonee Pack, throve and increased, and when there were about forty of them, masterless, full-voiced, clean-footed five-year-olds, Akela told them that they ought to gather themselves together and follow the Law, and run under one head, as befitted the Free People.

This was not a question in which Mowgli concerned himself, for, as he said, he had eaten sour fruit, and he knew the tree it hung from; but when Phao, son of Phaona* (his father was the Gray Tracker in the days of Akela's headship), fought his way to the leadership of the Pack, according to the Jungle Law, and the old calls and songs began to ring under the stars once more, Mowgli came to the Council Rock for memory's sake. When he chose to speak the Pack waited till he had finished, and he sat at Akela's side on the rock above Phao. Those were days of good hunting and good sleeping. No stranger cared to break into the jungles that belonged to Mowgli's people, as they called the Pack, and the young wolves grew fat and strong, and there were many cubs to bring to the Looking-over. Mowgli always attended a Looking-over, remembering the night when a black panther bought a naked brown baby into the pack, and the long call, 'Look, look well, O Wolves,' made his heart flutter. Otherwise, he would be far away in the Jungle with his four brothers, tasting, touching, seeing, and feeling new things.

One twilight when he was trotting leisurely across the ranges to give Akela the half of a buck that he had killed, while the Four jogged behind him, sparring a little, and tumbling one another over for joy of being alive, he heard a cry that had never been heard since the bad days of Shere

Khan. It was what they call in the Jungle the *pheeal*, a
hideous kind of shriek that the jackal gives when he is
hunting behind a tiger, or when there is a big killing afoot.
If you can imagine a mixture of hate, triumph, fear, and
despair, with a kind of leer running through it, you will get
some notion of the *pheeal** that rose and sank and wavered
and quavered far away across the Waingunga. The Four
stopped at once, bristling and growling. Mowgli's hand
went to his knife, and he checked, the blood in his face, his
eyebrows knotted.

'There is no Striped One dare kill here,' he said.

'That is not the cry of the Forerunner,' answered Gray
Brother. 'It is some great killing. Listen!'

It broke out again, half sobbing and half chuckling, just
as though the jackal had soft human lips. Then Mowgli
drew deep breath, and ran to the Council Rock overtaking
on his way hurrying wolves of the Pack. Phao and Akela
were on the Rock together, and below them, every nerve
strained, sat the others. The mothers and the cubs were
cantering off to their lairs; for when the *pheeal* cries it is no
time for weak things to be abroad.

They could hear nothing except the Waingunga rushing
and gurgling in the dark, and the light evening winds
among the tree-tops, till suddenly across the river a wolf
called. It was no wolf of the Pack, for they were all at the
Rock. The note changed to a long, despairing bay; and
'Dhole!' it said, 'Dhole! dhole! dhole!' They heard tired
feet on the rocks, and a gaunt wolf, streaked with red on
his flanks, his right fore-paw useless, and his jaws white
with foam, flung himself into the circle and lay gasping at
Mowgli's feet.

'Good hunting! Under whose Headship?' said Phao
gravely.

'Good hunting! Won-tolla* am I,' was the answer. He
meant that he was a solitary wolf, fending for himself, his
mate, and his cubs in some lonely lair, as do many wolves
in the south. Won-tolla means an Outlier—one who lies
out from any Pack. Then he panted, and they could see his
heart-beats shake him backward and forward.

'What moves?' said Phao, for that is the question all the Jungle asks after the *pheeal* cries.

'The dhole,* the dhole of the Dekkan*—Red Dog, the Killer! They came north from the south saying the Dekkan was empty and killing out by the way. When this moon was new there were four to me—my mate and three cubs. She would teach them to kill on the grass plains, hiding to drive the buck, as we do who are of the open. At midnight I heard them together, full tongue on the trail. At the dawn-wind I found them stiff in the grass—four, Free People, four when this moon was new. Then sought I my Blood-Right and found the dhole.'

'How many?' said Mowgli quickly; the Pack growled deep in their throats.

'I do not know. Three of them will kill no more, but at the last they drove me like the buck; on my three legs they drove me. Look, Free People!'

He thrust out his mangled fore-foot, all dark with dried blood. There were cruel bites low down on his side, and his throat was torn and worried.

'Eat,' said Akela, rising up from the meat Mowgli had brought him, and the Outlier flung himself on it.

'This shall be no loss,' he said humbly, when he had taken off the first edge of his hunger. 'Give me a little strength, Free People, and I also will kill. My lair is empty that was full when this moon was new, and the Blood Debt is not all paid.'

Phao heard his teeth crack on a haunch-bone and grunted approvingly.

'We shall need those jaws,' said he. 'Were there cubs with the dhole?'

'Nay, nay. Red Hunters all: grown dogs of their Pack, heavy and strong for all that they eat lizards in the Dekkan.'

What Won-tolla had said meant that the dhole, the red hunting-dog of the Dekkan, was moving to kill, and the Pack knew well that even the tiger will surrender a new kill to the dhole. They drive straight through the Jungle, and what they meet they pull down and tear to pieces. Though they are not as big nor half as cunning as the wolf, they are very strong and very numerous. The dhole, for instance, do not begin to call themselves a pack till they are a hundred strong; whereas forty wolves make a very fair pack indeed. Mowgli's wanderings had taken him to the edge of the high grassy downs of the Dekkan, and he had seen the fearless dholes sleeping and playing and scratching themselves in the little hollows and tussocks that they use for lairs. He despised and hated them because they did not smell like the Free People, because they did not live in caves, and, above all, because they had hair between their toes while he and his friends were clean-footed. But he knew, for Hathi had told him, what a terrible thing a dhole hunting-pack was. Even Hathi moves aside from their line, and until they are killed, or till game is scarce, they will go forward.

Akela knew something of the dholes, too, for he said to Mowgli quietly, 'It is better to die in a Full Pack than leaderless and alone. This is good hunting, and—my last. But, as men live, thou hast very many more nights and days, Little Brother. Go north and lie down, and if any live after the dhole has gone by he shall bring thee word of the fight.'

'Ah,' said Mowgli, quite gravely, 'must I go to the marshes and catch little fish and sleep in a tree, or must I ask help of the *Bandar-log* and crack nuts, while the Pack fight below?'

'It is to the death,' said Akela. 'Thou hast never met the dhole—the Red Killer. Even the Striped One——'

"*Aowa! Aowa!*" said Mowgli pettingly. 'I have killed one striped ape, and sure am I in my stomach that Shere Khan would have left his own mate for meat to the dhole if he had winded a pack across three ranges. Listen now: There was a wolf, my father, and there was a wolf, my mother, and there was an old gray wolf (not too wise: he is white now) was my father and my mother. Therefore I—' he raised his voice, 'I say that when the dhole come, and if the dhole come, Mowgli and the Free People are of one skin for that hunting; and I say, by the Bull that bought me—by the Bull Bagheera paid for me in the old days which ye of the Pack do not remember—*I* say, that the Trees and the River may hear and hold fast if I forget; *I* say that this my knife shall be as a tooth to the Pack—and I do not think it is so blunt. This is my Word which has gone from me.'

'Thou dost not know the dhole, man with a wolf's tongue,' said Won-tolla. 'I look only to clear the Blood Debt against them ere they have me in many pieces. They move slowly, killing out as they go, but in two days a little strength will come back to me and I turn again for the Blood Debt. But for *ye*, Free People, my word is that ye go north and eat but little for a while till the dhole are gone. There is no meat in this hunting.'

'Hear the Outlier!' said Mowgli with a laugh. 'Free People, we must go north and dig lizards and rats from the bank, lest by any chance we meet the dhole. He must kill out our hunting-grounds, while we lie hid in the north till it please him to give us our own again. He is a dog—and the pup of a dog—red, yellow-bellied, lairless, and haired between every toe! He counts his cubs six and eight at the litter, as though he were Chikai, the little leaping rat. Surely we must run away, Free People, and beg leave of the peoples of the north for the offal of dead cattle! Ye know the saying: "North are the vermin; south are the lice. *We* are the Jungle." Choose ye, O choose. It is good hunting! For the Pack—for the Full Pack—for the lair and the litter; for the in-kill and the out-kill; for the mate that drives the doe and the little, little cub within the cave; it is met!—it is met!—it is met!'

The Pack answered with one deep, crashing bark that sounded in the night like a big tree falling 'It is met!' they cried.

'Stay with these,' said Mowgli to the Four. 'We shall need every tooth. Phao and Akela must make ready the battle. I go to count the dogs.'

'It is death!' Won-tolla cried, half rising. 'What can such a hairless one do against the Red Dog? Even the Striped One, remember——'

'Thou art indeed an Outlier,' Mowgli called back; 'but we will speak when the dholes are dead. Good hunting all!'

He hurried off into the darkness, wild with excitement, hardly looking where he set foot, and the natural consequence was that he tripped full length over Kaa's great coils where the python lay watching a deer-path near the river.

'*Kssha!*' said Kaa angrily. 'Is this jungle-work, to stamp and tramp and undo a night's hunting—when the game are moving so well, too?'

'The fault was mine,' said Mowgli, picking himself up. 'Indeed I was seeking thee, Flathead, but each time we meet thou art longer and broader by the length of my arm. There is none like thee in the Jungle, wise, old, strong, and most beautiful Kaa.'

'Now whither does *this* trail lead?' Kaa's voice was gentler. 'Not a moon since there was a Manling with a knife threw stones at my head and called me bad little tree-cat names, because I lay asleep in the open.'

'Ay, and turned every driven deer to all the winds, and Mowgli was hunting, and this same Flathead was too deaf to hear his whistle, and leave the deer-roads free,' Mowgli answered composedly, sitting down among the painted coils.

'Now this same Manling comes with soft, tickling words to this same Flathead, telling him that he is wise and strong and beautiful, and this same old Flathead believes and makes a place, thus, for this same stone-throwing Manling, and——Art thou at ease now? Could Bagheera give thee so good a resting-place?'

Kaa had, as usual, made a sort of soft half-hammock of himself under Mowgli's weight. The boy reached out in the darkness, and gathered in the supple cable-like neck till Kaa's head rested on his shoulder, and then he told him all that had happened in the Jungle that night.

'Wise I may be,' said Kaa at the end; 'but deaf I surely am. Else I should have heard the *pheeal*. Small wonder the Eaters of Grass are uneasy. How many be the dhole?'

'I have not yet seen. I came hot-foot to thee. Thou art

older than Hathi. But oh, Kaa,'—here Mowgli wriggled with sheer joy,—'it will be good hunting. Few of us will see another moon.'

'Dost *thou* strike in this? Remember thou art a Man; and remember what Pack cast thee out. Let the Wolf look to the Dog. *Thou* art a Man.'

'Last year's nuts are this year's black earth,' said Mowgli. 'It is true that I am a Man, but it is in my stomach that this night I have said that I am a Wolf. I called the River and the Trees to remember. I am of the Free People, Kaa, till the dhole has gone by.'

'Free People,' Kaa grunted. 'Free thieves! And thou hast tied thyself into the death-knot for the sake of the memory of the dead wolves? This is no good hunting.'

'It is my Word which I have spoken. The Trees know, the River knows. Till the dhole have gone by my Word comes not back to me.'

'*Ngssh!* This changes all trails. I had thought to take thee away with me to the northern marshes, but the Word—even the Word of a little, naked, hairless Manling—is the Word. Now I, Kaa, say——'

'Think well, Flathead, lest thou tie thyself into the death-knot also. I need no Word from thee, for well I know——'

'Be it so, then,' said Kaa. 'I will give no Word; but what is in thy stomach to do when the dhole come?'

'They must swim the Waingunga. I thought to meet them with my knife in the shallows, the Pack behind me; and so stabbing and thrusting, we a little might turn them down-stream, or cool their throats.'

'The dhole do not turn and their throats are hot,' said Kaa. 'There will be neither Manling nor Wolf-cub when that hunting is done, but only dry bones.'

'*Alala!* If we die, we die. It will be most good hunting. But my stomach is young, and I have not seen many Rains. I am not wise nor strong. Hast thou a better plan, Kaa?'

'I have seen a hundred and a hundred Rains. Ere Hathi cast his milk-tushes* my trail was big in the dust. By the

First Egg, I am older than many trees, and I have seen all that the Jungle has done.'

'But *this* is new hunting,' said Mowgli. 'Never before have the dhole crossed our trail.'

'What is has been. What will be is no more than a forgotten year striking backward. Be still while I count those my years.'

For a long hour Mowgli lay back among the coils, while Kaa, his head motionless on the ground, thought of all that he had seen and known since the day he came from the egg. The light seemed to go out of his eyes and leave them like stale opals, and now and again he made little stiff passes with his head, right and left, as though he were hunting in his sleep. Mowgli dozed quietly, for he knew that there is nothing like sleep before hunting, and he was trained to take it at any hour of the day or night.

Then he felt Kaa's back grow bigger and broader below him as the huge python puffed himself out, hissing with the noise of a sword drawn from a steel scabbard.

'I have seen all the dead seasons,' Kaa said at last, 'and the great trees and the old elephants, and the rocks that were bare and sharp-pointed ere the moss grew. Art *thou* still alive, Manling?'

'It is only a little after moonset,' said Mowgli. 'I do not understand——'

'*Hssh!* I am again Kaa. I knew it was but a little time. Now we will go to the river, and I will show thee what is to be done against the dhole.'

He turned, straight as an arrow, for the main stream of the Waingunga, plunging in a little above the pool that hid the Peace Rock, Mowgli at his side.

'Nay, do not swim. I go swiftly. My back, Little Brother.'

Mowgli tucked his left arm round Kaa's neck, dropped his right close to his body, and straightened his feet. Then Kaa breasted the current as he alone could, and the ripple of the checked water stood up in a frill round Mowgli's neck, and his feet were waved to and fro in the eddy under the python's lashing sides. A mile or two above the Peace

Rock the Waingunga narrows between a gorge of marble rocks from eighty to a hundred feet high, and the current runs like a mill-race between and over all manner of ugly stones. But Mowgli did not trouble his head about the water; little water in the world could have given him a moment's fear. He was looking at the gorge on either side and sniffing uneasily, for there was a sweetish-sourish smell in the air, very like the smell of a big ant-hill on a hot day. Instinctively he lowered himself in the water, only raising his head to breathe from time to time, and Kaa came to anchor with a double twist of his tail round a sunken rock, holding Mowgli in the hollow of a coil, while the water raced on.

'This is the Place of Death,' said the boy. 'Why do we come here?'

'They sleep,' said Kaa. 'Hathi will not turn aside for the Striped One. Yet Hathi and the Striped One together turn aside for the dhole, and the dhole they say turn aside for nothing. And yet for whom do the Little People of the Rocks turn aside? Tell me, Master of the Jungle, who is the Master of the Jungle?'

'These,' Mowgli whispered. 'It is the Place of Death. Let us go.'

'Nay, look well, for they are asleep. It is as it was when I was not the length of thy arm.'

The split and weatherworn rocks of the gorge of the Waingunga had been used since the beginning of the Jungle by the Little People of the Rocks—the busy, furious, black wild bees of India; and, as Mowgli knew well, all trails turned off half a mile before they reached the gorge. For centuries the Little People had hived and swarmed from cleft to cleft, and swarmed again, staining the white marble with stale honey, and made their combs tall and deep in the dark of the inner caves, where neither man nor beast nor fire nor water had ever touched them. The length of the gorge on both sides was hung as it were with black shimmery velvet curtains, and Mowgli sank as he looked, for those were the clotted millions of the sleeping bees. There were other lumps and festoons and things like decayed tree-trunks studded on the face of the rock, the old combs of past years, or new cities built in the shadow of the windless gorge, and huge masses of spongy, rotten trash had rolled down and stuck among the trees and creepers that clung to the rock-face. As he listened he heard more than once the rustle and slide of a honey-loaded comb turning over or falling away somewhere in the dark galleries; then a booming of angry wings, and the sullen drip, drip, drip, of the wasted honey, guttering along till it lipped over some ledge in the open air and sluggishly trickled down on the twigs. There was a tiny little beach, not five feet broad, on one side of the river, and that was piled high with the rubbish of uncounted years. There were dead bees, drones, sweepings, and stale combs, and wings of marauding moths that had strayed in after honey, all tumbled in smooth piles of the finest black dust. The mere sharp smell of it was enough to frighten anything that had no wings, and knew what the Little People were.

Kaa moved up-stream again till he came to a sandy bar at the head of the gorge.

'Here is this season's kill,' said he. 'Look!'

On the bank lay the skeletons of a couple of young deer and a buffalo. Mowgli could see that neither wolf nor jackal had touched the bones, which were laid out naturally.

'They came beyond the line; they did not know the Law,' murmured Mowgli, 'and the Little People killed them. Let us go ere they wake.'

'They do not wake till the dawn,' said Kaa. 'Now I will tell thee. A hunted buck from the south, many, many Rains ago, came hither from the south, not knowing the Jungle, a Pack on his trail. Being made blind by fear, he leaped from above, the Pack running by sight, for they were hot and blind on the trail. The sun was high, and the Little People were many and very angry. Many, too, were those of the Pack who leaped into the Waingunga, but they were dead ere they took water. Those who did not leap died also in the rocks above. But the buck lived.'

'How?'

'Because he came first, running for his life, leaping ere the Little People were aware, and was in the river when they gathered to kill. The Pack, following, was altogether lost under the weight of the Little People.'

'The buck lived?' Mowgli repeated slowly.

'At least he did not die *then*, though none waited his coming down with a strong body to hold him safe against the water, as a certain old fat, deaf, yellow Flathead would wait for a Manling—yea, though there were all the dholes of the Dekkan on his trail. What is in thy stomach?' Kaa's head was close to Mowgli's ear; and it was a little time before the boy answered.

'It is to pull the very whiskers of Death, but—Kaa, thou art, indeed, the wisest of all the Jungle.'

'So many have said. Look now, if the dhole follow thee——'

'As surely they will follow. Ho! ho! I have many little thorns under my tongue to prick into their hides.'

'If they follow thee hot and blind, looking only at thy shoulders, those who do not die up above will take water either here or lower down, for the Little People will rise up and cover them. Now the Waingunga is hungry water, and they will have no Kaa to hold them, but will go down, such as live, to the shallows by the Seeonee Lairs, and there thy Pack may meet them by the throat.'

'*Ahai! Eowawa!* Better could not be till the Rains fall in the dry season. There is now only the little matter of the run and the leap. I will make me known to the dholes, so that they shall follow me very closely.'

'Hast thou seen the rocks above thee? From the land-ward side?'

'Indeed, no. That I had forgotten.'

'Go look. It is all rotten ground, cut and full of holes. One of thy clumsy feet set down without seeing would end the hunt. See, I leave thee here, and for thy sake only I will carry word to the Pack that they may know where to look for the dhole. For myself, I am not of one skin with *any* wolf.'

When Kaa disliked an acquaintance he could be more unpleasant than any of the Jungle People, except perhaps Bagheera. He swam down-stream, and opposite the Rock he came on Phao and Akela listening to the night noises.

'*Hssh!* Dogs,' he said cheerfully. 'The dholes will come down-stream. If ye be not afraid ye can kill them in the shallows.'

'When come they?' said Phao. 'And where is my Man-cub?' said Akela.

'They come when they come,' said Kaa. 'Wait and see. As for *thy* Man-cub, from whom thou hast taken a Word and so laid him open to Death, *thy* Man-cub is with *me*, and if he be not already dead the fault is none of thine, bleached dog! Wait here for the dhole, and be glad that the Man-cub and I strike on thy side.'

Kaa flashed up-stream again, and moored himself in the middle of the gorge, looking upward at the line of the cliff. Presently he saw Mowgli's head move against the stars, and then there was a whizz in the air, the keen, clean *schloop* of a body falling feet first, and the next minute the boy was at rest again in the loop of Kaa's body.

'It is no leap by night,' said Mowgli quietly. 'I have jumped twice as far for sport; but that is an evil place above—low bushes and gullies that go down very deep, all full of the Little People. I have put big stones one above the other by the side of three gullies. These I shall throw down with my feet in running, and the Little People will rise up behind me, very angry.'

'That is Man's talk and Man's cunning,' said Kaa. 'Thou art wise, but the Little People are always angry.'

'Nay, at twilight all wings near and far rest for a while. I will play with the dhole at twilight, for the dhole hunts best by day. He follows now Won-tolla's blood-trail.'

'Chil does not leave a dead ox, nor the dhole the blood-trail,' said Kaa.

'Then I will make him a new blood-trail, of his own blood, if I can, and give him dirt to eat. Thou wilt stay here, Kaa, till I come again with my dholes?'

'Ay, but what if they kill thee in the Jungle, or the Little People kill thee before thou canst leap down to the river?'

'When to-morrow comes we will kill for to-morrow,' said Mowgli, quoting a Jungle saying; and again, 'When I am dead it is time to sing the Death Song. Good hunting, Kaa!'

He loosed his arm from the python's neck and went down the gorge like a log in a freshet, paddling toward the far bank, where he found slack-water, and laughing aloud from sheer happiness. There was nothing Mowgli liked better than, as he himself said, 'to pull the whiskers of Death,' and make the Jungle know that he was their overlord. He had often, with Baloo's help, robbed bees' nests in single trees, and he knew that the Little People hated the smell of wild garlic. So he gathered a small bundle of it, tied it up with a bark string, and then followed Won-tolla's blood-trail, as it ran southerly from the Lairs, for some five miles, looking at the trees with his head on one side, and chuckling as he looked.

'Mowgli the Frog have I been,' said he to himself; 'Mowgli the Wolf have I said that I am. Now Mowgli the Ape must I be before I am Mowgli the Buck. At the end I shall be Mowgli the Man. Ho!' and he slid his thumb along the eighteen-inch blade of his knife.

Won-tolla's trail, all rank with dark blood-spots, ran under a forest of thick trees that grew close together and stretched away north-eastward, gradually growing thinner and thinner to within two miles of the Bee Rocks.* From the last tree to the low scrub of the Bee Rocks was open country, where there was hardly cover enough to hide a wolf. Mowgli trotted along under the trees, judging distances between branch and branch, occasionally climbing up a trunk and taking a trial leap from one tree to another till he came to the open ground, which he studied very carefully for an hour. Then he turned, picked up Won-tolla's trail where he had left it, settled himself in a tree with an outrunning branch some eight feet from the ground, and sat still, sharpening his knife on the sole of his foot and singing to himself.

A little before mid-day, when the sun was very warm, he heard the patter of feet and smelt the abominable smell of the dhole-pack as they trotted pitilessly along Won-tolla's trail. Seen from above, the red dhole does not look half the size of a wolf, but Mowgli knew how strong his feet and jaws were. He watched the sharp bay head of the leader snuffing along the trail, and gave him 'Good hunting!'

The brute looked up, and his companions halted behind him, scores and scores of red dogs with low-hung tails, heavy shoulders, weak quarters, and bloody mouths. The dholes are a very silent people as a rule, and they have no manners even in their own Jungle. Fully two hundred must have gathered below him, but he could see that the leaders sniffed hungrily on Won-tolla's trail, and tried to drag the Pack forward. That would never do, or they would be at the Lairs in broad daylight, and Mowgli meant to hold them under his tree till dusk.

'By whose leave do ye come here?' said Mowgli.

'All Jungles are our Jungle,' was the reply, and the dhole that gave it bared his white teeth. Mowgli looked down with a smile, and imitated perfectly the sharp chitter-chatter of Chikai, the leaping rat of the Dekkan, meaning the dholes to understand that he considered them no better than Chikai. The Pack closed up round the tree-trunk and the leader bayed savagely, calling Mowgli a tree-ape. For an answer Mowgli stretched down one naked leg and wriggled his bare toes just above the leader's head. That was enough, and more than enough, to wake the Pack to stupid rage. Those who have hair between their toes do not care to be reminded of it. Mowgli caught his foot away as the leader leaped up, and said sweetly: 'Dog, red dog! Go back to the Dekkan and eat lizards. Go to Chikai thy brother—dog, dog—red, red dog! There is hair between every toe!' He twiddled his toes a second time.

'Come down ere we starve thee out, hairless ape!' yelled the Pack, and this was exactly what Mowgli wanted. He laid himself down along the branch, his cheek to the bark, his right arm free, and there he told the Pack what he thought and knew about them, their manners, their customs, their mates, and their puppies. There is no speech in the world so rancorous and so stinging as the language the Jungle People use to show scorn and contempt. When you come to think of it you will see how this must be so. As Mowgli told Kaa, he had many little thorns under his tongue, and slowly and deliberately he drove the dholes from silence to growls, from growls to yells, and from yells to hoarse slavery ravings. They tried to answer his taunts, but a cub might as well have tried to answer Kaa in a rage; and all the while Mowgli's right hand lay crooked at his side, ready for action, his feet locked round the branch. The big bay leader had leaped many times in the air, but Mowgli dared not risk a false blow. At last, made furious beyond his natural strength, he bounded up seven or eight feet clear of the ground. Then Mowgli's hand shot out like the head of a tree-snake, and gripped him by the scruff of his neck, and the branch shook with the jar as his weight fell back, almost wrenching Mowgli to the ground. But he never loosed his grip, and inch by inch he hauled the beast, hanging like a drowned jackal, up on the branch. With his left hand he reached for his knife and cut off the red, bushy tail, flinging the dhole back to earth again. That was all he needed. The Pack would not go forward on Won-tolla's trail now till they had killed Mowgli or Mowgli had killed them. He saw them settle down in circles with a quiver of the haunches that meant they were going to stay, and so he climbed to a higher crotch, settled his back comfortably, and went to sleep.

After three or four hours he waked and counted the Pack. They were all there, silent, husky, and dry, with eyes of steel. The sun was beginning to sink. In half an hour the Little People of the rocks would be ending their labours, and, as you know, the dhole does not fight best in the twilight.

'I did not need such faithful watchers,' he said politely, standing up on a branch, 'but I will remember this. Ye be true dholes, but to my thinking over much of one kind. For that reason I do not give the big lizard-eater his tail again. Art thou not pleased, Red Dog?'

'I myself will tear out thy stomach!' yelled the leader, scratching at the foot of the tree.

'Nay, but consider, wise rat of the Dekkan. There will now be many litters of little tailless red dogs, yea, with raw red stumps that sting when the sand is hot. Go home, Red Dog, and cry that an ape had done this. Ye will not go? Come, then, with me, and I will make you very wise!'

He moved, *Bandar-log* fashion, into the next tree, and so on into the next and the next, the Pack following with lifted hungry heads. Now and then he would pretend to fall, and the Pack would tumble one over the other in their haste to be at the death. It was a curious sight—the boy with the knife that shone in the low sunlight as it sifted through the upper branches, and the silent Pack with their red coats all aflame, huddling and following below. When he came to the last tree he took the garlic and rubbed himself all over carefully, and the dholes yelled with scorn. 'Ape with a wolf's tongue, dost thou think to cover thy scent?' they said. 'We follow to the death.'

'Take thy tail,' said Mowgli, flinging it back along the course he had taken. The Pack instinctively rushed after it. 'And follow now—to the death.'

He had slipped down the tree-trunk, and headed like the wind in bare feet for the Bee Rocks, before the dholes saw what he would do.

They gave one deep howl, and settled down to the long, lobbing canter that can at the last run down anything that runs. Mowgli knew their pack-pace to be much slower than that of the wolves, or he would never have risked a two-mile run in full sight. They were sure that the boy was theirs at last, and he was sure that he held them to play with as he pleased. All his trouble was to keep them sufficiently hot behind him to prevent their turning off too soon. He ran cleanly, evenly, and springily; the tailless leader not five yards behind him; and the Pack tailing out over perhaps a quarter of a mile of ground, crazy and blind with the rage of slaughter. So he kept his distance by ear, reserving his last effort for the rush across the Bee Rocks.

The Little People had gone to sleep in the early twilight,

for it was not the season of late blossoming flowers; but as Mowgli's first foot-falls rang hollow on the hollow ground he heard a sound as though all the earth were humming. Then he ran as he had never run in his life before, spurned aside—one—two—three of the piles of stones into the dark, sweet-smelling gullies; heard a roar like the roar of the sea in a cave; saw with the tail of his eye the air grow dark behind him; saw the current of the Waingunga far below, and a flat, diamond-shaped head in the water; leaped outward with all his strength, the tailless dhole snapping at his shoulder in mid-air, and dropped feet first to the safety of the river, breathless and triumphant. There was not a sting upon him, for the smell of the garlic had checked the Little People for just the few seconds that he was among them. When he rose Kaa's coils were steadying him and things were bounding over the edge of the cliff—great lumps, it seemed, of clustered bees falling like plummets; but before any lump touched water the bees flew upward and the body of a dhole whirled downstream. Overhead they could hear furious short yells that were drowned in a roar like breakers—the roar of the wings of the Little People of the Rocks. Some of the dholes, too, had fallen into the gullies that communicated with the underground caves, and there choked and fought and snapped among the tumbled honeycombs, and at last, borne up, even when they were dead, on the heaving waves of bees beneath them, shot out of some hole in the river-face, to roll over on the black rubbish-heaps. There were dholes who had leaped short into the trees on the cliffs, and the bees blotted out their shapes; but the greater number of them, maddened by the stings, had flung themselves into the river; and, as Kaa said, the Waingunga was hungry water.

Kaa held Mowgli fast till the boy had recovered his breath.

'We may not stay here,' he said. 'The Little People are roused indeed. Come!'

Swimming low and diving as often as he could, Mowgli went down the river, knife in hand.

'Slowly, slowly,' said Kaa. 'One tooth does not kill a hundred unless it be a cobra's and many of the dholes took water swiftly when they saw the Little People rise.'

'The more work for my knife then. *Phai!* How the Little People follow!' Mowgli sank again. The face of the water was blanketed with wild bees, buzzing sullenly and stinging all they found.

'Nothing was ever yet lost by silence,' said Kaa—no sting could penetrate his scales—'and thou hast all the long night for the hunting. Hear them howl!'

Nearly half the pack had seen the trap their fellow rushed into, and turning sharp aside had flung themselves into the water where the gorge broke down in steep banks. Their cries of rage and their threats against the 'tree-ape' who had brought them to their shame mixed with the yells and growls of those who had been punished by the Little People. To remain ashore was death, and every dhole knew it. Their pack was swept along the current, down to the deep eddies of the Peace Pool, but even there the angry Little People followed and forced them to the water again. Mowgli could hear the voice of the tailless leader bidding his people to hold on and kill out every wolf in Seeonee. But he did not waste his time in listening.

'One kills in the dark behind us!' snapped a dhole. 'Here is tainted water!'

Mowgli had dived forward like an otter, twitched a struggling dhole under water before he could open his mouth, and dark rings rose as the body plopped up, turning on its side. The dholes tried to turn, but the current prevented them, and the Little People darted at their heads and ears, and they could hear the challenge of the Seeonee Pack growing louder and deeper in the gathering darkness. Again Mowgli dived, and again a dhole went under, and rose dead, and again the clamour broke out at the rear of the pack; some howling that it was best to go ashore, others calling on their leader to lead them back to the Dekkan, and others bidding Mowgli show himself and be killed.

'They come to the fight with two stomachs and several

voices,' said Kaa. 'The rest is with thy brethren below yonder. The Little People go back to sleep. They have chased us far. Now I, too, turn back, for I am not of one skin with any wolf. Good hunting, Little Brother, and remember the dhole bites low.'

A wolf came running along the bank on three legs, leaping up and down, laying his head sideways close to the ground, hunching his back, and breaking high into the air, as though he were playing with his cubs. It was Won-tolla, the Outlier, and he said never a word, but continued his horrible sport beside the dholes. They had been long in the water now, and were swimming wearily, their coats drenched and heavy, their bushy tails dragging like sponges, so tired and shaken that they, too, were silent, watching the pair of blazing eyes that moved abreast.

'This is no good hunting,' said one, panting.

'Good hunting! said Mowgli, as he rose boldy at the brute's side, and sent the long knife home behind the shoulder, pushing hard to avoid his dying snap.

'Art thou there, Man-cub?' said Won-tolla across the water.

'Ask of the dead, Outlier,' Mowgli replied 'Have none come down-stream? I have filled these dogs' mouths with dirt; I have tricked them in the broad daylight, and their leader lacks his tail, but here be some few for thee still. Whither shall I drive them?'

'I will wait,' said Won-tolla. 'The night is before me.'

Nearer and nearer came the bay of the Seeonee wolves. 'For the Pack, for the Full Pack it is met!' and a bend in the river drove the dholes forward among the sands and shoals opposite the Lairs.

Then they saw their mistake. They should have landed half a mile higher up, and rushed the wolves on dry ground. Now it was too late. The bank was lined with burning eyes, and except for the horrible *pheeal* that had never stopped since sundown, there was no sound in the Jungle. It seemed as though Won-tolla were fawning on them to come ashore; and 'Turn and take hold!' said the leader of the dholes. The entire Pack flung themselves at the shore, threshing and squattering through the shoal water, till the face of the Waingunga was all white and torn, and the great ripples went from side to side, like bow-waves from a boat. Mowgli followed the rush, stabbing and slicing as the dholes, huddled together, rushed up the river-beach in one wave.

Then the long fight began, heaving and straining and splitting and scattering and narrowing and broadening along the red, wet sands, and over and between the tangled tree-roots, and through and among the bushes, and in and out of the grass clumps; for even now the dholes were two to one. But they met wolves fighting for all that made the Pack, and not only the short, high, deep-chested, white-tusked hunters of the Pack, but the anxious-eyed lahi-nis*—the she-wolves of the lair, as the saying is—fighting for their litters, with here and there a yearling wolf, his first coat still half woolly, tugging and grappling by their sides. A wolf, you must know, flies at the throat or snaps at the flank, while a dhole, by preference, bites at the belly; so when the dholes were struggling out of the water and had to raise their heads, the odds were with the wolves. On dry land the wolves suffered; but in the water or ashore, Mowgli's knife came and went without ceasing. The Four had worried their way to his side. Gray Brother, crouched between the boy's knees, was protecting his stomach, while the others guarded his back and either side, or stood over him when the shock of a leaping yelling dhole who had thrown himself full on the steady blade bore him down. For the rest, it was one tangled confusion—a locked and swaying mob that moved from right to left and from left to right along the bank; and also ground round and round slowly on its centre. Here would be a heaving mound, like a water-blister in a whirlpool, which would break like a water-blister, and throw up four or five mangled dogs, each striving to get back to the centre; here would be a single wolf borne down by two or three dholes, laboriously dragging them forward, and sinking the while; here a yearling cub would be held up by the pressure round him, though he had been killed early, while his mother, crazed with dumb rage, rolled over and over, snapping, and passing on; and in the middle of the thickest

press, perhaps, one wolf and one dhole, forgetting everything else, would be manœuvring for first hold till they
were whirled away by a rush of furious fighters. Once
Mowgli passed Akela, a dhole on either flank, and his all
but toothless jaws closed over the loins of a third; and once
he saw Phao, his teeth set in the throat of a dhole, tugging
the unwilling beast forward till the yearlings could finish
him. But the bulk of the fight was blind flurry and smother
in the dark; hit, trip, and tumble, yelp, groan, and worry-
worry-worry,* round him and behind him and above him.
As the night wore on, the quick, giddy-go-round motion
increased. The dholes were cowed and afraid to attack the
stronger wolves, but did not yet dare to run away. Mowgli
felt that the end was coming soon, and contented himself
with striking merely to cripple. The yearlings were growing bolder; there was time now and again to breathe, and
pass a word to a friend, and the mere flicker of the knife
would sometimes turn a dog aside.

'The meat is very near the bone,' Gray Brother yelled.
He was bleeding from a score of flesh-wounds.

'But the bone is yet to be cracked,' said Mowgli.
'*Eowawa! Thus* do we do in the Jungle!' The red blade ran
like a flame along the side of a dhole whose hind-quarters
were hidden by the weight of a clinging wolf.

'My kill!' snorted the wolf through his wrinkled nostrils. 'Leave him to me.'

'Is thy stomach still empty, Outlier?' said Mowgli.
Won-tolla was fearfully punished, but his grip had
paralysed the dhole, who could not turn round and reach
him.

'By the Bull that bought me,' said Mowgli, with a bitter
laugh, 'it is the tailless one!' And indeed it was the big bay-
coloured leader.

'It is not wise to kill cubs and lahinis,' Mowgli went on
philosophically, wiping the blood out of his eyes, 'unless
one has also killed the Outlier; and it is in my stomach that
this Won-tolla kills thee.'

A dhole leaped to his leader's aid; but before his teeth
had found Won-tolla's flank, Mowgli's knife was in his
throat, and Gray Brother took what was left.

'And thus do we do in the Jungle,' said Mowgli.

Won-tolla said not a word, only his jaws were closing and closing on the backbone as his life ebbed. The dhole shuddered, his head dropped, and he lay still, and Won-tolla dropped above him.

'*Huh!* the Blood Debt is paid,' said Mowgli. 'Sing the song, Won-tolla.'

'He hunts no more,' said Gray Brother; 'and Akela, too, is silent this long time.'

'The bone is cracked!' thundered Phao, son of Phaona. 'They go! Kill, kill out, O hunters of the Free People!'

Dhole after dhole was slinking away from those dark and bloody sands to the river, to the thick Jungle, up-stream or down-stream as he saw the road clear.

'The debt! The debt!' shouted Mowgli. 'Pay the debt! They have slain the Lone Wolf! Let not a dog go!'

He was flying to the river, knife in hand, to check any dhole who dared to take water, when, from under a mound of nine dead, rose Akela's head and fore-quarters, and Mowgli dropped on his knees beside the Lone Wolf.

'Said I not it would be my last fight?' Akela gasped. 'It is good hunting. And thou, Little Brother?'

'I live, having killed many.'

'Even so. I die, and I would—I would die by thee, Little Brother.'

Mowgli took the terrible scarred head on his knees, and put his arms round the torn neck.

'It is long since the old days of Shere Khan, and a Man-cub that rolled naked in the dust.'

'Nay, nay, I am a wolf. I am of one skin with the Free People,' Mowgli cried. 'It is no will of mine that I am a man.'

'Thou art a man, Little Brother, wolfling of my watching. Thou art a man, or else the Pack had fled before the dhole. My life I owe to thee, and to-day thou hast saved the Pack even as once I saved thee. Hast thou forgotten? All debts are paid now. Go to thine own people. I tell thee again, eye of my eye, this hunting is ended. Go to thine own people.'

'I will never go. I will hunt alone in the Jungle. I have said it.'

'After the summer come the Rains, and after the Rains comes the spring. Go back before thou art driven.'

'Who will drive me?'

'Mowgli will drive Mowgli. Go back to thy people. Go to Man.'

'When Mowgli drives Mowgli I will go,' Mowgli answered.

'There is no more to say,' said Akela. 'Little Brother, canst thou raise me to my feet? I also was a leader of the Free People.'

Very carefully and gently Mowgli lifted the bodies aside, and raised Akela to his feet, both arms round him, and the Lone Wolf drew a long breath, and began the Death Song that a leader of the Pack should sing when he dies. It gathered strength as he went on, lifting and lifting, and ringing far across the river, till it came to the last 'Good hunting!' and Akela shook himself clear of Mowgli for an instant, and, leaping into the air, fell backward dead upon his last and most terrible kill.

Mowgli sat with his head on his knees, careless of anything else, while the remnant of the flying dholes were being overtaken and run down by the merciless lahinis. Little by little the cries died away, and the wolves returned limping, as their wounds stiffened, to take stock of the losses. Fifteen of the Pack, as well as half a dozen lahinis, lay dead by the river, and of the others not one was unmarked. And Mowgli sat through it all till the cold daybreak, when Phao's wet, red muzzle was dropped in his hand, and Mowgli drew back to show the gaunt body of Akela.

'Good hunting!' said Phao, as though Akela were still alive, and then over his bitten shoulder to the others: 'Howl, dogs! A Wolf has died to-night!'

But of all the Pack of two hundred fighting dholes, whose boast was that all Jungles were their Jungle, and that no living thing could stand before them, not one returned to the Dekkan to carry that word.

Chil's Song

[This is the song that Chil sang as the kites dropped down one after another to the river-bed, when the great fight was finished. Chil is good friends with everybody, but he is a cold-blooded kind of creature at heart, because he knows that almost everybody in the Jungle comes to him in the long-run.]

THESE were my companions going forth by night—
   (*For Chil! Look you, for Chil!*)
Now come I to whistle them the ending of the fight.
   (*Chil! Vanguards of Chil!*)
Word they gave me overhead of quarry newly slain,
Word I gave them underfoot of buck upon the plain.
Here's an end of every trail—they shall not speak again!

They that called the hunting-cry—they that followed fast—
   (*For Chil! Look you, for Chil!*)
They that bade the sambhur wheel, and pinned him as he
      passed—
   (*Chil! Vanguards of Chil!*)
They that lagged behind the scent—they that ran before,
They that shunned the level horn—they that overbore.
Here's an end of every trail—they shall not follow more.

These were my companions. Pity 'twas they died!
   (*For Chil! Look you, for Chil!*)
Now come I to comfort them that knew them in their pride.
   (*Chil! Vanguards of Chil!*)
Tattered flank and sunken eye, open mouth and red,
Locked and lank and lone they lie, the dead upon their dead.
Here's an end of every trail—and here my hosts are fed!

The Spring Running

Man goes to Man! Cry the challenge through the Jungle!
  He that was our Brother goes away.
Hear, now, and judge, O ye People of the Jungle,—
  Answer, who shall turn him—who shall stay?

Man goes to Man! He is weeping in the Jungle:
  He that was our Brother sorrows sore!
Man goes to Man! (Oh, we loved him in the Jungle!)
  To the Man-Trail where we may not follow more.

THE second year after the great fight with Red Dog and the death of Akela, Mowgli must have been nearly seventeen years old. He looked older, for hard exercise, the best of good eating, and baths whenever he felt in the least hot or dusty, had given him strength and growth far beyond his age. He could swing by one hand from a top branch for half an hour at a time, when he had occasion to look along the tree-roads. He could stop a young buck in mid-gallop and throw him sideways by the head. He could even jerk over the big, blue wild boars that lived in the Marshes of the North. The Jungle People who used to fear him for his wits feared him now for his strength, and when he moved quietly on his own affairs the mere whisper of his coming cleared the wood-paths. And yet the look in his eyes was always gentle. Even when he fought, his eyes never blazed as Bagheera's did. They only grew more and more interested and excited; and that was one of the things that Bagheera himself did not understand.

He asked Mowgli about it, and the boy laughed and said: 'When I miss the kill I am angry. When I must go empty for two days I am very angry. Do not my eyes talk then?'

'The mouth is hungry,' said Bagheera, 'but the eyes say nothing. Hunting, eating, or swimming, it is all one—like a stone in wet or dry weather.' Mowgli looked at him lazily from under his long eyelashes, and, as usual, the panther's head dropped. Bagheera knew his master.

They were lying out far up the side of a hill overlooking the Waingunga, and the morning mists hung below them in bands of white and green. As the sun rose it changed into bubbling seas of red gold, churned off, and let the low rays stripe the dried grass on which Mowgli and Bagheera were resting. It was the end of the cold weather, the leaves and the trees looked worn and faded, and there was a dry, ticking rustle everywhere when the wind blew. A little leaf tap-tap-tapped furiously against a twig, as a single leaf caught in a current will. It roused Bagheera, for he snuffed the morning air with a deep, hollow cough, threw himself on his back, and struck with his fore-paws at the nodding leaf above.

'The year turns,' he said. 'The Jungle goes forward. The Time of New Talk is near. That leaf knows. It is very good.'

'The grass is dry,' Mowgli answered, pulling up a tuft. 'Even Eye-of-the-Spring [that is a little trumpet-shaped, waxy red flower that runs in and out among the grasses]— even Eye-of-the-Spring is shut, and . . . Bagheera, *is* it well for the Black Panther so to lie on his back and beat with his paws in the air, as though he were the tree-cat?'*

'Aowh?' said Bagheera. He seemed to be thinking of other things.

'I say, *is* it well for the Black Panther so to mouth and cough, and howl and roll? Remember, we be the Masters of the Jungle, thou and I.'

'Indeed, yes; I hear, Man-cub.' Bagheera rolled over hurriedly and sat up, the dust on his ragged black flanks. (He was just casting his winter coat.) 'We be surely the Masters of the Jungle! Who is so strong as Mowgli? Who so wise?' There was a curious drawl in the voice that made Mowgli turn to see whether by any chance the Black Panther were making fun of him, for the Jungle is full of words that sound like one thing, but mean another. 'I said we be beyond question of the Masters of the Jungle,' Bagheera repeated. 'Have I done wrong? I did not know that the Man-cub no longer lay upon the ground. Does he fly, then?'

Mowgli sat with his elbows on his knees, looking out across the valley at the daylight. Somewhere down in the woods below a bird was trying over in a husky, reedy voice the first few notes of his spring song. It was not more than a shadow of the liquid, tumbling call he would be pouring later, but Bagheera heard it.

'I said the Time of New Talk is near,' growled the panther, switching his tail.

'I hear,' Mowgli answered. 'Bagheera, why dost thou shake all over? The sun is warm.'

'That is Ferao,* the scarlet woodpecker,' said Bagheera. '*He* has not forgotten. Now I, too, must remember my song,' and he began purring and crooning to himself, harking back dissatisfied again and again.

'There is no game afoot,' said Mowgli.

'Little Brother, are *both* thine ears stopped? That is no killing-word, but my song that I make ready against the need.'

'I had forgotten. I shall know when the Time of New Talk is here, because then thou and the others all run away and leave me alone.' Mowgli spoke rather savagely.

'But, indeed, Little Brother,' Bagheera began, 'we do not always——'

'I say ye do,' said Mowgli, shooting out his forefinger angrily. 'Ye *do* run away, and I, who am the Master of the Jungle, must needs walk alone. How was it last season, when I would gather sugar-cane from the fields of a Man-Pack? I sent a runner—I sent thee!—to Hathi, bidding him to come upon such a night and pluck the sweet grass for me with his trunk.'

'He came only two nights later,' said Bagheera, cowering a little; 'and of that long, sweet grass that pleased thee so he gathered more than any Man-cub could eat in all the nights of the Rains. That was no fault of mine.'

'He did not come upon the night when I sent him the word. No, he was trumpeting and running and roaring through the valleys in the moonlight. His trail was like the trail of three elephants, for he would not hide among the trees. He danced in the moonlight before the houses of the

Man-Pack. I saw him, and yet he would not come to me; and *I* am the Master of the Jungle!'

'It was the Time of New Talk,' said the panther, always very humble. 'Perhaps, Little Brother, thou didst not that time call him by a Master-word? Listen to Ferao, and be glad!'

Mowgli's bad temper seemed to have boiled itself away. He lay back with his head on his arms, his eyes shut. 'I do not know—nor do I care,' he said sleepily. 'Let us sleep, Bagheera. My stomach is heavy in me. Make me a rest for my head.'

The panther lay down again with a sigh, because he could hear Ferao practising and repractising his song against the Springtime of New Talk, as they say.

In an Indian Jungle the seasons slide one into the other almost without division. There seem to be only two—the wet and the dry; but if you look closely below the torrents of rain and the clouds of char* and dust you will find all four going round in their regular ring. Spring is the most wonderful, because she has not to cover a clean, bare field with new leaves and flowers, but to drive before her and to put away the hanging-on, over-surviving raffle of half-green things which the gentle winter has suffered to live, and to make the partly-dressed stale earth feel new and young once more. And this she does so well that there is no spring in the world like the Jungle spring.

There is one day when all things are tired, and the very smells, as they drift on the heavy air, are old and used. One cannot explain this, but it feels so. Then there is another day—to the eye nothing whatever has changed—when all the smells are new and delightful, and the whiskers of the Jungle People quiver to their roots, and the winter hair comes away from their sides in long, draggled locks. Then, perhaps, a little rain falls, and all the trees and the bushes and the bamboos and the mosses and the juicy-leaved plants wake with a noise of growing that you can almost hear, and under this noise runs, day and night, a deep hum. *That* is the noise of the spring—a vibrating boom which is neither bees, nor falling water, nor the wind in tree-tops, but the purring of the warm, happy world.

Up to this year Mowgli had always delighted in the turn of the seasons. It was he who generally saw the first Eye-of-the-Spring deep down among the grasses, and the first bank of spring clouds, which are like nothing else in the Jungle. His voice could be heard in all sorts of wet, star-lighted, blossoming places, helping the big frogs through their choruses, or mocking the little upside-down owls that hoot through the white nights. Like all his people, spring was the season he chose for his flittings—moving, for the mere joy of rushing through the warm air, thirty, forty, or fifty miles between twilight and the morning star, and coming back panting and laughing and wreathed with strange flowers. The Four did not follow him on these wild ringings of the Jungle, but went off to sing songs with other wolves. The Jungle People are very busy in the spring, and Mowgli could hear them grunting and scream-ing and whistling according to their kind. Their voices then are different from their voices at other times of the year, and that is one of the reasons why spring in the Jungle is called the Time of New Talk.

But that spring, as he told Bagheera, his stomach was changed in him. Ever since the bamboo shoots turned spotty-brown he had been looking forward to the morning when the smells should change. But when the morning came, and Mor* the Peacock, blazing in bronze and blue and gold, cried it aloud all along the misty woods, and Mowgli opened his mouth to send on the cry, the words choked between his teeth, and a feeling came over him that began at his toes and ended in his hair—a feeling of pure unhappiness, so that he looked himself over to be sure that he had not trod on a thorn. Mor cried the new smells, the other birds took it over, and from the rocks by the Waingunga he heard Bagheera's hoarse scream—some-thing between the scream of an eagle and the neighing of a horse. There was a yelling and scattering of *Bandar-log* in the new-budding branches above, and there stood Mowgli, his chest, filled to answer Mor, sinking in little gasps as the breath was driven out of it by this unhappiness.

He stared all round him, but he could see no more than the mocking *Bandar-log* scudding through the trees, and Mor, his tail spread in full splendour, dancing on the slopes below.

'The smells have changed,' screamed Mor. 'Good hunting, Little Brother! Where is thy answer?'

'Little Brother, good hunting!' whistled Chil the Kite and his mate, swooping down together. The two baffed* under Mowgli's nose so close that a pinch of downy white feathers brushed away.

A light spring rain—elephant-rain they call it—drove across the Jungle in a belt half a mile wide, left the new leaves wet and nodding behind, and died out in a double rainbow and a light roll of thunder. The spring hum broke out for a minute, and was silent, but all the Jungle Folk seemed to be giving tongue at once. All except Mowgli.

'I have eaten good food,' he said to himself. 'I have drunk good water. Nor does my throat burn and grow small, as it did when I bit the blue-spotted root that Oo the Turtle said was clean food. But my stomach is heavy, and I have given very bad talk to Bagheera and others, people of the Jungle and my people. Now, too, I am hot and now I am cold, and now I am neither hot nor cold, but angry with that which I cannot see. Huhu! It is time to make a running! To-night I will cross the ranges; yes, I will make a spring running to the Marches of the North, and back again. I have hunted too easily too long. The Four shall come with me, for they grow as fat as white grubs.'

He called, but never one of the Four answered. They were far beyond earshot, singing over the spring songs— the Moon and Sambhur Songs—with the wolves of the Pack; for in the spring-time the Jungle People make very little difference between the day and the night. He gave the sharp, barking note, but his only answer was the mocking *maiou* of the little spotted tree-cat winding in and out among the branches for early birds' nests. At this he shook all over with rage, and half drew his knife. Then he became very haughty, though there was no one to see him, and stalked severely down the hillside, chin up and eye-brows down. But never a single one of his people asked him a question, for they were all too busy with their own affairs.

'Yes,' said Mowgli to himself, though in his heart he knew that he had no reason. 'Let the Red Dhole come from the Dekkan, or the Red Flower dance among the bamboos, and all the Jungle runs whining to Mowgli, calling him great elephant-names. But now, because Eye-of-the-Spring is red, and Mor, forsooth, must show his naked legs in some spring dance, the Jungle goes mad as Tabaqui.* ... By the Bull that bought me! am I the Master of the Jungle, or am I not? Be silent! What do ye here?'

A couple of young wolves of the Pack were cantering down a path, looking for open ground in which to fight. (You will remember that the Law of the Jungle forbids fighting where the Pack can see.) Their neck-bristles were as stiff as wire, and they bayed furiously, crouching for the first grapple. Mowgli leaped forward, caught one out-stretched throat in either hand, expecting to fling the creatures backward as he had often done in games or Pack hunts. But he had never before interfered with a spring fight. The two leaped forward and dashed him aside, and without word to waste rolled over and over close locked.

Mowgli was on his feet almost before he fell, his knife and his white teeth were bared, and at that minute he would have killed both for no reason but that they were fighting when he wished them to be quiet, although every wolf has full right under the Law to fight. He danced round them with lowered shoulders and quivering hand, ready to send in a double blow when the first flurry of the scuffle should be over; but while he waited the strength seemed to ebb from his body, the knife-point lowered, and he sheathed the knife and watched.

'I have surely eaten poison,' he sighed at last. 'Since I broke up the Council with the Red Flower—since I killed Shere Khan—none of the Pack could fling me aside. And these be only tail-wolves in the Pack, little hunters! My strength is gone from me, and presently I shall die. Oh, Mowgli, why dost thou not kill them both?'

The fight went on till one wolf ran away, and Mowgli was left alone on the torn and bloody ground, looking now at his knife, and now at his legs and arms, while the feeling of unhappiness he had never known before covered him as water covers a log.

He killed early that evening and ate but little, so as to be in good fettle for his spring running, and he ate alone because all the Jungle People were away singing or fighting. It was a perfect white night,* as they call it. All green things seemed to have made a month's growth since the morning. The branch that was yellow-leaved the day before dripped sap when Mowgli broke it. The mosses curled deep and warm over his feet, the young grass had no cutting edges, and all the voices of the Jungle boomed like one deep harp-string touched by the moon—the Moon of New Talk, who splashed her light full on rock and pool, slipped it between trunk and creeper, and sifted it through a million leaves. Forgetting his unhappiness, Mowgli sang aloud with pure delight as he settled into his stride. It was more like flying than anything else, for he had chosen the long downward slope that leads to the Northern Marshes through the heart of the main Jungle, where the springy ground deadened the fall of his feet. A man-taught man would have picked his way with many stumbles through the cheating moonlight, but Mowgli's muscles, trained by years of experience, bore him up as though he were a feather. When a rotten log or a hidden stone turned under his foot he saved himself, never checking his pace, without effort and without thought. When he tired of ground-going he threw up his hands monkey-fashion to the nearest creeper, and seemed to float rather than to climb up into the thin branches, whence he would follow a tree-road till his mood changed, and he shot downward in a long, leafy curve to the levels again. There were still, hot hollows surrounded by wet rocks where he could hardly breathe for the heavy scents of the night flowers and the bloom along the creeper buds; dark

avenues where the moonlight lay in belts as regular as
checkered marbles in a church aisle; thickets where the
wet young growth stood breast-high about him and threw
its arms round his waist; and hilltops crowned with broken
rock, where he leaped from stone to stone above the lairs of
the frightened little foxes. He would hear, very faint and
far off, the *chug-drug* of a boar sharpening his tusks on a
bole; and would come across the great gray brute all alone,
scribing* and rending the bark of a tall tree, his mouth
dripping with foam, and his eyes blazing like fire. Or he
would turn aside to the sound of clashing horns and
hissing grunts, and dash past a couple of furious sambhur,
staggering to and fro with lowered heads, striped with
blood that showed black in the moonlight. Or at some
rushing ford he would hear Jacala the Crocodile bellowing
like a bull, or disturb a twined knot of the Poison People,
but before they could strike he would be away and across
the glistening shingle, and deep in the Jungle again.

So he ran, sometimes shouting, sometimes singing to
himself, the happiest thing in all the Jungle that night, till
the smell of the flowers warned him that he was near the
marshes, and those lay far beyond his farthest hunting-
grounds.

Here, again, a man-trained man would have sunk overhead in three strides, but Mowgli's feet had eyes in them,
and they passed him from tussock to tussock and clump to
quaking clump without asking help from the eyes in his
head. He ran out to the middle of the swamp, disturbing
the duck as he ran, and sat down on a moss-coated tree-
trunk lapped in the black water. The marsh was awake all
round him, for in the spring the Bird People sleep very
lightly, and companies of them were coming or going the
night through. But no one took any notice of Mowgli
sitting among the tall reeds humming songs without
words, and looking at the soles of his hard brown feet in
case of neglected thorns. All his unhappiness seemed to
have been left behind in his own Jungle, and he was just
beginning a full-throat song when it came back again—ten
times worse that before.

This time Mowgli was frightened. 'It is here also!' he said half aloud. 'It has followed me,' and he looked over his shoulder to see whether the It were not standing behind him. 'There is no one here.' The night noises of the marsh went on, but never a bird or beast spoke to him, and the new feeling of misery grew.

'I have surely eaten poison,' he said in an awe-stricken voice. 'It must be that carelessly I have eaten poison, and my strength is going from me. I was afraid—and yet it was not *I* that was afraid—Mowgli was afraid when the two wolves fought. Akela, or even Phao, would have silenced them; yet Mowgli was afraid. That is true sign I have eaten poison. . . . But what do they care in the Jungle? They sing and howl and fight, and run in companies under the moon, and I—*Hai-mai!*—I am dying in the marshes, of that poison which I have eaten.' He was so sorry for himself that he nearly wept. 'And after,' he went on, 'they will find me lying in the black water. Nay, I will go back to my own Jungle, and I will die upon the Council Rock, and Bagheera, whom I love, if he is not screaming in the valley—Bagheera, perhaps, may watch by what is left for a little, lest Chil use me as he used Akela.'

A large, warm tear splashed down on his knee, and, miserable as he was, Mowgli felt happy that he was so miserable, if you can understand that upside-down sort of happiness. 'As Chil the Kite used Akela,' he repeated, 'on the night I saved the Pack from Red Dog.' He was quiet for a little, thinking of the last words of the Lone Wolf, which you, of course, remember. 'Now Akela said to me many foolish things before he died, for when we die our stomachs change. He said . . . None the less, I *am* of the Jungle!'

In his excitement, as he remembered the fight on Waingunga bank, he shouted the last words aloud, and a wild buffalo-cow among the reeds sprang to her knees, snorting, 'Man!'

'Uhh!' said Mysa the Wild Buffalo (Mowgli could hear him turn in his wallow), '*that* is no man. It is only the hairless wolf of the Seeonee Pack. On such nights runs he to and fro.'

'Uhh!' said the cow, dropping her head again to graze, 'I thought it was Man.'

'I say no. Oh, Mowgli, is it danger?' lowed Mysa.

'Oh, Mowgli, is it danger?' the boy called back mockingly. 'That is all Mysa thinks for: Is it danger? But for Mowgli, who goes to and fro in the Jungle by night, watching, what do ye care?'

'How loud he cries!' said the cow.

'Thus do they cry,' Mysa answered contemptuously, 'who, having torn up the grass, know not how to eat it.'

'For less than this,' Mowgli groaned to himself,—'for less than this even last Rains I had pricked Mysa out of his wallow, and ridden him through the swamp on a rush halter.' He stretched a hand to break one of the feathery reeds, but drew it back with a sigh. Mysa went on steadily chewing the cud, and the long grass ripped where the cow grazed. 'I will not die *here*,' he said angrily. 'Mysa, who is of one blood with Jacala and the pig, would see me. Let us go beyond the swamp and see what comes. Never have I run such a spring running—hot and cold together. Up, Mowgli!'

He could not resist the temptation of stealing across the reeds to Mysa and pricking him with the point of his knife. The great dripping bull broke out of his wallow like a shell exploding, while Mowgli laughed till he sat down.

'Say now that the hairless wolf of the Seeonee Pack once herded thee, Mysa,' he called.

'Wolf! *Thou?*' the bull snorted, stamping in the mud. 'All the Jungle knows thou wast a herder of tame cattle—such a man's brat as shouts in the dust by the crops yonder. *Thou* of the Jungle! What hunter would have crawled like a snake among the leeches, and for a muddy jest—a jackal's jest—have shamed me before my cow? Come to firm ground, and I will—I will . . .' Mysa frothed at the mouth, for Mysa has nearly the worst temper of any one in the Jungle.

Mowgli watched him puff and blow with eyes that never

changed. When he could make himself heard through the spattering mud, he said: 'What Man-Pack lair here by the marshes, Mysa? This is new Jungle to me.'

'Go north, then,' roared the angry bull, for Mowgli had pricked him rather sharply. 'It was a naked cow-herd's jest. Go and tell them at the village at the foot of the marsh.'

'The Man-Pack do not love jungle-tales, nor do I think, Mysa, that a scratch more or less on thy hide is any matter for a council. But I will go and look at this village. Yes, I will go. Softly now. It is not every night that the Master of the Jungle comes to herd thee.'

He stepped out to the shivering ground on the edge of the marsh, well knowing that Mysa would never charge over it, and laughed, as he ran, to think of the bull's anger.

'My strength is not altogether gone,' he said. 'It may be that the poison is not to the bone. There is a star sitting low yonder.' He looked at it between his half-shut hands. 'By the Bull that bought me, it is the Red Flower—the Red Flower that I lay beside before—before I came even to the first Seeonee Pack! Now that I have seen, I will finish the running.'

The marsh ended in a broad plain where a light twinkled. It was a long time since Mowgli had concerned himself with the doings of men, but this night the glimmer of the Red Flower drew him forward.

'I will look,' said he, 'as I did in the old days, and I will see how far the Man-Pack has changed.'

Forgetting that he was no longer in his own Jungle, where he could do what he pleased, he trod carelessly through the dew-loaded grasses till he came to the hut where the light stood. Three or four yelping dogs gave tongue, for he was on the outskirts of a village.

'Ho!' said Mowgli, sitting down noiselessly, after sending back a deep wolf-growl that silenced the curs. 'What comes will come. Mowgli, what hast thou to do any more with the lairs of the Man-Pack?' He rubbed his mouth, remembering where a stone had struck it years ago when the other Man-Pack had cast him out.

The door of the hut opened, and a woman stood peering out into the darkness. A child cried, and the woman said over her shoulder, 'Sleep. It was but a jackal that waked the dogs. In a little time morning comes.'

Mowgli in the grass began to shake as though he had fever. He knew that voice well, but to make sure he cried softly, surprised to find how man's talk came back, 'Messua! O Messua!'

'Who calls?' said the women, a quiver in her voice.

'Hast thou forgotten?' said Mowgli. His throat was dry as he spoke.

'If it be *thou*, what name did I give thee? Say!' She had half shut the door, and her hand was clutching at her breast.

'Nathoo! Ohé Nathoo!' said Mowgli, for, as you remember, that was the name Messua gave him when he first came to the Man-Pack.

'Come, my son,' she called, and Mowgli stepped into the light, and looked full at Messua, the woman who had been good to him, and whose life he had saved from the Man-Pack so long before. She was older, and her hair was gray, but her eyes and her voice had not changed. Woman-like, she expected to find Mowgli where she had left him, and her eyes travelled upward in a puzzled way from his chest to his head, that touched the top of the door.

'My son,' she stammered; and then, sinking to his feet: 'But it is no longer my son. It is a Godling of the Woods! Ahai!'

As he stood in the red light of the oil-lamp, strong, tall, and beautiful, his long black hair sweeping over his shoulders, the knife swinging at his neck, and his head crowned with a wreath of white jasmine, he might easily have been mistaken for some wild god of a jungle legend. The child half asleep on a cot sprang up and shrieked aloud with terror. Messua turned to soothe him, while Mowgli stood still, looking in at the water-jars and the cooking pots, the grain-bin, and all the other human belongings that he found himself remembering so well.

'What wilt thou eat or drink?' Messua murmured. 'This

is all thine. We owe our lives to thee. But art thou him I called Nathoo, or a Godling, indeed?'

'I am Nathoo,' said Mowgli, 'I am very far from my own place. I saw this light, and came hither. I did not know thou wast here.'

'After we came to Khanhiwara,' Messua said timidly, 'the English would have helped us against those villagers that sought to burn us. Rememberest thou?'

'Indeed, I have not forgotten.'

'But when the English Law was made ready, we went to the village of those evil people, and it was not more to be found.'

'That also I remember,' said Mowgli, with a quiver of his nostril.

'My man, therefore, took service in the fields, and at last—for, indeed, he was a strong man—we held a little land here. It is not so rich as the old village, but we do not need much—we two.'

'Where is he—the man that dug in the dirt when he was afraid on that night?'

'He is dead—a year.'

'And he?' Mowgli pointed to the child.

'My son that was born two Rains ago. If thou art a Godling, give him the Favour of the Jungle, that he may be safe among thy—thy people, as we were safe on that night.'

She lifted up the child, who, forgetting his fright, reached out to play with the knife that hung on Mowgli's chest, and Mowgli put the little fingers aside very carefully.

'And if thou art Nathoo whom the tiger carried away,' Messua went on choking, 'he is then thy younger brother. Give him an elder brother's blessing.'

'*Hai-mai!* What do I know of the thing called a blessing? I am neither a Godling nor his brother, and—O mother, mother, my heart is heavy in me.' He shivered as he set down the child.

'Like enough,' said Messua, bustling among the cooking-pots. 'This comes of running about the marshes by night. Beyond question, the fever has soaked thee to the marrow.' Mowgli smiled a little at the idea of anything in the Jungle hurting him. 'I will make a fire, and thou shalt drink warm milk. Put away the jasmine wreath: the smell is heavy in so small a place.'

Mowgli sat down, muttering, with his face in his hands. All manner of strange feelings that he had never felt before were running over him, exactly as though he had been poisoned, and he felt dizzy and a little sick. He drank the warm milk in long gulps, Messua patting him on the shoulder from time to time, not quite sure whether he were her son Nathoo of the long ago days, or some wonderful Jungle being, but glad to feel that he was at least flesh and blood.

'Son,' she said at last,—her eyes were full of pride,— 'have any told thee that thou art beautiful beyond all men?'

'Hah?' said Mowgli, for naturally he had never heard anything of the kind. Messua laughed softly and happily. The look in his face was enough for her.

'I am the first, then? It is right, though it comes seldom, that a mother should tell her son these good things. Thou art very beautiful. Never have I looked upon such a man.'

Mowgli twisted his head and tried to see over his own hard shoulder, and Messua laughed again so long that Mowgli, not knowing why, was forced to laugh with her, and the child ran from one to the other, laughing too.

'Nay, thou must not mock thy brother,' said Messua, catching him to her breast. 'When thou art one-half as fair we will marry thee to the youngest daughter of a king, and thou shalt ride great elephants.'

Mowgli could not understand one word in three of the talk here; the warm milk was taking effect on him after his long run, so he curled up and in a minute was deep asleep, and Messua put the hair back from his eyes, threw a cloth over him, and was happy. Jungle-fashion, he slept out the rest of that night and all the next day; for his instincts, which never wholly slept, warned him there was nothing to fear. He waked at last with a bound that shook the hut, for the cloth over his face made him dream of traps; and there he stood, his hand on his knife, the sleep all heavy in his rolling eyes, ready for any fight.

Messua laughed, and set the evening meal before him. There were only a few coarse cakes baked over the smoky fire, some rice, and a lump of sour preserved tamarinds— just enough to go on with till he could get to his evening kill. The smell of the dew in the marshes made him hungry and restless. He wanted to finish his spring running, but the child insisted on sitting in his arms, and Messua would have it that his long, blue-black hair must be combed out. So she sang, as she combed, foolish little baby-songs, now calling Mowgli her son, and now begging him to give some of his jungle power to the child. The hut door was closed, but Mowgli heard a sound he knew well, and saw Messua's jaw drop with horror as a great gray paw came under the bottom of the door, and Gray Brother outside whined a muffled and penitent whine of anxiety and fear.

'Out and wait! Ye would not come when I called,' said Mowgli in Jungle-talk, without turning his head, and the great gray paw disappeared.

'Do not—do not bring thy—thy servants with thee,' said Messua. 'I—we have always lived at peace with the Jungle.'

'It is peace,' said Mowgli, rising. 'Think of that night on the road to Khanhiwara. There were scores of such folk before thee and behind thee. But I see that even in springtime the Jungle People do not always forget. Mother, I go.'

Messua drew aside humbly—he was indeed a wood-god, she thought; but as his hand was on the door the mother in her made her throw her arms round Mowgli's neck again and again.

'Come back!' she whispered. 'Son or no son, come back, for I love thee—Look, he too grieves.'

The child was crying because the man with the shiny knife was going away.

'Come back again,' Messua repeated. 'By night or by day this door is never shut to thee.'

Mowgli's throat worked as though the cords in it were

being pulled, and his voice seemed to be dragged from it as he answered, 'I will surely come back.'

'And now,' he said as he put by the head of the fawning wolf on the threshold, 'I have a little cry against thee, Gray Brother. Why came ye not all four when I called so long ago?'

'So long ago? It was but last night. I—we—were singing in the Jungle the new songs, for this is the Time of New Talk. Rememberest thou?'

'Truly, truly.'

'And as soon as the songs were sung,' Gray Brother went on earnestly, 'I followed thy trail. I ran from all the others and followed hot-foot. But, O Little Brother, what hast *thou* done, eating and sleeping with the Man-Pack?'

'If ye had come when I called, this had never been,' said Mowgli, running must faster.

'And now what is to be?' said Gray Brother.

Mowgli was going to answer when a girl in a white cloth came down some path that led from the outskirts of the village. Gray Brother dropped out of sight at once, and Mowgli backed noiselessly into a field of high-springing crops. He could almost have touched her with his hand when the warm, green stalks closed before his face and he disappeared like a ghost. The girl screamed, for she thought she had seen a spirit, and then she gave a deep sigh. Mowgli parted the stalks with his hands and watched her till she was out of sight.

'And now I do not know,' he said, sighing in his turn. '*Why* did ye not come when I called?'

'We follow thee—we follow thee,' Gray Brother mumbled, licking at Mowgli's heel. 'We follow thee always, except in the Time of the New Talk.'

'And would ye follow me to the Man-Pack?' Mowgli whispered.

'Did I not follow thee on the night our old Pack cast thee out? Who waked thee lying among the crops?'

'Ay, but again?'

'Have I not followed thee to-night?'

'Ay, but again and again, and it may be again, Gray Brother?'

Gray Brother was silent. When he spoke he growled to himself, 'The Black One spoke truth.'

'And he said?'

'Man goes to Man at the last. Raksha, our mother, said——'

'So also said Akela on the night of Red Dog,' Mowgli muttered.

'So also says Kaa, who is wiser than us all.'

'What dost thou say, Gray Brother?'

'They cast thee out once, with bad talk. They cut thy mouth with stones. They sent Buldeo to slay thee. They would have thrown thee into the Red Flower. Thou, and not I, hast said that they are evil and senseless. Thou, and not I—I follow my own people—didst let in the Jungle upon them. Thou, and not I, didst make song against them more bitter even than our song against Red Dog.'

'I ask thee what *thou* sayest?'

They were talking as they ran. Gray Brother cantered on a while without replying, and then he said,—between bound and bound as it were,—'Man-cub—Master of the Jungle—Son of Raksha, Lair-brother to me—though I forget for a little while in the spring, thy trail is my trail, thy lair is my lair, thy kill is my kill, and thy death-fight is my death-fight. I speak for the Three. But what wilt thou say to the Jungle?'

'That is well thought. Between the sight and the kill it is not good to wait. Go before and cry them all to the Council Rock, and I will tell them what is in my stomach. But they may not come—in the Time of New Talk they may forget me.'

'Hast thou, then, forgotten nothing?' snapped Gray Brother over his shoulder, as he laid himself down to gallop, and Mowgli followed, thinking.

At any other season the news would have called all the Jungle together with bristling necks, but now they were busy hunting and fighting and killing and singing. From one to another Gray Brother ran, crying, 'The Master of

the Jungle goes back to Man! Come to the Council Rock.'
And the happy, eager People only answered, 'He will
return in the summer heats. The Rains will drive him to
lair. Run and sing with us, Gray Brother.'

'But the Master of the Jungle goes back to Man,' Gray
Brother would repeat.

'*Eee—Yoawa?* Is the Time of New Talk any less sweet
for that?' they would reply. So when Mowgli, heavy-
hearted, came up through the well-remembered rocks to
the place where he had been brought into the Council, he
found only the Four, Baloo, who was nearly blind with
age, and the heavy, cold-blooded Kaa coiled around
Akela's empty seat.

'Thy trail ends here, then, Manling?' said Kaa, as
Mowgli threw himself down, his face in his hands. 'Cry
thy cry. We be of one blood, thou and I—man and snake
together.'

'Why did I not die under Red Dog?' the boy moaned.
'My strength is gone from me, and it is not any poison. By
night and by day I hear a double step upon my trail. When
I turn my head it is as though one had hidden himself from
me that instant. I go to look behind the trees and he is not
there. I call and none cry again; but it is as though one
listened and kept back the answer. I lie down, but I do not
rest. I run the spring running, but I am not made still. I
bathe, but I am not made cool. The kill sickens me, but I
have no heart to fight except I kill. The Red Flower is in
my body, my bones are water—and—I know not what I
know.'

'What need of talk?' said Baloo slowly, turning his head
to where Mowgli lay. 'Akela by the river said it, that
Mowgli should drive Mowgli back to the Man-Pack. I said
it. But who listens now to Baloo? Bagheera—where is
Bagheera this night?—he knows also. It is the Law.'

'When we met at Cold Lairs, Manling, I knew it,' said
Kaa, turning a little in his mighty coils. 'Man goes to Man
at the last, though the Jungle does not cast him out.'

The Four looked at one another and at Mowgli, puzzled
but obedient.

'The Jungle does not cast me out, then?' Mowgli stammered.

Gray Brother and the Three growled furiously, beginning, 'So long as we live none shall dare——' But Baloo checked them.

'I taught thee the Law. It is for me to speak,' he said; 'and, though I cannot now see the rocks before me, I see far. Little Frog, take thine own trail; make thy lair with thine own blood and pack and people; but when there is need of foot or tooth or eye, or a word carried swiftly by night, remember, Master of the Jungle, the Jungle is thine at call.'

'The Middle Jungle is thine also,' said Kaa. 'I speak for no small people.'

'*Hai-mai*, my brothers,' cried Mowgli, throwing up his arms with a sob. 'I know not what I know! I would not go; but I am drawn by both feet. How shall I leave these nights?'

'Nay, look up, Little Brother,' Baloo repeated. 'There is no shame in this hunting. When the honey is eaten we leave the empty hive.'

'Having cast the skin,' said Kaa, 'we may not creep into it afresh. It is the Law.'

'Listen, dearest of all to me,' said Baloo. 'There is neither word nor will here to hold thee back. Look up! Who may question the Master of the Jungle? I saw thee playing among the white pebbles yonder when thou wast a little frog; and Bagheera, that bought thee for the price of a young bull newly killed, saw thee also. Of that Looking Over we two only remain; for Raksha, thy lair-mother, is dead with thy lair-father; the old Wolf-Pack is long since dead; thou knowest whither Shere Khan went, and Akela died among the dholes, where, but for thy wisdom and strength, the second Seeonee Pack would also have died. There remains nothing but old bones. It is no longer the Man-cub that asks leave of his Pack, but the Master of the Jungle that changes his trail. Who shall question Man in his ways?'

'But Bagheera and the Bull that bought me,' said Mowgli. 'I would not——'

His words were cut short by a roar and a crash in the thicket below, and Bagheera, light, strong, and terrible as always, stood before him.

'*Therefore*,' he said, stretching out a dripping right paw, 'I did not come. It was a long hunt, but he lies dead in the bushes now—a bull in his second year—the Bull that frees thee, Little Brother. All debts are paid now. For the rest, my word is Baloo's word.' He licked Mowgli's foot. 'Remember, Bagheera loved thee,' he cried, and bounded away. At the foot of the hill he cried again long and loud, 'Good hunting on a new trail, Master of the Jungle! Remember, Bagheera loved thee.'

'Thou hast heard,' said Baloo. 'There is no more. Go now; but first come to me. O wise Little Frog, come to me!'

'It is hard to cast the skin,' said Kaa as Mowgli sobbed and sobbed, with his head on the blind bear's side and his arms round his neck, while Baloo tried feebly to lick his feet.

'The stars are thin,' said Gray Brother, snuffing at the dawn wind. 'Where shall we lair to-day? for, from now, we follow new trails.'

And this is the last of the Mowgli stories.

The Outsong

[This is the song that Mowgli heard behind him in the Jungle till he came to Messua's door again.]

BALOO

For the sake of him who showed
One wise Frog the Jungle-Road,
Keep the Law the Man-Pack make—

For thy blind old Baloo's sake!
Clean or tainted, hot or stale,
Hold it as it were the Trail,
Through the day and through the night,
Questing neither left nor right.
For the sake of him who loves
Thee beyond all else that moves,
When thy Pack would make thee pain,
Say: 'Tabaqui sings again.'
When thy Pack would work thee ill,
Say: 'Shere Khan is yet to kill.'
When the knife is drawn to slay,
Keep the Law and go thy way.
(Root and honey, palm and spathe,
Guard a cub from harm and scathe!)
Wood and Water, Wind and Tree,
Jungle-Favour go with thee!

KAA

Anger is the egg of Fear—
Only lidless eyes are clear.
Cobra-poison none may leech;
Even so with Cobra-speech.
Open talk shall call to thee
Strength, whose mate is Courtesy.
Send no lunge beyond thy length;
Lend no rotten bough thy strength.
Gauge thy gape with buck or goat,
Lest thine eye should choke thy throat.
After gorging, wouldst thou sleep,
Look thy den is hid and deep,
Lest a wrong, by thee forgot,
Draw thy killer to the spot.
East and West and North and South,
Wash thy hide and close thy mouth.
(Pit and rift and blue pool-brim,
Middle-Jungle follow him!)
Wood and Water, Wind and Tree,
Jungle-Favour go with thee!

BAGHEERA

In the cage my life began;
Well I know the worth of Man.
By the Broken Lock that freed—
Man-cub, 'ware the Man-cub's breed!
Scenting-dew or starlight pale,
Choose no tangled tree-cat trail.
Pack or council, hunt or den,
Cry no truce with Jackal-Men.
Feed them silence when they say:
'Come with us an easy way.'
Feed them silence when they seek
Help of thine to hurt the weak.
Make no *bandar's** boast of skill;
Hold thy peace above the kill.
Let nor call nor song nor sign
Turn thee from thy hunting-line.
(Morning mist or twilight clear,
Serve him, Wardens of the Deer!)
Wood and Water, Wind and Tree,
Jungle-Favour go with thee!

THE THREE

On the trail that thou must tread
To the thresholds of our dread,
Where the Flower blossoms red;
Through the nights when thou shalt lie
Prisoned from our Mother-sky,
Hearing us, thy loves, go by;
In the dawns when thou shalt wake
To the toil thou canst not break,
Heartsick for the Jungle's sake:
Wood and Water, Wind and Tree,
Wisdom, Strength, and Courtesy,
Jungle-Favour go with thee!

APPENDIX A

In the Rukh*

The Only Son lay down again and dreamed that he dreamed
    a dream.
The last ash dropped from the dying fire with the click of a
    falling spark,
And the Only Son woke up again and called across the
    dark:–
'Now, was I born of womankind and laid in a mother's
    breast?
For I have dreamed of a shaggy hide whereon I went to rest.
And was I born of womankind and laid on a father's arm?
For I have dreamed of long white teeth that guarded me from
    harm.
Oh, was I born of womankind and did I play alone?
For I have dreamed of playmates twain that bit me to the
    bone.
And did I break the barley bread and steep it in the tyre?*
For I have dreamed of a youngling kid new riven from the
    byre.
An hour it lacks and an hour it lacks to the rising of the
    moon—
But I can see the black roof-beams as plain as it were noon!
'Tis a league and a league to the Lena Falls where the trooping
    sambhur* go,
But I can hear the little fawn that bleats behind the doe!
'Tis a league and a league to the Lena Falls where the crop and
    the upland meet,
But I can smell the warm wet wind that whispers through the
    wheat!'

The Only Son

Of the wheels of public service that turn under the Indian
Government, there is none more important than the Department
of Woods and Forests. The reboisement* of all India is in its
hands; or will be when Government has the money to spend. Its
servants wrestle with wandering sand-torrents and shifting
dunes: wattling them at the sides, damming them in front, and
pegging them down atop with coarse grass and spindling pine
after the rules of Nancy.* They are responsible for all the timber

in the State Forests of the Himalayas, as well as for the denuded hillsides that the monsoons wash into dry gullies and aching ravines; each cut a mouth crying aloud what carelessness can do. They experiment with battalions of foreign trees, and coax the blue gum* to take root and, perhaps, dry up the Canal fever. In the plains the chief part of their duty is to see that the belt fire-lines in the forest reserves are kept clean, so that when drought comes and the cattle starve, they may throw the reserve open to the villager's herds and allow the man himself to gather sticks. They poll and lop* for the stacked railway-fuel along the lines that burn no coal; they calculate the profit of their plantations to five points of decimals; they are the doctors and midwives of the huge teak forests of Upper Burma, the rubber of the Eastern Jungles, and the gall-nuts of the South; and they are always hampered by lack of funds. But since a Forest Officer's business takes him far from the beaten roads and the regular stations, he learns to grow wise in more than wood-lore alone; to know the people and the polity of the jungle; meeting tiger, bear, leopard, wild-dog, and all the deer, not once or twice after days of beating, but again and again in the execution of his duty. He spends much time in saddle or under canvas—the friend of newly-planted trees, the associate of uncouth rangers and hairy trackers—till the woods, that show his care, in turn set their mark upon him, and he ceases to sing the naughty French songs he learned at Nancy, and grows silent with the silent things of the underbrush.

Gisborne of the Woods and Forests had spent four years in the service. At first he loved it without comprehension, because it led him into the open on horseback and gave him authority. Then he hated it furiously, and would have given a year's pay for one month of such society as India affords. That crisis over, the forests took him back again, and he was content to serve them, to deepen and widen his fire-lines, to watch the green mist of his new plantation against the older foliage, to dredge out the choked stream, and to follow and strengthen the last struggle of the forest where it broke down and died among the long pig-grass. On some still day that grass would be burned off, and a hundred beasts that had their homes there would rush out before the pale flames at high noon. Later, the forest would creep forward over the blackened ground in orderly lines of saplings, and Gisborne, watching, would be well pleased. His bungalow, a thatched white-walled cottage of two rooms, was set at one end of the great *rukh* and overlooking it. He made no pretence at keeping a garden, for the *rukh* swept up to his door, curled over in a thicket of bamboo, and he rode from his verandah into its heart without the need of any carriage-drive.

Abdul Gafur, his fat Mohammedan butler, fed him when he was at home, and spent the rest of the time gossiping with the little band of native servants whose huts lay behind the bungalow. There were two grooms, a cook, a water-carrier, and a sweeper, and that was all. Gisborne cleaned his own guns and kept no dog. Dogs scared the game, and it pleased the man to be able to say where the subjects of his kingdom would drink at moonrise, eat before dawn, and lie up in the day's heat. The rangers and forest-guards lived in little huts far away in the *rukh*, only appearing when one of them had been injured by a falling tree or a wild beast. There Gisborne was alone.

In the spring the *rukh* put out few new leaves, but lay dry and still untouched by the finger of the year, waiting for rain. Only there was then more calling and roaring in the dark on a quiet night; the tumult of a battle-royal among the tigers, the bellowing of arrogant buck, or the steady wood-chopping of an old boar sharpening his tushes against a bole. Then Gisborne laid aside his little-used gun altogether, for it was to him a sin to kill. In summer, through the furious May heats, the *rukh* reeled in the haze, and Gisborne watched for the first sign of curling smoke that should betray a forest fire. Then came the Rains with a roar, and the *rukh* was blotted out in fetch after fetch of warm mist, and the broad leaves drummed the night through under the big drops; and there was a noise of running water, and of juicy green stuff crackling where the wind struck it, and the lightning wove patterns behind the dense matting of the foliage, till the sun broke loose again and the *rukh* stood with hot flanks smoking to the newly-washed sky. Then the heat and the dry cold subdued everything to tiger-colour again. So Gisborne learned to know his *rukh* and was very happy. His pay came month by month, but he had very little need for money. The currency notes accumulated in the drawer where he kept his home-letters and the recapping-machine.* If he drew anything, it was to make a purchase from the Calcutta Botanical Gardens, or to pay a ranger's widow a sum that the Government of India would never have sanctioned for her man's death.

Payment was good, but vengeance was also necessary, and he took that when he could. One night of many nights a runner, breathless and gasping, came to him with the news that a forest-

guard lay dead by the Kanye stream, the side of his head smashed
in as though it had been an eggshell. Gisborne went out at dawn
to look for the murderer. It is only travellers and now and then
young soldiers who are known to the world as great hunters. The
Forest Officers take their *shikar** as part of the day's work, and no
one hears of it. Gisborne went on foot to the place of the kill: the
widow was wailing over the corpse as it lay on a bedstead, while
two or three men were looking at footprints on the moist ground.
'That is the Red One,' said a man. 'I knew he would turn to man
in time, but surely there is game enough even for him. This must
have been done for devilry.'

'The Red One lies up in the rocks at the back of the *sal* trees,'*
said Gisborne. He knew the tiger under suspicion.

'Not now, Sahib, not now. He will be raging and ranging to
and fro. Remember that the first kill is a triple kill always. Our
blood makes them mad. He may be behind us even as we speak.'

'He may have gone to the next hut,' said another. 'It is only
four *koss*.* Wallah, who is this?'

Gisborne turned with the others. A man was walking down the
dried bed of the stream, naked except for the loin-cloth, but
crowned with a wreath of the tasselled blossoms of the white
convolvulus creeper. So noiselessly did he move over the little
pebbles, that even Gisborne, used to the soft-footedness of
trackers, started.

'The tiger that killed,' he began, without any salute, 'has gone
to drink, and now he is asleep under a rock beyond that hill.' His
voice was clear and bell-like, utterly different from the usual
whine of the native, and his face as he lifted it in the sunshine
might have been that of an angel strayed among the woods. The
widow ceased wailing above the corpse and looked round-eyed at
the stranger, returning to her duty with double strength.

'Shall I show the Sahib?' he said simply.

'If thou are sure—' Gisborne began.

'Sure indeed. I saw him only an hour ago—the dog. It is before
his time to eat man's flesh. He has yet a dozen sound teeth in his
evil head.'

The men kneeling above the footprints slunk off quietly, for
fear that Gisborne should ask them to go with him, and the
young man laughed a little to himself.

'Come, Sahib,' he cried, and turned on his heel, walking
before his companion.

'Not so fast. I cannot keep that pace,' said the white man. 'Halt there. Thy face is new to me.'

'That may be. I am but newly come into this forest.'

'From what village?'

'I am without a village. I come from over there.' He flung out his arm towards the notth.

'A gipsy then?'

'No, Sahib. I am a man without caste, and for matter of that without a father.'

'What do men call thee?'

'Mowgli, Sahib. And what is the Sahib's name?'

'I am the warden of this *rukh*—Gisborne is my name.'

'How? Do they number the trees and the blades of grass here?'

'Even so; lest such gipsy fellows as thou set them afire.'

'I! I would not hurt the jungle for any gift. That is my home.'

He turned to Gisborne with a smile that was irresistible, and held up a warning hand.

'Now, Sahib, we must go a little quietly. There is no need to wake the dog, though he sleeps heavily enough. Perhaps it were better if I went forward alone and drove him down wind to the Sahib.'

'Allah! Since when have tigers been driven to and fro like cattle by naked men?' said Gisborne, aghast at the man's audacity.

He laughed again softly. 'Nay, then, come along with me and shoot him in thy own way with the big English rifle.'

Gisborne stepped in his guide's track, twisted, crawled, and clomb* and stooped and suffered through all the many agonies of a jungle-stalk. He was purple and dripping with sweat when Mowgli at the last bade him raise his head and peer over a blue baked rock near a tiny hill pool. By the waterside lay the tiger extended and at ease, lazily licking clean again an enormous elbow and fore paw. He was old, yellow-toothed, and not a little mangy, but in that setting and sunshine, imposing enough.

Gisborne had no false ideas of sport where the man-eater was concerned. This thing was vermin, to be killed as speedily as possible. He waited to recover his breath, rested the rifle on the rock and whistled. The brute's head turned slowly not twenty feet from the rifle-mouth, and Gisborne planted his shots, business-like, one behind the shoulder and the other a little below the eye. At that range the heavy bones were no guard against the rending bullets.

'Well, the skin was not worth keeping at any rate,' said he, as the smoke cleared away and the beast lay kicking and gasping in the last agony.

'A dog's death for a dog,' said Mowgli quietly. 'Indeed there is nothing in that carrion worth taking away.'

'The whiskers.* Does thou not take the whiskers?' said Gisborne, who knew how the rangers valued such things.

'I? Am I a lousy *shikarri** of the jungle to paddle with a tiger's muzzle? Let him lie. Here come his friends already.'

A dropping kite whistled shrilly overhead, as Gisborne snapped out the empty shells, and wiped his face.

'And if thou are not a *shikarri*, where didst thou learn thy knowledge of the tiger-folk?' said he. 'No tracker could have done better.'

'I hate all tigers,' said Mowgli curtly. 'Let the Sahib give me his gun to carry. Arré, it is a very fine one. And where does the Sahib go now?'

'To my house.'

'May I come? I have never yet looked within a white man's house.'

Gisborne returned to his bungalow, Mowgli striding noiselessly before him, his brown skin glistening in the sunlight.

He stared curiously at the verandah and the two chairs there, fingered the split bamboo shade curtains with suspicion, and entered, looking always behind him. Gisborne loosed a curtain to keep out the sun. It dropped with a clatter, but almost before it touched the flagging of the verandah Mowgli had leaped clear, and was standing with heaving chest in the open.

'It is a trap,' he said quickly.

Gisborne laughed. 'White men do not trap men. Indeed thou art altogether of the jungle.'

'I see,' said Mowgli, 'it has neither catch nor fall. I—I never beheld these things till to-day.'

He came in on tiptoe and stared with large eyes at the furniture of the two rooms. Abdul Gafur, who was laying lunch, looked at him with deep disgust.

'So much trouble to eat, and so much trouble to lie down after you have eaten!' said Mowgli with a grin. 'We do better in the jungle. It is very wonderful. There are very many rich things here. Is the Sahib not afraid that he may be robbed? I have never seen such wonderful things.' He was staring at a dusty Benares brass plate on a rickety bracket.

'Only a thief from the jungle would rob here,' said Abdul

Gafur, setting down a plate with a clatter. Mowgli opened his eyes wide and stared at the white-bearded Mohammedan.

'In my country when goats bleat very loud we cut their throats,' he returned cheerfully. 'But have no fear, thou. I am going.'

He turned and disappeared into the *rukh*. Gisborne looked after him with a laugh that ended in a little sigh. There was not much outside his regular work to interest the Forest Officer, and this son of the forest, who seemed to know tigers as other people know dogs, would have been a diversion.

'He's a most wonderful chap,' thought Gisborne; 'he's like the illustrations in the Classical Dictionary.* I wish I could have made him a gun-boy. There's no fun in shikarring alone, and this fellow would have been a perfect *shikarri*. I wonder what in the world he is.'

That evening he sat on the verandah under the stairs smoking as he wondered. A puff of smoke curled from the pipe-bowl. As it cleared he was aware of Mowgli sitting with arms crossed on the verandah edge. A ghost could not have drifted up more noiselessly. Gisborne started and let the pipe drop.

'There is no man to talk to out there in the *rukh*,' said Mowgli; 'I came here, therefore.' He picked up the pipe and returned it to Gisborne.

'Oh,' said Gisborne, and after a long pause, 'What news is there in the *rukh*? Hast thou found another tiger?'

'The nilghai are changing their feeding-ground against the new moon, as is their custom. The pig are feeding near the Kanye river now, because they will not feed with the nilghai, and one of their sows has been killed by a leopard in the long grass at the water-head. I do not know any more.'

'And how didst thou know all these things?' said Gisborne, leaning forward and looking at the eyes that glittered in the starlight.

'How should I not know? The nilghai has his custom and his use, and a child knows that pig will not feed with him.'

'I do not know this,' said Gisborne.

'Tck! Tck! And thou art in charge—so the men of the huts tell me—in charge of all this *rukh*.' He laughed to himself.

'It is well enough to talk and to tell child's tales,' Gisborne retorted, nettled at the chuckle. 'To say that this and that goes on in the *rukh*. No man can deny thee.'

'As for the sow's carcase, I will show thee her bones

to-morrow,' Mowgli returned, absolutely unmoved. 'Touching the matter of the nilghai, if the Sahib will sit here very still I will drive one nilghai up to this place, and by listening to the sounds carefully, the Sahib can tell whence that nilghai has been driven.'

'Mowgli, the jungle has made thee mad,' said Gisborne. 'Who can drive nilghai?'

'Still—sit still, then. I go.'

'Gad, the man's a ghost!' said Gisborne; for Mowgli had faded out into the darkness and there was no sound of feet. The *rukh* lay out in great velvety folds in the uncertain shimmer of the star-dust—so still that the least little wandering wind among the tree-tops came up as the sigh of a child sleeping equably. Abdul Gafur in the cook-house was clicking plates together.

'Be still there!' shouted Gisborne, and composed himself to listen as a man can who is used to the stillness of the *rukh*. It had been his custom, to preserve his self-respect in his isolation, to dress for dinner each night, and the stiff white shirt-front creaked with his regular breathing till he shifted a little sideways. Then the tobacco of a somewhat foul pipe began to purr, and he threw the pipe from him. Now, except for the night-breath in the *rukh*, everything was dumb.

From an inconceivable distance, and drawled through immea-surable darkness, came the faint, faint echo of a wolf's howl. Then silence again for, it seemed, long hours. At last, when his legs below the knees had lost all feeling, Gisborne heard some-thing that might have been a crash far off through the under-growth. He doubted till it was repeated again and yet again.

'That's from the west,' he muttered; 'there's something on foot there.' The noise increased—crash on crash, plunge on plunge—with the thick grunting of a hotly pressed nilghai, flying in panic terror and taking no heed to his course.

A shadow blundered out from between the tree-trunks, wheeled back, turned again grunting, and with a clatter on the bare ground dashed up almost within reach of his hand. It was a bull nilghai, dripping with dew—his withers hung with a torn trail of creeper, his eyes shining in the light from the house. The creature checked at sight of the man, and fled along the edge of the *rukh* till he melted into the darkness. The first idea in Gisborne's bewildered mind was the indecency of thus dragging out for inspection the big blue bull of the *rukh*—the putting him through his paces in the night which should have been his own.

Then said a smooth voice at his ear as he stood staring:

'He came from the water-head where he was leading the herd. From the west he came. Does the Sahib believe now, or shall I bring up the herd to be counted? The Sahib is in charge of this *rukh*.'

Mowgli had reseated himself on the verandah, breathing a little quickly. Gisborne looked at him with open mouth. 'How was that accomplished?' he said.

'The Sahib saw. The bull was driven—driven as a buffalo is. Ho! ho! He will have a fine tale to tell when he returns to the herd.'

'That is a new trick to me. Canst thou run as swiftly as the nilghai, then?'

'The Sahib has seen. If the Sahib needs more knowledge at any time of the movings of the game, I, Mowgli, am here. This is a good *rukh*, and I shall stay.'

'Stay then, and if thou hast need of a meal at any time my servants shall give thee one.'

'Yes, indeed, I am fond of cooked food,' Mowgli answered quickly. 'No man may say that I do not eat boiled and roast as much as any other man. I will come for that meal. Now, on my part, I promise that the Sahib shall sleep safely in his house by night, and no thief shall break in to carry away his so rich treasures.'

The conversation ended itself on Mowgli's abrupt departure. Gisborne sat long smoking, and the upshot of his thoughts was that in Mowgli he had found at last that ideal ranger and forest-guard for whom he and the Department were always looking.

'I must get him into the Government service somehow. A man who can drive nilghai would know more about the *rukh* than fifty men. He's a miracle—a *lusus naturæ**—but a forest-guard he must be if he'll only settle down in one place,' said Gisborne.

Abdul Gafur's opinion was less favourable. He confided to Gisborne at bedtime that strangers from God-knew-where were more than likely to be professional thieves, and that he personally did not approved of naked outcastes who had not the proper manner of addressing white people. Gisborne laughed and bade him go to his quarters, and Abdul Gafur retreated growling. Later in the night he found occasion to rise up and beat his thirteen-year-old daughter. Nobody knew the cause of dispute, but Gisborne heard the cry.

Through the days that followed Mowgli came and went like a shadow. He had established himself and his wild house-keeping close to the bungalow, but on the edge of the *rukh*, where Gisborne, going out on to the verandah for a breath of cool air, would see him sometimes sitting in the moonlight, his forehead on his knees, or lying out along the fling* of a branch, closely pressed to it as some beast of the night. Thence Mowgli would throw him a salutation and bid him sleep at ease, or descending would weave prodigious stories of the manners of the beasts in the *rukh*. Once he wandered into the stables and was found looking at the horses with deep interest.

'That,' said Abdul Gafur pointedly, 'is sure sign that some day he will steal one. Why, if he lives about this house, does he not take an honest employment? But no, he must wander up and down like a loose camel, turning the heads of fools and opening the jaws of the unwise to folly.' So Abdul Gafur would give harsh orders to Mowgli when they met, would bid him fetch water and pluck fowls, and Mowgli, laughing unconcernedly, would obey.

'He has no caste,' said Abdul Gafur. 'He will do anything. Look to it, Sahib, that he does not do too much. A snake is a snake, and a jungle-gipsy is a thief till the death.'

'Be silent, then,' said Gisborne. 'I allow thee to correct thy own household if there is not too much noise, because I know thy customs and use. My custom thou does not know. The man is without doubt a little mad.'

'Very little mad indeed,' said Abdul Gafur. 'But we shall see what comes thereof.'

A few days later on his business took Gisborne into the *rukh* for three days. Abdul Gafur being old and fat was left at home. He did not approve of lying up in rangers' huts, and was inclined to levy contributions in his master's name of grain and oil and milk from those who could ill afford such benevolences. Gisborne rode off early one dawn a little vexed that his man of the woods was not at the verandah to accompany him. He liked him—liked his strength, fleetness, and silence of foot, and his ever-ready open smile; his ignorance of all forms of ceremony and salutations, and the child-like tales that he would tell (and Gisborne would credit now) of what the game was doing in the *rukh*. After an hour's riding through the greenery, he heard a rustle behind him, and Mowgli trotted at his stirrup.

'We have a three days' work toward,' said Gisborne, 'among the new trees.'

'Good,' said Mowgli. 'It is always good to cherish young trees.

They make cover if the beasts leave them alone. We must shift the pig again.'

'Again? How?' Gisborne smiled.

'Oh, they were rooting and tusking among the young *sal* last night, and I drove them off. Therefore I did not come to the verandah this morning. The pig should not be on this side of the *rukh* at all. We must keep them below the head of the Kanye river.'

'If a man could herd clouds he might do that thing; but, Mowgli, if as thou sayest, thou art herder in the *rukh* for no gain and for no pay——'

'It is the Sahib's *rukh*,' said Mowgli, quickly looking up.

Gisborne nodded thanks and went on: 'Would it not be better to work for pay from the Government? There is a pension at the end of long service.'

'Of that I have thought,' said Mowgli, 'but the rangers live in huts with shut doors, and all that is all too much a trap to me. Yet I think——'

'Think well then and tell me later. Here we will stay for breakfast.'

Gisborne dismounted, took his morning meal from his home-made saddle-bags, and saw the day open hot above the *rukh*. Mowgli lay in the grass at his side staring up at the sky.

Presently he said in a lazy whisper: 'Sahib, is there any order at the bungalow to take out the white mare to-day?'

'No, she is fat and old and a little lame beside. Why?'

'She is being ridden now and *not* slowly on the road that runs to the railway line.'

'Bah, that is two *koss* away. It is a woodpecker.'

Mowgli put up his forearm to keep the sun out of his eyes.

'The road curves in with a big curve from the bungalow. It is not more than a *koss*, at the farthest, as the kite goes; and sound flies with the birds. Shall we see?'

'What folly! To run a *koss* in this sun to see a noise in the forest.'

'Nay, the pony is the Sahib's pony. I meant only to bring her here. If she is not the Sahib's pony, no matter. If she is, the Sahib can do what he wills. She is certainly being ridden hard.'

'And how wilt thou bring her here, madman?'

'Has the Sahib forgotten? By the road of the nilghai and no other.'

'Up then and run if thou art so full of zeal.'

'Oh, I do not run!' He put out his hand to sign for silence, and still lying on his back called aloud thrice—with a deep gurgling cry that was new to Gisborne.

'She will come,' he said at the end. 'Let us wait in the shade.' The long eyelashes dropped over the wild eyes as Mowgli began to doze in the morning hush. Gisborne waited patiently: Mowgli was surely mad, but as entertaining a companion as a lonely Forest Officer could desire.

'Ho! ho!' said Mowgli lazily, with shut eyes. 'He has dropped off. Well, first the mare will come and then the man.' Then he yawned as Gisborne's pony stallion neighed. Three minutes later Gisborne's white mare, saddled, bridled, but riderless, tore into the glade where they were sitting, and hurried to her companion.

'She is not very warm,' said Mowgli, 'but in this heat the sweat comes easily. Presently we shall see her rider, for a man goes more slowly than a horse—especially if he chance to be a fat man and old.'

'Allah! This is the devil's work,' cried Gisborne leaping to his feet, for he heard a yell in the jungle.

'Have no care, Sahib. He will not be hurt. He also will say that it is devil's work. Ah! Listen! Who is that?'

It was the voice of Abdul Gafur in an agony of terror, crying out upon unknown things to spare him and his gray hairs.

'Nay, I cannot move another step,' he howled. 'I am old and my turban is lost. Arré! Arré! But I will move. Indeed I will hasten. I will run! Oh, Devils of the Pit, I am a Mussulman!'

The undergrowth parted and gave up Abdul Gafur, turban-less, shoeless, with his waist-cloth unbound, mud and grass in his clutched hands, and his face purple. He saw Gisborne, yelled anew, and pitched forward, exhausted and quivering, at his feet. Mowgli watched him with a sweet smile.

'This is no joke,' said Gisborne sternly. 'The man is like to die, Mowgli.'

'He will not die. He is only afraid. There was no need that he should have come out of a walk.'

Abdul Gafur groaned and rose up, shaking in every limb.

'It was witchcraft—witchcraft and devildom!' he sobbed, fumbling with his hand in his breast. 'Because of my sin I have been whipped through the woods by devils. It is all finished. I repent. Take them, Sahib!' He held out a roll of dirty paper.

'What is the meaning of this, Abdul Gafur?' said Gisborne, already knowing what would come.

'Put me in the jail-khana—the notes are all here—but lock me up safely that no devils may follow. I have sinned against the Sahib and his salt* which I have eaten; and but for those accursed wood-demons, I might have bought land afar off and lived in peace all my days.' He beat his head upon the ground in an agony of despair and mortification. Gisborne turned the roll of notes over and over. It was his accumulated back-pay for the last nine months—the roll that lay in the drawer with the home-letters and the recapping machine. Mowgli watched Abdul Gafur, laughing noiselessly to himself. 'There is no need to put me on the horse again. I will walk home slowly with the Sahib, and then he can send me under guard to the jail-khana. The Government gives many years for this offence,' said the butler sullenly.

Loneliness in the *rukh* affects very many ideas about very many things. Gisborne stared at Abdul Gafur, remembering that he was a very good servant, and that a new butler must be broken into the ways of the house from the beginning, and at the best would be a new face and a new tongue.

'Listen, Abdul Gafur,' he said. 'Thou hast done great wrong, and altogether lost thy *izzat** and thy reputation. But I think that this came upon thee suddenly.'

'Allah! I had never desired the notes before. The Evil took me by the throat while I looked.'

'That also I can believe. Go then back to my house, and when I return I will send the notes by a runner to the Bank, and there shall be no more said. Thou are too old for the jail-khana. Also thy household is guiltless.'

For answer Abdul Gafur sobbed between Gisborne's cowhide riding-boots.

'Is there no dismissal then?' he gulped.

'That we shall see. It hangs upon thy conduct when we return. Get upon the mare and ride slowly back.'

'But the devils! The *rukh* is full of devils.'

'No matter, my father. They will do thee no more harm unless, indeed, the Sahib's orders be not obeyed,' said Mowgli. 'Then, perchance, they may drive thee home—by the road of the nilghai.'

Abdul Gafur's lower jaw dropped as he twisted up his waist-cloth, staring at Mowgli.

'Are they *his* devils? His devils! And I had thought to return and lay the blame upon this warlock!'*

'That was well thought of, Huzrut;* but before we make a trap we see first how big the game is that may fall into it. Now I thought no more than that a man had taken one of the Sahib's horses. I did not know that the design was to make me a thief before the Sahib, or my devils had haled thee here by the leg. It is not too late now.'

Mowgli looked inquiringly at Gisborne; but Abdul Gafur waddled hastily to the white mare, scrambled on her back and fled, the woodways crashing and echoing behind him.

'That was well done,' said Mowgli. 'But he will fall again unless he holds by the mane.'

'Now it is time to tell me what these things mean,' said Gisborne a little sternly. 'What is this talk of thy devils? How can men be driven up and down the *rukh* like cattle? Give answer.'

'Is the Sahib angry because I have saved him, his money?'

'No, but there is trick-work in this that does not please me.'

'Very good. Now if I rose and stepped three paces into the *rukh* there is no one, not even the Sahib, could find me till I choose. As I would not willingly do this, so I would not willingly tell. Have patience a little, Sahib, and some day I will show thee everything, for, if thou wilt, some day we will drive the buck together. There is no devil-work in the matter at all. Only ... I know the *rukh* as a man knows the cooking-place in his house.'

Mowgli was speaking as he would speak to an impatient child. Gisborne, puzzled, baffled, and a great deal annoyed, said nothing, but stared on the ground and thought. When he looked up the man of the woods had gone.

'It is not good,' said a level voice from the thicket, 'for friends to be angry. Wait till the evening, Sahib, when the air cools.'

Left to himself thus, dropped as it were in the heart of the *rukh*, Gisborne swore, then laughed, remounted his pony, and rode on. He visited a ranger's hut, overlooked a couple of new plantations, left some orders as to the burning of a patch of dry grass, and set out for a camping-ground of his own choice, a pile of splintered rocks roughly roofed over with branches and leaves, not far from the banks of the Kanye stream. It was twilight when he came in sight of his resting-place, and the *rukh* was waking to the hushed ravenous life of the night.

A camp-fire flickered on the knoll, and there was the smell of a very good dinner in the wind.

'Um,' said Gisborne, 'that's better than cold meat at any rate. Now the only man who'd be likely to be here'd be Muller,* and, officially, he ought to be looking over the Changamanga *rukh*. I suppose that's why he's on my ground.'

The gigantic German who was the head of the Woods and Forests of all India, Head Ranger from Burma to Bombay, had a habit of flitting bat-like without warning from one place to another, and turning up exactly where he was least looked for. His theory was that sudden visitations, the discovery of short-comings and a word-of-mouth upbraiding of a subordinate were infinitely better than the slow processes of correspondence, which might end in a written and official reprimand—a thing in after years to be counted against a Forest Officer's record. As he explained it: 'If I only talk to my boys like a Dutch uncle, dey say, "It was only dot damned old Muller," and dey do better next dime. But if my fat-head clerk he write and say dot Muller der Inspecdor-General fail to onderstand and is much annoyed, first dot does no goot because I am not dere, and, second, der fool dot comes after me he may say to my best boys: "Look here, you haf been wigged by my bredecessor." I tell you der big brass-hat* pizness does not make der trees grow.'

Muller's deep voice was coming out of the darkness behind the firelight as he bent over the shoulders of his pet cook. 'Not so much sauce, you son of Belial! Worcester sauce* he is a gondi-ment and not a fluid. Ah, Gisborne, you haf come to a very bad dinner. Where is your camp?' and he walked up to shake hands.

'I'm the camp, sir,' said Gisborne. 'I didn't know you were about here.'

Muller looked at the young man's trim figure. 'Goot! That is very goot! One horse and some cold things to eat. When I was young I did my camp so. Now you shall dine with me. I went into Headquarters to make up my rebort last month. I haf written Half—ho! ho!—and der rest I haf leaved to my glerks and come out for a walk. Der Government is mad about dose reborts. I dold der Viceroy so at Simla.'

Gisborne chuckled, remembering the many tales that were told of Muller's conflicts with the Supreme Government. He was the chartered libertine of all the offices, for as a Forest Officer he had no equal.

'If I find you, Gisborne, sitting in your bungalow und hatch-ing reborts to me about der blantations instead of riding der blantations, I will dransfer you to der middle of der Bikaneer Desert* to reforest *him*. I am sick of reborts und chewing paper when we should do our work.'

'There's not much danger of my wasting time over my annuals. I hate them as much as you do, sir.'

The talk went over at this point to professional matters. Muller had some questions to ask, and Gisborne orders and hints to receive, till dinner was ready. It was the most civilized meal Gisborne had eaten for months. No distance from the base of supplies was allowed to interfere with the work of Muller's cook; and that table spread in the wilderness began with devilled small fresh-water fish, and ended with coffee and cognac.

'Ah!' said Muller at the end, with a sigh of satisfaction as he lighted a cheroot and dropped into his much worn camp-chair. 'When I am making reborts I am Freethinker und Atheist, but here in der *rukh* I am more than Christian. I am Bagan also.' He rolled the cheroot-butt luxuriously under his tongue, dropped his hands on his knees, and stared before him into the dim shifting heart of the *rukh*, full of stealthy noises; the snapping of twigs like the snapping of the fire behind him; the sigh and rustle of a heat-bended branch recovering her straightness in the cool night; the incessant mutter of the Kanye stream, and the under-note of the many-peopled grass uplands out of sight beyond a swell of hill. He blew out a thick puff of smoke, and began to quote Heine* to himself.

'Yes, it is very goot. Very goot. "Yes, I work miracles, and, by Goot, dey come off too."* I remember when dere was no *rukh* more big than your knee, from here to der plough-lands, und in drought-time der cattle ate bones of dead cattle up and down. Now der trees haf come back. Dey were planted by a Free-thinker, because he know just de cause dot made der effect. But der trees dey had der cult of der old gods—"und der Christian Gods howl loudly."* Dey could not live in der *rukh*, Gisborne.'

A shadow moved in one of the bridle-paths—moved and stepped out into the starlight.

'I haf said true. Hush! Here is Faunus* himself come to see der Insbector-General. Himmel, he is der god! Look!'

It was Mowgli, crowned with his wreath of white flowers and walking with a half-peeled branch—Mowgli, very mistrustful of the fire-light and ready to fly back to the thicket on the least alarm.

'That's a friend of mine,' said Gisborne. 'He's looking for me. Ohé, Mowgli!'

Muller had barely time to gasp before the man was at Gisborne's side, crying: 'I was wrong to go. I was wrong, but I did not know then that the mate of him that was killed by this river was awake looking for thee. Else I should not have gone away. She tracked thee from the back-range, Sahib.'

'He is a little mad,' said Gisborne, 'and he speaks of all the beasts about here as if he was a friend of theirs.'

'Of course—of course. If Faunus does not know, who should know?' said Muller gravely. 'What does he say about tigers—dis god who knows you so well?'

Gisborne relighted his cheroot, and before he had finished the story of Mowgli and his exploits it was burned down to moustache-edge. Muller listened without interruption. 'Dot is not madness,' he said at last when Gisborne had described the driving of Abdul Gafur. 'Dot is not madness at all.'

'What is it, then? He left me in a temper this morning because I asked him to tell how he did it. I fancy the chap's possessed in some way.'

'No, dere is no bossession, but it is most wonderful. Normally they die young*—dese beoble. Und you say now dot your thief-servant did not say what drove der poney, and of course der nilghai he could not speak.'

'No, but, confound it, there wasn't anything. I listened, and I can hear most things. The bull and the man simply came headlong—mad with fright.'

For answer Muller looked Mowgli up and down from head to foot, then beckoned him nearer. He came as a buck treads a tainted trail.

'There is no harm,' said Muller in the vernacular. 'Hold out an arm.'

He ran his hand down to the elbow, felt that, and nodded. 'So I thought. Now the knee.' Gisborne saw him feel the knee-cap and smile. Two or three white scars just above the ankle caught his eye.

'Those came when thou wast very young?' he said.

'Ay,' Mowgli answered with a smile. 'They were love-tokens from the little ones.' Then to Gisborne over his shoulder. 'This Sahib knows everything. Who is he?'

'That comes after, my friend. Now where are *they*?' said Muller.

Mowgli swept his hand round his head in a circle.

'So! And thou canst drive nilghai? See! There is my mare in her pickets. Canst thou bring her to me without frightening her?'

'Can I bring the mare to the Sahib without frightening her!'

Mowgli repeated, raising his voice a little above its normal pitch. 'What is more easy if the heel-ropes are lose?'

'Loosen the head and heel-pegs,' shouted Muller to the groom. They were hardly out of the ground before the mare, a huge black Australian, flung up her head and cocked her ears.

'Careful! I do not wish her driven into the *rukh*,' said Muller.

Mowgli stood still fronting the blaze of the fire—in the very form and likeness of that Greek god who is so lavishly described in the novels. The mare whickered, drew up one hind leg, found that the heel-ropes were free, and moved swiftly to her master, on whose bosom she dropped her head, sweating lightly.

'She came of her own accord. My horses will do that,' cried Gisborne.

'Feel if she sweats,' said Mowgli.

Gisborne laid a hand on the damp flank.

'It is enough,' said Muller.

'It is enough,' Mowgli repeated, and a rock behind him threw back the word.

'That's uncanny, isn't it?' said Gisborne.

'No, only wonderful—most wonderful. Still you do not know, Gisborne?'

'I confess I don't.'

'Well then, I shall not tell. He says dot some day he will show you what it is. It would be gruel if I told. But why he is not dead I do not understand. Now listen thou.' Muller faced Mowgli, and returned to the vernacular. 'I am the head of all the *rukhs* in this country of India and others across the Black Water. I do not know how many men be under me—perhaps five thousand, perhaps ten. Thy business is this,—to wander no more up and down the *rukh* and drive beasts for sport or for show, but to take service under me, who am the Government in the matter of Woods and Forests, and to live in this *rukh* as a forest-guard; to drive the villagers' goats away when there is no order to feed them in the *rukh*; to admit them when there is an order; to keep down, as thou canst keep down, the boar and the nilghai when they become too many; to tell Gisborne Sahib how and where tigers move, and what game there is in the forests; and to give sure warning of all the fires in the *rukh*, for thou canst give warning more quickly than any other. For that work there is a payment each month in silver, and at the end, when thou hast gathered a wife and cattle and, may be, children, a pension. What answer?'

'That's just what I——' Gisborne began.

'My Sahib spoke this morning of such a service. I walked all day alone considering the matter, and my answer is ready here. I serve, *if* I serve in this *rukh* and no other: *with* Gisborne Sahib and with no other.'

'It shall be so. In a week comes the written order that pledges the honour of the Government for the pension. After that thou wilt take up thy hut where Gisborne Sahib shall appoint.'

'I was going to speak to you about it,' said Gisborne.

'I did not want to be told when I saw that man. Dere will never be a forest-guard like him. He is a miracle. I tell you, Gisborne, some day you will find it so. Listen, he is blood-brother to every beast in der *rukh*!'

'I should be easier in my mind if I could understand him.'

'Dot will come. Now I tell you dot only once in my service, and dot is thirty years, haf I met a boy dot began as this man began. Und he died. Sometimes you hear of dem in der census reports, but dey all die. Dis man haf lived, and he is an anachronism, for he is before der Iron Age, and der Stone Age. Look here, he is at der beginnings of der history of man—Adam* in der Garden, und now we want only an Eva! No! He is older than dot child-tale, shust as der *rukh* is older dan der gods. Gisborne, I am a Bagan now, once for all.'

Through the rest of the long evening Muller sat smoking and smoking, and staring and staring into the darkness, his lips moving in multiplied quotations, and great wonder upon his face. He went to his tent, but presently came out again in his majestic pink sleeping-suit, and the last words that Gisborne heard him address to the *rukh* through the deep hush of midnight were these, delivered with immense emphasis:–

'Dough we shivt und bedeck und bedrape us,*
    Dou art noble und nude und andeek;
Libidina* dy moder, Briapus*
    Dy fader, a God und a Greek.

Now I know dot, Bagan *or* Christian, I shall nefer know der inwardness of der *rukh*!'

It was midnight in the bungalow a week later when Abdul Gafur, ashy gray with rage, stood at the foot of Gisborne's bed and whispering bade him awake.

'Up, Sahib,' he stammered. 'Up and bring thy gun. Mine honour is gone. Up and kill before any see.'

The old man's face had changed, so that Gisborne stared stupidly.

'It was for this, then, that that jungle outcaste helped me to polish the Sahib's table, and drew water and plucked fowls. They have gone off together for all my beatings, and now he sits among his devils dragging her soul to the Pit. Up, Sahib, and come with me!'

He thrust a rifle into Gisborne's half-wakened hand and almost dragged him from the room on to the verandah.

'They are there in the *rukh*; even within gun-shot of the house. Come softly with me.'

'But what is it? What is the trouble, Abdul?'

'Mowgli, and his devils. Also my own daughter,' said Abdul Gafur. Gisborne whistled and followed his guide. Not for nothing, he knew, had Abdul Gafur beaten his daughter of nights, and not for nothing had Mowgli helped in the housework a man whom his own powers, whatever those were, had convicted of theft. Also, a forest wooing goes quickly.

There was the breathing of a flute in the *rukh*, as it might have been the song of some wandering wood-god, and, as they came nearer, a murmur of voices. The path ended in a little semicircular glade walled partly by high grass and partly by trees. In the centre, upon a fallen trunk, his back to the watchers and his arm round the neck of Abdul Gafur's daughter, sat Mowgli, newly crowned with flowers, playing upon a rude bamboo flute, to whose music four huge wolves danced solemnly on their hind legs.

'Those are his devils,' Abdul Gafur whispered. He held a bunch of cartridges in his hand. The beasts dropped to a long-drawn quavering note and lay still with steady green eyes, glaring at the girl.

'Behold,' said Mowgli, laying aside the flute. 'Is there anything of fear in that? I told thee, little Stout-heart, that there was not, and thou didst believe. Thy father said—and oh, if thou couldst have seen thy father being driven by the road of the nilghai!—thy father said that they were devils; and by Allah,* who is thy God, I do not wonder that he so believed.'

The girl laughed a little rippling laugh, and Gisborne heard Abdul grind his few remaining teeth. This was not at all the girl that Gisborne had seen with a half-eye slinking about the compound veiled and silent, but another—a woman full blown in a night as the orchid puts out in an hour's moist heat.

'But they are my playmates and my brothers, children of that mother that gave me suck, as I told thee behind the cook-house,' Mowgli went on. 'Children of the father that lay between me and the cold at the mouth of the cave when I was a little naked child. Look'—a wolf raised his gray jowl, slavering at Mowgli's knee—'my brother knows that I speak of them. Yes, when I was a little child he was a cub rolling with me on the clay.'

'But thou hast said that thou are human-born,' cooed the girl, nestling closer to the shoulder. 'Thou are human-born?'

'Said! Nay, I know that I am human born, because my heart is in thy hold, little one.' Her head dropped under Mowgli's chin. Gisborne put up a warning hand to restrain Abdul Gafur, who was not in the least impressed by the wonder of the sight.

'But I was a wolf among wolves none the less till a time came when Those of the jungle bade me go because I was a man.'

'Who bade thee go? That is not like a true man's talk.'

'The very beasts themselves. Little one, thou wouldst never believe that telling, but so it was. The beasts of the jungle bade me go, but these four followed me because I was their brother. Then was I a herder of cattle among men, having learned their language. Ho! ho! The herds paid toll to my brothers, till a woman, an old woman, beloved, saw me playing by night with my brethren in the crops. They said that I was possessed of devils, and drove me from that village with sticks and stones, and the four came with me by stealth and not openly. That was when I had learned to eat cooked meat and to talk boldly. From village to village I went, heart of my heart, a herder of cattle, a tender of buffaloes, a tracker of game, but there was no man that dared lift a finger against me twice.' He stooped down and patted one of the heads. 'Do thou also like this. There is neither hurt nor magic in them. See, they know thee.'

'The woods are full of all manner of devils,' said the girl with a shudder.

'A lie. A child's lie,' Mowgli returned confidently. 'I have lain out in the dew under the stars and in the dark night, and know. The jungle is my house. Shall a man fear his own roof-beams or a woman her man's hearth? Stoop down and pat them.'

'They are dogs and unclean,' she murmured, bending forward with averted head.

'Having eaten the fruit, now we remember the Law!' said

Abdul Gafur bitterly. 'What is the need of this waiting, Sahib? Kill!'

'H'sh, thou. Let us learn what has happened,' said Gisborne.

'That is well done,' said Mowgli, slipping his arm round the girl again. 'Dogs or no dogs, they were with me through a thousand villages.'

'Ahi, and where was thy heart then? Through a thousand villages. Thou hast seen a thousand maids. I—that am—that am a maid no more, have I thy heart?'

'What shall I swear by? By Allah, of whom thou speakest?'

'Nay, by the life that is in thee, and I am well content. Where was thy heart in those days?'

Mowgli laughed a little. 'In my belly, because I was young and always hungry. So I learned to track and to hunt, sending and calling my brothers back and forth as a king calls his armies. Therefore I drove the nilghai for the foolish young Sahib, and the big fat mare for the big fat Sahib, when they questioned my power. It were as easy to have driven the men themselves. Even now,' his voice lifted a little—'even now I know that behind me stand thy father and Gisborne Sahib. Nay, do not run, for no ten men dare more a pace forward. Remembering that thy father beat thee more than once, shall I give the word and drive him again in rings through the *rukh*?' A wolf stood up with bared teeth.

Gisborne felt Abdul Gafur tremble at his side. Next, his place was empty, and the fat man was skimming down the glade.

'Remains only Gisborne Sahib,' said Mowgli, still without turning; 'but I have eaten Gisborne Sahib's bread, and presently I shall be in his service, and my brothers will be his servants to drive game and carry the news. Hide thou in the grass.'

The girl fled, the tall grass closed behind her and the guardian wolf that followed, and Mowgli turning with his three retainers faced Gisborne as the Forest Officer came forward.

'That is all the magic,' he said, pointing to the three. 'The fat Sahib knew that we who are bred among wolves run on our elbows and our knees for a season. Feeling my arms and legs, he felt the truth which thou didst not know. Is it so wonderful, Sahib?'

'Indeed it is all more wonderful than magic. These then drove the nilghai?'

'Ay, as they would drive Eblis* if I gave the order. They are my eyes and feet to me.'

'Look to it, then, that Eblis does not carry a double rifle. They have yet something to learn, thy devils, for they stand one behind the other, so that two shots would kill the three.'

'Ah, but they know they will be thy servants as soon as I am a forest-guard.'

'Guard or no guard, Mowgli, thou hast done a great shame to Abdul Gafur. Thou hast dishonoured his house and blackened his face.'

'For that, it was blackened when he took thy money, and made blacker still when he whispered in thy ear a little while since to kill a naked man. I myself will talk to Abdul Gafur, for I am a man of the Government service, with a pension. He shall make the marriage by whatsoever rite he will, or he shall run once more. I will speak to him in the dawn. For the rest, the Sahib has his house and this is mine. It is time to sleep again, Sahib.'

Mowgli turned on his heel and disappeared into the grass, leaving Gisborne alone. The hint of the wood-god was not to be mistaken; and Gisborne went back to the bungalow, where Abdul Gafur, torn by rage and fear, was raving in the verandah.

'Peace, peace,' said Gisborne, shaking him, for he looked as though he were going to have a fit. 'Muller Sahib has made the man a forest-guard, and as thou knowest there is a pension at the end of that business, and it is Government service.'

'He is an outcaste—a *mlech*—a dog among dogs; an eater of carrion! What pension can pay for that?'

'Allah knows; and thou hast heard that the mischief is done. Wouldst thou blaze it to all the other servants? Make the *shadi** swiftly, and the girl will make him a Mussulman. He is very comely. Canst thou wonder that after thy beatings she went to him?'

'Did he say that he would chase me with his beasts?'

'So it seemed to me. If he be a wizard, he is at least a very strong one.'

Abdul Gafur thought awhile, and then broke down and howled, forgetting that he was a Mussulman:—

'Thou art a Brahmin. I am thy cow.* Make thou the matter plain, and save my honour if it can be saved!'

A second time then Gisborne plunged into the *rukh* and called Mowgli. The answer came from high overhead, and in no submissive tones.

'Speak softly,' said Gisborne, looking up. 'There is yet time to strip thee of thy place and hunt thee with thy wolves. The girl must go back to her father's house to-night. To-morrow there will be the *shadi*, by the Mussulman law, and then thou canst take her away. Bring her to Abdul Gafur.'

'I hear.' There was a murmur of two voices conferring among the leaves. 'Also, we will obey—for the last time.'

A year later Muller and Gisborne were riding through the *rukh* together, talking of their business. They came out among the rocks near the Kanye stream; Muller riding a little in advance. Under the shade of a thorn thicket sprawled a naked brown baby, and from the brake immediately behind him peered the head of a gray wolf. Gisborne had just time to strike up Muller's rifle, and the bullet tore spattering through the branches above.

'Are you mad?' thundered Muller, 'Look!'

'I see,' said Gisborne quietly. 'The mother's somewhere near. You'll wake the whole pack, by Jove!'

The bushes parted once more, and a woman unveiled snatched up the child.

'Who fired, Sahib?' she cried to Gisborne.

'This Sahib. He had not remembered thy man's people.'

'Not remembered? But indeed it may be so, for we who live with them forget that they are strangers at all. Mowgli is down the stream catching fish. Does the Sahib wish to see him? Come out, ye lacking manners. Come out of the bushes, and make your service to the Sahibs.'

Muller's eyes grew rounder and rounder. He swung himself off the plunging mare and dismounted, while the jungle gave up four wolves who fawned round Gisborne. The mother stood nursing her child and spurning them aside as they brushed against her bare feet.

'You were quite right about Mowgli,' said Gisborne. 'I meant to have told you, but I've got so used to these fellows in the last twelve months that it slipped my mind.'

'Oh, don't apologise,' said Muller. 'It's nothing. Gott in Himmel!* "Und I work miracles—und dey come off too!"'*

APPENDIX B

Professor Aubrey Manning, Professor of Natural History in the University of Edinburgh, writes (4 April 1986):
'In the strict sense I have to say that Kipling was wrong. Animals will easily make eye contact with humans under many circumstances. One can check this out easily with our pet cats and dogs. Yet behind the strict interpretation Kipling was, perhaps intuitively or perhaps from his own observation, right to lay stress on the power and emotional content of eye-to-eye contact.

In general with carnivores and primates ... eye contact is highly significant. During encounters which may develop aggressively, subordinate animals will not make eye contact—at least more than momentarily—with animals they regard as superior in the hierarchy. A cringing dog averts its gaze—often turns its whole head away—from its angry master. It behaves in just the same way towards a higher ranking animal in the pack. Battles between cats (or symbolic battles between lion-tamers and their animals) involve prolonged staring—the lion often averts its gaze as it finally submits to the threat of the whip. In primates direct gaze is widely regarded as a threat. The stares of dominant animals are often enhanced by the fact that upper eyelids and orbits are pale-coloured, often very conspicuously, so that you can easily tell if a rival is staring at you—he flashes his eyebrows. The people who work with gorillas and have managed to accustom them to human presence know never to look directly at one of the apes—it must always be sideways glances...

Perhaps the point Kipling misses is that there can be friendly eye contact as well as aggressive. Dogs wanting to be taken out for a walk do not avoid the eyes of humans; nor monkeys who hope you will feed them a grape. I had to spend some time watching caged domestic cats with their kittens. The mothers were absolutely delighted to see me, and I sometimes found it impossible to make good observations of their maternal behaviour because they paid more attention to me than to their offspring. In such cases it was essential to avoid eye contact. If one looked directly at the mother she would instantly meet my eyes and come towards the front of the cage, purring and rubbing herself against the bars. It is a remarkable fact that, for all the more advanced mammals, the eyes are indeed recognized as the key part of the face.'

EXPLANATORY NOTES

FIRST JUNGLE BOOK

CONSIDERABLE use has been made in the compilation of these Notes of James McG. Stewart, *Rudyard Kipling: A Bibliographical Catalogue*, ed. A. W. Yeats (Toronto, 1959), and of *The Readers' Guide to Rudyard Kipling's Works* ed. R. E. Harbord, to both of whom I express my gratitude. I should also like to thank Mr O. D. Edwards, Reader in History in the University of Edinburgh, for help with two notes on 'Rikki-tikki-tavi', and Mr Jonathan Katz, Librarian of the Indian Institute at Oxford, for help with a note on 'Toomai of the Elephants'.

ABBREVIATIONS

'(K)' indicates that the note is taken from 'Author's Notes on the Names in the Jungle Books', first published in volume 12 of the Sussex Edition (1937).

'(Sterndale)' indicates that the name annotated has been taken, or adapted, from the list of 'Native Names' given by Robert Armitage Sterndale in *Seonee, or Camp Life on the Satpura Range* (1st edn London, 1877; 2nd edn Calcutta, 1887).

K   Kipling

JB   *The Jungle Book*

2JB   *The Second Jungle Book*

THE TEXT

The text is that of the Uniform Edition, with a few changes which are indicated in the Notes. The first English edn of *The Jungle Book* was published in 1894, and the first American edn in the same year.

PREFACE TO *THE JUNGLE BOOK*

The Preface is of course a parody of a scholarly Editor acknowledging the expert help of 'specialists', who include two elephants, a monkey, a dancing wolf, and (probably) a mongoose, as well as a fellow-passenger on a ship of the Canadian Pacific Line. After this lapse of time some of the allusions are now indecipherable (if, indeed, they were ever meant to be deciphered). The tone (of playfulness) is more important than the content here.

xxxix *Bahadur Shah*: means 'Great King'.

Pudmini: appears in 'Toomai of the Elephants'.

a Hindu gentleman: this probably refers to a langur or sacred Indian monkey, inhabiting the Jakko hill slopes (above Simla).

Presbytes: from Greek *presbys*, an old man.

Sahi: this wolf does not appear in the JBs.

herpetologist: a zoologist who deals with reptiles. (The jocular manner does not suggest that a human being is referred to.)

Thanatophidia: K's word for poisonous snakes: Greek *thanatos* (death) + *ophis* (snake).

MOWGLI'S BROTHERS

Completed November 1892 (first Mowgli story to be written, except possibly 'In the Rukh'). First appeared in *St. Nicholas Magazine* (January 1894). This magazine was the best known of US children's periodicals. It was edited by Mary Mapes Dodge (1831–1905), now remembered as the author of *Hans Brinker, or the Silver Skates* (1865).

1 *Seeonee*: usually spelt 'Seoni', a district of Central India (Sterndale).

Tabaqui: 'Pronounced *Tabarky*. I think I made up this name myself (accent on *bar*)' (K).

2 *Gidur-log*: 'Pronounced *Geeder*—Indian name for Jackal. *Log* rhymes with *vogue*' (K; Sterndale). The meaning of *log* is 'people'.

Shere Khan: 'Pronounced *Sheer Karn*. "Shere" = "tiger" in some Indian dialects. "Khan" a title, to show that he was a chief among tigers' (K; Sterndale).

Waingunga River: 'A real river in Central India. Pronounced *wine-gunger* (accent on *gung*, I think)' (K).

Lungri: 'Pronounced as spelt' (K). Presumably to rhyme with 'hungry'. 'Literally "lame", as S.K. was' (K).

5 *Raksha*: 'Pronounced *Rúk-sher*' (K).

Sambhur: a large Indian deer.

6 *Mowgli*: 'Made up. Doesn't mean "frog" in any language I know. Pronounced *Mów-gli*' (K).

Akela: 'Means Alone. Pronounced *Uk-kay-la* (accent on *kay*)' (K).

8 *Baloo*: 'Hindustani for Bear. Pronounced '*Bár-loo*' (K). Sterndale gives *Bhaloo* as the native name for the Black Bear (not the Brown Bear).

Bagheera: 'Hindustani for panther or leopard? Diminutive of *Bagh* (Hindustani for Tiger). Pronounced *Bug-eer-a*' (K). Not in Sterndale.

11 *look him between the eyes*: cf. 'How Fear Came', in 2JB, pp. 8, 16, and 'Letting in the Jungle', in 2JB, p. 50. This is a leitmotif in the Mowgli stories. Its function is to give 'biological' legitimation to Mowgli's right to rule. But see Appendix.

Ikki: 'I think I made this up. Rhyme with *sticky*. "Ho-Igo" a real native name for him' (K). Called 'Kanta Siah' in Sterndale. In early edns K called him 'Sahi'—cf. the name of the wolf in the Preface to JB.

KAA'S HUNTING

First published in *Today* of 31 March and 7 April 1894, with illustrations by H. R. Millar. Next appeared in *McClure's Magazine*, June 1894. Also printed in USA under the title 'Mowgli among the Monkeys'.

22 *Kaa*: 'Pronounced *Kar*. Made up (from queer open-mouthed hiss of a big snake)' (K). Sterndale has no list of snakes.

the Law of the Jungle: see 2JB, pp. 17–19, where it is put into verse. Also see Introduction.

Mang: 'is *Mung*, a made-up name' (K).

24 *Hathi*: 'Pronounced *Huttee* ... An Indian name for Elephant' (K).

25 *Bandar-log*: 'Pronounced *Bunder* ... *Log* rhymes with *vogue*' (K). The native name for the Bengal Monkey is given by Sterndale as *Bundar*.

27 *think now*: there was a saying in K's time: 'What Manchester thinks to-day, England will think to-morrow.'

29 *Rann*: the kite is elsewhere called 'Chil'—'pronounced *Cheel*' (K). 'Cheel' in Sterndale.

30 *Ikki*: the porcupine.

34 *Cold Lairs*: 'There are lots of old deserted cities in India which look very much like the Cold Lairs in the *Jungle Books*. It is called Cold Lairs because when any animal leaves its lair or den the place becomes cold, of course. Same with men as with animals' (K). A famous example is Fatehpur-Sikri, near Agra; but two visited by Kipling himself were Amber and Chitor in Rajputana.

35 *Broken Lock*: see 'Mowgli's Brothers', p. 12.

45 *fascination*: apparently folklore rather than science.

'TIGER! TIGER!'

First published in *St. Nicholas Magazine*, February 1894.

48 *title*: from 'The Tyger', in *Songs of Experience* (etched 1789–94) by William Blake (1757–1827).

pariah dogs: dogs of a domesticated breed that have reverted to a half wild state. A 'pariah' is a social outcast. Various pronunciations are current in English, some stressing the first, some the second syllable. The word is of Tamil origin.

49 *Meswa*: 'Pronounced *Mess-wa*' (K).

51 *caste*: an Indian concept, meaning (approximately) group or tribe or social grading.

52 *low-caste*: see above.

as possible: in earlier edns there are 9 or 10 extra lines, in which the priest tells Mowgli that the god will be angry if Mowgli steals the priest's mangoes, whereupon Mowgli takes the god's image from the temple to the priest's house and asks that the god be made angry so that he can fight him.

Buldeo: stress on first syllable. 'Almost as spelt, but the -o isn't sounded very much' (K).

Tower musket: a flintlock of *c*.1800.

53 *Khanhiwara*: 'A real place. *Kan-i-war-rer*, I think' (K).

a hundred rupees: meant by K as equivalent to about £7 in his time.

Rama: 'Pronounced *Rár-mer*' (K).

54 *dhâk-tree*: which has 'golden-red' flowers (see p. 155).

56 *ladies'-chain fashion*: from square-dancing: female partners moving in procession one after the other, in and out between male partners formed up into a line or circle.

62 *tulsi*: a variety of the basil family of aromatic herbs: sacred to the Hindu God Vishnu.

64 *a story for grown-ups*: it had already been told in 'In the Rukh', collected in *Many Inventions* (1893): included in 2JB in this edn.

THE WHITE SEAL

Begun 3 May 1893, at Brattleboro, Vermont, USA. First appeared in *National Review*, August 1893. K had never crossed the Arctic Circle. All the names in 'The White Seal' are taken from H. W. Elliott, *The Seal Islands of Alaska* (1881). The story is about a seal rookery in the Pribilof Islands in the Bering Sea, about 250 miles north of the Aleutian Islands.

Readers interested in the geography of the story should consult a map, as K advises in the Sussex edn.

67 *Verse heading*: the 'Seal Lullaby' alludes to Sir Walter Scott's 'Lullaby of an Infant Chief' (1815), beginning 'O hush thee, my babie, thy sire was a knight . . .'.

Novastoshnah: 'I don't know how this should be pronounced. It is a Russian name' (K).

Limmershin: ?disguise for Elliott (also source of 'Quiquern' in 2JB).

Sea Catch: '*Sea Catchee*' is the Russian word for a full-grown seal' (K).

68 *holluschickie*: a less-than-adult seal (also from a Russian word).

Matkah: 'Pronounced *Mut-ker*. A mother seal' (K).

69 *Killer Whale*: otherwise grampus: a cetacean.

Lukannon: not on the map. 'There is a Lukannon Beach not far from Cape Town' (K).

Kotick: 'Pronounced *Kó-tick*. Baby seal' (K).

72 *by his side*: in a discussion in the *Kipling Journal* (no. 58, p. 24, July 1941) it is authoritatively stated that baby seals do not sleep like this. (They do not talk English, either.)

75 *Sea-Lion*: a larger type of seal.

76 *Sea Vitch*: 'Russian for *walrus*' (K). i.e. 'sivitch'.

78 *Sea Cow*: 'manatee, or dugon' (K). 'Dugong' is more usual. A member of the mammalian order *Sirenia*.

79 *the Gallapagos*: the Galapagos Islands, a group of islands on the Equator, 98°W, belonging to Ecuador.

80 *the Great Combers of Magellan*: a comber is a long curly wave. Ferdinand Magellan (?1440–1521) was the first man to undertake a voyage round the globe; and the Straits of Magellan, between S. America and Tierra del Fuego, are named after him.

Frog-Footman: In Lewis Carroll's *Through the Looking-Glass* (1871), chapter 9.

82 *My wig*: the hairs on the back of the neck of the 'Sea-catch' form a 'wig' or mane.

84 *Northern Lights*: the atmospheric phenomenon known as the Aurora Borealis.

86 *shark's egg*: The larger sharks are viviparous, but there are smaller varieties who do lay eggs.

'RIKKI-TIKKI-TAVI'

Completed 1893. First appeared in England and USA in November 1893, in *The Pall Mall Magazine* and *St. Nicholas Magazine*. The setting was based on a garden at Allahabad, surrounding the bungalow ('Belvedere') where K lived as a paying guest for his last year in India with his American friends Professor and Mrs Hill. She was known as 'Ted'—cf. the boy 'Teddy' in the story. But cf. also note on p. 87.

87 *title*: 'Pronounced *Rikky-tikky-tarvi*' (K). Many readers seem to have pronounced the *tavi* part of the name to rhyme with 'gravy', as Bernard Shaw did: see Act I of *Man and Superman* (published 1903) in which Jack Tanner, speaking of Ann Whitefield, tells Octavius ('Tavy') Robinson: 'Why, man, your head is in the lioness's mouth: you are half swallowed already—in three bites—Bite One, Ricky; Bite Two, Ticky; Bite Three, Tavy; and down you go.'

Darzee: from Indian word for 'tailor'. 'Pronounced *Dar-zy*' (K).

Chuchundra: 'Pronounced *Chew-chun-drer*' (K; Sterndale).

musk-rat: it appears that the musk-rat is peculiar to America. The timid Chuchundra was probably a musk-shrew.

87 *mongoose*: a weasel-like Indian mammal of the genus *Herpes-ter*. 'Mongooses are as bold and clever as I have tried to describe, and they often come into a house or even into an office with people going in and out all the time, and make friends with men there. A perfectly wild mongoose used to come in and sit on my shoulder in my office in India, and burn his inquisitive nose on the end of my cigar, just as Rikki did in the tale' (K). For more on mongooses see Lockwood Kipling's *Beast and Man in India* (1891).

In A. Conan Doyle's Sherlock Holmes story 'The Crooked Man', first published in *The Strand Magazine*, London, July 1893, and in *Harpers Weekly*, New York, 8 July 1893, a mongoose figures prominently: his name is Teddy, the name of the boy in Kipling's story. K is known to have read and enjoyed the Sherlock Holmes stories as they came out. If any borrowing took place, it cannot have been Doyle's.

89 *kerosene*: usually called paraffin in Britain.

Marshal Niel: yellow rose named after Adolphe Niel (1822–69), Marshal of France.

90 *Nag*: 'Native name for the Cobra. Pronounced *Narg*' (K). Poisonous Colubrine snake (*Naja tripudians*).

Brahm: in Sanskrit 'Brahma' (masculine) is the Supreme God. The final vowel is often omitted.

91 *Nagaina*: 'Pronounced *Na-gý-na*' (K).

grow red: not true, apparently.

92 *Karait*: 'Pronounced *Ker-ite*' (K). The krait belongs to the sub-family of snakes called *Micruridae*, a notorious killer in India. The murderer in K's story 'The Return of Imray' (1891) dies of krait-bite. (See *Life's Handicap*.)

93 *Chua*: 'Pronounced *Chew-er*' (K; Sterndale).

TOOMAI OF THE ELEPHANTS

Begun May 1892. Thought to be the first written of the JB stories. First published in *St. Nicholas Magazine*, December 1893. In K's Preface to JB, Bahadur Shah (baggage elephant 174) and his sister Pudmini are stated to have provided the material for this story. In the story, in which the animals do not speak, unlike the Mowgli tales, K has been compared to Ernest Thompson Seton (1860–1946). For discussion of Seton see R. L. Green, *Kipling and the Children* (1965). Seton himself wrote:

'Since Kipling had no knowledge of natural history, and made no effort to present it, and since furthermore his animals talk and live like men, his stories are not animal stories in the realistic sense, they are wonderful, beautiful fairy tales.' (*Trail of an Artist–Naturalist*, 1951).

104 *Kala Nag*: black Snake, a reference to the elephant's trunk.

elephant: this animal occurs in two species of *Proboscidea*. This story concerns the Asian elephant, *Elephas maximus*. It can reach a shoulder height of 11 feet in the wild state, and can live up to 100 years.

Theodore: Negus of Abyssinia (1816–68); died by his own hand at the capture of Magdala by the British Expedition under General Napier in April 1868.

105 *Moulmein*: port in Burma. Where George Orwell said he shot an elephant. (See *Shooting an Elephant*, 1950.)

The British Army in India used elephants for its guns and commissariat till *c*.1900.

stockade: a method of capturing elephants known as the *Khedda* (spelt 'Keddah' in this story).

109 *mahout*: an elephant driver. Accent on second syllable: rhyme to 'doubt'.

111 *ball-rooms*: These are now known to be maternity wards rather than ball-rooms, according to J. H. Williams ('Elephant Bill') in *Bandoola* (1953).

112 *Bapree-Bap!*: 'Expresses surprise, amazement, sometimes grief . . . not only in Hindustani but some other vernaculars' (Jonathan Katz).

Dihang River: The Brahmaputra.

113 *tom-tom* (or Tam-Tam): native word for a drum used in signalling.

Shiv (or 'Shiva' or 'Siva'): in Hinduism, one of the Brahminical triad of gods. Mahadeo (the great god) is another of his names.

guddee: throne.

115 *coir*: made with yarn spun from fibre of a coconut-tree.

hog-boar: more usually 'boar-hog', the male of the wild boar of India (*Sus cristatus*). Uniform Edition reads 'hog-bear', probably a misprint.

116 *swashed*: dashed with a splashing sound (*OED*). Echoic.

119 *trip-hammers*: mechanical hammers.

121 *there too*: *The Readers' Guide* notes Machua Appa's remarkable feat in recognizing this slashed bark as done by a particular elephant.

122 *Gunga*: the Ganges (after which the elephant was named). *Hira Guj, Birchi Guj, Kuttar Guj*: authentic elephant names.

HER MAJESTY'S SERVANTS

First appeared in *Harper's Weekly*, 3 March 1894, and in *The Pall Mall Magazine* March 1894. Collected in JB, 1894. The setting is the Rawalpindi Durbar (public audience or levee) which the Viceroy (much admired by K) Lord Dufferin called in honour of the Amir Abdurrahman of Afghanistan. K attended it as a special reporter and sent detailed accounts to *The Civil and Military Gazette*.

125 *Verse-heading*: *Rule of Three* e.g. 'As 2 is to 4, 6 is to x: hence x = 12'.

Tweedle-dum ... Tweedle-dee: names invented by John Byrom (1692–1763) to satirize the partisans of two composers. Cf. also *Through the Looking-Glass* (1871), by Lewis Carroll, chapter 4.

Pilly-Winky ... Winkie-Pop: cf. K's 'The Song of the Banjo' (1894).

camels: 'Nervous and stupid when all caged together. They stampede at night sometimes for no reason, and fall all over the tents and horse-lines' (K).

Rawal Pindi: one of the two great military stations of the Punjab (the other was Lahore). Both are now in Pakistan.

126 *stacked*: parked.

plowter: splash messily (a Scotticism).

rammers: rods for ramming home charges in muzzle-loading guns.

127 *Screw Battery*: screw guns, much used in mountain warfare, could be dismantled, loaded on mules, and reassembled where required.

128 *number-one*: slang for 'first class'.

yoke: i.e. two bullocks yoked together.

130 *hock*: the joint in the hind leg between the knee and the fetlock.

a hen's ear: i.e. never (the hen having no visible external ear).

131 *crupper*: a strap buckled to the back of the saddle, and passing under the tail, to keep the saddle from slipping down.

breastplate: a strap passing under the breast of a cavalry horse.

132 *twenty yoke*: i.e. 40 bullocks.

Hapur: a district and town 40 miles east of Delhi.

133 *mule*: hybrid between horse and ass (horse is the female parent).

Brumby: Australian slang for a wild horse.

Sunol: a winner of an Australian classic race.

car-horse: American slang for the lowest category of horse. Cf. American 'street-horse' and 'tram-horse'.

'skate': American slang, used by the Deacon in abuse of the yellow horse in K's story about horses in Vermont, 'A Walking Delegate' (1894). (See *The Day's Work*.)

Malaga: a port in Southern Spain. (Spanish donkeys were perhaps supposed to be exceptionally stupid.)

Carbine: a famous racehorse, winner of the Melbourne Cup (the Australian Derby) and other classic races in Australia.

134 *Pachydermatous*: thick-skinned.

136 *dog*: apparently no evidence for this.

138 *eat beef*: forbidden to Hindus.

139 *'Bonnie Dundee'*: should be 'Bonny Dundee': a tune used by most of the cavalry regiments of the British Army. The words of the song are by Sir Walter Scott.

dog-cart: a carriage or trap with a special compartment underneath for the conveyance of sporting dogs.

140 *two by two*: adapted from an old (anonymous) song about Noah's Ark beginning 'The animals went in two by two'—probably itself adapted from a Negro Spiritual.

141 *Elephants of the Gun-Teams*: this verse and 'Gun-Bullocks' echo 'The British Grenadiers'. 'Cavalry Horses' echoes 'Bonny Dundee'.

142 *Screw-Gun Mules*: echoes the rhythm of 'The Lincolnshire Poacher'.

EXPLANATORY NOTES

SECOND JUNGLE BOOK

CONSIDERABLE use has been made in the compilation of these Notes of James McG. Stewart, *Rudyard Kipling: A Bibliographical Catalogue* ed. A. W. Yeats, Toronto, 1959, and of *The Readers' Guide to Rudyard Kipling's Works*, ed. R. E. Harbord, to both of whom I express my gratitude. I should also like to thank Dr J. L. Brockington, Department of Sanskrit, University of Edinburgh, for help with a note on 'The Miracle of Purun Bhagat', and Professor S. S. Prawer, of Oxford University, for help with a note on 'In the Rukh'.

Abbreviations:
'(K)' indicates that the note is taken from 'Author's Notes on the Names in the Jungle Books', first published in volume 12 of the Sussex Edition (1937).
'Sterndale' refers to Robert Armitage Sterndale's *Seeonee, or Camp Life on the Satpura Range*, 1st edn London, 1877; 2nd edn Calcutta, 1887.

K	Kipling
JB	*The Jungle Book*
2JB	*The Second Jungle Book*

The Text:
The text is that of the Uniform Edition, with a few changes which are indicated in the Notes. The first and second English edns of *The Second Jungle Book* were published in 1895, and the first American edn in the same year.

HOW FEAR CAME

First published in *The Pall Mall Budget*, 7 and 14 June 1894; and in *The Pall Mall Gazette*, 14 and 5 June 1894, and *The New York World*, 10 June 1894, as 'A Strange Tale of the Jungle'. For famine in India caused by drought, cf. K's story 'William the Conqueror' (1895), collected in *The Day's Work* (1898).

149 *Mowgli*: 'Made up. Doesn't mean "frog" in any language I know. Pronounced *Mów-gli*' (K).

149 *Baloo*: 'Hindustani for Bear. Pronounced *Bár-loo* (K). '*Bha-loo*' in Sterndale.

Ikki: 'The Porcupine. I think I made this up. Rhymes with *sticky*. *Ho-Igoo* a real native name for him' (K).

150 *mohwa*: 'Pronounced *mower*, to rhyme with *cower*. A tree that bears sweet sticky smelly blossoms which some native tribes in the Jungle make into a strong drink' [i.e. arrack]. 'Latin name *Bassia Longifolia*, I believe' (K).

151 *Chil*: 'The Indian Kite. Pronounced *Cheel*' (K).

Waingunga: 'A real river in Central India. Pronounced *Wine-gunger* (accent on *gung*, I think)' (K).

Hathi: 'Pronounced *Huttee*. An Indian name for Elephant' (K).

152 *Bagheera*: 'Hindustani for panther or leopard. ?diminutive of *bagh* (Hindustani for tiger). Pronounced *Bug-eér-a*' (K).

Shere Khan: 'Pronounced *Sheer Karn*. "Shere" = Tiger in some Indian dialects. "Khan" a title to show that he was a chief among tigers' (K).

155 *paddy paw*: with claws retracted.

156 *Look at me, Man-cub!*: see Appendix B.

158 *Tha*: 'Pronounced *Tar*. A made up name' (K).

160 *Mysa*: 'Made up. *Mý-ser*' (K).

163 *Gonds*: their kingdom was in the Central Provinces of India.

Red Flower: JB term for fire.

164 *If Man looked at him*: see Appendix B.

THE MIRACLE OF PURUN BHAGAT

Written May 1894, while K was on holiday from Vermont and living near his parents at Tisbury, Wiltshire. First published (under the title 'A Miracle of the Present Day') in *The New York World*, 14 October 1894; and in *The Pall Mall Gazette* and *Pall Mall Budget*, 18 October 1894.

168 *Title: Purun Bhagat*: 'Pronounced *Poor-un Bhuggat*. Purun the Holy Man' (K).

Langurs: 'Pronounced *Lun-goors*. Big monkeys of the Hima-layas' (K). Name in Sterndale, Cf. 'The Creeping Man' in A. C. Doyle, *The Case-Book of Sherlock Holmes* (1927).

168 *Brahmin*: member of the highest priestly class.

169 *Pioneer*: a leading daily newspaper in India at that time, British-owned, and published at Allahabad. K worked on it for a year and a half before leaving India, having previously worked for five years for its associated newspaper *The Civil and Military Gazette* of Lahore.

Star of India: an Order instituted by Queen Victoria in 1861.

170 *General Post*: a parlour game involving much changing of seats.

Dewan: chief minister of Native State.

coco-de-mer: 'Very big coconut shell that I believe comes from the Seychelles Islands: does not grow in India' (K).

171 *Kala Pir*: K does not locate this shrine on Purun Bhagat's (quite exactly detailed) route. The term *pir* is one of the standard terms for a Muslim holy man. But the most obvious interpretation of *Kala* would be as the Sanskrit and Hindi term meaning 'dark', of which the feminine form is *Kali*, the name of the Hindu goddess mentioned a little later in the story (p. 25), in whose shrine Purun Bhagat takes lodging. And it may be noted that 'Kala Pir' is linked by K with the Yogis (see next note), who are at least nominally Hindu, though by this time often rather syncretistic. Possibly some local Muslim saint is meant; but it may be that the name as K gives it is the corruption of some other name, originally without Muslim associations.

Jogis or Yogis: adherents of the Yoga philosophy, meditation and ascetic practices.

Kulu: A district in the Himalayas, 70 miles north of Simla. The Sahiba in *Kim* was a Kula woman.

Hill blood: cf. K's poem 'The Sea and the Hills' (1902), on how 'hillmen desire their Hills'.

Simla: hill-station and summer capital of all India under British administration, until independence (1947).

172 *Chota Simla*: i.e. '*Little Simla*, native quarter of the town of Simla' (K).

borax: used as a mild disinfectant.

173 *Kali*: 'Pronounced *Kár-li*' (K). The name means 'dark'. Usually regarded as a goddess of death and destruction.

174 *turmeric*: formerly used as a medicine.

bannocks: home-made loaves (in Scotland and the North of England).

a Name: cf. the repetitions of the name 'Kim' in *Kim*. ('What is Kim?' etc.)

Ladakhi: from Ladakh, a mountainous district in Kashmir, about 100 miles north of Simla.

175 *blanket*: note that there is no question of a 'Bandar-log' here: the apes share the Saint's blanket.

176 *barasingh*: 'Native for "Big Horn". Pronounced *burra sing*' (K).

mushick-nabha: thought to be the Kashmiri stag, which lives in the Western Himalayas.

Bhai: brother.

181 *scarp*: the steep face of a hillside.

cross-legged: i.e. in the posture of the Buddha when he attained Enlightenment.

D.C.L.: Doctor of Civil Law.

Ph.D.: Doctor of Philosophy.

182 *Mohiniwala*: a fictitious name.

the next: the close of the story has been the object of some adverse criticism, e.g. by H. E. Bates in *The Modern Short Story* (1941) and, more mildly, by J. M. S. Tompkins in *The Art of Rudyard Kipling* (1959), where she refers to it as 'two sentences that are like a hot fingermark on glass, and fade in the memory as quickly' (Tompkins, p. 27).

Kabir: a religious teacher, who flourished in the fifteenth century, claimed by both Hindus and Muslims. Associated by K with religious tolerance. See 'The Prayer', from *Kim*:

> My brother kneels, so saith Kabir,
> To stone and brass in heathen wise,
> But in my brother's voice I hear
> My own unanswered agonies.
> His God is as the fates assign,
> His prayer is all the world's—and mine.

guddee: throne; seat of justice.

bairagi: mendicant.

sal: a valuable timber-tree, with wood resembling teak.

182 *kikar*: 'Pronounced *kee-kar*. A scrubby, spiny tree that belongs to the Acacia family' (K).

the Way: a brief explanation is impossible. The Way is the road to heaven, or Nirvana, or eternal beatitude. It has no necessary connexion with any particular religious creed.

LETTING IN THE JUNGLE

First published in *The Pall Mall Gazette*, 12, 13 December 1894, and *The Pall Mall Budget*, 13 December 1894; and in *McClure's Magazine*, January 1895. The only Mowgli story not completed in Vermont. It was written, along with two or three other 2JB stories, at Tisbury, Wiltshire, his parents' home.

183 *Akela*: '(Means Alone.) Pronounced *Uk-kay-la* (accent on *kay*') (K).

184 *Raksha*: '("The demon"). Pronounced *Rúk-sher*' (K).

Mang: 'The bat. Pronounced *Mung*. A made-up name' (K).

hawking: catching insects.

185 *Buldeo*: stress on first syllable. 'Almost as spelt, but the -o isn't sounded very much' (K).

186 *cages*: first mentioned by Bagheera in JB as the place of his captivity.

188 *Messua*: 'Pronounced *Mess-wa*' (K).

190 *nilghai* '(Pronounced *neal-guy*. Literally "blue bull", a wild antelope as big as a small pony' (K).

191 *talao*: lake or pond (rhymed by K with 'plough').

192 *dhâk-tree*: a red-flowered tree from which lac dye comes: ultimate source of shellac.

194 *peepul-tree*: fig-tree.

Bandar-log: the monkey folk: cf. 'Kaa's Hunting' in JB. 'Pronounced *bunder*' (K). *Log* rhymes with *vogue*, and means 'people'.

195 *Khanhiwara*: 'A real place. *Kan-i-war-rer*, I think' (K).

198 *Mowgli stared*: see Appendix B.

gentled: stroked.

201 *Bhurtpore*: similar to the name of an Indian state in Rajputana, and of its capital city, but the 'Sack' seems to be imaginary.

205 *Kaa*: 'Pronounced *Kar*. Made up (from queer open-mouthed hiss of a big snake') (K).

207 *leeped*: ?cemented up.

208 *Karela*: 'A wild melon' (K).

209 *destructive*: this can be documented. See *Kipling Journal*, no. 14, December 1962.

THE UNDERTAKERS

Written at Tisbury, Wiltshire. First published in *The Pall Mall Budget*, 8 & 15 November 1894, *The New York World*, 8, 9, 10 and 12 November 1894; and *The Pall Mall Gazette*, 14 & 15 November 1894. The chief characters are three predators: the Mugger, or marsh crocodile (*Crocodylus palaestris*), the best known Indian species of crocodile; the Adjutant bird, a large stork of genus *Leptophilus*, an efficient scavenger; and the Jackal (*Canis aereus*), wolf-like member of the dog family, inhabiting South Asia and eastern Europe: 'an endearing and intelligent creature', according to Joy Adamson, *The Spotted Sphinx* (1969), but with an unpleasant reputation in folklore as a hanger-on who performs vile services for a great one. For the bridge which is the setting of the story, cf. 'The Bridge-Builders' in *The Day's Work*. The period of the story is 1887, i.e. 30 years after the Sepoy Mutiny of 1857. This story qualifies the statement by K. Bhaskara Rao in *Rudyard Kipling's India* (University of Oklahoma Press, 1967) that K 'wrote nothing about the Mutiny'.

212 *scour*: action of a current or flow of water in clearing away deposits.

Brahmins: this is flattery; (the Brahmins were the highest of all the castes.)

Mugger-Ghaut: 'Pronounced *Gort*. The Crocodile's Ferry, or bankside' (K).

213 *flying-foxes*: fruit-eating bats.

Ally Sloper: the first British strip-cartoon hero (or anti-hero); made his first appearance in the humorous magazine *Judy* on 14 August 1867; ugly, bulbous red nose, bald, with a battered top hat; a morally seedy character, and so an appropriate comparison for the Adjutant. See Maurice Horn, *World Encyclopaedia of Comics* (New York, 1976).

217 *Gavial*: or Ghavial. 'A sharp-nosed alligator, who does not

generally eat men. The Mugger's nose is as blunt as a boot' (K).

221 *lathis*: 'clubs' does not quite suggest what these are, i.e. stout bamboos used by Indian police against rioters.

Jats: Punjabi peasants: see *Kim*, chapter 11.

Malwais: i.e. from Malwa, a large area of land in the Punjab.

Bêt: a farming district.

223 *Wenham Lake*: near Salem, Massachusetts, USA.

225 *Sirhind*: a tract of land in the Punjab.

229 *Purbeeahs*: men from the Oudh, Benares, Behar regions of upper India, much used for recruitment of sepoys to the pre-Mutiny army: these were the corpses of the mutineers.

232 *Martini*: 'An old make of rifle, firing black powder. The four-bore was a gun used for shooting elephant, very heavy, and firing a bullet about an inch in diameter' (K). The Martini-Henry rifle was issued to the British (and later to the Indian) Army in the 1870s.

four-bore: see K's note above on 'Martini'.

234 *A Ripple Song*: requires knowledge of 'The Undertakers' for comprehension.

THE KING'S ANKUS

Mostly written September 1894. First published in *St. Nicholas Magazine*, March 1895. See discussion in *The Kipling Journal*, no. 173, March 1970, of possible sources and analogues of the story.

235 *title: ankus*: elephant-goad.

two-hundredth: pythons are said normally to live about 50 years.

Cold Lairs: see 'Kaa's Hunting' in JB.

237 *buffaloes*: see 'Tiger! Tiger!' in JB.

238 *White Hood*: there is apparently no reason to think that a snake could be turned white by confinement in the dark.

240 *Salomdhi* etc., and *Kurrun Raja*: appear to be all fictional.

241 *jackal*: a well-known transmitter of rabies (hence of madness).

242 *howdah*: seat on the back of an elephant (often richly decorated).

245 *Thuu*: 'Pronounced *Thoo-oo*' (K).

251 *dhatura*: *Datura stramonium*: plant of the nightshade family.

QUIQUERN

Written in Tisbury, Wiltshire, in 1894, when K and his wife were spending a holiday near his parents. First published in *The Pall Mall Gazette*, 24 & 25 October 1895, then in *McClure's Magazine*, November 1895. K had never crossed the Arctic Circle. His information about the Seal Islands of Alaska, in which the story is set, came from a book on them by H. W. Elliott (published in Washington, DC, USA, in 1881.) Elliott visited K in Vermont. Readers interested in the geography of the story should take K's advice in the Sussex Edition and consult a map.

254 *title*: 'Pronounced *Kawi-kwern*' (K). The word was invented by him.

255 *Northern Lights*: the Aurora Borealis.

256 *Labrador*: now administratively part of Newfoundland (Canada).

Inuit: plural of 'inuk'.

Esquimau: the spelling 'Eskimo' is more usual.

offing: what can be seen of the sea from the shore.

257 *musk-ox*: a ruminant of Arctic America (*Ovibos moschatus*).

dog-sleighs: Eskimo sledges.

narwhal: an Arctic whale.

Bhendy Bazaar: in Calcutta.

258 *kit-fox*: a small fox.

buckle: explained later; see p. 114, about the *tutareang*.

260 *toodle-kiyi*: onomatopoeic word invented by K.

262 *wolverine*: also known as glutton (*Gulo luscus*), a member of the weasel family.

264 *hydrophobia*: generally used only for the human manifestation of the disease (rabies).

something else: i.e. for food.

266 *Great Bear*: the constellation *Ursa Major*, largest and brightest in the northern skies (also called Charles's Wain, the Plough, the Dipper).

268 *a Thing*: i.e. a mirage. These are apparently caused by the

refraction of light by layers of air of varying temperature and density.

270 *floe*: a sheet of floating ice.

274 (*boiled meat*): i.e. a special treat for people who usually ate their meat raw.

275 *Cingalese*: a native of Ceylon (now 'Sinhalese').

RED DOG

Written at Brattleboro, Vermont, February and March 1895. First published (with the title 'Good Hunting: a Story of the Jungle') in *The Pall Mall Gazette*, 29 and 30 July 1895, and *McClure's Magazine* (August 1895).

276 *paying debts*: here as in much of his work K thinks of revenge as something that does a person good.

279 *Phao, son of Phaona*: 'Pronounced *Fay-ou*, son of *Fay-owner*. Made up' (K).

280 *pheeal*: 'Pronounced *fe-arl*: noise a jackal sometimes makes when full or going behind a hunting tiger. Quite different from his regular cry, not nice to listen to' (K).

   Won-tolla: 'Pronounced *Woon-toller*' (K).

281 *dhole*: 'Pronounced *dole* (a native name for the Wild Hunting Dog of India' (K).

   the Dekkan or Deccan: from Sanskrit 'Dakshina', the South.

285 *tushes*: archaic form of 'tusks'. (Elephants, it seems, do not actually have milk-tusks.)

291 *Bee Rocks*: 'Some rocks above a river near Jubbulpore' (K).

298 *lahini*: 'Pronounced *lar-hee-ney*. Made-up name for she-wolves' (K).

299 *worry-worry-worry*: a term taken from foxhunting.

THE SPRING RUNNING

First published (with the title 'Mowgli Leaves the Jungle for Ever') in *The Pall Mall Gazette*, 25 September 1895, and *Cosmopolitan Magazine*, October 1895.

304 *tree-cat*: possibly the jungle cat, *Felis chaus*.

305 *Ferao*: 'Pronounced *feer-ow*, made-up name for "Come back again, like Spring does"' (K).

306 *char*: (noun) a charred substance (*OED*).

307 *Mor*: 'Mohr' in Sterndale.

308 *baffed*: a baff is a blow with something flat or soft (*OED*).

309 *Tabaqui*: the jackal. 'Pronounced *Tabarky*. I think I made up this name myself (accent on *bar*)' (K).

310 *white night*: cf. French *nuit blanche* (a night when sleep is impossible).

311 *scribing*: marking with a pointed instrument.

325 *bandar*: monkey.

APPENDIX A

IN THE RUKH

First appeared in *Many Inventions* (1893). Republished with illustrations, and several explanatory notes by K, in *McClure's Magazine*, June 1896. The first Mowgli story to be published.

326 *title*: *Rukh*: forest. Pronounced like the English word 'ruck'.

tyre: curdled milk (from Tamil *tayir*).

Sambhur: elk found in forest-clad parts of India.

reboisement: re-afforestation (from French).

Nancy: a town in north-eastern France. The first French national school of forestry was opened there in 1824.

327 *blue-gum*: the eucalyptus.

poll and lop: cut the top and trim the branches.

328 *recapping-machine*: for inserting new percussion caps into spent shot-gun cartridge cases.

329 *shikar*: hunting (usually of big game).

sal trees: resembling teak.

koss: about 2000 yards.

330 *clomb*: archaic past tense of 'climb'.

331 *whiskers*: valued as an alleged aphrodisiac. (Does Mowgli reject them because he is virile enough already? or because he is not interested in sex? or because he does not believe in their powers?.)

shikarri: hunter.

332 *Classical Dictionary*: perhaps that by John Lemprière (1788), used by John Keats.

334 *lusus naturæ*: sport of nature (Latin).

335 *fling*: extension. cf. 'our far-flung battle-line' in K's poem 'Recessional' (1897).

338 *salt*: hospitality.

lost thy izzat: lost face. The Anglo-Indian official Ronnie Heaslop talks with unpleasant knowledgeableness about *izzat* in E. M. Forster's *A Passage to India* (1924).

warlock: sorcerer, in league with the devil.

339 *Huzrut*: Highness.

Muller: said to be based on the Inspector-General of Forests at that time, one Ribbentrop (his relationship, if any, to Hitler's Foreign Minister is not known).

340 *brass-hat*: a (usually somewhat hostile) description of a senior staff officer.

Worcester sauce: apparently an 'in-joke', handed down in the forestry service.

Bikaneer Desert: part of the Great India Desert of North-West India.

341 *Heine*: Heinrich Heine (1797–1856), German poet and journalist.

dey come off too ... und der Christian Gods howl loudly: Professor S. S. Prawer has kindly identified these allusions to Heine. Muller was 'quoting' from Heine's *Buch der Lieder*, the section called 'Die Heimkehr', no. 66 (see Heine's *Poems*, ed. Elster, I. 125–6). In the second half of the poem there is a description of the culinary miracles a non-Christian God would perform. The same section also includes the 'Almansor' poem in which the 'Christian gods whimper' (*wimmern*)—rather than 'howl'.

'Der cult of der old gods', as Muller calls it, is a frequent theme in Heine. Cf. A. I. Sandor's book, *The Exile of Gods* (The Hague & Paris, 1967).

These allusions, together with the reference to 'Faunus' (see below) and Swinburne's 'Dolores' (p. 230), make it clear that neo-Pagan, explicitly anti-Christian, ideas were in K's mind when he arrived at his first conception of Mowgli.

Faunus: one of the oldest of the Italian gods, the protective deity of agriculture and shepherds. When Pan was introduced (from Greek religion) into Italian mythology Faunus was identified with Pan and given horns and goat's feet. Pan enjoyed great popularity in the work of Late Victorian and Edwardian writers, e.g. J. M. Barrie, E. M. Forster, Kenneth Grahame, Saki, etc. Often there is a 'twee' element about him which may not be entirely absent from 'In the Rukh', but which is not present in *The Jungle Books*.

342 *die young*: see Introduction to this edition, for C. E. Carrington's comments on 'wolf children'.

343 *Adam*: Hebrew 'man'. In Genesis 1: 26 it appears to mean the human species, but in Genesis 2: 25 and 5: 1 it is probably a proper name, and certainly so in Genesis 5: 2–6.

'*Dough we ...*': verse from 'Dolores', by Algernon Charles Swinburne (1837–1909). Without Muller's (atrociously rendered) German pronunciation, and misquotation, the original reads:

> Though we shift and bedeck and bedrape us
> Thou art noble and nude and antique;
> Libitina thy mother, Priapus
> Thy father, a Tuscan and Greek.

Libitina: an Italian divinity, goddess of the earth, especially gardens; identified with Venus.

Priapus: son of Dionysus and Aphrodite. Originally worshipped in the image of the phallus as a fertility god (especially associated with gardens, vineyards, and trees).

345 *Allah*: Arabic name used by all Muslims for the one true God: = *al* (definite article) + *ilah* (god).

347 *Eblis*: in Arabian mythology a fallen angel.

348 *shadi*: ceremonial in preparation for marriage.

thy cow: a common form of self-abasement. For this and other examples of K's experiments with non-English idiom see D. H. Stewart's article on *Kim*, in *The Journal of Narrative Technique*, volume 15, no. 1 (Eastern Michigan University), Winter 1985.

349 *Gott in Himmel*: God in Heaven.

come off too: see note to p. 341.

American Literature

British and Irish Literature

Children's Literature

Classics and Ancient Literature

Colonial Literature

Eastern Literature

European Literature

Gothic Literature

History

Medieval Literature

Oxford English Drama

Poetry

Philosophy

Politics

Religion

The Oxford Shakespeare

A complete list of Oxford World's Classics, including Authors in Context, Oxford English Drama, and the Oxford Shakespeare, is available in the UK from the Marketing Services Department, Oxford University Press, Great Clarendon Street, Oxford OX2 6DP, or visit the website at www.oup.com/uk/worldsclassics.

In the USA, visit www.oup.com/us/owc for a complete title list.

Oxford World's Classics are available from all good bookshops. In case of difficulty, customers in the UK should contact Oxford University Press Bookshop, 116 High Street, Oxford OX1 4BR.

TROLLOPE IN OXFORD WORLD'S CLASSICS

ANTHONY TROLLOPE

An Autobiography

The American Senator

Barchester Towers

Can You Forgive Her?

The Claverings

Cousin Henry

Doctor Thorne

The Duke's Children

The Eustace Diamonds

Framley Parsonage

He Knew He Was Right

Lady Anna

The Last Chronicle of Barset

Orley Farm

Phineas Finn

Phineas Redux

The Prime Minister

Rachel Ray

The Small House at Allington

The Warden

The Way We Live Now